I0770491

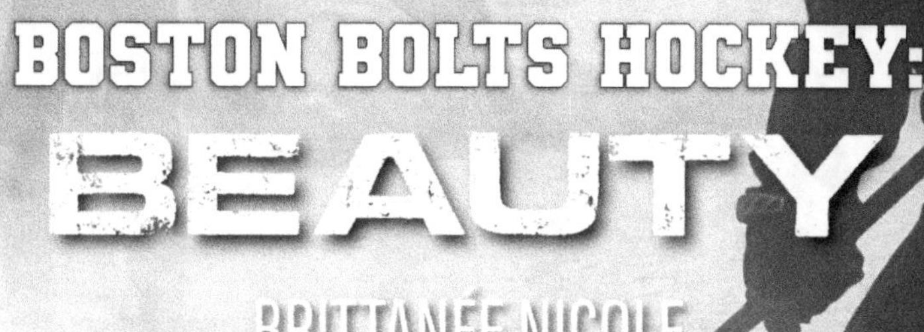

BOSTON BOLTS HOCKEY:
BEAUTY
BRITTANÉE NICOLE

PLAYLIST

Blue Jeans - Lana Del Ray
GRAVITY - Matt Hansen
Betting on Us - Myles Smith
Tidal - Noah Kahan
Solo - Myles Smith
Before You - Benson Boone
I Found - Amber Run
Daydream - Lily Meola
A Little Bit Yours - JP Saxe
back to friends - sombr
savior - sombr
This Love - Taylor Swift
You Are In Love - Taylor Swift
Turning Page - Sleeping At Last
Slow It Down - Benson Boone
would've been you - sombr
Blurred Lines - Robin Thicke
Roar - Katy Perry
Wildest Dreams - Taylor Swift
Save Tonight - Eagle Eye Cherry
feelslikeimfallinginlove - Coldplay
Thing of Beauty - Danger Twins
The Fate of Ophelia - Taylor Swift

DEDICATION

For the dreamers.

FOREWORD

Dear Reader,

With each book I write, the world I build becomes more connected and complex. This book, like all the books in this series, can be read as a standalone. However, you will see some character overlap and since I know many of you enjoy the easter eggs I hide and prefer to read in order, here is a suggested reading order as it comes to this world:

Revenge Era: Ford Hall and Lake Paige
Mother Faker: Beckett Langfield and Olivia Maxwell
Pucking Revenge: Brooks Langfield and Sara Case
A Major Puck Up: Gavin Langfield and Millie Hall
Hockey Boy: Aiden Langfield and Lennox Kennedy
Trouble: Cade Fitzgerald, Declan Everhart and Melina Rodriguez
War: Tyler Warren and Ava Erickson
Playboy: Daniel Hall and Hannah Prescott
Beauty: Noah Harrison and Sienna Langfield

This is simply a suggestion. You can start with any book and work your way through the series in any order you prefer.

Want more of the Langfields? Check out the 8 chapter epilogue, _Seasons of Love_ in the Langfield Brothers Boxset.

All of these books take place in the Boston Billionaire World so you will see or hear about those characters as well.

I hope you enjoy this world as much as I enjoy writing it.

XO,
Brittanée

CONTENTS

1. Sienna	1
2. Noah	7
3. Sienna	12
4. Noah	17
5. Sienna	20
6. Noah	30
7. Sienna	43
8. Noah	49
9. Sienna	56
10. Noah	65
11. Sienna	79
12. Noah	91
13. Sienna	107
14. Noah	114
15. Sienna	118
16. Noah	121
17. Sienna	129
18. Sienna	133
19. Noah	144
20. Sienna	154
21. Noah	166
22. Sienna	169
23. Noah	176
24. Sienna	181
25. Sienna	190
26. Sienna	194
27. Noah	202
28. Noah	210
29. Sienna	214
30. Noah	217
31. Sienna	226
32. Noah	231
33. Sienna	237
34. Noah	250
35. Sienna	259
36. Noah	266

37. Sienna 276
38. Noah 283
39. Sienna 289
40. Sienna 294
41. Sienna 309
42. Noah 313
43. Sienna 316
44. Noah 320
45. Noah 324
46. Sienna 334
47. Noah 341
48. Sienna 351
49. The Langfield Brothers 354
50. Noah 365
51. Noah 368
52. Sienna 374
53. Noah 380
54. Sienna 389
Epilogue 398

Acknowledgments 417
Also by Brittanée Nicole 419

Chapter 1
SIENNA

"WHY DON'T we call your brother? He'll fix this."

Frustration flares to life inside me. Everywhere I go, people think it's the most logical answer. *Call your brothers. Use your family name.*

For years, I've taken that advice, and look where it landed me. I'm two seconds from signing away the right to do the one thing I love.

I glare at the piece of paper in front of me, refusing to even glance at my attorney. "I paid you to resolve this, and you resolved it." As the pen slides against the settlement documents, a boulder presses down on my chest.

Wasn't a settlement supposed to make this feeling go away? The mediator said that if everyone was unhappy, then he'd done his job.

I feel beyond miserable, so he's succeeded there. Yet the people on the other side of the table are all smiles.

I would be too if the finalization of this settlement meant my bank account balance had just increased by more than a million dollars.

A million fucking dollars. It's certainly worth more than their designs.

Fuck, my head throbs from going over every step that led me to this moment.

The moment I agreed never to open another fashion house and

promised never to sell another design. A thirty-year prison sentence wouldn't feel this harsh.

But it had to be done. The vultures sitting across from me know what my family is worth. This is about dollar signs and revenge. Revenge that is rightfully sought. All they've worked for is gone. It isn't their fault. It's mine, so this is my punishment. An eye for an eye, I suppose. But not quite, because they'll get to design again. They'll have to start over, but they'll have that chance.

I won't.

Money isn't enough for them. They've taken my livelihood and my passion too.

"I want to thank you all—" the mediator starts in French.

But I've heard enough. I have no fucks left to give. So I push back from the table and walk out of his office without a backward glance.

Behind me, people I once considered friends snicker. Friends? More like back-stabbing bottom-feeders.

I don't stop. I keep walking until I hit the street corner where my favorite café is located. After ordering a cappuccino with a shot of sambuca, I slide into an uncomfortable black metal chair. Parisians don't care about comfort. They care about appearances. The way the gorgeous black lines of the chair contrast with the cream-colored cushion. The highest of heels and the tightest of belts cinched around waists.

I love everything about this city, yet five minutes ago, I gave up any reason to stay.

It feels like only days ago when Catherine Bouvier offered me my own television show, a show that would follow me as a bright, up-and-coming designer in the cutthroat world of fashion.

And now, here I am, almost six years later, left with nothing. I still can't figure out how it all went so wrong. Or what I'll do with my life.

So I close my eyes, take a sip of coffee, and try like hell to forget.

Six Years Ago

"Surely you can find someone with more experience."

A flight attendant appears with the glass of champagne I ordered, and I mouth a *thank you*, though my focus remains on Catherine Bouvier, the acting editor for the best fashion magazine on the market, *Jolie*.

Through the screen, Cat spears me with a glare. She's famous for the expression, really. She's also famous for being insanely gorgeous. She's tall, with long black hair, oversized natural lips that always look glossy, and eyes the color of whiskey.

The eye color is fitting, I suppose, since whiskey is what made her family rich. A whiskey company, in fact, that closely rivaled that of her husband's. For years, their families were enemies, though lately they all seem to get along. Cat and Jay recently married, and they have a teenage daughter and a toddler.

The whole family will be joining me in Paris next week to start filming our television show.

Cat and I both come from money. From large well-known families in Boston too. We're the only daughters surrounded by billionaire brothers. Women who have chosen to buck the family business and go after our true passions. Though that's where our similarities end.

While Cat is a go-getter and an incredible businesswoman, I'm a dreamer. An artist. The art comes easy, but actually turning it into a business is a challenge. Though, with a last name like Langfield nothing has ever been too difficult. My family's reputation alone opens more doors than most people find, but monetizing my passion has been the trickier part.

"The people want you. Remember that," Cat says, her features softening a little. "Your story is inspiring. People want to know how the Langfield princess who grew up surrounded by pro athletes ended up one of the top fashion designers of our generation."

I snort. "First of all, not a princess."

She lets out a scoff.

"Second, I'm just starting out. No one is declaring me a top designer."

"Hello." She leans closer to the screen. "I'm Catherine Bouvier. If I say Sienna Langfield is one of the top fashion designers of our generation, then it's fact."

Lips pursed, I look away, letting out an uncomfortable breath through my nose. Because she's right. As editor of *Jolie*, she decides what's in style each season. Their winter list is every influencer's dream. Even scoring an item on that list can make a person a legend. To be seen in it, an icon. And for some reason, a year ago, she saw something in me. So now here I am, a terrified twenty-four-year-old about to embark on the wildest year of my life.

"Fine, Your Majesty." I huff. "Thank you for believing in me."

With a raspy laugh, she spins in her office chair. Behind her, the Boston skyline is visible. If I squint, I can pick out Lang Field and Bolts Arena, the sports facilities that house my family's teams.

My brothers and I originally planned to spend the weekend at my family's compound in the Keys. One last hurrah before I leave for Paris. Unfortunately, my father summoned them all at the last minute, apparently calling in reinforcements to charm Cortney Miller into signing with our family's baseball team, the Boston Revs. Miller plays catcher for the New York Metros, and my brother Beckett has been trying to get him to agree to a trade. Miller's family is well-known in the highest echelons of society in New York, so it's been a challenge, but the trade would be huge for the Revs.

Gavin made me promise I'd fly to the Keys anyway, insisting that I deserve a few days in the sun to celebrate and swearing they'd all fly to Paris to visit next month.

I won't hold my breath.

My brothers are incredible. I couldn't ask for better siblings, but they're all ridiculously busy. Aiden, who is two years older than me, is the Bolts' center and well-known throughout the NHL as the guy to be watched. He's incredible. Brooks is too. He's two years older than Aiden and the team's goalie. Gavin is the Bolts' general manager. Though our dad owns both teams, he turned over the Revs reins to Beckett.

The MLB and NHL seasons are both ridiculously long, and between the two, they span the entire year, so when my brothers aren't attending a hockey game, they're supporting the baseball team.

I grew up doing both, though I was normally doodling designs on any scrap of paper I could find.

"Have fun in the Keys," Cat says. "I'll see you next week. No working until then."

I burst into laughter, and she follows suit. The notion that either of us could go a week without working is absurd.

"Thanks, Cat, and seriously, thanks for believing in me." I click out of the call and set my phone on the armrest. Then I finally take a sip of my champagne.

I haven't flown commercial more than a couple of times in my life, and if my brothers were with me, we'd definitely be on one of our family's jets. But since I'm alone, I'm more than happy in first class.

After my brothers bailed, I scrapped my plans to stay at our place in the Keys. Rather than sitting on our private beach all alone, I'll spend this weekend at an all-inclusive resort in the Bahamas.

My brothers would lose their minds if they knew about my change in plans.

All my life, I've been sheltered, and it's come at a cost.

It's cliché, I suppose. Here I am, a wealthy girl complaining about how she has all kinds of money but no love. The love part isn't true, really. Though I've never been in love, I *know* love. My brothers show it to me all the time. Being raised by nannies meant that the five of us always banded together because our parents were always too busy. My brothers have been my best friends all my life. Leaving them will be difficult, even though they're all so busy that we don't see each other much anymore.

I drop my head back against the seat and close my eyes. Why am I doing this? Why am I reflecting on my life like it's suddenly going to end?

Maybe in a sense it is. Leaving Boston, leaving my family and the only home I've ever known, is a big deal. And honestly, I'm not sure I'm ready for it. Or that I even deserve the opportunity.

The masses believe I'm only given these opportunities because of my name. And they wouldn't be completely wrong. Cat never would have heard of me if her über-wealthy husband didn't run in the same circles as my brothers.

But I'm also a twenty-four-year-old that's been completely sheltered for most of her life. I've never been in love. Never even come close to it. I've never had a chance to make really bad decisions, like having a one-night stand or fucking a stranger.

Maybe hot sex with a stranger is exactly what I need for this trip.

I settle back into my seat, and with another sip of champagne, I promise myself that I'll say yes to every opportunity the universe gives me this weekend.

The instant after I make that promise to myself, a man steps into the aisle, and my heart stutters just a little. He's tall, with the body of an athlete. His black T-shirt hugs his broad shoulders, muscular chest, and impressive arms like it was tailor made for him. His thick, sandy brown hair is perfectly messy, adding to his natural swagger. His cheekbones belong on a fashion model, and his irises are the exact color of a tropical wave. The color is only emphasized by the thick black frames of his glasses.

Who knew glasses were my personal kryptonite?

The guy is a sexy nerd, and I'm officially interested. What a perfect way to start my last hurrah.

Please let him sit next to me. Pretty freaking please.

Chapter 2
NOAH

I'M PREGNANT, *but I don't expect anything from you.*

Jen's words echo in my head once again as I step onto the plane. Honestly, they've haunted me since she uttered them a month ago. She's having my baby four weeks from now. Meaning she waited until she was seven months along to tell me. Why? Because she and her boyfriend, Ted, got back together and she didn't know how to tell him that the baby isn't his.

Now they're getting married. He's all-in. He works a steady nine-to-five. He doesn't spend more days on the road than at home ten months out of the year. They love each other and *he's* ready for fatherhood.

The implication there? *I'm not.*

She's not wrong. I'm at the height of my career. In a month, when my baby enters this world, I'll be starting my eighth season in the NHL. Jen is from Boston, and she's mentioned wanting to raise the baby there. Her future husband is from Minnesota, thank fuck, so for now, they're staying put.

If one day the idea of moving comes around again, will I even have a say?

That's my kid. The reply was immediate, forceful. My mom died when I was young, but my father is the best damn single dad that ever existed. With a role model like that, I know I can do it. How, I haven't worked out yet.

"You can't just flit in and out of his life when it suits you," she'd said. That's when I found out I was having a son.

There's no chance in hell I'll miss out on his life.

> War: I can't believe you're going to the Bahamas without me.

> War: And in July.

> War: Who the fuck goes to the Bahamas in July?

With a chuckle, I slide my phone into my pocket. Then I check the ticket in my hand against the numbers listed on the aisles.

4B. And so far, *4A* is open.

I scan the mostly full first-class cabin, my attention snagging on a woman seated in the row behind me. The second our eyes meet, she drops her gaze.

A fan? Maybe. Based on the reaction, she's not one that'll pester me during the flight.

I dig Hannah's debut novel from my carry-on as well as my glasses case and then settle into the aisle seat.

Hannah is actually the reason I'm headed to the Bahamas in July. I was in Boston for the offseason when Jen called, and after I had a full-on freak out, my stepsister told me I needed to *have a day*. She came up with the concept when she was a kid. When a friend or loved one is going through a breakup or having a major crisis like I am, she sends them on a trip.

In the middle of summer, flights to the Bahamas are cheap. Accommodations too. If they hadn't been, I never would have allowed her to pay. She booked the flight, and I was more than happy with sitting in coach until I realized just how uncomfortable I'd be in a middle seat at the back of the plane. While I'm not the biggest guy in the NHL, four hours stuck between two people in those little seats would be pure torture.

Since this is supposed to be my last big hurrah, I upgraded.

I take out my phone and type out a response to my best friend.

Me: I can't believe you left me to play for Boston. Without your miserable ass on the ice by my side, who the fuck is going to make me look good?

War: Ha ha. Come to Boston, brother. The weather's slightly warmer.

Me: You know I can't.

War: Yeah, yeah. I just hope all those zeros that contract gave you will keep you warm on those cold, lonely nights.

Doubtful. After Jen's news, all those zeros feel like a noose. If she moves back to Boston, I'll have to find a way to get out of my contract.

I haven't told War about the baby. In fact, Hannah and my dad are the only people I've told.

Jen and Ted's friends and family probably know by now, but I have a feeling that most of them think the baby is Ted's.

Closing my eyes, I pinch the bridge of my nose and will the headache that's formed to abate. My head pounds every time I think of all of this.

I promised Hannah I'd give myself this long weekend. I'd take this break and put aside the things I can't control. Because in a month, I'll be a parent. In a month, I'll be spending all the evenings I'm not traveling or playing raising a child.

There will be little time for a break for the next ten to eighteen-ish years.

"Nervous flier?" The question comes from a silky-soft voice.

I open my eyes, expecting to come face to face with a concerned flight attendant. Instead, I find myself struck stupid, unable to talk. The woman before me is stunning. Drop-dead gorgeous. The type of beauty that leaves a man tongue-tied.

Her hair is dark and pulled back from her face by the oversized black sunglasses perched on the top of her head. Her lashes are long and thick, emphasizing the most dazzling green eyes I've ever seen.

The eyes that were locked on me only moments ago. I glance over my seat back and find the row occupied by two people who look nothing like the woman now hovering over me. So I was either hallucinating before, or I've conjured her now.

"Are you okay?" she asks slowly, her brow furrowed with concern.

I blink up at her, my attention snagging on the beauty mark to one side of her cupid's bow lips. Lips that are covered in fuck-me red lipstick.

Fuck me is right.

She's dressed in all black, the dark fabric only emphasizing the large diamonds in her ears and the thick gold chain around her neck.

One look is all it takes to know that she comes from money. A lot of it.

"S-sorry." I clear my throat. "I'm fine. Just have a bit of a headache. Is this your seat?" I point to the window seat beside me.

She nods once. "The couple behind us are on their honeymoon, but they didn't have seats together. I offered to swap."

"Do you need help with your carry-on?" I unbuckle and step out into the aisle, trying my best not to brush up against her.

She's tiny, probably a foot shorter than I am, with high cheek-bones and creamy skin. Everything about her screams out of my league.

I'm just stupid enough to take a shot anyway.

She holds up her glass of champagne and shrugs. "This is all I have. Bag's already up top."

"Right. Of course." I hold out a hand, motioning for her to sit first. I follow, keeping my focus fixed ahead, suddenly at a loss for how to behave. Do people normally introduce themselves on planes? Should I? And if so, what the fuck do I say? I can't really start with hello because, well, we've already said that.

My phone vibrates in my pocket, interrupting my thoughts. I dig it out, and as I read the text, I'm reminded that I no longer have the freedom to just flirt with a girl.

Jen: Just left the doctor's office. The baby's measurements are on track with my due date. Just keeping you in the loop like you wanted. Here's a picture.

As I tap on the sonogram image, everything around me falls away. That's my son.

Chapter 3
SIENNA

THE MAN IS PRACTICALLY MUTE. Beautiful, handsome, and gorgeous, but uncomfortably quiet. He's polite. He takes my garbage and passes it to the flight attendant, and he hands me the drinks I order. But after staring at me like he was going to devour me, he went silent.

This is so not the kind of energy I was hoping the universe would give me.

Since I was a child, I've had a shadow. Usually security or at least one of my brothers. My whole life, there's always been someone there, watching me like a hawk.

Because my brothers think I'm going to our home in the Keys—on our private plane—no one bothered to assign someone to watch over me.

The freedom feels incredible.

When I move to Paris, I'll make sure I have more privacy. I'm a nobody outside of Boston. Really, when my brothers aren't around, the only people who recognize me work in the fashion industry. Alone, I could walk down the street without being recognized. It's the security —or my brothers—that cause people to look.

Here on this plane, not a single person recognizes me. I can be whoever I want.

Even in college, I never had the opportunity to be reckless. There were always eyes everywhere.

I've never even had a boyfriend. Who the hell would date a girl with four wildly overprotective older brothers? Two of whom play hockey professionally and can clearly fight, one with a scowl that can kill, and Gavin. Okay, funny, charming Gavin may not be as intimidating.

Anyone who does show interest is usually in it to get close to my brothers.

But for once, I can let loose. No one will recognize me or feign interest because of my family.

I can just be Sienna. I can relax and maybe, finally, find out what it's like to have mind-blowing sex.

I stumbled through bad sex with a guy near the end of my senior year of high school, only to later read in *Jolie* that most boys don't even know where the clit is, let alone a woman's G-spot. In college I invested in a really good vibrator and focused on my designs instead.

It only takes one look at the man beside me to determine that he knows what he's doing in the bedroom. Maybe it's the glasses, though he took them off and put them away when he pulled out a paperback. I wonder if he takes them off during sex?

Perhaps it's the romance novel he's unabashedly reading in public. Or maybe it's how he taps his finger gently against his tongue before he delicately turns each page. Anyone who reads with such reverence is sure to know what else he can do with that finger or that tongue.

God, I'm horny.

I squeeze my legs and thank my former self for packing toys for this trip. It's clear as day that this man will not be showing me what he can or can't do with either of those appendages.

Since he's determined to ignore me, I turn my focus to the little screen in front of me. When I find the title of my favorite movie, *Serendipity*, nostalgia blossoms inside me, warm and comforting. For the next two hours, I'll lose myself in the familiar story.

After the turquoise waters of the Bahamas come into view and we finally touch down, my seatmate takes my carry-on out of the overhead compartment and hands it to me.

Well, I guess that's that. No mind-blowing orgasm from him. Bachelor number one was a dud. The universe really blew that one.

Beckett: Why is the family jet still parked at Logan?

Gavin: And why did O'Ryan think O'Rourke was traveling with you and that you gave him the weekend off?

Gavin: And how come O'Rourke says you canceled your flight and promised you were staying put in Boston with O'Ryan?

Aiden: Do we really have to go to this dinner tonight? I was looking forward to the Keys.

Brooks: For once I'm with Aiden. Why do WE have to come to your baseball wooing dinner, Beckett? Hundred bucks says Miller doesn't even show up. AGAIN.

Gavin: Sienna!

Beckett: Found her. She's in the Bahamas.

Aiden: How the hell did you do that?

Beckett: Tracked her phone. I know where all you bozos are at all times.

Aiden: Shit.

Gavin: Sienna! Answer your phone!

As my car service takes me to my hotel, I glare at the traitorous device that gave away my location and actually consider tossing it into the turquoise waters.

Hell no am I answering when they call. And they sure do call.

Incessantly. They love me, I get that, but they're so damn uptight. So controlling.

Though I do feel a modicum of guilt.

Fine. I sigh and open the text thread again. I'll let them know I'm okay and then tell them to leave me the hell alone for the next four days. They're going to have to get used to easing up on the reins anyway. What are they going to do, track my every move from another continent?

> Me: Hi, my annoying, overbearing brothers. I'm fine. Yes, I'm in the Bahamas. Beckett, turn the tracking off on my phone or I'll toss it into the ocean so you can't find me. Love you all. See you on Tuesday!

Before they can respond, I power down the device. When the screen goes black, the last of my stress eases out of me like a wave returning to the ocean. Unfortunately, just like those waves, it will return.

I need to figure out how to let it all go. No amount of boundary-setting will keep them from caring. That means it's time to learn not to let it bother me so much. It's time to discover who I am without them.

As the car turns into the resort parking lot, a spark ignites inside me, sending goose bumps skittering across my skin. Maybe it's because I've never done this kind of thing alone, but at the sight of the white and turquoise buildings, I can't help but feel like this is a new beginning.

I've just stepped out of the car when a man rushes toward me, wearing a large, professional smile. "Ms. Langfield!"

My heart sinks.

There's no way this isn't my oldest brother's doing. His emergent energy screams "Beckett Langfield threatened to do unspeakable things to me if I don't follow his instructions to the T." Fuck.

The man approaches me, practically tripping over his own feet. "Welcome to Blu. We were just informed of your arrival. Please accept my apologies for not sending our service to pick you up." He gives the perfectly fine sedan behind me a look of disgust while a second man rushes over and takes my luggage from the driver.

With a conciliatory smile at the driver, I rummage in my purse so I can tip him. But before I can pull out cash, I'm guided away. "Miguel will handle that for you," the concierge says. "Let me show you to the private lobby. I'll bring you a drink and get you settled there while housekeeping gets your new villa ready."

I sigh. It's pointless to ask, but I do it anyway. "*Villa?*"

"Oh, yes." His eyes light up. "You've been upgraded. Congratulations." The man looks at me like he expects to find me jubilant over this information. I suppose most people would.

So I paste on a smile and force a cheery tone. "Thank you so much. I hope it wasn't too much trouble."

Chapter 4
NOAH

"I'VE BEEN UPGRADED?"

As I take in the marble lobby with views out to the ocean, I wait for someone to jump out and tell me I've been punked.

I make a lot of money, especially after signing my new contract, so I can afford to upgrade, but I grew up in a middle-class home with a single parent. My dad put every extra dime we had into my hockey career.

It wasn't until I was a junior in high school that he literally won the lottery. After that, we had more than enough to splurge, but my dad's focus then shifted to funding my education and paying off debt. Now he lives in a simple apartment in Boston and maintains a bank balance that'll allow him to retire any time he wants.

After growing up that way, and with the influence of my frugal father, the tropical vacation itself is an upgrade in my life. Being told I've been moved into a villa suite is quite honestly shocking.

And unnecessary.

What the hell am I going to do in a full suite?

"Yes, Mr. Harrison," the pretty attendant says, lashes fluttering. She's been flirtatious since she pulled up my reservation and discovered the upgrade. "Follow me." She comes around the desk, tablet clutched to her chest, and leads me through the lobby. Rolling my small suitcase behind me, I follow, taking in the colorful plants that pop against the white backdrop. This place is so Hannah. I'm determined to pay her back for this trip, though I know she won't accept money.

My stepsister is my closest friend, and I miss the shit out of her. She works for Boston's major league baseball team, which just so happens to be under the same ownership as War's new team. Though she recently published her first book and one day hopes to write full time.

In a perfect world, I'd be living in Boston too, raising my son, spending time with Hannah, and playing for the Bolts with Tyler Warren and Brooks Langfield, another good buddy from college.

I banish the thought. Because where I live is solely dependent on Jen. I'm not going to miss out on anything when it comes to my son.

I blow out a breath. Why the hell are all my thoughts so doom and gloom? I've got this one weekend to enjoy myself. I'm not a dad yet.

My phone buzzes in my hand, and when I hold it up, a text notification appears.

> War: Did you get your new room?

Chuckling, I type a quick response.

> Me: You did this? Why?

> War: Congrats on the deal, buddy. I'm proud of you. I'll miss playing with you, though.

Tears prick my eyes. I've always been an emotional guy. Maybe it's because I was raised by a single dad who made a point of always being open and vulnerable with me. He was always affectionate and made sure I knew how much he loved me. That he was proud of me.

War wasn't so lucky. He lost his mom at a young age too, but his father couldn't have been less interested in being a parent. During college, he typically spent the holidays with either Brooks or me. Now that he's in Boston and playing for the Langfields, he's got a good support system. I'm glad he'll be so close to Brooks's family, but damn, will I miss this guy.

> Me: You didn't have to do this, but I appreciate it, man. Hockey isn't going to be the same without you.

> War: Don't go getting emotional on me now. You'll still get to see me on the ice. You know, when I skate by you and score.

Just like that, the tears clear and I'm laughing. War's one of the kindest people I know, but he's also the cockiest.

Just as I look up from my phone, a figure appears directly in front of me. So close that I have to throw my hands out and grasp her arms to keep from walking into her. "Shit. Sorry." I steady her, and when she tips her head and I get a look at her face, I can't help but break into a smile.

Pretty green eyes widen in shock and those fuck-me red lips drop open.

My seat mate from the plane.

"Hi," I force out past where my heart has lodged itself in my throat.

"Sir," the attendant calls from several feet ahead of me.

The woman from the plane bites down on her bottom lip and pulls out of my grip. Then she offers me the tiniest of waves, her fingers dancing subtly, and walks away.

I turn, watching her disappear from view for the second time, only looking away when I crane my neck so far it cracks.

This is going to be a problem.

Chapter 5
SIENNA

AS THE DOOR closes with a loud snick behind the attendant, I blow out a relieved breath.

Finally.

I take my time examining my home for the next few days, exhausted but also excited and beyond ready to check out the minibar and relax. The villa is decorated in colors fitting for a tropical location. White walls, turquoise rug, white bedding with turquoise stitching on the pillows, white couch, and turquoise vases stacked on the minibar. The highlight of the space, though, is the enormous set of double doors leading to the expansive deck that looks out over the turquoise waters. The vibe here is perfect. Well, almost perfect. A little music will fix that.

I power on my phone, set it to do not disturb, and tap the Spotify icon. As I scan my playlists, I make my way to the bar, where the attendant left an open bottle of champagne sitting inside a—yes, you guessed it—turquoise ice bucket. Once I settle on a little Lana Del Rey mix, I set my phone down and pour myself a glass. The bubbles cause the liquid to foam to the top, but because I've mastered the art of drinking champagne, it doesn't spill over.

After a sip of the crisp liquid, I head for my suitcase, already feeling lighter, and pull out the first bathing suit I find. It's a cherry-red set of strings. Thank god my brothers aren't here. If they were, I'd have hideous tan lines from the one-pieces I would have been forced to wear. Once I discovered I'd be on my own, I gladly packed several more indecent options.

The deck is private, but I pluck out a sheer black wrap skirt as well. If someone shows up at the door, at least it will cover my ass. Then I strip off my travel clothes and get comfortable.

Within minutes of settling on the chaise lounge, with my head tilted toward the sun, I'm bored out of my mind.

What do people do on vacation? Is there a trick to turning off an overactive mind?

What I want to do is take out a sketchpad and get lost in designing, but Cat's insistence that I not work this week is valid. I haven't slowed down since I started my fashion line. For the last two years, my brain and my body have been in high gear, always working, always pushing.

And in Paris, there will be cameras and a film crew following my every move. I'll barely have time for bathroom breaks, let alone free afternoons to lie in the sun and relax.

Eyes closed, I tap my red-painted toes to the beat of the music. I can do this. I can lie here and clear my mind. This is enjoyable. This is fine.

I count to ten, and when that doesn't work, I hum along with the song, focusing on the lyrics.

Oh, fuck this shit.

Two songs in, I heave myself up and storm through the open double doors, causing the sheer turquoise curtains to fan dramatically. I snag the book on the coffee table and dig my journal out of my suit-case, then head back outside.

With a mission in mind, relief washes over me. I'll peruse the activities the resort offers, check out the room service menu, and make plans for the weekend. If I sit here any longer, staring at the ocean, I'll lose my mind.

And when I'm done with all that, I'm going to draw.

Just as the sky is turning a vibrant red, room service knocks on my door with the bottle of Sirah and the cheese platter I ordered. "Where would you like it?" he asks, as if there's any question of what my answer will be.

The view outside my villa is incredible. The sight of it from here causes design idea after design idea to spark to life in my mind. I guide him outside to the table and two chairs. Yes, two. Because who stays in a place like this alone?

Life is meant to be spent in twos. Or so the world tells us.

There's never been a person to occupy that second chair in my life. Not a person I wanted there anyway.

Though right now, I don't need anyone. I've got my sketchpad, some sustenance, and a gorgeous view to keep me company.

Once I've tipped the man and he's gone, I cut a piece of the creamy white cheese and smear it onto a cracker. As I'm adding a little apricot spread, the doors to the villa beside mine open.

Two male voices discuss where to put the food one must be delivering. After a *thank you* and a farewell greeting, I'm blanketed in silence again.

Nosy, I pop the first bite of my dinner into my mouth and shift in my seat to get a look at my new neighbor. When I realize it's *him*, I practically choke on the cracker.

Familiar black glasses and light brown hair. It's messy, like he just woke from a nap. His face is shadowed in a way it wasn't this morning, reminding me that he's at least a few years older than I am.

And the man is shirtless. Damn. Every inch of muscle I imagined when he first walked onto that plane is on full display.

But my imagination has nothing on the real thing.

It hits me as I soak in the sight of all his bare skin, covered in a few tattoos, just how underdressed I am myself.

As if he can sense my scrutiny, he turns in my direction. Clearly he's noticing just how little I'm wearing as well. Though I'm still wearing the sheer skirt, I suddenly feel naked. My skin heats as he takes me in, his eyes scanning every inch of me as if I'm a mirage and he's worried I'll vanish.

Emboldened by the desire in his gaze, I clear my throat and put on my proverbial big-girl pants. "Third time's a charm, right?" I stand and sidle over to the white metal railing separating his deck from mine. "I'm Sienna. It seems the universe really wanted me to tell you that."

That does it. The man's lips tip up into a half smile, and my stomach swoops. "The universe, eh?" He holds out a hand in greeting.

The moment our fingers touch, electricity zaps through me. He feels it too, if the way his eyes drop to our hands and his jaw hangs open are any indication.

His palms are rough, his calluses brushing against my soft, smooth skin, sending a shiver through me.

"Canadian?" I ask as I let go.

He scans my face, his brows pulling together. "Uh, no, but I play hockey with a few of them."

Amusement flares inside me and a snort escapes before I can stop it. Of course he's a hockey player.

My reaction has the lines on his forehead deepening.

Cringing, I shake my head. "Sorry. It's just that the second I saw you, I clocked you as an athlete."

This makes him smirk. "Oh yeah, and what was it about me that screamed athlete?" He folds his arms across his broad chest.

It's impossible not to ogle him. Damn, he's gorgeous. "Muscular arms. Abs for days." I lift my chin, gesturing to his face. "Scar above your eye, though you must have had good plastics, because I'm just now noticing it."

His lip curls in a hint of a smile, and those blue eyes practically sparkle, but he doesn't say a word.

So I go on, dragging my focus to where his thighs are covered by a pair of gray shorts. "Incredible thighs and…" I press my teeth into my bottom lip. "Fuck, could you turn around for a sec?"

He chuckles, his brows arching high, but he does what I ask.

Heat gathers low in my belly as I take in the view. I let out an exaggerated sigh. "Yup. Calf muscles that pop and an ass. God, you've got a good one."

"I'm not sure if I should say thank you or ask you to return the favor." He's smiling as he turns back around.

"Oh, I've got an excellent ass. You can ogle it whenever you want." I peek over my shoulder at my bum and give it a little wiggle.

He licks his lips, that grin still in place. "I'll take your word for it, sweet cheeks. I'm Noah."

"Oh, we're already at the nickname stage. Love it," I tease with a shimmy of my shoulders.

We both fall silent, though before it gets awkward, the plate on the table behind him catches my eye. The steak in the center is massive, and it's surrounded by a salad and vegetables. It's definitely the meal of a man who's working to stay in shape. "Your dinner looks a little healthier than mine," I tease, thumbing at my cheese platter.

He scoffs. "That's all you're having?"

I shrug. "I didn't want to go to the buffet by myself."

Lips twisting, he nods. "I get that." He takes half a step back and scratches at his nape. "I'll, uh, let you get back to your meal."

My heart sinks a little. I'm not ready to walk away from this conversation. From him. "It'd be kind of weird for us both to sit out here and not talk, wouldn't it?"

He shrugs. "I'm sure plenty of others have done it."

That makes my stomach drop right along with my heart. Shit. He's trying to politely get out of this conversation, and I'm only now catching the signs, I guess. "Shit, right. Sorry. Enjoy your dinner." I give him a stupid little finger wave and turn away. The moment my back is to him, I close my eyes and blow out a frustrated breath.

"Wait, Sienna—"

I whip back around without thinking it through, blinking like an idiot, trying to act totally normal. "Yeah?"

He swallows, his Adam's apple working. "That didn't come out right. What I said. Yes, I'm sure many guests have sat out here without talking to their neighbor. But I'd like to not do that with you."

My embarrassment morphs into confusion. "Huh?"

Eyes closing, he shakes his head. "Sorry, you're just really fucking beautiful, and I'm not making any sense."

Heat creeps into my cheeks, and I flush in response to the unexpected compliment.

His nostrils flare like he's trying to get control of himself, and then he breaks into a smile that's somehow both boyish and devastating. "Will you have dinner with me?"

"Yeah?"

He nods. "Yes." Another deep breath. "*Please.*"

Heart flipping, I beam at him. "Sure." I shrug. "Why not?"

I rush inside to tidy up quickly, kicking the black thong on the floor under the bed.

After that's taken care of, I give myself a quick assessment in the mirror. My shoulder-length hair is pulled back in a stubby ponytail and my cheeks are rosy from spending the afternoon in the sun—and from the wine—and my boobs look fantastic in my bikini top.

I should probably change. The bottoms are little more than a couple of strings tied together. Even with the skirt, my cute ass is out there for the world to see. Telling him it was nice was one thing; mooning him is another.

I toss my suitcase open and pull out a red dress packed near the top. The fabric is loosely woven, leaving the tiniest of holes. It's meant to be a cover-up. Perfect. Still flirty, still me, but a little less revealing. I tug it over my head, then shuffle back to the mirror and pull my hair out of its ponytail and give it a quick fluff.

I grimace at my reflection. Nope. Now I look like I'm trying too hard.

A knock sounds on the door, the sharp noise pulling a squeal from me. Bouncing on my toes, I eye the door in the mirror, then focus on myself again.

Up or down? *Make up your mind, woman.*

With a fortifying breath, I back away. I march to the door. But apprehension stops me an instant before I can pull it open. With a quiet groan, I scoop my hair back into the elastic. Then, shoulders pulled back, I throw the door open. "Hi, sorry. I was—"

Noah shakes his head. "I have a sister. I get it." He put on a shirt, like maybe he was having the same dilemma I was. Those damn glasses that make his blue eyes extra bright are in place, and he's got his plate in one hand and a bottle of wine under his arm.

I hold out my hands. "Can I take something for you?"

He shakes his head. "Just lead the way."

With another breath I hope will settle my nerves, I lead him inside. As I pass my suitcase, I slam it shut. Then I kick the sheer black skirt into the corner.

Beside me, his lips quirk up a bit, putting me at ease.

"So a sister, huh?" I hold open the turquoise curtains.

With a nod, he steps out onto the deck.

He sets his plate next to mine and holds up the bottle, though he nods at my already open Sirah. "Want me to open this too?"

I wave away the question and back toward the door. "Don't be silly. There's no way I'd finish this entire bottle on my own. Let me get another glass."

When both our glasses are full and he's cut a slice of his steak he insists I eat—because he's obviously a gentleman like that—he holds up his wine. "To the persistence of the universe."

I huff a laugh. "You're making fun of me."

Eyes widening, he rears back. "I would never. I take this universe business very seriously." He taps his glass against mine.

"How else could all this be explained?" I tease. "We ended up next to one another on the plane, only to then discover that not only are we staying at the same resort, but that our villas are side by side." I keep up with the light tone, even if, as I'm putting it all together, it sounds sort of romantic. Like fate keeps bringing him my way.

A little like serendipity.

My heart lifts at that thought.

Noah shrugs. "A bunch of happy coincidences?"

"So you're saying it's a good thing you keep running into me?"

He takes a slow sip of wine, his head tipped back enough to show off the lines of his thick neck. The way his Adam's apple moves is mesmerizing. So much so that when he dips his chin and holds my gaze, my breath catches. "A very good thing."

Sparks ignite inside me, dancing all the way down to my toes. I love the way he looks at me. And I really enjoy looking at him.

Needing a distraction from the overwhelming sensation, I cut into the steak he's set on my plate. The moment the flavor registers, I hum. It's the perfect temperature, and for room service, the taste is impressive.

"So what brings you to the Bahamas?" I ask.

His smile is subdued. "My sister wanted me to have a day."

"Have a day?"

He sighs like he's not really sure how to explain the concept. "She does this thing for the people she cares about. When one of us is having a bad day…" He rakes a hand through his hair. "Or several of them," he says, as if that's the case for him, "she forces us to have a day. A day where the focus is fixed on us only. You know, splurging, self-care, that sort of stuff."

A genuine affection for this woman I've never met blossoms inside me. "She sounds incredible. So she sent you here?"

He nods, attention drifting to the table.

"Which means you were having a bad day before you got here?" My heart aches a little at the thought.

He shrugs. "Seems things are looking up now."

A thrill zips through me. Is he flirting?

"How 'bout you?" he asks, straightening in his seat. "Why are you here?"

I set down my fork and take a sip of wine, considering how much I want to tell him. People look at me differently when they find out who I am, and he's a virtual stranger, so it doesn't seem wise to give him specific details about what I'm running from. "I have a big career thing happening soon." I lift one shoulder. "My sort-of boss told me to take a few days to relax because after next week, we'll be nonstop for the foreseeable future."

Noah's lips turn down in an impressed sort of frown. "Sounds like a nice boss."

That's an understatement. Cat has championed me since the moment she saw my designs. And while she loves and appreciates my work, she's also become a friend. I'm excited to spend the next few months with her in Paris. I only hope I make her proud. "She's incredible. Truly."

"There isn't someone back home you wanted to invite on this celebratory vacation?" The question is innocent enough, but he's definitely digging for information.

My responding smile is half relief and half sadness, really. "My brothers were supposed to come, but they had to cancel at the last minute."

"Brothers?"

I dip my chin once and pick up a cracker. "Four of them."

Focus averted, I wait for the typical response. The frown. The jokes. The backpedaling.

Instead, he simply nods. "Are you close?"

"Yeah, though they've all got busy careers, and I do too, so we don't see each other enough. But you should see the family chat," I tease with a grin.

He chuckles as he cuts another bite from his steak.

"So there's no girlfriend back home to bring along on your have a day trip?"

Noah's grin widens, though he quickly rubs a hand over his mouth, wiping it away. "No girlfriend." His expression is serious now as he studies me. "What about you?"

"Do I have a girlfriend?" Brows arched, I point to myself.

He chuckles. "Or a boyfriend?"

I shake my head. "No on both accounts. Just me."

"And me," he murmurs.

Silence creeps in as we focus on our food. Though every few seconds, I can't resist stealing a glance at him. And every time, I catch him doing the same.

The quiet isn't uncomfortable. In fact, it's strange how un-awkward the moment is. We eat, we sip our wine, we enjoy the view.

"How long are you here for?" Noah asks as we set the plates outside the front door to be collected.

I lean against the door, holding it open a couple of inches so I don't get locked out as he sets the stack on the floor. "Till Tuesday."

Crouched low, he looks up at me, surprise clear as day on his face. "Me too."

A bolt of excitement courses through me, and I bite down on my lip to quell the sensation. "Maybe I'll run into you again tomorrow."

Noah stands and clutches the doorframe, his eyes blazing with heat as he stares at me, his face closer to mine than could be considered just friendly. "Thanks for having dinner with me."

My pulse thrums, making my breaths a little ragged. "It was my pleasure."

He's so close I can smell the wine on his breath. I pull one corner of my lip between my teeth to temper the urge to lunge at him.

His eyes narrow on the movement, and my stomach swoops again. Is he…

Before I can finish the thought, he pushes back and gives me a cocky smile. "Night, sweet cheeks."

I stand frozen to the spot until the door clicks shut between us. Then I throw myself onto the bed, kicking my legs and squealing like the damn romantic I am.

Chapter 6
NOAH

FORGET FUCK-ME RED LIPS. Her ass in that red bathing suit will be the star of every single fantasy I have for the next year. And the peeks of skin the little holes in her dress gave me? Every damn inch of it—from her tits to her stomach to her goddamn thighs—teased me and taunted me, slashing at my restraint. I was a heartbeat away from slamming my lips to hers, then pressing them against every indecent hole.

By some miracle, the logical part of my brain came back online, and I rushed into my villa before I gave in to the temptation.

I've always prided myself on being a decent man. A good one, even. But I do love to make a woman come. I actually prefer it to my own pleasure.

However, I don't ogle women, and I don't hang out in strip clubs or even regular clubs, really. Sure, I've had a couple of one-night stands, though I've always been clear of my intentions going into them. Outside of those few incidents, I believe in taking a woman out on a date and treating her right before even thinking about seeing her naked.

Even before I discovered I had a child on the way, my schedule left no time for dating, which means I rarely have sex.

But Sienna?

Sienna has altered my brain chemistry. She's damaged the parts of my mind where self-control dominates, leaving me with all kinds of dirty thoughts. Fuck. The things I want to do to her. Suddenly, I've been overtaken with the need to make her moan my name, then chant it in that flirty fucking tone that has me hard as fucking stone right now.

She's young. Far too young for the things I want to do to her. She can't be more than a year or two out of college.

And in a matter of weeks, I'll be a single dad.

Could I lose myself in her for a few days? Enjoy the time we have together and never look back?

Unlikely. She's the type of woman a man doesn't forget.

The whole point of this trip was to get my head on straight. To relax. Unwind. And prepare for fatherhood.

There'd be nothing relaxing about this weekend if I spent it with her. I'm the opposite of relaxed right now. Wound tight thinking of all the things I want to do to her.

No. I won't sleep with her. I won't even see her again. Tomorrow morning, I'll go down to the concierge, thank them for this lovely upgrade, and politely beg them to move me to the room farthest from Sienna. Then I'll stay inside, ensuring I don't run into her again.

Yes. That's a plan.

With a relieved sigh, I grab a beer from the mini fridge—might as well enjoy the amenities of the villa while I've got them—and head outside to enjoy the warm night.

As I step outside, a breeze whips the curtains on Sienna's deck, catching my attention. Dammit. She's still too close.

Forcing myself to look away, I shuffle to the railing. I clutch the metal, still warm from the day, and take in the moon where it hangs just above the crashing waves.

With a swig of beer, I soak up the beauty in front of me.

This is the type of break I need. Just me and the ocean. A moment to get my head on straight.

Practice starts in two weeks. Coach is going to lose his shit when he finds out about the baby. My teammates might at first, but they'll be supportive. They're a good group, and we're set to have a good season, but it won't be the same without War.

For ten years, I've played almost every game with my best friend at my side.

That kind of shit never lasts, though. It was a miracle we ended up on the same pro team after college.

He'll freak the fuck out too when I tell him about the baby. Then, when I tell him about Sienna, he'll give me all kinds of hell. If he were in my place, he'd lose himself in the gorgeous woman next door. Then he'd man the fuck up and be the best damn father ever.

Maybe I should have lost myself in Sienna for the night. I picture the night going differently. What would she have done if I'd pushed her back through that door, scooped her into my arms, and carried her to the edge of her bed? If I'd slid that tease of a dress up her thighs and settled between them?

I'd have kissed her long and hard before lifting that dress over her head. Then I would have taken my time learning every inch of her body. The way her breasts would heave as I traced a line down her neck with my tongue. The way her nipples would pebble behind the flimsy red fabric of her suit as her back arched and she begged me to pull it off.

I'd finally know what she tastes like.

The sounds she'd make as I—

Wait, what the fuck is that sound?

I tilt my head, tuning out the waves in the distance, and sure enough, I hear the distinct echo of a moan. It's breathy and indecent. A *yes* followed by another whimper. Then a *fuck yes.*

All the air leaves my lungs in a whoosh. Holy shit, *that's* Sienna.

Eyes squeezed shut, I remind myself that storming back to her room and banging on her door is a bad idea. That jumping this gate and rushing through the open doors is wrong.

I take three steps closer, my free hand locked tight around the fence separating our decks, getting as close as I can. From here, I can hear every whimpering breath she lets out as she pleasures herself.

It's not quick. No, I should have known that Sienna would take her time. She edges herself, breathing out yeses over and over again, her tone sultry and dripping with need, until I'm leaking in my shorts. I don't dare touch myself. I should go inside and close the doors, but I can't pull myself away. I stand stock-still, listening as her voice carries over the ocean breeze until she's wrung every ounce of pleasure out of her body and comes with a loud moan.

Only when I'm sure she's finished, only as the wind teases her curtains, taunting me, telling me that if I'd leaned forward a little more, I could have seen her, do I go back into my bedroom and fist my cock until I'm spurting cum all over my goddamn stomach to thoughts of her and those damn sounds she made.

"I'm sorry, sir, but we're completely booked." The man behind the counter eyes me like I've lost my damn mind.

He's not wrong.

I've already gotten off twice this morning, thinking of Sienna, replaying her sounds. Once in bed because I was too damn hard to even walk after waking in the middle of a dream of her bouncing on my cock, then again in the shower as I fantasized about her red lips circling my crown.

If I have to hear those moans again, I won't survive. I'm already in danger of rubbing my dick raw.

"Give someone else the upgrade. I'll switch. I'm sure there's a couple here who'd be thrilled with a villa on the ocean."

Yes, I'm begging him to downgrade my accommodations. It's ridiculous, but I'm desperate. I haven't even tasted the woman, and already, I know she'd become an addiction. One taste could never be enough.

"A villa, huh?"

I turn and assess the two older gentlemen standing a couple of feet behind me. One is tall and bald, his head as shiny as a bowling ball, with a round face to match. His cheeks are red from the sun and his grin is wide. The other is even taller, with a full head of white hair like Ted Danson and wears a cocky smirk.

"Sure sounds nice," the man with the white hair says. "What's wrong with it? Infestation?"

A startled laugh escapes me. "Nope. Gorgeous room. Just too nice."

In unison, their smiles fall and their eyes go narrow, scrutinizing. "Too nice?" the bald man says.

Crossing my arms, I back up against the counter, leaning on it for support, and fully embrace the excuse. "Yup. The bed is too soft and the comforter is too silky against my skin. And the shower? Fuck, don't even get me started on the shower."

"And you don't want to stay there," Ted Danson's lookalike says. It's not really a question. There's no lilt to his tone. Just a plainly phrased statement.

"I'm used to crappy hotels. Hockey player." I raise a hand. "So it comes with the territory. My mattress at home is terrible, and the places they put us up while we travel are worse. If I stay in that villa, it'll throw off my sleep when I get back. Superstitions and all that."

"I don't even think that was a sentence," Baldy says.

Ted Danson shakes his head. "He said he plays hockey. Probably been hit in the head a few too many times."

I nod. "Definitely true. So where's your room?"

"Sir, we don't allow the bartering of rooms," the concierge says.

Ted Danson's twin holds up his hand. "No bartering happening. We'll leave you alone. Let you get back to your work." He drapes an arm over my shoulder and guides me away from the desk. "Does this room have two beds?"

I shake my head. "No, but it's a king."

The two men share a look, and movements in sync, they shrug. "Why don't you take us to it? I'm sure we can come to an agreement."

Clearly out of my mind, I guide them down the paths of the resort toward the villa. Did I mention they're both taller than I am? Like, ridiculously tall. "I'm Noah, by the way."

"Bert," Baldy says.

"Ernie," says Ted Danson.

Lip curling, I turn back and eye them.

They burst into laughter.

"We get that reaction a lot," Ernie says with a slap to my back. "But it's true."

"Fuck," I mutter, facing ahead again. "That's awful."

Bert chuckles. "Tell us about it. Not a selling point with the ladies."

"So one bed won't matter?"

"That's why we're coming to look," Ernie explains. "We'll test it out. See how we feel."

Shit. There's no way these two big guys will have enough room if they're not sleeping together. Well, sleeping together but not fucking.

An image of the two of them kissing overtakes me, and I practically shudder as I shake it loose. Why am I picturing them in an intimate way?

It's better than picturing Sienna, right?

On second thought, no. Not at all.

Fuck, what the hell is my problem, and why am I having so much trouble getting out of my own damn head?

As we approach my villa, I can't help but dart a look at Sienna's door.

Ernie eyes me, picking up on the move, but he says nothing as he steps inside.

Instantly, he sucks in a breath. "Bert, look at this view."

"Forget the view," the heavier man says as he heads to the minibar. "Look at all these labels." He lifts up a bottle of Hanson whiskey and grins.

"Don't touch the minibar," Ernie warns, heading out onto the deck.

Deflating, Bert sets the bottle down.

Angling in, I tap him on the shoulder. "You swap rooms, and I'll cover the bottle."

That grin creeps back up his face, and after a quick peek into the bathroom, he joins his friend on the deck.

Hands in my pockets, I wait for them to make a decision.

Will I miss this view? Sure. But this is for the best. I can sit on the beach at night. I don't need a private deck to myself. Hell, I can go off property for dinner. I probably should. It's likely the only way to avoid running into Sienna.

Yes. She mentioned not wanting to go to dinner alone. This is a good plan. I'll have to find something to do off property today so I don't risk running into her at the beach.

I'm slipping my phone from my pocket, intent on finding activities nearby, when a sweet voice filters in on the wind.

"Those are your real names?"

The low chuckles are harder to hear. I can imagine they're giving her the same spiel they gave me.

"What happened to Noah?" she asks them.

It takes everything in me to stay where I am. If I see her, I'll break. But if I can stay strong for the next ten minutes, then hopefully I can distance myself from the temptation for good.

"He doesn't like the room," Ernie explains. "So he asked if we'd swap. We haven't decided yet, though."

"Oh." The way she whispers the word, in understanding, pierces my heart.

Of course she sees right through my bullshit. Why the fuck would anyone dislike this room? It's a gorgeous beachfront villa. There's nothing to dislike. Now she knows I'm avoiding her.

Fuck.

"Well, I'll see you boys around, then." At least she sounds more upbeat again.

I rub at the ache in my chest, telling myself that this is for the best. But when the guys come inside, all smiles, ready to make the swap, the ache doesn't wane.

"Great," I say, even as that pain intensifies. "Let me just get my stuff packed up—"

Ernie shakes his head. "We've got a snorkeling trip booked this morning. We can swap when we get back."

I sigh. Dammit. I need to get out of here before I lose my mind. But it's only a few hours. I can avoid Sienna for that long.

"All right, I can give you my number, and when you get back—"

Bert is the one who shakes his head this time, the light from outside glinting off his bald head. "No can do. No phones. You'll just have to come with us."

I frown, looking from one man to the other. "Come with you?"

Nodding, Ernie slips his hands into his pockets. "Yup. Get changed quick. Otherwise we'll miss the boat."

"The boat," I parrot. "You want me to get changed?" With every word, I'm more lost.

"We saw the girl," Ernie explains. "She's gorgeous. We don't understand why that means you need to switch rooms, but obviously you've got your reasons, so—"

"We'll take you under our wing," Bert chimes in. "You'll snorkel with us. Then we'll swap rooms. Deal?"

I do need to avoid Sienna for the next few hours…

"I guess we're going snorkeling."

Turns out there was a single spot open for the snorkeling trip. "This works out well," the concierge said when Ernie put the phone in my room on speaker and called the front desk to get my name added to the list. "Another single booked last night as well."

"Great," I mumbled.

While it really was good news, since it meant I wouldn't be the only solo snorkeler, my mood had tanked.

With any luck, I told myself that would change when we got out there. Bert and Ernie had dived headfirst into this "taking me under their wing" nonsense and refused to leave my side, so I wouldn't have time to think about Sienna and the way she sounded this morning.

That one simple *oh* immediately played on repeat, pushing out even the sounds of her moans and leaving me feeling like absolute dogshit.

At the marina, multiple boats bob in the water ahead, and a sign directs us to the large catamaran where we'll spend the day.

A man wearing yellow shorts that come to his mid-thigh and a pink muscle shirt greets us with a smile. "Welcome aboard!" He's probably in his mid-twenties, with dark hair, dark eyes, and an insanely muscular body. If I met this guy anywhere else, I'd assume he was a model. "We're waiting on one more person, so we'll be heading out shortly." He guides us into the catamaran and shows us where the refreshments are, then quickly heads back to the dock, calling over his shoulder that he'll make a batch of his famous Caribbean punch once the last person arrives.

"The punch is always my favorite," Bert tells me.

"Don't have too much this early," Ernie says, pinning me with a look. "Otherwise you'll end up belly up while you're snorkeling like this guy did last time."

Bert barks out a laugh. "I don't see the issue. I didn't have to kick my feet, and I made it back to the boat just fine."

Ernie shoots him a glare. "But you missed the fish. That's the whole reason we're here."

"No, that's the reason you're here. I come for the free booze and sunshine." He bumps my shoulder and points to Ernie. "Definitely not the company."

Their banter quickly eases my anxiety. It's hard to focus on my intrusive thoughts when I have to use all my brain power to keep up with their conversation.

"Hi." A woman in her late forties appears, taking a drink from the table. "I'm Leslie. Where are you guys from?"

Ernie turns and faces her directly, immediately striking up a conversation.

Leslie's friend Gina appears next, and according to her, the two of them are visiting from Florida.

My two new friends are taken with them immediately. It makes sense. They're both good-looking, with bright smiles and easy laughter as Bert charms them.

Phil and Dana introduce themselves next. They're from Arkansas, and they're on their honeymoon. Dana spends several minutes rubbing lotion on her new husband's shoulders and shaking her head, mumbling, "He'd get a sun rash if it weren't for me."

They don't exactly give off newlywed vibes, but I've never been married, so what do I know?

With my towel under one arm, I'm eyeing the front of the catamaran, considering where I should set myself up, when Eddy, our model tour guide, claps his hands. "All right, our straggler has arrived. I'll start on the drinks, and then we'll go over the rules of the ship. You stay by me, beautiful Sienna," he says, his tone pure flirtation. "Your drink is first."

At the sound of her name, my muscles lock up. Every cell in my body urges me to turn, to look at the newcomer. Even knowing what I'll find, the sight before me still takes my breath away.

The woman the universe keeps pushing my way stands several feet away, her skin glistening in the sun. She's dressed in another one of those cover-ups that aren't cover-ups, this one white. And she looks downright delectable.

The oversized glasses she had perched on her head yesterday now cover half her face, making it difficult to read her expression, but she's turned in my direction, and the way her fingers tighten over the black bag on her shoulder tells me that she's just as surprised as I am to see her.

The white cover-up does little to hide the hot pink strings beneath, and I have no doubt that when she turns around, the ass I've so quickly become obsessed with will be on full display.

As Eddy motions for her to walk ahead of him, I have to stifle a growl. *Mine* is what I want to say. Or maybe *Keep your goddamn eyes on the fish and off her ass.*

I bite my tongue. In general, I'm not a fighter. I'm not possessive, and most importantly, *she's not mine.*

She's an adult who chose to wear a revealing bathing suit, knowing full well a boat full of people would see her ass. She's okay with that, and I have no right to an opinion. I can't go around like a damn hotheaded hockey player and beat people up for looking.

But I want to.

When she passes by, I clear my throat, and in the lightest tone I can muster, I say, "You again."

It's clear from the way she shrugs and waves as she continues forward that it didn't come out light at all.

No, it probably came out exactly how I feel: dejected, slightly irritated, and stupid.

Because who the hell fights the universe when it offers up a woman as perfect as Sienna?

Only an idiot like me.

"Isn't that the girl from the deck?" Bert asks, leaning in close.

Ernie, who's still chatting with Leslie and Gina, perks up and eyes Sienna's back as she walks away. With a bow of his head, he excuses himself and sidles over to us.

"That's her, right?" Bert prods.

Eyes squeezed shut, I pinch my brow. There's no avoiding this, so I might as well get it over with. "Yes."

Ernie tilts his head closer. "Why are we avoiding her?"

"I'm not," I grit out.

Both men eye me like I'm an idiot.

"Okay." I sigh. "I sort of am. Or I was." I shake my head. "Clearly I'm an idiot."

"Clearly," Ernie agrees.

Sienna's soft laughter echoes from where she stands beside Eddy, a drink in her hand. It's a performance laugh. One I bet she's used in polite conversation a thousand times. It only reinforces my assumption that she comes from money. She's practiced and rehearsed, but she was none of those things last night. She was flirtatious yet innocent, and her laugh was loud and contagious.

And none of that has anything on the way she acted when I left the room. Or the sounds she made when she thought no one could hear.

Squeezing my eyes shut, I try not to think about that. I try not to remember her sweet sounds and sensual moans. If I do, especially with the woman standing right before me in *that* bathing suit, I'm at risk of tenting my shorts and showing the whole group exactly how I feel.

Eddy appears in front of us, skillfully carrying two drinks in each hand. "Who wants my special punch?"

I shake my head. Hell no. I need to have all my brain cells if I want to survive this.

After the group has toasted to new friendships, Eddy returns to Sienna and lays her towel out on the front of the catamaran. By some miracle, before he can blatantly hit on her or ogle her ass, the captain calls him over to help undo the lines.

Bert nudges me. "Now's your time."

I shake my head. "Let her relax. This is a four-hour trip. I've got plenty of time to talk to her."

"Plenty of time." Ernie tuts. "That's what Bert thought about his first and second marriages."

"And now my dog calls someone else Daddy, and I share holidays with my ex and her husband."

I scowl. "I barely know the woman. There's no need to even mention divorce."

"It's not about divorce. It's about wasting time. Ask me how I know," Ernie says in a tone that tells me my friend who looks like Ted Danson never found his Mary.

As the catamaran cruises out of the marina, tropical music floats around us. I can't look away from Sienna, who's now lying on her back, sunglasses still hiding her face.

She's not my Mary. That's not a real thing. Even if it were, we met yesterday. So what if we keep running into one another?

It could be that the two of us are just meant to spend the next few days having a bit of fun, right? Maybe it's the universe's way of telling me to relax and enjoy myself. That's a theory I could get behind.

But more? I've got more than I can handle heading my way already. My son and my career are my only long-term priorities. They're all I have room for in my life.

Eddy dances by us, hips swinging and arms rolling. "Enjoy the ride out. We've got thirty minutes before we reach the first diving spot." He turns in a circle, still moving to the rhythm. "Let me know if you want a refill."

With that, he makes his way to the front of the catamaran where he kneels beside Sienna.

She looks up at him as he speaks, and in response to whatever he asks her, she nods and then reaches into her bag. She produces a small bottle and passes it to him.

I know before he squeezes the sunscreen into his hand what it is, and when Sienna sits up and leans forward and Eddy begins lathering her with lotion, a low growl rumbles from my chest. I don't want him touching her.

I don't want *anyone* touching her.

"Barely know her, huh?" Ernie says, a knowing glint in his eye.

Fuck.

Chapter 7
SIENNA

WELL, this was an epic failure. Last night, when the itch to work almost overtook me, when I was struggling to just be, I booked this snorkeling trip. This morning, when I found out that Noah was switching rooms, I felt like the earth was going to swallow me whole.

Or maybe I wished it would.

Because a woman knows when a man wants her, and it's clear as day that Noah does not want me. So much so that he's given up a beautiful villa to get away from me. So that I won't bother him? Is that it? So that I don't throw myself at him and beg him to spend time with me?

Yes, I flirted last night, but did I go too far? Did I miss some sign that he wasn't interested?

I don't have the first clue, and now here we are, on the same catamaran. He probably thinks I followed him on this snorkeling trip. Especially If the *you again* he greeted me with is anything to go by.

Maybe while we're out here, a whale will swallow me whole. Or maybe there's a life raft nearby, and I can drift off to sea.

While I wait for either opportunity to arise, I do what any properly chastised girl would do and relegate myself to the corner of the catamaran, away from Noah, away from the crowd and the drinks and the dancing.

So much for distractions. I might as well be on my deck by myself, because it's just as easy to freak out about Paris here as it was there. The show too, and my impending move. How I'll be halfway around the world all by myself for the first time in my life.

No, instead, that's all I can think about.

That and Noah. He's probably groaning to everyone about the desperate young girl who won't leave him alone.

Gah, this is embarrassing.

"Sienna," Eddy sings as he bounces onto the netting beside me.

I paste on a grin and slide my glasses up, giving the flirty tour guide my full attention. The man's muscles have muscles. He's a delicious specimen, and I can't help but preen when he discreetly checks me out.

"We've got a half hour until the first stop. Would you like another punch?"

I hold up the drink he made for me a few minutes ago, which is still pretty full. "I think I'm good for now." Though in this heat, I will eventually want another.

His eyes wander, maybe a little too brazenly this time, reminding me that in my celebratory *my brothers aren't coming on vacation* packing, I didn't bring a single suit that covers my ass. This one is a hot pink string bikini. And when I say string, I mean it's truly nothing but a lot of strings and the smallest bits of fabric. Whoops.

"The sun is very strong down here. Did you put on sunscreen?"

I did properly sunscreen my body before I left my villa. I'm twenty-four, not sixteen. But I can picture what it will look like from where Noah is standing if I tell sweet Eddy that I missed a spot. And after the shit Noah has pulled, I'm feeling like a petty bitch.

If he doesn't want to see me, then he'll look away. But even after all the signs he's thrown out, I have an inkling that it isn't so much that he doesn't find me attractive as it is that he can't make up his mind. And on this boat, surrounded by a crowd of people who are much older than we are—and Eddy, of course—his focus will be easily caught.

So I dig into my bag, pluck out the lotion, and hand it to Eddy. Then, propping myself up on my knees, I ensure I'm providing Noah with the perfect view of my *sweet cheeks*.

The man beside me hisses, then curses under his breath, but from the heat burning into my back from the attention focused there, he's not the only one feeling that way.

When Eddy is finished lathering my shoulders and back, I take the bottle and thank him. "How long have you worked here?" I ask as I settle back into my spot on my towel.

He crosses his legs, resting his forearms on his knees and lacing his fingers, and tells me how he's been with the tour company for a year. He's polite, making sure to ask me about my job too, but I gloss over the specifics and turn the conversation back to him. By the time we arrive at the first stop, I've learned that he was raised by a single mom and has two sisters, and on his nights off, he loves to dance.

He jumps up with ease, going from sitting to standing in one move, and holds out a hand to me. "Let's get you a mask and flippers."

I polish off the last of my drink, then let him help me up. Though I'm not the teensiest bit tipsy, my feet get caught in the netting and I lose my balance. Just as I'm certain I'm going down, Noah appears, stopping my fall.

He loops an arm around my waist and pulls me against his chest, then eases me onto my feet. "You okay?" he asks, his brows furrowed.

Annoyed, but well-practiced in the art of not letting such negative reactions show, I suck in a breath and nod. "Yes, thank you."

His body is so much bigger than mine. His one arm wraps almost completely around my waist, his large hand practically touching my back.

Like this, with his forearm draped across my torso, his olive skin looks incredible against mine. I never hold a tan. My skin is always this creamy color. Though fortunately, I rarely burn.

He sucks in a quick breath, his chest expanding, and when I tip my head back to make sure he's okay, I get caught on the most beautiful pair of eyes. Fuck, that was a bad idea. They're endless, beguiling. The sparkling ocean surrounding us has nothing on their blue depths.

I may be drowning in the Caribbean pools, but he's locked in on the space between us. Only then do I notice the way my practically bare ass is tucked up tight against his board shorts. It's his fault, really, because he's the one who caught me and pulled me in. Because he's the one who hasn't let go.

But he doesn't step away, and neither do I.

I could say it's because I'm not quite steady on this netting, but that'd be a lie, and if I can't be honest in my own head, what's the point?

I like the feel of him against me. I like how his lips have fallen open and he's trying to breathe without making it obvious how hard he's working for that simple necessity.

And I really like the sensation of his arousal against the globes of my ass.

It's proof that I'm not alone in this moment.

He wants me. Maybe he doesn't want to want me, but there's no denying he does.

"I've got flippers." Eddy's voice pulls me from my thoughts, but it's the loss of this man's touch that sends me teetering forward again. Shocked. Stupid.

He grips my thigh, his movement just as quick as the last, and sucks in another exaggerated breath. "Why don't you get off the netting?"

I laugh lightly, maintaining an unbothered appearance. "Right. Thank you."

He steps back, keeping his arm outstretched so I can use it for support as I climb onto the solid teak surface.

"Come on, Noah. Last person in is a rotten egg," one of the men I met on the deck this morning—the rounder one, with the bald head—calls. Then he catapults himself off the side of the boat and tucks his legs, cannonball style, creating an enormous splash.

The other man shakes his head and points at the water. "Your goggles."

"Sienna," Eddy says, cradling my elbow. "Let me get everyone set up, and then I'll go in with you." He holds out the flippers he fetched for me. "Everyone must have a buddy. And don't swim too far from the boat."

"I'll go with her." Noah reaches into the bucket of goggles at Eddy's feet and plucks a set out, shaking off another pair that's tangled around them. He turns toward me, but instead of handing them to me like I expect, he steps close, loops the strap around his wrist and uses both hands to push my hair behind my ears.

I can't help but stare at his lips, one of which he has caught between his teeth. He drags his hands down my jaw, his thumbs brushing over my cheeks, the blue of his irises suddenly stormy.

The warm air crackles between us, and my pulse picks up. Is he going to kiss me? And if so, what would those lips feel like? What would he taste like if he pressed his mouth to mine?

Between one heartbeat and the next, his hands are gone and he's pulling back. He holds up the goggles, and when I nod, he fits them over my head and adjusts them on my face.

When I reach up to tighten them, he shakes his head. It's the tiniest of movements. Then, with his tongue in his cheek, he tightens each side.

"This okay?" he asks.

I'm beginning to hate that question, because I swear every time he asks, his next move is to pull back. Despite that, the simple words light me up inside. The check-ins are as endearing as they are sexy. He's clearly a guy who thrives on consent.

Heat swirls in my core at the thought, and my nipples pebble.

Shit.

Why the hell did I let my mind wander there?

I have to step back. I have to get away from his heady scent and that mouth. It's too damn expressive, his thoughts written all over it rather than in his eyes. Biting down when he's apprehensive, licking his lips when he's turned on, the corners tipped up when he's surprised to find himself happy.

I barely know him, and already I see so much.

And he's made a point of putting space between us.

Clearing my throat, I give him a nod. And with a quick thanks, I take my flippers to the edge of the boat where a ladder is located.

Like any stubborn younger sister to a whole slew of boys would, I don't wait for him or Eddy. I slip the flippers onto my feet and drop into the water. The cool temperature is as much a shock as it is refreshing, and when I surface, I can't help but smile. I can't remember the last time I did something like this. Joining a tour with people I don't know. Spending the day on a boat that isn't private.

The thought makes me stupidly giddy and defiant and free. I tip forward, kicking my feet, and put my face in the water to confirm my goggles won't leak and that my snorkel is clear. Rather than coming right back up, I'm sidetracked by the kaleidoscope of color beneath me. Orange and deep blue fish with the prettiest black and white fins dart below me. I drift, enraptured, until I catch sight of a reef only a few feet away. With excitement coursing through me, I kick my way over to it, taking in the variety of fish and sea creatures.

The sight is incredible. The colors, the beauty, the whole world that exists beneath the surface. This is why people should snorkel in pairs, not just for safety, but because right now, I wish I could share this with someone. I've always hoped to one day fall in love, but I've never truly craved a relationship. But as I note a starfish close by, I get it. This is the kind of moment that I want to share with someone. It's an experience to look back on.

A fish peeks out of a cavernous cave within the reef, and when my shadow passes over it, its body puffs wide. I gasp, the sound strange in my ears. I'm practically giddy at the sight.

When there's a tap on my shoulder, I turn and find Noah's goggled face beside mine. My instinct is to smile at the gorgeous man, but before I can end up with a mouthful of saltwater, I school the expression and give him a thumbs-up.

He grasps my hand and tugs me forward, and we spend the next twenty minutes pointing out the fish and coral we see, each prettier and more exciting than the last. As the minutes go by, I'm not sure if it's the bright tropical fish or Noah's firm hand in mine that makes me feel lighter than I have in a long time.

Chapter 8
NOAH

A WOMAN I barely know shouldn't have the ability to silence every thought in my head. Her mere presence shouldn't push me into living in the moment in a way that only hockey ever has. I don't have the patience or capacity to sit and watch television or a movie. If I want to relax, I'm better off with a crossword puzzle challenging enough to require deep focus.

Topics that require studying before I can understand them. Sometimes even a good book.

But never a person.

Yet here Sienna is, an exception to that rule.

Spending hours going from spot to spot, taking in one incredible view after another, leaves my mind empty of everything but her. My entire focus is fixed on her, the rainbow-colored fish swimming below us, the coral, and the salt water that drips from her lips when we surface so we can board the catamaran. The track it takes down her chin, onto her neck, and between her breasts is a line I'd like to trace with my tongue.

The second the thought crosses my mind, I blow out a breath and look away from her. If I don't get myself under control, I'm liable to pull her flush to my body and kiss the ever-loving shit out of her.

It's insane that I'm more attracted to her right now, with a set of goggles covering her face and a snorkel dangling beside her cheek, than I've ever been to another person.

"You are a man of mixed signals," she says, her tone flat as we tread water to stay afloat while we wait for our turn near the ladder.

Aggravated with myself, I turn my eyes to the cloudless sky and consider how deep my explanation should go.

She slides the goggles off and dips beneath the water, coming up with her head tipped back so her wet hair cascades down and clings to her shoulders. "Forget it. You were very clear when you moved rooms. Thanks for swimming with me."

Fuck.

She turns, but before she can slip away, I grab her hand. "It's not what you think."

With one brow arched, she peers at me over her shoulder, silently saying *Yeah, buddy, really?*

"I had fun last night. I did, really. I just—" I tug on her hand until she turns back, then I pull the goggles off my head, feeling like an idiot for having this conversation through the glass.

She frowns, her green eyes not nearly as bright as they should be when surrounded by tropical waters.

I rough a hand through my hair, then drag it down my face. "But then I heard something I shouldn't have last night, and I had all these thoughts—" I snap my mouth shut and swallow past the lump that's formed in my throat.

I know she knows exactly what I'm talking about, though her expression gives nothing away. She doesn't even blush.

After several silent heartbeats, her mouth kicks up on one side and she nibbles ever so slightly on her bottom lip. "Did you consider that maybe I left my doors open on purpose? That I *wanted* you to hear?"

Without waiting for a response, she dips beneath the water and swims back to the boat.

I stay where I am, every kick that keeps me from sinking below the water painful as I wait for the boner that's just sprung to dissipate.

Even long after we've gotten out of the water, she holds my attention, and I don't know what to do about that.

The ride back on the catamaran is rough. The wind has picked up, and the waves force us to the back of the boat. I'm irrationally annoyed because I hoped I could have a few minutes up front with Sienna to talk about what she said. Figure out what she meant.

My attitude is absurd. We're not in a relationship. I barely know the woman. We shouldn't need to talk anything out. Yet I crave her words. Crave her nearness.

Instead, Eddy hovers at her side, chatting away. Entertaining her.

"Tell Eddy you need a drink," I mumble to Ernie.

"So you can talk to the girl?" He cocks a brow. "Nah, I'd rather you let your balls drop and go interrupt them yourself."

I'm used to crude comments and locker room talk. I just don't normally engage. Today is no different. Rather than argue with him, I lean back, hoping someone, anyone, will need something from Eddy and do the interrupting for me.

Though as I sit and wait and scan the group, it seems like they all have full drinks and are happy to flirt among themselves. So before long, I find myself watching, once again, as Eddy chats up Sienna, making her eyes dance and pulling genuine laughs from her. She's holding the straw of her drink to her mouth, biting down on it every few seconds and smiling.

Thank fuck she pulled a sweatshirt on when the wind picked up. If I had to watch him flirt with her while she was nearly naked, I might actually lose it.

As we get close to port, Eddy gets up. But before I can collect myself and move closer, the two women in their forties approach Sienna and fall into conversation.

I'm hanging back until I can get a moment alone when Eddy calls out to the group. "Ride is over. You don't have to go home, but you can't stay here!" Around me, laughs ring out, and one by one, the other snorkelers step off the boat, all smiles. As we shuffle closer to the exit point, I make sure I slide in behind Sienna. Once we're on the dock, I'll apologize and explain. But before I can, Eddy grabs her arm and pulls her to the side. "There's a dance party tonight on the beach. I'm working it. Will you come?"

With no more than a second's hesitation and a big smile, she says, "That sounds fun."

I fight back a shudder and bow my head. It sounds miserable. Sand, alcohol, sweaty bodies, and loud music? All I want is to sit in a quiet corner with this woman. To talk to her for hours like we did last night. I want to laugh with her, and maybe, *fuck*, maybe hear those sounds she made last night from a little closer. Say, while I'm inside her.

Yes, my dick thickens at the image that pops into my head.

Whether we get to that last part or not, I need to talk to her. Determined, I lift my head. Only to find she's gone.

I'm still looking around, searching for her, when Ernie squeezes my shoulder. "Come on, son. Let us show you to your new room."

It takes Ernie and Bert half an hour to pack up and another half hour for the cleaning crew to come through. The guys asked me to meet them for a late dinner. I should go. If I don't, I'll end up sitting in this small room with one lone window looking out at the air conditioning unit and the building next door.

Really, I should go to the beach party. Find the woman I can't stop thinking about. I could stop her from dancing with anyone else. I could, I don't know, ask her to dance with me.

I scoff and drop my head back against the headboard. What am I, fifteen? Why is this so hard?

Rather than make a decision, I scroll through Instagram. War posted a photo of himself with Brooks and a few other guys who look vaguely familiar at what looks like a cookout. The caption reads *New team, who dis?*

I chuckle, take a screenshot, and shoot him a text.

Me: You're an idiot.

His response is immediate.

War: You know you miss me.

With a sigh, I lie back on one of the beds. Because, yeah, there are two. The empty one beside me is a painful reminder of just how alone I am. When traveling for the last few years, War and I always shared a room.

Until now, I hadn't considered who I might bunk with. Hopefully not one of the rookies. Maybe I'll get my own room. It's been a long time since I've had a roommate other than when we traveled. War was easy to put up with. We liked hanging out together. If he brought a woman back to the hotel—which happened pretty often, actually— he'd kick a pair of rookies out of their room for a few hours.

Asshole.

War: How's the upgrade? Send me a pic.

I scan the room. Shit. This isn't going to cut it.

Before I can come up with an excuse, my phone vibrates, and the screen flashes with a FaceTime request.

Groaning, I accept it. If I don't answer, he'll keep calling until I do. "Hello?"

"Harry!" War yells.

The nickname is immediately echoed by another familiar voice. When he flips the camera, Brooks is grinning at me, a spoonful of ice cream inches from his lips.

"Hi, guys." I offer a stupid wave and settle back in the bed.

"Show us the digs," War says.

"Where are you?" I ask in a lame attempt to distract him.

"The pad. Most of the team lives here. Moneybags over here owns the whole building." War nods at Brooks, who's now beside him so I can see both guys at once.

Brooks rolls his eyes. "My brothers own it; I do not."

"Not me." Aiden Langfield pops up on War's other side, upside down, like he's hovering over the guys, wearing a wide smile.

Even if he weren't Brooks's brother, I'd recognize him. He's one of the greats at our game. He's a couple of years younger than the rest of us, but the guy is already slated to end up in the hall of fame.

With a grunt, War pulls the phone back. "As I was saying…" He glares over the top of his phone, probably at Aiden. "Their family owns it and we all live here. Like a bunch of monkeys. This way they can keep an eye on us."

"I'm watching you," a female calls from close by.

"Oh, we know," War mumbles. He gets real close to the screen and whisper-hisses, "Sara is the head of PR. She's wicked hot but super scary."

Brooks punches him in the arm. "Don't be a dick."

Blue eyes dancing with mischief, War throws a thumb toward Brooks. "And he's in love with her."

"I'm going to kill you," my gentle giant of a friend curses. A second later, he's gone.

War drops his head back and chuckles. "So I'm making friends and settling in. What are *you* doing? Or better yet, *who* are you doing?"

A sigh slips out of me without my permission. "I'm just hanging in the room."

War frowns, bringing the phone closer to his face. "That's—dude, why the fuck aren't you outside? Or inside a woman?"

"Gross," Sara, I assume, calls off screen.

Huffing a laugh, I shake my head. "Calm yourself. I spent the day snorkeling. With a woman," I add for good measure.

"Oh." He sits up straighter, his dark brows high on his forehead. "Are you in her room?"

"Yes," I lie. "She's in the shower."

His lips kick up on one side. "Fuck yes. Is she hot?"

Mouth shut tight, I glare at him. He knows I don't talk like that.

He gives up quickly, leaning back against the cushions behind him. "Whatever. All right, go get in that shower. And don't call me again until you get home."

"You called me," I argue.

He chuckles. "Don't pick up next time. Go fuck. Swim. Do something. Stop being such an old man. And if I see one goddamn crossword puzzle the next time we video chat, you're a dead man."

I huff out a breath, but I'm smiling. He knows me well.

The screen goes dark before I have a chance to respond, and the room goes silent again.

With a sigh, I navigate to Jen's contact and send her a text, checking in and ensuring she's still feeling okay. Then I type out a message to Hannah. She's on the Boston Revs PR team, so this is her busy season. She's traveling, which it seems she does even more than I do, but she says things are good. She loves her job. Now that I think about it, she probably knows Sara, and from the way Sara handled War and Brooks, I bet she and my sister get along well.

That makes me smile. Hannah deserves the world. She hasn't had the easiest life, but she's one of the best people I know.

My phone buzzes, and a notification banner appears, so I tap on it.

> Jen: Feeling good. Based on what the doctor said yesterday, it's not likely I'll have this baby until you're back for summer camp.

Right. Because preseason training starts next week. And in a matter of weeks after that, I'll be a dad.

War's right. Why the fuck am I sitting in this room like an old man? Yes, I have a kid on the way, and yes, my life is about to change. But I'm not a dad *yet*.

I've got two more days in paradise. After that, trips like this will be impossible, so I better make the time worth remembering.

I'm going after Sienna. Fuck it.

Chapter 9
SIENNA

THE SUN TAKES a swan dive into the ocean, turning the water a shimmery pink and gold as the sky shifts from a teal that nearly matches the water to a deep red. Is the sky a reflection of the sea or the opposite? I can't remember.

Either way, the way they meet in a soft dance reminds me of silky fabric, and suddenly, a design creates itself in my mind and I'm itching for a sketchpad so I can get it down before the details evaporate. I grab my phone from my clutch and power it on. Ignoring the slew of texts that flood in, I tap on the app I use when I don't have a pad handy. Quickly, but with precision, I bring the image in my mind to life.

School was never easy for me. Even peopling takes effort, since I've always had a role to play. But this—drawing, envisioning, designing— is second nature. I can't imagine what I'd do without it.

Feeling lighter than I have all day, I take a screenshot, then send the image to Cat. This way, I can all but guarantee she'll have the fabric in Paris when I arrive. A design like this is too beautiful not to be shown off by a woman like her. No, it should be shown off by Cat and Cat alone. There isn't another woman in the world like her. She's *it*. And she loves my designs.

I'm still pinching myself over that.

My phone buzzes almost immediately, so I slide my finger over the screen and accept the FaceTime request, expecting her to tease me about working while I'm on vacation.

When my brothers appear on the screen, I shift, ensuring they'll see the sunset behind me rather than the hotel.

"Settle a debate for us," Aiden, the youngest of my brothers, says. No *Hi*, no *How are you?*

Maybe I don't have to bother hiding where I am. At least not with Aiden. He's barely paying attention.

At twenty-six, he's still got a boyish look about him. I'm not sure he'll ever grow out of it, honestly. It might be the way his hair curls at the ends or the permanent sparkle in his eyes and the smile he's always wearing.

For a second, I find myself wondering what it's like to always be that happy. I envy him for the way he can make even the worst days enjoyable. If I'm tired, he'll break into a song about how it's a bright sunshiny day, though he usually changes the lyrics to make them more fitting for the occasion. If I'm sad, I can always count on him to tell a joke or force me to my feet to dance.

"What's the debate?" I find myself smiling. It's hard not to with my happy-go-lucky brother.

"*That* doesn't match, correct?"

He squints at the screen, and a second later, the camera is flipped, and I'm looking at another man from the waist down. Like this, I can't tell who it is. I almost don't want to know anyway. All the men my brothers hang out with play hockey, and I've always kept myself far, far away from them.

Mostly because my brothers would kill me. But also because if I dated a man affiliated with the Bolts or the Revs, I'd never know whether he was interested in me or the connections he could make because of me.

Noah mentioned playing hockey. Does that mean he plays professionally? If so, that's one more huge reason to avoid telling him my last name.

Though why would I even have the opportunity? The man has made it abundantly clear he's not interested in me.

After the room swap today, I probably won't see him again anyway.

Aiden appears on the screen again, wearing a frown. "Well? It's awful, right?"

I chuckle. "I only saw the bottom half, as in black pants."

"It's the sandals!" he yells as he flips his phone again and zeros in on a pair of very white, very large feet in blue slip-on sandals.

I make a face. I can't help it. That's just...*no.*

"Ha," my brother says, loud and obnoxious. "Told you."

"She didn't see the whole thing," the man in the sandals complains. "Show her everything."

"No, because if she sees all your *War* hotness, it will negate the sandals issue."

I snort. "I assure you, no one is hot enough to negate those sandals."

"That's what I'm saying."

"Show her my face," the man taunts.

Oh, he's a cocky one.

"Not happening." Aiden gives him a death glare that, on him, doesn't look even remotely threatening. "All right, beautiful Sienna, what are you doing?"

His refusal to let me see his friend sparks a hint of curiosity inside me. Now I want to know what the cocky guy looks like.

The thought has just entered my mind when the image on my phone screen goes blurry, then dark. A second later, a thump echoes through the speaker. The device lights up again quickly, though all I can make out are snapshots of black pants, then the floor, then what could be a wall, like I'm being run around the room. My brother shrieks, and then a gorgeous man appears and winks at me.

And hot damn, he wasn't kidding. I could actually forgive him for the crime he's committing with those sandals. He's insanely hot. And the way his blue eyes dance with mirth, like he knows I think he's gorgeous, somehow only makes him hotter.

But he's not my type.

Once again, images of Noah, the man with the glasses and sweet disposition, infiltrate my brain. I bite my lip. I've never been so infatuated with seeking out the attention of another person. I've never had to work for it, if I'm honest. Because if a guy isn't really in it for me, he's still in it for my money or connections or to gain notoriety. So really, men are never *not* after me.

I affect the most unimpressed expression and shake my head. "Change the sandals. Oh, and take your arm off my brother's neck. I assume you play hockey with him, so I'd think you'd know that you need him breathing in order to win this season."

"Aw, she doesn't remember me." He pushes out his lips in a big pout. "Tyler Warren." His eyes dance like he knows I'll remember that name. And I do. He played hockey with Brooks long before they went pro. "Little Langfield grew up hot," he tells my brother as he releases him.

"She's off-limits," Aiden coughs. When he appears on the screen again, his face is red. "You having fun?"

I giggle. "Yes, I'm having a good time."

"You dancing?"

My heart thumps a little at the question. "You know, I haven't yet. But I'm about to do just that."

With a boyish grin, he says, "Good. Have fun. I'll see you in a few days."

The screen goes dark, and when I get a glimpse of my reflection looking back at me, I see the big smile I'm wearing. And then I remember the promise I just made.

I'm going dancing. I'm going to have fun, whether I'm on my own or not. It's what Aiden would do.

An hour later, I've found Eddy and a drink, and I'm swaying to the music from the live band on stage.

Eddy mentioned it was a white party when he asked me to come, and though I was pretty sure I hadn't brought anything acceptable, it was like fate intervened. Because as I headed to my room after talking to Aiden, I passed by the resort boutique and discovered a white tube top and a long, white gauzy skirt in the window. The turquoise bib-style necklace I brought works perfectly with it, the combination making the white even crisper and the turquoise brighter.

After a day in the sun, my cheeks are pink and my skin is glowing, so I put the tiniest swipe of mascara on my lashes and a clear gloss on my lips, then headed out.

I didn't bring a hair tie, since my hair is barely long enough to pull up, so within minutes of stepping onto the dance floor, it clings to the sheen of sweat collecting on my brow.

Since he's working the party, Eddy checks on me periodically but spends most of his time bouncing around, entertaining the crowd and encouraging people to dance.

I don't mind being on my own. The night sky, lit up by millions of stars, is beautiful, and the warm air against my skin is soothing. I push my hair out of my face and tip my head back as the band begins to play "Blurred Lines" by Robin Thicke. As the chorus starts, I sway my hips and close my eyes, losing myself to the beat.

Though my heart is thumping and the music is loud, the slightest tickle rolls down my spine and an awareness needles at me. It's the sound of magic, like the strum of tiny wind chimes floating through the air, announcing his presence.

So when a warm body slides in close, I'm not the least bit surprised. He doesn't touch me. Of course he doesn't. He's a gentleman. But he stays close, choosing to be in my presence, like that alone could ever be enough for us. I open my eyes and tilt my head slightly so I can look behind me. When Noah's lips lift shyly, like he's not quite sure how I'll react, my heart does a little tap dance I worry is detrimental to my health.

He doesn't say anything, and neither do I, but I step back and drape my arm around his neck, pulling him closer.

His hands find my waist, his touch tentative.

Hell no. He sought me out. He approached me. There's no room for uncertainty anymore. I push back into him. At first, his body stiffens, but after a breath, he loosens up and tugs me flush against him, one hand now splayed over my abdomen.

With the first roll of my hips to the beat, he lets out a grunt. It's guttural. Deep in his throat. Animalistic.

Intrigue and desire spark to life in my veins. So this sweet, respectful man does have another side.

A smile finds its way to my face as I hum to the music, my fingers tugging at the hair at his nape. He tips his head, his cheek brushing against mine, and a shiver runs through me. No sensation has ever felt so good. The slight roughness on my sun-kissed skin reminds me of the itch I really need to scratch. An itch that, surely, he can take care of far better than any of the toys I brought.

One song turns into three, and when my drink is empty and I'm a sweaty mess, I turn to him. "Can we get a drink?"

With his hand on my back, he guides me through the throng of people toward the bar. Secretly, I'm glad Eddy hasn't returned. Or maybe he has, and he saw us dancing. Either way, I'm glad that Noah showed up.

"What happened to your friends?" I ask him.

He shrugs. "I think they went to dinner."

"You think? You gave away your room, and in return, they ditched you?" I chuckle.

He shakes his head, his lips quirking in a hint of a smile. "I'm an idiot; I know."

At the bar, I set down my empty drink.

In seconds, the bartender is in front of us. "Margarita?"

Once we've ordered two, I lean against the bar and face the man I can't stop thinking about. In the sea of white clothing, he stands out in teal shorts and a black polo. Maybe he'd stand out anyway, with the way his shirt tugs against his muscles. The sight of him alone makes my mouth water.

I'm familiar with his body from snorkeling today. He's clearly a man who takes care of himself, and I appreciate that.

What I appreciate more, though, are his loafers. They're Italian leather and a sign that he's far more mature than most men I know.

The contrast between his shoes and the damn sandals Tyler Warren was wearing makes me snort.

"What's so funny?" Noah asks, dipping in a little closer, his face lit up with curiosity.

"My brother—" I shake my head. It's stupid.

He arches a brow, expectant.

"He called me earlier," I explain, "because he and his friend were going out, and that friend was wearing black slacks and sandals."

Noah feigns an affronted scowl. "Terrible."

"It is." I press my hand against his chest, pushing him back. Or at least I mean to push him back. But once my palm is against his chest and I feel the way his heart is beating, I can't pull away.

With his lip pressed between his teeth and his eyes locked on mine, he rests his own heavy hand over mine, holding it there.

The blue of his eyes seems to grow more vibrant as he shifts infinitely closer. For a moment I think he's going to kiss me. My heart thuds wildly at his proximity, but when he leans over my shoulder, then steps back, holding a margarita between us, a small sigh of disappointment escapes me. When I don't take the drink, he arches a brow and sips it himself. Then, with his focus locked on my face, he turns the glass and brings it to my lips, pressing my mouth to the spot where his was only seconds ago.

"Open," he commands.

Holy fuck. That single word is enough to make me simultaneously combust and whimper.

He tips the glass, and my lips part to allow the smallest sip of liquid in. He eases it back again, his gaze trailing down my throat as I swallow.

I melt into a damn puddle under his scrutiny. My panties are so damp it's embarrassing.

"Want to take our drinks to go?" The question is a low rumble from deep within his chest.

Surprised by the boldness, I nod woodenly and blink several times.

With the smallest of smiles, he hands me the fresh margarita, then settles the tab.

"I'm surprised you showed up," I admit as we meander down the path toward the beach. This is the easiest way to my villa, though I'm not sure that's our destination. I don't want to be presumptuous, and with a little thought, I realize that I also don't know that I'm ready to go back to my room with him anyway.

"I don't want to want you," he admits, his voice soft but his focus steady on my face. He meant for me to hear it, but he's tempering his tone to dampen the harshness of the statement.

I lift my chin and study his face in the moonlight. "Why?"

He glances out at the now midnight blue waves, at the shimmering crests as they roll in. "My life is complicated."

Affronted, a light scoff escapes me. "I'm not asking for a ring. Hell, I'm not really asking for anything. I was just flirting, enjoying myself. You don't have to be here."

He grasps my hand, stopping me, and faces me head-on. "That's just it, though. I want to be." He wets his lips, his gaze trailing over me with reverence. "I want more than to be here, honestly," he rasps.

My heart stutters. "Why?"

He blows out a heavy breath, then breaks into a shy smile. "Have you ever met a person and thought, *God, I want to know them*? Like—" He gently tugs on a tendril of my hair, his fingers smoothing over it, back and forth, back and forth, like he doesn't even realize he's doing it.

When his eyes meet mine again, I know exactly what he wants to say. I understand him.

"I need to know you. It's impossible to walk away, knowing you exist in this world." He sighs like the admission has sapped all his energy. "Have you ever felt that before?"

I dip my chin as tingles course through me. "Yes."

"I have nothing to offer. My life—" He shakes his head. "But the idea of not knowing you is untenable."

After such raw honesty from him, I give him a little of my own. Maybe this will settle his nerves. "I'm moving to Paris next week. There's no possibility after this weekend for me either."

His hopeful expression slips, and I swear a look of devastation sweeps across his face before he forces a crooked smile. "Well, look at me getting ahead of myself."

I bite my lip and offer a small laugh. "I suppose we'll see what the universe has planned for us next."

He threads his fingers through my hair and swipes his thumb against my cheek, tipping my chin up. I'm prepared when he lowers his mouth to mine. I've wanted to kiss him since the moment he stepped onto that plane. Since he looked at me through those thick frames, that book in his hand. Every moment since, my desire has grown, morphing into lust and now need. A need to know whether the sparks that have been bouncing between us—the tension that's electrified the air we share—will make us combust. Or if instead, we'll dance within the flames of this affair.

I hope it's the latter. With any luck, we'll figure out how to enjoy the heat.

He angles in, and when he presses his lips against mine and a soft sigh escapes him, the reality of this moment washes over me. Kissing him feels like sinking into a comfortable bed. Like a warm blanket, a book, and a glass of wine on a rainy day. Like a sketchpad and a stack of colored pencils and hours with nothing on the agenda. It's perfect and cozy and familiar and new and exciting. It's all the things a woman could want in a first kiss.

And everything I don't want in a first kiss with someone I'll soon be saying goodbye to.

Noah has a complicated life, and mine hasn't even begun. We're a blip in time. A cataclysmic slip created by the universe. But I take it anyway.

I take what he's offering, because for a girl who's been offered almost everything in life, I've never been given anything that was so perfectly made for me.

Chapter 10
NOAH

SAYING GOODBYE TO SIENNA—AND not begging to spend the whole night kissing her—took herculean effort. We only have two days. This is going nowhere. I shouldn't be taking this slow. Fuck romance. I should be diving in headfirst.

And yet romance is all I see when I look at that woman.

It's a living, breathing thing, guiding my every move. It sets a pace I can't help but take. Nothing has ever felt this right. It's terrifying, since we're meant for a one-night stand, if we're lucky, and nothing more.

Despite the fear there, it's impossible not to enjoy every tension-filled moment.

I contemplate showing up at her room with breakfast this morning but determine it's a little too presumptuous. Better to wait for lunchtime. If I haven't run into her by then, it'll be the perfect excuse to check in. She has to eat, so why not eat with me?

I'm heading out for a run along the beach when Bert and Ernie appear, blocking my path. "Thought you were going to meet us for dinner last night. Where'd you disappear to?"

I run my hands through my hair and dart a look around. "Ended up going to the party on the beach."

Ernie's eyes light up. "Oh, our next-door neighbor told us she was going there too, didn't she, Bert?"

The rounder of the two men nods. "Yup. She did say that. Did you happen to run into her?"

I try to wipe the grin off my face, but it's no use. "Yeah, I did, actually."

Ernie, white hair styled perfectly, claps me on the shoulder with a little too much force, turning me around and leading me back the way I came. "That's great. Walk with us. Tell us what happened."

I glance over my shoulder. "I was just going for a run."

He waves a hand. "You can do that later."

I suppose he's right. So I give them a very brief overview of the night, quickly touching on how Sienna and I danced and talked.

"But she was by herself this morning," Bert states.

"Yeah, when we left, she was having breakfast on her deck. *Alone,*" Ernie emphasizes.

I duck my head and chuckle. "I walked her back to her place and haven't seen her since."

Without stopping, Ernie looks at me head-on, his face twisted in confusion. "Why?"

"Because—" I shake my head. "Wait, why are you pushing this?"

In unison, they let out obnoxious sighs.

"You really like her," Ernie says.

I shrug. "Yeah, why's that bad?"

"Because we thought this was a vacation fling." Bert runs a hand over his shiny bald head. "If we'd realized you liked her like this, we'd have turned you down when you asked to switch rooms. Now we feel bad."

I frown. "What difference does it make?"

"Because now you're less likely to casually 'run into' her," Bert explains like I'm an idiot.

"I appreciate the concern, but I'll be okay."

"No you won't," Ernie grumbles. He stops, so Bert and I do the same.

Ahead on the beach, a dozen or so women sit on towels, lined up in rows. Between them and the ocean, a man with his own beach towel laid out beside him stands, gesturing like he's speaking.

"But fortunately for you," Bert says, "we're here to help."

I scratch my head, still surveying the scene. "Huh?"

Just as the word leaves my mouth, it hits me. Because there, in the back row, pushing to her feet on her towel, is Sienna. "So you're my fairy godfathers?"

Ernie throws his head back and guffaws. "I kind of like that title."

Bert mouths the words a few times and shrugs. "It works."

Now that I've spotted the woman who's occupied all my thoughts since we touched down in the Bahamas, it's as if there's a tether connecting me to her, tugging, insisting I get closer. "Thanks, guys."

I hustle onto the beach, though I only make it a few steps before Ernie calls my name.

"You need this." He tosses a turquoise towel to me.

With a grin, I snag it out of the air. When I turn back around, Sienna is looking our way. And when our eyes meet, her lips lift like I'm the greatest surprise.

"You found me," she says as I place my towel beside hers.

I nod. "Yup. I found you."

My body feels surprisingly good after yoga. It's nothing like the workouts I'll be doing in a matter of weeks, nor the training I follow even in the offseason, but the stretches loosened up my muscles, and since I'm supposed to be relaxing during this trip, I guess that's fitting.

"Would you maybe want to run into each other for lunch?" I ask her as we shake out our towels.

Sienna shrugs, but she's smiling. "Maybe. What did you have in mind?"

I glance around the resort, then point at the beach bar. "There work for you?" I don't want to waste time traveling, so that place is probably our best bet. "We can go back to our rooms and change, then meet at the restaurant in thirty minutes?"

"Sure." She folds her towel in half, then in half again, and drapes it over her arm. "I can do that."

"Want me to walk you back to your room?"

She rolls her eyes. "If you hadn't given up your nice room to avoid me, we could walk back together. But no, I can get back myself okay. Unless…" She trails off, scanning the beach before blinking up at me.

The look is weighted, heavy. Like she has something other than lunch in mind.

Stomach tightening and heart racing, I force myself to respond. "Unless?"

She presses her teeth into her lip. "I can walk back with you, and then you can come to my room."

Maybe it's my imagination, but it almost sounds like she doesn't want to leave me any more than I want to leave her. Like spending thirty minutes apart is a terrible waste of the limited time we have here.

"Okay, though it probably makes sense to stop at your room first, since you're near the water."

With a shrug, she turns toward the path that winds along the beach and to the villas.

"So, Paris," I hedge.

Last night, once I finally found the strength to stop kissing her, I got the hell out of there, worried about what would happen next if I didn't, so I never had a chance to ask about her move.

Sienna hums, her focus on the sidewalk ahead. "Yes, Paris."

"Why are you moving?"

"Job. It's a big move for my career. But I'm nervous. Being the youngest of five siblings means that I've always been kind of cocooned."

Amused, I parrot her words. "Cocooned?"

She giggles. "Like I can't go anywhere without someone being in my business. They all care. They only do it because they love me. But I'm ready to fly, ya know?"

I nod, smiling. "Yeah, butterfly, I think you are."

"Butterfly." She hums. "I like that."

"Better than sweet cheeks?"

Her already flushed face goes red. Most of the time, she's sassy, but then she has soft moments like this, almost like the sexy clothes and sharp tongue are a front. A defense mechanism, perhaps. Like the intricate designs on a butterfly. The colorful attitude protects her. It allows her to stand out, or blend in, depending upon the role required of her at that moment.

One of my strengths is my ability to read people. It's served me well in my career. I study my opponents' tells so I know when they're about to deke left or glide right. I know when a goalie has taken his focus off a certain spot. It takes a second of indecision on his part and a fake-out on mine to get the puck into the back of his net.

Though I don't normally use that intuition in my day-to-day life. I've never really had reason to, I guess. My focus has always been fixed solely on hockey. If I'm not studying tape, training, or working out, I'm keeping my brain occupied with crossword puzzles or a documentary. I like learning and I like studying, but I've never been interested enough in a woman to use those skills to discover more about her.

But with Sienna, I want to know everything and I'm studying every detail. It takes work, and I've got to really focus on the little comments, the body language, and the facial expressions, because she's not giving me much to go on.

"In what industry is this big career move happening?"

Sienna stares off toward the ocean, those green eyes going distant, and shakes her head. "Can we not do that whole thing?"

"What whole thing?"

Head tilted, she sighs. "The careers, the last names. I don't want any of that to influence the way you look at me."

I frown. "Why would your last name influence the way I look at you?"

"It influences how everyone looks at me," she says, a soft sadness to her voice.

My hackles rise a little, an unfamiliar defensiveness overtaking me. "I'm not everyone."

I don't get hung up on wealth. I already know she comes from money anyway. It was obvious the moment I saw her. I couldn't care less about fame either. Could she be an actress? I'd be the last person to recognize her if that were the case. Honestly, none of it matters to me.

"Please?" Her tone is soft but full of desperation. "It changes how people look at me. I know it's asking a lot, but can we just be Noah and Sienna here? I need to be my own person this week. I'm so damn nervous about next week. I have no idea what life will look like when I'm no longer living in my brothers' shadows. It'll be good to practice."

I thread my fingers through hers and squeeze. "You're going to soar, butterfly. I don't know your last name, and I don't know a damn thing about your life, but from what I've witnessed over the last couple of days, I know you'll be amazing. So yeah, we can just be Noah and Sienna this weekend. I think I'd like that, actually."

With a relieved sigh, she smiles. "Well." She peers back at her villa. "I know you had to switch rooms since the accommodations were so terrible, but you'll have to slum it with me for a few minutes while I change."

I chuckle. "I already told you why I switched rooms."

"Ah, yes," she teases. "Because you were trying to stay away from little old me. How's that working out for you?"

With a grunt, I pull her into a bear hug and lumber toward her door. "You're a brat, you know that?"

Sienna stares up at me, wide-eyed, like she's shocked by how freely I'm touching her.

Truth is, if this caught her off guard, then I may need to rethink all the things I want to do with her. I may not sleep around, but like everything else in my life, I've studied how the human body experiences pleasure—and pain—and I like to utilize both to take sex to a higher level.

I ache to explore it all with Sienna. It won't just be sex. Our connection is too strong, and I'm already too invested.

Ready to get our time together rolling, I release her and hold out my hand, silently requesting she give me her key card. With any luck, in the time it takes for me to open the door, she'll recover.

In a matter of seconds, she's back to copping an attitude, swaying her hips and taunting me as she walks into the bedroom. She points to the bed and tells me to make myself comfortable while she gets changed.

Then, being the tease she is, she leaves the bathroom door open. From my position on the bed, I could very easily catch her reflection in the mirror while she strips out of her clothes. It's hard not to look. Not because I want to get a glimpse of her body—though that would be a bonus—but because I want to know if she's watching for me.

I give in quickly, though I keep my attention on her face. Sure enough, her eyes are searching for mine, her teeth sinking into her bottom lip.

The moment she catches me watching her in return, she breaks into a brilliant smile. Then, to my fucking delight, she turns and saunters toward me. She's in another red bikini. The bottoms are already in place, but the top? She's holding it to her chest with her hands, lifting and pressing her breasts together, giving me an eyeful of cleavage.

"Tie this for me? I normally do it from the front and then turn it around, but since you're here…" She spins, giving me the perfect view of the sweet cheeks that have been taunting me since day one. They're practically bare, with only a red string between them.

This fucking woman is toying with my resistance.

I suck in air through my teeth, garnering all the control I've got left. Then I grasp the straps dangling at her sides. "Lift your hair for me."

She could easily do it with one hand, yet she chooses to torture me further by releasing her hold on her top completely before pulling her hair up, causing the fabric of her bikini top to hang limply in my hands.

I squeeze my eyes shut and inhale through my nose.

She shifts, the move tugging on the straps I'm still clinging to. "This okay?" she asks over her shoulder, her tone one degree from a sexual purr.

I open my eyes and glare. "*Sienna.*" The word is a warning. To both of us. My patience is threadbare by now, and she's calling to a side of me I'm not sure she's ready for.

"Yes, Noah?" The brat is back, faking a sweet, coy attitude, like she has an inkling of how this will go.

Despite her brazenness, she doesn't have a clue. But she's about to find out.

I release the straps, and her top floats to the floor.

"Oops," she says, her voice breathy. "I'll get it." She bends, grinding her practically bare ass against my dick. If the move had been brief, it could have been considered an accident. Maybe. Though it would have taken a stretch of the imagination. But as she remains bent over, her ass taunting me, she's making it clear that she has no interest in lunch or a day on the beach.

"You have five seconds to change your mind, Sienna. Stand up and get dressed like a good girl, and we'll go to lunch, or—" I inhale, cataloging her mouthwatering curves and the tantalizing red line separating her cheeks. I consider pulling on it. I consider running my teeth over it.

I'm lost in all my options when she says, "Or?"

My heart rate skyrockets. That's truly the only answer I needed, but I detail it for her. "Or I'll put you face down on the bed and spank you for taunting me. And then I'll spend every minute between now and when we leave on Tuesday learning all the ways I can make you come."

"I pick that one," she says without even a moment to think it through.

Even still, I count backward from five, giving her a warning of what's to come. Giving her those few extra seconds to consider what she's agreeing to. To ratchet up the tension between us.

"Five." My words are slow and enunciated, my muscles taut. "Four." I can't look away from her ass as it sways back and forth sensually, but I don't dare touch. "Three." I exhale loudly. "Two. Last chance."

She waggles her ass in response, begging to be punished.

"One." The word is hoarse, rough, as it escapes me.

She lets out a long, shuddering breath, waiting.

And fuck do I make her wait. I close my eyes and savor this moment. The seconds before I finally touch her. Before I discover what kinds of sounds she makes. All the ways she likes to be touched, teased, pleasured. The way she tastes. The next time we leave this room, I'll know all of it.

I settle against the headboard, still not having touched her. Maybe I'm a fucking idiot, but I need a moment to think. I'm still not convinced this is the right move with her. I want her too much. I want to control her pleasure, her orgasms. Never in my life have I experienced the effervescent need flowing through my blood. It's all-consuming and suddenly making me question whether, once I have her, I'll have the strength to walk away. Whether anyone will ever compare.

So I lace my fingers in my lap and call her to me. "Show me that you want this."

When she turns toward me, her top long forgotten, it isn't her tits I focus on; it's her face. Those green eyes, to be exact. Her pupils are blown wide with pure lust, but there's a hint of uneasiness there too.

"I do want this," she says, her chin held high. "But if you don't, that's fine. I'm sure I could call Eddy—"

I reach for her hand before she can finish that sentence and tug her to me. She falls onto the mattress between my legs and studies my expression. She's so fucking beautiful. I could stare at her for hours. Study the various golden circles in her emerald irises. Near the outside, they're dark, but each smaller ring is a little lighter, like the many facets of a jewel held up to the sun.

"Wanting you is not the problem," I say, finally allowing my hands to explore. First her hips, then over the smooth expanse of her ass. I tug her up onto my lap, and without hesitation, she straddles my thighs, her hands on my shoulders for balance.

"Then what is the problem?" she whispers, focusing on my mouth.

"Ever making it stop." The moment the words are out, the moment the truth is set free, her lips are on mine. Our time may be limited, and I may spend the rest of my life reliving the forty-eight hours I have with her, but the memories will be damn good ones, at least.

For now, that's enough.

"Touch me, please." She swirls her hips over me, the heat of her pussy soaking through the fabric of my shorts and briefs. Fuck, she's already burning for me.

I slide my palms up her sides, letting them wander to her tits, squeezing and tweaking and playing as she writhes.

"Yes," she mumbles, dipping lower for another kiss. They're drugging, and the way she tastes and the little whimpers she makes as she grinds against me are explosive.

Lightheaded, already out of my mind, I tease her nipples. Her tits fit perfectly in my hands, and they're so goddamn lush, so plump, I can't wait to get them in my mouth. When I pinch one nipple and roll it between my fingers, her breathy moan turns to a whine.

"Ah, fuck. Why do I like that?" She slows the movement of her hips, like she's extending her pleasure.

"Because your body was made for this. It was made to be pleasured and teased. Is that what you want, Sienna? You want me to show you the right way to *fuck*? The right way to come?"

She moans, but her bratty attitude makes an appearance. "I didn't know there was a wrong way."

I pinch her nipple, harder this time, then lap at it, finally getting my mouth on her.

"Holy shit. The glasses, the book, the *pleases* and *thank yous*? I thought you were polite."

With a shake of my head, I bite down on her taut peak and suck it into my mouth, making her squeal. "You won't make that mistake again."

"Oh." Her breath comes out quicker and her irises flare to a green so rich I swear the color doesn't exist in the real world. Then she's rolling her hips with more urgency.

I meet the movement, bucking up into her. Holy fuck. We're dry-humping, nothing more, yet I don't think I've ever experienced this kind of bliss.

It's too good. If I'm not careful, this is going to end far too soon. I clutch her upper thighs, slowing her movements.

"Fuck, I need—" she whines, fighting against me, her head thrown back.

My control snaps. "You don't need a goddamn thing except what I'm giving you. *I* control the pace." I drag her over my length. "I control your pleasure." I tease her clit with the head of my cock and am rewarded by a breathy sigh as she drops her head back. "I don't need an instruction manual to make you come," I grit out as my spine begins to tingle, the pleasure almost unbearable. "I'm not your good boy that you can boss around."

"No, I don't think you are," she says almost breathless. "But still," she whines. "I need your cock, right now, inside me. Please, I need *you* inside me."

Bringing my mouth to her ear, I rasp, "I don't fuck a lot because when I do, I like to do it a certain way. Sex isn't just sex to me."

Her body tenses a fraction and her green eyes meet mine. They're boundless. "You make love?"

I shake my head, even as that thought burrows into my brain. If she were the one I was fucking, could it be that way?

"No, baby, I don't make love. I ravage. I fuck. Hard. I will draw orgasm after orgasm out of you. I'll make them last so long you won't know when one ends and the next begins. It won't be sweet. It won't be gentle. And for the rest of your life, you'll crave it. But you'll never find it again. If you want my cock inside you, then you have to know that's what you're signing up for," I grit out, my spine already tingling. "Or—"

She shakes her head. "I want the first thing."

Need and relief course through me. That's my needy girl, already willing to submit. To take what I'm offering. If we had more time, I have a feeling she'd be everything I'd ever need.

"Or I make you come on my lap right now. Then I lay you down and fuck you with my tongue. With my fingers. I'll let you ride my face. I'll get you off again and again and leave it at that. I'll kiss you, cherish you, make you feel like you're walking on clouds. But I won't fuck you."

"I don't know," she says, her voice taunting, "you moved rooms just to get away from me. We already know I can make myself come. So I want your cock inside me, I want you to fuck me until I don't remember my own name. And if you don't—" She sits up straight and swats away my hand, then replaces it with her own as she rolls her hips against my raging erection. "I'll rub this hot pussy all over your dick, I'll play with my tits like this." She writhes on top of me, rolling her nipples and crying out. "And after I come," she breathes out, licking her lips which turn up into a delicious smile, "I'll send you back to your new room."

I'm so lost in the way she's bringing herself to the precipice that I've lost the ability to even sense the way my own release builds.

"Fuck, baby. You need to—"

Lost in her own pleasure, she glides her hand down her stomach and pushes the red fabric of her bikini to the side, exposing her glistening pink flesh. As she slides two fingers past her opening, my mouth waters, and when she pulls them out, soaked, and presses them to my lips, I swear my soul leaves my body.

"Suck," she commands.

In absolute awe of the sexual being hovering above me, I obey, savoring the taste of her arousal. She swirls them, taunting, teasing, essentially fingering my mouth. My balls tighten and my ab muscles seize, and for the first time in my life, I come in long, hot spurts, right in my fucking shorts. Sienna falls apart on top of me, letting loose the sweetest sounds, her skin turning the prettiest shade of pink.

"Holy fuck." I loop my arms around her back and pull her to my chest, panting. "Never in my life have I come in my shorts. You're a fucking dream."

Head tipped back, she surveys me, her eyes dancing like she's just getting started. "Now who's craving who?"

My brain is a scrambled mess. As are my pants. Holy shit. With a laugh, I admit defeat. "You win. But I already told you wanting you wasn't an issue." I brush her hair back. "If we're going to do this—"

She inhales sharply. "Oh, we're doing this."

I smile. "Then we need condoms. You need to eat too, and I need my glasses."

Brow lifted, she coos, "Condoms? As in plural."

I cuff her neck and pull her mouth to mine, kissing her like she's my oxygen. "Yes, I'm going to fuck you repeatedly, and I don't plan on coming in my pants again."

A wickedly delighted smile creeps up her face as she trails her fingers down my chest. "I've never made a man do that."

"Well, you did it." I ease her onto the mattress beside me. "Now I need to shower and gather necessities. We aren't leaving this room until you're as well and truly fucked as I am."

She giggles. "Impossible."

I pinch her nipple. "Brat."

With a squeal, she rolls away and hops off the bed. "I didn't bring condoms, and your shorts are a mess." She gives the wet spot on my crotch a pointed look. "So you'll have to be resourceful." With a giggle, she spins and saunters to the bathroom.

When the shower turns on, I stand and shuck my damp shorts. I take the time to fold them and leave them in the corner of the room to ensure they don't get anything else dirty. Then I call the front desk and ask them to have all my belongings brought here. Now that I've had Sienna, I have no intention of leaving her side. For the next forty-some-odd hours, she's mine.

After perusing the room service options, I wander to the bathroom door so I can check in with Sienna about food allergies and preferences. She tells me she's easy—not true—and that she'll eat whatever I order. I place an order for a salad, a charcuterie, and a burger and fries for us to split. That should get us through at least round one. Then I pluck a fluffy white robe from a hanger in her closet, steal the key card off her bureau, and head out the door.

A few quick strides later, I'm standing outside the villa I gave up.

After I knock, there's movement inside, and an instant later, the door opens and Ernie appears.

I plaster on a smile. "Need a favor."

He points at me and barks out a laugh. "I knew you had it in you."

Hands jammed into the pockets of my robe, I rock back on my heels. "Get it out. I'll give you a few seconds."

"Bert," he hollers over his shoulder. "Looks like lover boy actually made it happen."

I roll my eyes.

Bert appears at the doors to the deck, the white curtains floating in the breeze around him. "Really? Hmm." He grins. "Looks like we actually did it. Our first successful match."

"The fairy godfathers, at your service," Ernie says, tipping an imaginary hat.

I sigh. "Done yet?"

They look at one another, brows lifted, and nod in unison. "What do you need?"

"Condoms." It's an easy enough request, and based on the way my friends here were flirting with the ladies yesterday, I'm betting on them having come prepared.

After my last one-night stand and the child created that night, I'm not taking any chances. So if they don't have them, I'll march my ass to the front desk to get them.

"Coming right up. Any specific size or flavor you'd like?" Bert spins on his heel and heads to his bag.

"Size or flavor?" I mutter, head lowered.

Ernie winks at me. "I've got the magnums; he's got the regular size."

I close my eyes, shuddering. If only I could bleach the images those words have created in my mind. "Magnum," I croak.

"My guy." Ernie squeezes my shoulder. "He needs the big ones, Bert."

"Keep it down," I hiss, glancing over my shoulder. Each villa is offset by several steppingstones from a path that meanders through lush green palm trees and flowering bushes. Four villas down, a cleaning crew hovers around their cart, readying to enter the unit, but no one looks our way, so I don't think they heard the comment about my big dick.

Bert returns with a whole strip, holding the edge of one so the rest dangle. "How many do you—"

I snatch the entire pack and back up. "Consider it part of the room trade." I wink. Then, teasing, I add, "Oh, you may want to keep the doors closed tonight so we don't keep you up."

Both men break into laughter as I give them a salute and stride back to Sienna's place. Maybe I should have taken a moment to really say goodbye, since I don't plan to leave her room until Tuesday. I have a feeling the second I'm finally inside her, I'll never want to leave.

Chapter 11
SIENNA

"FOOD SHOULD BE HERE in twenty, along with my stuff," Noah says as I step out of the bathroom. "And I got these." He drops a strip of condoms on the bed. "Figure they'll last us a few hours."

My body heats, and the urge to drop the towel wrapped around my torso is strong. But I keep my cool. I cock a brow and say, "I'm glad you made yourself comfortable."

Despite my outward calm, I'm squealing on the inside. I've never done this before and I half expected him to be getting dressed and leaving when I came out of the shower.

Instead, the man had the hotel staff move his stuff to my room.

I won't wake up at two a.m. to an empty bed. He'll be here. With me.

My stomach is alight with butterflies, and I try to hide my smile.

I'm still drunk on the orgasm he gave me earlier. Still reeling over the fact that all we did was dry hump and it was the best *O* I'd ever had. It's pathetic, I know. But if that simple encounter is anything to go by, I have a feeling he's going to destroy me in the best way.

Noah struts toward me wearing a fluffy white robe, his hair mussed. I have this itch to run my fingers through it again, though it's quickly followed by a sense of unease. I shouldn't feel this comfortable with him. I shouldn't be this needy for him.

It's just a vacation fling. Nothing more. I can totally do this. I can be chill and detached about this hot man who's given me the best orgasm of my life and plans to continue until I can't walk. Totally. We're not going to fall for the vacation fling, Sienna. Even if he wears hot glasses and he's got tattoos and his dirty talk could be categorized as its own language…Okay fine, I'm totally fucked.

As if he can read every one of my thoughts, he smirks. Then, without warning, he tugs on my towel. I've got no choice but to fall into his chest. If I don't, he'll take the towel right from my body.

"Would you prefer it if I pretend I don't plan to sleep here for the next two nights?" His mouth kicks up on one side. "I can fake it for a bit, prepare to do the walk of shame. But if I do that, then you'll have to beg me to stay later."

With an eye roll, I drape my arms around his neck. "I'm no good at begging."

Noah leans down, his lips ghosting against mine, sending a thrill through me. "I'll teach you how to beg, sweet cheeks. Don't you worry."

"Says the man who came in his shorts." I force a scoff, pretending I'm unaffected by his charm when, in fact, my pussy is already fluttering like the hussy she is. She and I would both willingly pant on the floor for this man. He won't need to teach me to beg.

"And I loved every second of it," he rasps against my lips. "I'm going to shower." He presses his mouth to mine in a surprisingly sweet kiss. "Put on a robe, nothing under it. I want easy access while we eat."

I huff a breath. "Now you're dictating what I wear?" That's the one thing in my life I've always had full control over. It goes against my instincts to give that up. Yet the idea of him slipping his fingers inside me at any given moment is tempting.

Noah tilts his head and sucks on the skin below my ear, then kisses that same spot. "Only if you want me to."

"Hmm?" It's a question, but it escapes sounding like a moan.

"I want to try something with you." He tugs on the towel, his mouth raining kisses down my neck and across my clavicle. When he pulls the terry cloth away from my body, he bends slightly and sucks my nipple into his mouth.

"What kind of something?" The words are surprisingly clear for the state I'm in. I'm completely naked, and he's slowly unraveling me with soft kisses everywhere.

His hand ghosts over my abdomen, then as he takes my mouth again, he thrusts a finger inside me. All the air escapes my lungs, leaving my body with a moan. The instant my mouth drops open, he licks and sucks at my tongue.

Knees wobbling, I manage to pop up on my toes and wrap my arms around him, practically clawing at his body, needing more.

"Shh," he murmurs against my mouth. "Let me watch you come first." He adds a second finger and sets a rhythm, dangerous in his pursuit of my pleasure. "Fuck, I love it so much."

My vision goes hazy. How is it possible he knows exactly the type of ministrations it takes to get me to the edge? Within seconds, I'm there, and when he grinds his thumb against my clit without slowing, then curls against the inside wall, finding a spot no one has ever touched and adding pressure, I lose all control. An explosion rocks through my body. My limbs go weak, but he lifts me off the ground with one arm, his fingers still playing, and carries me to the bed. With another kiss to my lips, he settles me there, leaning over me with the most relaxed smile on his face.

"That's my girl. Look at how pretty you are, flushed pink because of me. You're glowing."

My lips tingle, the feel of his kisses still haunting me, as I struggle to keep my eyes open. "What did you do to me?" I murmur. And can he do it again?

"I ruined you, butterfly, and I intend to do it again and again and again."

A sigh escapes me. He's right. It's only been an hour since we walked into my villa, and already I crave him like a drug.

With a wink, he presses one more kiss to my mouth. Gently, he slides his fingers out of my pussy, causing aftershocks that make my core spasm, and brings them to his mouth. As he sucks them clean, my stomach swoops. And the raw hunger in his eyes as he fixes his focus on the space between my thighs sends a shudder through me. He's starved. If the heat in his eyes is any indication, he wants to lick me dry.

Instead, he pulls the covers up to my shoulders and insists I close my eyes for a few minutes. A moment after he disappears into the bathroom, the water kicks on, and within seconds, the soft sound lulls me to sleep.

I wake to murmured voices, then the clang of metal. As I force my heavy eyelids open, I spot Noah rolling a cart toward the deck, the silver platters on top of it glinting in the sunlight. On cue, my stomach rumbles. It hits me then that I haven't eaten yet today, and based on the brightness of the room, it's got to be afternoon.

Noah appears again a moment later, the curtains billowing around him. He's wearing his robe again, but his hair is damp and his face is dewy. And he's wearing his glasses. Holy fuck, is he hot in those glasses. Their black rims brighten the blue of his irises, making it impossible to look away.

"How long was I out?"

His lips tip up on one side. "Only about twenty minutes."

I yawn. Felt like longer. "You seem to have sent me into a comatose state." I hold out my arms, beckoning him.

He's there a heartbeat later, hovering over me. My pulse picks up at his proximity, my body coming alive, ready for another round. But rather than join me in bed, he pulls the sheet back and scoops me up.

"Hey," I practically whine. Damn him for dashing the fantasies I've conjured in a matter of seconds.

Wearing a cocky smile, he snags the second robe from the end of the bed and heads for the deck. "You need to eat."

"I do not. I need—"

My stomach growls loudly, proving him right.

He peers down at me, those eyes as blue as the ocean outside. "You were saying?"

As soon as we step out into the warm afternoon sun, my body hums to life. The light breeze coming off the water wakes me further, invigorating me. From here, we can see the ocean but not the populated beach area of the resort. It's like this space is just for us.

And the neighbors, if they come out on their deck. With any luck, Noah's request for condoms was the hint they needed to disappear for the day.

He sets me on my feet and helps me slip my arms into the second robe. Then he guides me into a chair at the table and presses a kiss to my forehead. "I'll give you everything you need, but first, I'm feeding you."

"Feeding me, eh?" I tease. A sensation I've never experienced before swirls in my chest. It's not butterflies; it's warmer than that. It's not lust, either. It's familiarity and trust and longing for more of this every day. It's foreign but absolutely welcome. Though it's quickly followed by a niggle of worry in my brain. One that tells me I shouldn't be this comfortable, that I shouldn't have such strong feelings for or attachment to a man I've just met.

The hopeless romantic in me is louder, pushing to the forefront. This side of me—the one that loves old rom-coms, the girl who's spent her life wondering if it's possible to be both successful and in love— can't help but hope that this is exactly what that feels like. That this weekend was fated. That I was meant to be here. I was meant to meet this man. That he could be my soulmate.

I look away from him and focus on the cloches before us, silently chiding myself for being such a hopeless study in silly girls.

Noah lifts several silver domes, revealing more food than the two of us could possibly eat. "Yes, for the next two days you're mine to take care of." He slides a knife through the cheeseburger and puts half on a plate, along with fries and a small portion of salad. Then he picks up one of those fries and guides it to my lips. "Open."

I snort. "I figured you'd be trying to feed me something completely different while giving me such a command." I blatantly stare at his hips. A spark of desire lights inside me. I may have rubbed myself against a certain appendage to get off already today, but I've yet to see it.

"You're shameless," he says, his eyes dancing, and brings the fry closer to my mouth. "Now," he adds, the single word rough. That grating tone sends a shiver through me. It's so at odds with the hot, quiet nerd thing he has going for him.

My insides go molten at the command. I open my mouth, peeking up at him from beneath my lashes, and slide my tongue out, giving him quite the visual. He hisses out a *fuck* and drags the fry across it. Mouth watering in response to the salty flavor, I close around it and hum.

Noah licks his lips, his pupils blown out, his breaths coming so quickly I can make out the way his chest rises and falls beneath his robe.

I tug my plate closer and focus on my food. If I don't, I'm liable to drop to my knees right here.

My first bite of the cheeseburger leaves me ravenous. Without looking up, I take another. When I pluck a napkin off the table and wipe at my mouth, Noah is watching me from his own seat, a smile on his face and his half of the burger held aloft.

"You mentioned wanting to try something with me," I hedge. The words have been swirling in my head since he put them out there, but I've yet to decipher them. The potential is limitless, so it's better to just be up-front and ask than to get ahead of myself and freak out.

Noah strikes me as the kind of person who knows precisely what he likes. I, on the other hand, haven't had enough experience in the bedroom to have a clue where my interests lie.

It's odd, really, how comfortable I am with this near stranger. It's odder still that he doesn't feel like one. There isn't much he could toss my way that would make me hesitate.

He takes another bite of his burger, watching me thoughtfully. The silence is suddenly unnerving, and now the scenarios I was trying to avoid freaking out about run through my head. Though in a matter of seconds, I realize I don't even know enough about sex to come up with more than one or two crazy ideas.

I'm picking at my salad, holding back from begging him to put me out of my misery and tell me, when he finishes the last bite of his burger, wipes his mouth with a napkin, and sets his hands flat on the table.

"I don't fuck just anyone."

The matter-of-fact way the crass word comes out of his deliciously polite mouth ignites heat in my core once more. I clench my thighs and press my lips together so I don't whimper while I wait for him to continue.

"I've discovered several things that interest me. I've read about them…" He blows out a breath, suddenly looking a little nervous. "Because I like to read." He dips his head, his cheeks going rosy at the admission.

My heart warms at his tone, at the shyness there. How is it possible for him to be so brazen one second and endearing the next?

He shrugs. "But I've never had the opportunity to try most of them, since I've never been in a relationship."

The confession, said with such a straight face, and his openness, urge me to be honest as well. "I haven't either."

Noah's eyes flash with what I think is delight.

"I like to please a woman. It's my—" He wets his lips and angles a fraction closer. "It pleases me to please a woman. Simply playing with you could make me come."

My breath escapes me in a quiet gasp. "Huh?"

"I don't need to fuck. Because I get off on touching you. On watching you come. That's normally enough. I rarely have sex because, in the past, when I've been with women, it's felt like they're performing for me. Like they've been trained to please men rather than seek their own pleasure. And that doesn't do it for me." He closes his eyes, a pained expression flitting across his face, though it's gone quickly. "I don't want to do that with you."

My stomach sinks, and there's no hiding the devastation in my tone when I ask, "You don't want to fuck me?" This is not where I thought this was going.

Noah's lips curl up, as if he's pleased by how bothered I am. "Oh, I want to fuck you. And I *will* fuck you." He beckons me with the crook of one finger. "Come sit on my lap. I want to touch you while you eat."

That heat in my belly turns to liquid, slicking my thighs as I slide my chair back. Who knew talking so plainly about sex could be so hot? This man's openness and honesty may be the sexiest things about him, and that's saying something. He flat-out told me that he wants to experience something with me he never has with another woman.

The thought consumes me, blooms inside me, encourages me to be brazen myself. Maybe that makes me a *pick me* girl but in this moment, I don't give a fuck. I'll gladly wear the title of a hopeless romantic.

Noah pushes his plate back and drags mine across the table until it's in front of him. Then he spreads his thighs and sets his hands on them, waiting.

Eyes locked on his, I stand and shuffle into the slot he's created for me between his knees.

"Sit," he says, guiding me to sit sideways on his lap with a shoulder pressed against his chest. "Now eat."

I peer up at him, only to find him surveying the ocean. Confusion swirls in my belly, tempering the arousal there. I thought he was going to touch me. I wait a beat, and when he still doesn't look at me, I pick up a fry.

As I bring it to my mouth, he slides a hand beneath my robe and cups one of my breasts, though he's still intent on watching the waves roll in. He dusts a finger across my nipple, then circles back, lightly teasing me, and the zap of electricity that shoots straight to my core makes me hiss.

"I want to make you come over and over. Until you're begging me to stop. But I need you to tell me right now that even when you beg, you understand that I won't stop. I want to spend the next forty-eight hours using your body, pleasuring you in every way, even when it's too much for your senses. Telling me to stop will only spur me on, so pick another word, and only use it if you truly don't want me to continue."

As he speaks, he doesn't stop playing with my nipples. It takes concerted effort to understand the rules he's laying out with the way my core tightens and my pussy begs to be filled and fucked. Arousal drips from me, coating my thighs and soaking through my robe as I work hard to decipher his words.

"Will you fuck me to please me?" I need to know. If he wants me to agree to be the equivalent of his sex toy, then I need to know that what he has in mind will involve actual sex. Like penetration. My body is a slut for him right now, and I'd agree to just about anything, but only if it means I get his dick.

I stare up at him, desperate for him to look at me. But he keeps his attention fixed on the water. He pinches my nipple, and my hips roll in response, searching for relief.

"I'm going to stick my cock in whatever hole will make you squirt for me. Then I'll drink your cum."

My mind spins, his dirty words leaving me dizzy. "Holy shit."

His hand drifts to my other breast, and he starts his ministrations over. In seconds, I swear I'm on the brink of release. It's impossible, yet here I am, my limbs tingling and need coiling tight in my belly.

As if he knows better, as if he knows he can work my body over in a way that'll send me hurtling into the abyss without touching my pussy, he finally zeroes in on me. By the way his pupils are blown out, one would think I was on my knees for him. That I was the one pleasuring him, touching him. He pinches my nipple and rolls it.

"Say yes. Tell me I can have free rein over your body. Give me permission to make you come over and over. Please tell me I can stick my cock in you whenever I want, wherever we are, so I can watch your skin take on that gorgeous golden flushed hue. I want you soaked for me. Coated in sweat and panting."

"Yes," I cry out. The single word isn't meant to be an answer to his question. It passes my lips with force as my body crests a wave of need. He's done it. He's sent me over the edge with nothing more than nipple play.

He curls around me, pushing my robe aside with a rough sideways thrust of his chin. Then he laps at one breast and bites down on the nipple while he continues teasing the other.

Desire washes over me, flooding me, overtaking me, dripping down my legs. "Holy shit. Don't stop," I babble. "Please, please."

Vision spotty, I thrash against him. I need to be fucked. I need to be filled.

But he holds me in place, refusing to give me what I'm literally begging for and instead taking what he wants. He sucks on my tits, drawing out my orgasm. As he takes and takes and takes some more, my mind swirls and understanding finally dawns. This is what he wants. He wants the control, and he wants to give me this insane pleasure.

As my trembling limbs settle and my orgasm ebbs, he drags his mouth up my chest, up my neck, and seals his lips over mine.

Gasping for air, still desperate to be filled with him, I drop my head against his chest. He presses kisses to my forehead, adjusts the robe so I'm covered again, and picks up one of the glasses of water from the table. He brings the straw to my mouth and waits for me to open.

I obey easily, catching on to how much he likes to take care of me. Once I've taken a few sips, he sets the glass down. Then he snakes a hand beneath my robe and settles his warm palm against the burning skin of my thigh.

My mind is a jumbled mess. Every second of what he just did was pure bliss, yet he still hasn't even touched my pussy. How is that possible? He's made me come three times now, and I've yet to even see the man's cock. It's incredible. It's—

"Butterfly," I whisper.

"Hmm?" The sound rumbles through his chest.

"My word. If I say butterfly, you stop."

The only indication that he's heard me is a slight inhale of breath, followed by a thick swallow. Then he's back to staring out at the ocean. He remains like that, silent, contemplative, for so long that I think I must have imagined the way he just worked me over. Just as I'm getting restless, his fingers move. A tiny adjustment. I freeze, holding my breath, worrying I imagined it. But then it happens again. This time, his fingers twitch a little more obviously, and then he slides his palm up my thigh and between my legs.

The grin that spreads across his face is wicked. "You're soaked."

A surprised laugh rips through me. "I'm pretty sure I need to shower. My thighs are coated."

"In your cum," he rumbles, looking at me with an intensity that sets my skin on fire. "I'm going to bring you inside and lick up every single drop." Then his finger is prodding at my entrance, the slickness there allowing it to slip in without resistance.

I moan, my head tipped back against his bicep.

He thrusts in and out slowly, deliberately, as if he has a plan and refuses to deviate from it, studying me, brow furrowed, like he's memorizing every detail, as if each freckle, each line, is knowledge he needs for a test he intends to ace.

I'm catching on. This focus, this determination, means I'm going to come again. So I will my body to relax and focus on the sensations.

"I'm going to settle you on the bed." He presses his thumb to my clit without stopping his ministrations. "And I'm going to tell you to open your knees for me." He licks his lips, heat flaring in his irises. "Then I'm gonna tell you to take those dainty fingers of yours and spread your cunt wide so I can lean over and get my fill." A shaky breath escapes him, but when he speaks again, his tone is just as stern. "My glasses have to come off when we fuck, but I want to see every inch of what's mine before I do that." He drags his gaze down my body, to my breasts, which are fully exposed to the midday sun now that my robe has fallen open down to where he's working me over.

Like this, I'm exposed. It sends a thrill through me, even though there's not a soul in sight. If the control he craves is anything to go by, he wouldn't let anyone see me like this, but the idea that a person could walk up on us at any time doesn't exactly bother me. In fact, the thought makes me gush around his fingers.

He lets out a low, rough moan of his own. "Then once I've gotten my fill, once I've cataloged every inch of you, I'll put my glasses on the bedside table and hand you a condom. While you rip it open, I'll take out my cock for you."

I imagine it. Every second. The way he'd carefully fold up his glasses and gently set them down. That simple move shouldn't be such a turn-on. Maybe it's the dichotomy of it all. The dirty words, the demands, paired with the exquisite thought and care in his every movement, especially when it comes to my pleasure.

The desperate need to finally see his cock helps. The vision I've already conjured of rolling the condom over his shaft, pulling a desperate groan from him in the process.

"Help me, Sienna, spread that cunt wide open for me just like you will in there, let me see everything."

I do as I'm told without hesitation. I'm wanton, aching for his touch, aching for more of him. My fingers brush over his knuckles, and when I pull myself open for him, he leans forward and sighs.

"Look at how beautiful you are. How your blood has all rushed to this spot, making you so pink and lovely for me." He blows air against my exposed pussy, and I shudder violently in his arms. "That's my girl," he rasps. "Come for me so I can take you inside and drink from you."

His words are all it takes to send me over the edge. I come hard, liquid gushing from me. Unashamed, I give in, moaning loudly. He leans over me, transfixed, enraptured, his focus completely set, like he can't get enough of watching me pulse around his fingers.

The chuckle that leaves him is pure sex. "You squirted all over my glasses. Fuck," he hisses, like he's lost control. Like he's so taken aback that he's lost the script for a moment.

With a final curl of his finger, he slips out of me and hauls me into the villa, like he can't move quick enough.

The world around me is a blur. It only comes back into focus when I'm on my back, watching the ceiling fan rotate lazily above, and he's suctioning his lips over my clit and drinking my orgasm from my body. He works me through the last of my release, and even as it abates, he doesn't stop. He licks and sucks and finger-fucks me straight into another. And as I enter a state of ecstasy I never could have imagined, I can only hope he does every single thing he's promised.

Chapter 12
NOAH

THIS WOMAN WAS MADE for me. I hover over her, taking her in, knowing that what I plan to do next will ruin me in the best and worst ways. After this, no other woman will ever come close to satisfying me.

I've lost track of time, though I know exactly how many orgasms I've given her. While I licked, sucked, and teased one after another from her body, I made her count them. We're up to nine. And I've yet to give her my cock. I've explored her tits, her cunt, and her ass with my hands and fingers, and I've never in my life been so gloriously edged.

This is the type of pleasure I never allow myself. It's too addicting. As her skin flushes and she cries out and babbles, the animalistic need takes over. It's terrifying how singularly focused I am on her pleasure. It makes me want to give up everything and spend my life worshipping her.

The looming deadline is the only reason I'm giving in to my cravings. I can get lost in her for two days, and then I'll never see her again. I can go back to my life. Back to hockey and, soon, parenthood.

I tell myself I'm allowed to have this. I'm allowed to have her.

Even if I'll forever look back on this week and know I did it to myself. I ruined it all.

She ruined me.

"Please take off the robe," she begs.

She's been good. She's given me exactly what I demanded. Free rein over her body. It'll be even more fucking incredible tonight when I take her out of the room. When I guide her into a bar and find a dark corner where we can fuck. The possibilities are endless. The list of things I want to do to her is long, but I'm going to cross off every fucking one. Every reckless, depraved act I've ever been intrigued by.

I don't make a show of stripping out of my robe. I simply shrug it off my shoulders and settle a knee on the bed beside her.

But her rough intake of breath tells me I'm not going nearly slow enough.

"You are huge." A slow smile curls her lips.

My cock strains, the head nearly purple and coated in precum. I want her so badly. In another life, I'd take her bare. I'd do anything to keep her. Toss birth control out the window and impregnate her. Spend my life fucking her.

Which is why I can't keep her. She's addicting. I have to work for a living. I have a career to get back to. But if I had access to Sienna like this, there's no way I'd leave my bed. Especially when she's leaning forward, her tongue darting out and those damn innocent eyes locking on my face while she says, "Can I taste you now?"

The air leaves my lungs, making it impossible to speak.

I manage a wooden nod, and in response, she wets her lips with that lascivious tongue.

Anticipation floods me, sending a shiver up my spine and making my heart race.

She plucks a red silicone vibrator from the sheets and cocks a brow. It's still coated in her release, and it's not the only toy she pulled out in the short time I gave her to recover between rounds. My naughty, perfect woman has quite the collection. A vibrator, a dildo I worked into her as she soaked me in her arousal, and a rose for her clit.

"Can I use this on your balls while I suck you?"

My cock pulses at the idea. "Fuck, baby. You're perfect."

As she presses the button at the bottom of the vibrator, I settle my other knee on the bed and wait. When it buzzes to life, my balls tighten in anticipation. For a moment, she only studies my dick, and my heart pumps harder. As she leans in, the silicone toy getting close to my crown, I have the fleeting fear that she'll use it there and I'll blow my load in her face. Instead, she licks at my tip, then slides that hot mouth around me and takes me deep, only stopping when she gags. The sounds she makes cause my vision to fade in and out. Holy fuck. I scrape her hair back gently, gathering it into my fist, and take a deep breath in. I exhale slowly, finding my bearings, and give her hair a little tug. "Go slow, sweetheart. We've got all night."

She looks up at me, my dick in her mouth, and places the vibrator against my balls. My knees wobble at the sensation, and I nearly collapse onto the bed.

"Remember your word," I growl.

Now that I've been let in, my body is thrumming with the need to take. To use. To come.

I've never been unraveled like this before. It's obvious from the need in her eyes that she's enjoying this even more than I am. It's addictive, knowing that she's getting off on my pleasure just like I've been getting off on hers. I'll need every ounce of willpower I possess to fight the urge to come down her throat.

With a roll of my pelvis, I test her, ensuring she can handle what I'm about to give her. When she moans and sucks harder, I do it again, this time with more force. I find a rhythm, fucking her mouth roughly, hips snapping.

She's on her knees, bent over for me, tears in her bright, eager eyes. With one hand flat on the mattress, she uses the other to tease my balls with the vibrator.

"I need your cunt in my mouth," I grit out as I drop onto my back and flip her around so she straddles my face.

Barely breaking the rhythm she's created, she gets back to working me over, vibrator in place once again.

She's so fucking sweet. I've wrung orgasm after orgasm from her body, but it's not enough.

I'm fucking up into her throat, lost in the way she tastes and the way her hot mouth envelops me when she slides the vibrator from my balls down my perineum. I shudder once, and when she continues, dragging it between my cheeks, my breath stalls out.

She pops off my dick, her breathing ragged, and grinds against my face. "Is this okay?"

She's got the vibrator pressed against my asshole, causing sparks to shoot down my legs and scrambling my brain. I have no idea if it's okay. I've never done it.

While my mind is working overtime to come up with an answer, my hips take over, bucking wildly. The move causes the vibrator to slip past the tight ring of muscle there, and yeah, I fucking like that.

"Please," I plead, my lips brushing against her cunt and my hips rolling, searching for more. "Put your mouth on my dick and fuck me with that vibrator, baby."

She gasps, and an instant later, she soaks my face. I double down in response, so fucking turned on by her reaction, sucking hard on her clit and thrusting my hips. When the vibrator slips deeper, the resulting burn is startling at first, but it's quickly replaced by a coiling sensation deep inside me. As if my body is winding up, preparing to detonate. When she sheathes my length with her warm, wet mouth again, hollowing her cheeks and sucking me while she fucks my ass, that tension breaks and an orgasm rips through my body. Toes curling, I fuck up into her mouth, licking and sucking her like my life depends on it. In this moment, I'm certain it does. She's my life raft as a tidal wave rushes over me.

With a hand on the back of her head, I hold her down, needing her as deep as I can get her. She doesn't fight me; she doesn't protest. Her throat opens, and she guides the toy deeper, hitting what must be my fucking prostate, and finally my balls release all that tension and I come down her throat.

I come for what feels like an eternity, and when the pulsing finally stops and she flips over and presses her lips to mine, I'm a sputtering mess, breathless and in fucking love with her body.

"Next time I stick that in your ass," she pants, "I want your cock in my pussy."

Chuckling, I pull her against me. "Give me a few minutes, baby. I'm pretty sure my soul just left my body."

As I massage the expanse of Sienna's gorgeous body, steam and the scent of her body wash engulfing me, my mind is still orbiting somewhere in space.

Without thinking, I dip low and press my mouth to hers. She nips at my lip in return, and only then, as the sharp sting registers, do I return to my senses.

Need and longing swirl through me, but those sensations are quickly followed by dread. Fuck. This is so much more than sex. I can't keep doing this. I can't take her back into that bedroom and sink inside her gently. If I do, if I rock into her while staring into her eyes, I know I'll topple right over the edge into a dangerous type of emotion.

Despite that, I can't pull myself away. My fingers tingle as they skate down her body and dip between her thighs. When I force my finger in, she gasps into my mouth.

"Sore," she mumbles, eyes closed.

I don't stop. "Remember your word," I murmur, dragging my lips across her cheek. I push her wet hair behind her ear and kiss the sensitive spot just below it. "Work through it with me. Let me use this tight cunt. Let me pull one more orgasm from you. Then we're going out to dinner. We'll dance, and then I'll pull you onto my lap while we eat dinner and fuck you in a room full of people."

She clenches around my fingers, already gushing.

"Feel better?" I ask as I add another finger.

She responds by humping my hand.

I stop my movements and pull back. Yes, her actions make her answer clear, but I want her to tell me. I crave her words.

"Yes. Please, Noah. I need your cock. Fuck me."

Groaning, cock straining against her thigh, I pull my hand free and suck her taste from my fingers. "Put your hands on the wall and bend over for me."

As she obeys, her movements languid, I step out of the shower and dart into the bedroom for a condom. I roll it on and give my length a tug as I step back into the bathroom and survey her through the foggy glass separating us.

Impatience swirls through me, so I quickly step back into the shower, my dick still in my hand, and clutch her hip. "I'm going to fuck you now."

The warning is more for me than for her. I've never needed someone or something more in my entire life. It's terrifying. I should stop. I should back away. She's going to wreck me for anyone else in the future, but fuck if I don't want to be wrecked by her.

So, hand shaking, I grip her a little harder and notch myself at her entrance. Like she can sense my nerves, and probably feel my shaking hand, she adjusts so she's resting her weight on one elbow and then she rests her other hand over mine, threads our fingers and squeezes.

As my heart cracks open and warmth floods my body, I slide inside her.

It's too late to go back now. She owns me.

Warmth rushes through me as her walls clamp down. She feels so fucking right. I curl over her, pressing a kiss to her shoulder, then her neck, and we both sigh in relief.

I'll never come back from this. I'll never recover. She's completely and irrevocably changed me. And as I sink inside her repeatedly, I relish it. Because why the fuck would I ever want to undo what I've just done?

For the next twenty-four hours, Sienna allows me, and encourages me, to use her over and over again. I pleasure her with my fingers at dinner, teasing her beneath the table while the waiter takes our order. As we listen to live music, I push inside her while she sits on my lap. While the people around us sway to the beat, she writhes on my dick, coming with her teeth sunken into my shoulder. I wake her in the middle of the night with my tongue on her clit and a toy shoved into her ass. She squirts all over the sheets, and while she's still a whimpering mess, I shove my dick inside her and fuck her until she's begging for me to stop.

She doesn't say butterfly. Not even when I flip her over, cover my sheathed dick in lube, and slide inside her other hole. No, the wanton thing pushes back against me and rubs her clit until she comes again.

We sleep late into the morning, have lunch on the beach, and do it all over again. When she turns on her phone to check in for her flight, a million messages pop up, and she disappears out the door, telling me she needs to make a few calls.

My stomach ties itself in knots as I realize I only have a matter of hours left with her. Tomorrow we leave this island, and I'm not even close to ready. With a long breath out, I walk out onto the deck and stare up at the midnight sky. The moon and the stars sparkle so damn bright here. Just like Sienna.

In a matter of days, I'll be back in Minnesota. Back in the cold. The winters are brutal. So dark and long.

Fuck. *Get out of your head.*

The last thing I want is to ruin the night with this shitty mood. She's not gone yet. We're not done.

I pull out my phone and FaceTime War. Talking to him always puts me in a better mood.

"Ah shit, the Bahamas must really suck if you're calling me," he says in greeting. He's lying on a couch, phone held above him, shirtless.

Dammit. I hope he's wearing pants, but this wouldn't be the first time he picked up the phone minutes after sex, so there's a solid chance he isn't.

"The vacation's awesome. Thank you very much."

His chuckle is a low rumble. "Good. And the girl?"

I scrub a palm over my face. "She's fucking perfect."

"Ah shit."

My gut clenches in agreement with the sentiment. "Exactly."

He blows out a breath and shrugs. "If she's cool, maybe keep in touch? I hear relationships aren't terrible."

I roll my eyes. That's a ringing endorsement for monogamy if I've ever heard one. "It would never work," I say, as much to myself as him.

His blue eyes narrow, like he's studying me. Then he nods. "Nothing good ever came easy to us. You want her, you think she's worth it, you make it work."

"Who?" Brooks asks from somewhere off screen.

"Harry's vacation girl. He's in *love*." War drags the word out obnoxiously. "Your sister good?"

I frown. "Mine?"

He shakes his head. "Nah, Brooks's baby sister has been MIA. She just called, though."

"She's fine. Aiden's on the phone with her now. She needs help avoiding Beckett. Overbearing ass tried to send a plane to pick her up. She wants us to talk him out of his insanity." He chuckles. "Like the man can be controlled."

War huffs a laugh. "I'm trying to convince Harry he can have a girl and play hockey too. What do you think?" He looks past his phone, a glint in his eye I don't understand.

"I wouldn't know. Hockey is my life," our other best friend grumbles.

The main door opens and closes, and Sienna walks in. "I gotta go. Thanks for the vote of confidence. And Brooks can't wait to catch up in person and score some goals on you."

He shakes his head, never one to entertain shit talk.

Just as I'm tapping the *End* button, Sienna steps out onto the deck.

Wearing a red dress that follows every one of her curves, she looks absolutely gorgeous, though her expression is one of annoyance.

"Everything okay?" I straighten and slip my phone into my pocket.

She forces a smile. "Yeah, just my brothers being"—she lets out a breath and shakes her head—"my brothers."

I nod once, going for supportive, though I don't have the first clue what she means and she wouldn't want me to ask.

She's made her boundaries clear. We're limited to the bubble we've created here. As much as I want more, I have to honor her requests.

Still, I can't say nothing. So I hold out my arms. "Do you want to talk about it?"

To my relief, she darts for me, holding me tight and resting her head on my chest.

She melts in my hold, and fuck, I can't explain how it feels to be the person she feels safe with. My heart simultaneously skips and settles as I cradle her against me. The warm weight of her pressed against me is like a balm to my soul.

How the fuck am I going to let her go?

She props her chin on my chest and offers me a crooked smile. "I like when you hold me."

My chest constricts, making it hard to breathe. "I love holding you."

Her muscles relax and her smile grows. "I wanna do something reckless."

"Whatever you want, butterfly."

She sighs, relieved, and damn, knowing that I've given her exactly what she needs makes my heart race faster.

With a quick glance to the left, she runs her teeth over her bottom lip. "Let's go swimming."

"Right now?" I bury my face in her neck and inhale. "It's midnight. Pool's closed."

Stepping out of my hold, she tilts her head, and reaches behind her, tugging on the knot at her nape . Her red dress practically floats off her body, leaving her in a black strapless bra and a scrap of fabric that could barely be considered a thong. "Who said anything about a pool?"

For a moment I'm struck stupid by her. By the way her skin glows in the moonlight. Her long dark hair flows around her, ruffled gently by the breeze, and those emerald eyes of hers brighten with excitement.

She takes a step back, then another, and before I can make sense of what's happening, she squeals, "Come and get me!" and hops over the railing and onto the sand a foot or so lower than the deck.

Only as she scurries off does my brain reboot. Without hesitation, I launch myself after her and take off.

Shit. If any of her neighbors are out, I have no doubt they're about to get a show.

She rushes forward, heading toward the deserted beach and the fathomless, lapping waters.

"Maybe we should try the pool," I call, figuring that's probably safer.

Her giggles carry on the wind as she hurdles over a beach chair without slowing.

By the time I make it to the water, she's ankle-deep, walking backward, staring right at me.

"Sienna," I warn.

My stern tone does nothing but spur her on. This woman likes to be punished, and clearly she's decided to use my love for punishing her against me.

"Come on, Noah. Play with me." She puts her hands behind her back and then tosses her bra at me. As it lands at my feet with a soft plop, I zero in on her tits, on her pebbled nipples, then her gorgeous face, relishing the joy radiating from her.

I shake my head. "What are you doing, baby?"

"I told you." She hooks her thumbs into the strips of elastic at her hips and drags her thong down her gorgeous legs before kicking them off. They land at the water's edge, but I snag them before they drift away.

I inspect the beach once more, making sure we're alone, then throw my head back and sigh. What the fuck am I doing? We've got one night left. Why am I worried about anyone but her? Let them fucking see us.

I pull off my shirt, and as I drop it to the sand, Sienna sinks back into the water. Unwilling to let her get any farther from me, I shuck off my shorts quickly, nearly falling in the process, then dive for her, pulling her under the waves with me.

When we surface, she's laughing.

"Fuck, it's cold," I mutter, hugging her to my body to keep her warm.

She wraps her legs around my waist, and when her hot cunt brushes against me, I hiss.

"Want me to warm you up?" Her words are anything but innocent, but her eyes? Fuck, they're wide and bright. She blinks, her lashes wet and sticking together, as she waits.

I can do nothing but nod.

But it's enough. With the smallest of smiles, she lines herself up with my length and welcomes me home.

With my forehead pressed to hers, I sigh in relief.

"That better?" she murmurs.

"I've never been inside anyone bare." The words practically claw their way out of me.

Her breathing hitches. "Good. I've never gone without a condom either."

We stare at one another as I hold her close, the water lapping against us. This isn't fucking. Not a single moment of it is for that type of pleasure, yet this is the most satisfying moment of my life.

Just being inside Sienna is heaven. Knowing that I'm giving her the same comfort—the same pleasure—alters my brain chemistry.

She tips her head back, face turned to the night sky, as I hold her in the water. "I'm not ready to leave," she whispers, almost like she's telling the universe though and not me.

Emotion floods me as I stare at her. She's lying back, arms outstretched, her nipples breaching the surf, the long lines of her hips disappearing where they meet mine. How could the universe introduce me to this perfect woman, and then take her away?

"If you could have anything," I ask, "what would it be?"

She arches up, grasping my shoulders, and presses a kiss to my lips. "I'd want people to know me for who I am rather than because of my family name."

And what is that family name?

It takes everything in me not to ask.

"I'd want a little boutique in Boston, maybe."

"What kind of boutique?"

She shakes her head, brushing her nose against mine. "We're not supposed to tell each other what we do."

As she moves, her pussy clenches around me, pulling a moan from deep in my chest.

"Fuck, baby. I don't care about our rules. I just want—I need—"

She bites down on my lip and tugs. "You need whatever I give you."

Heat sears through me, along with amusement. Is she seriously using my own words against me again?

"I'm going to miss you," I croak. It's the most honest admission I've ever made.

She ghosts her lips over mine. "What about you? What would your life look like if you could have anything?"

The moment she asks, an intense vision hits me, nearly knocking beneath the surf. In it, a brick home set on a rolling hill. Walking distance to downtown Boston. A little boy smiling up at me. My wife standing in the doorway with her hand on her rounded belly.

Sienna.

That's what I picture. A life with her. Not hockey. Not saying goodbye to her.

Shit.

Chest tight, I force the words out, taking my time to keep my voice from shaking. "A family. My mom passed when I was a baby, so I missed out on a lot. But I'd really like to have that. Children, a home."

She strokes my cheek, studying every inch of my face. "I'm so sorry."

I shrug. "I don't remember her. And I have a great dad."

She nibbles on her lip, her attention drifting. "I hope you find it. What you want. I hope you get that family."

"I hope you get your boutique."

I want to tell her I could have all those things, that I could give her everything she wants, but none of her woes are caused by a shortage of money. That's not the issue, so mine can't solve her problems. She has a vision, a hunger for a career. She has a plan, and she's set to dive into it next week. She's just beginning. I can't keep her from chasing those dreams.

She brings her lips to mine, and as she deepens the kiss, she silently tells me she wants all of it too. She wants a future, she wants those dreams.

At least I tell myself that's what she's saying. I kiss her back. For long moments, we're lost like that. Eventually the warmth of her isn't enough, so I fuck up into her, focusing on things we can have. I walk backward, and at the ocean's edge, I settle my ass in the sand. "Ride me. I want to watch you come. I want to watch the most beautiful woman fall apart around me in the light of the moon."

Sienna rolls her hips, the move sending tingles up my spine. "I'm on birth control," she rasps against my mouth.

My chest grows tight. "Fuck, baby. Don't say things like that."

"I want you to come inside me," she begs. "Be mine." Her eyes search mine, desperate. "Just for tonight."

I lose all sense then. As I fuck up into her, I unleash a piece of myself, implanting it deep, knowing I'll never get it back. Forget being wrecked. I'm shattered and I don't give a fuck.

The moment the world goes hazy, my vision blurring from the intense pleasure, she imprints herself on my retinas. She tattoos herself on my brain. When I come apart with her name on my lips, I can only hope that for the rest of my life, the image of her under the moonlit sky is all I'll see.

The sound of wheels on the floor wakes me, and I jackknife out of bed. "You're leaving?" I rasp, glaring at the woman standing near the door. I'm naked and hard—which should be impossible at this point—and I'm pissed. "You were just going to leave?"

She strides over and cups my cheek. "No, I was just collecting my things before I came to say goodbye to you properly."

My racing heart calms. There's nothing but sincerity in her eyes. "Let me get dressed and wait for your car with you."

I tried to change my travel plans so we could fly out of here together, but her flight was completely booked.

She took that as a sign that it's best that we part for good here in the Bahamas. I took it as a sign that I should pay someone to take their seat, but that's not what she wants, so here we are.

It's like a punch to the gut, really, to have found this woman, a woman who is, for all intents and purposes, made for me, who's as filthy as I am and so fucking brilliant—a woman I could get lost in—only to be hit with the reality that she doesn't have time to get lost in me.

Could we make it work? A big part of me wants to try. Yeah, hockey keeps me busy, and soon, the rest of my time will be consumed with the ups and downs of parenthood. But even if Sienna and I could sneak away and see each other once or twice in the next year, it'd be a whole lot better than parting for good.

"Give me your number," I say, cradling her face.

Lashes lowered, she shakes her head.

My stomach twists painfully. "Please," I urge, my voice grating. "Your last name, at least? Give me something that'll allow me to reach out to you when life isn't so complicated."

She sags, her eyes darting away. "It's better this way," she whispers.

"How?"

How could never seeing her again be *better*? How could she be so okay with saying goodbye?

"I did something." She straightens and lifts her chin. "Ever heard of the movie *Serendipity*?"

I shrug. "I don't watch TV."

"It's a movie, you dork. With Kate Beckinsale and John Cusack. God, it's so good." She smiles, her expression wistful, and for a moment I forget how angry I am over how easily she's willing to walk away after she went and made me fall for her.

"Give me your number." I brush my mouth over hers.

She pulls back and licks her lips. "In the movie, a man and a woman meet unexpectedly and spend a perfect day together. But they're both in relationships with other people—"

"You told me you were single," I force out, my throat suddenly tight.

Her smile is soft. "I am, but our lives are complicated. We're not ready for this," she whispers.

This. As if that word could encompass what exists between us. I'm not sure the word *love* would either. It feels pedestrian and overused, and yet it's the only thing that comes close to what I feel for this woman.

Still, the devastation in her expression kills me. I know she's right.

If she gave me her name and number, there's no way I could resist calling, and I'd be so fucking tempted to visit during any break in the season. But I can't. I'm about to be a father.

I don't have time to be in love, yet she's wormed her way under my skin and soaked into my bones, and now I can't imagine letting her go.

With a sigh, I drag a hand down my face. "What happens in the movie?"

"Kate's character has John's character write his name and number on a dollar bill. She spends the money, believing that if it comes back to her, she'll know they're meant to be."

A thread of irritation works its way through me. "That's ridiculous," I huff. "I'm not putting my number on a dollar bill when I could give it to you now. Let me do that. Take it. You can decide whether you want to call. You may never use it, but at least that way, there'd be a chance."

"I've written my number on a dollar bill already. I'll use it when I get back to Boston."

"Sienna," I plead, grasping her wrists, desperate to change her mind.

"And the book you were reading on the plane?"

I frown. "What about it?"

"In the movie, she writes her number in a book, then sells it. That way, they have double the chance." She worries her bottom lip and searches my eyes. "Put your name and number in the book, and when you get back to Boston, sell it."

"But you'll be in Paris." I pull her closer. I can't get close enough. Why did the universe throw us together like this only to take her away so quickly? Why is my life so damn complicated?

"I snapped a picture of the book. The universe will bring us back together when the time is right." She's so sure of herself. So innocent and pure. So fucking perfect.

Frustration floods me. I hate this plan. I hate it so freaking much.

She snaps me out of my stewing with a nip to my lip. "It's

serendipity. We're meant to be. We'll find each other again when the timing is right."

What if serendipity isn't real and this weekend was nothing but a bunch of happy coincidences? What if we never find each other again?

I keep those thoughts to myself, choosing instead to believe like she does that we're meant to be. That the universe will bring her back to me.

With her arms draped around my neck, she kisses me slowly, deeply.

I savor the taste of her. The feel of her in my arms, cataloging every detail, set on memorizing them all.

Before I'm ready to let her go, her phone rings and she pulls back.

The person on the other end—the concierge, I assume—reminds her that her car is ready. With a simple *okay*, she ends the call. Then she's peering up at me again. "I have to go."

I nod, swallowing back the devastation that threatens to burst from me. "Have a safe flight."

"Thank you, Noah. This weekend." She shakes her head and sucks in a long breath. "It was everything."

I cuff the back of her neck and kiss her again. Eyes closed, soaking her in one last time, I will her to be right. But most of all, I silently pray she'll be happy. "You're going to do amazing things, butterfly. You're going to soar. I can't wait to see what you do with this life." I press my forehead to hers and inhale deeply. "And I'm going to find you again."

With a step back, she gives me a melancholy smile. "I'm counting on it."

And then she's gone.

Chapter 13
Sienna

AS I SETTLE into my first-class seat, I survey every person who steps onto the plane. I'm almost certain that I made the biggest mistake of my life last week.

Why didn't I give Noah my phone number? Or get his last name? Something, *anything*. I was a fool, believing in fate, and now I'm heading to Paris for god only knows how long, pretty certain I'll never see him again.

While I waited for my flight from the Bahamas, I was tempted to call the hotel and ask for his information. And I came close to calling my room number to see if he was still there. But the romantic in me believed he'd find that dollar bill when the time was right. Believed I'd find that book.

Now I'm coming to terms with the fact that I'm the dumbest girl alive. What kind of woman finds a hot, articulate, intellectual man who knows how to make her body melt and says *hope you find my dollar bill*? Only an idiot, that's who.

As a woman in business attire walks down the aisle past me, I look away and remind myself that it's better this way. I'm about to embark on the kind of endeavor every fashion designer dreams of. Soon, I'll have my own line and my own show. Not to mention an unlimited budget to create whatever I want.

I'm twenty-four. I still have plenty of time for love.

And if Noah and I are meant to be, we'll find each other again.

Noah

Me: Meet my son, Oliver George Harrison.

War: Holy shit! You're a dad?? What the hell, Harry? Call me when you can.

War: Oh shit. Forgot to add a big fucking CONGRATS! Can't wait to meet the little guy and teach him how to skate. Love you, bro.

The moment my son was placed in my arms was officially the greatest moment of my life.

But when I had to hand him back, so much of the hopefulness his presence infused me with drained right back out. Because my first instinct was to call Sienna. But I don't have her fucking number. Not only that, but I never told her about him. She had no idea I was about to become a dad, so finding out about a baby would really be a surprise.

Probably an unwelcome one.

Still, I can't help but feel that agreeing to her plan was the biggest mistake I've ever made. About two minutes after she left, regret engulfed me. I knew without a doubt I shouldn't have let her leave without getting her full name.

I went so far as to offer a hundred-dollar bill to any employee who could give me her name.

No one who was tempted by the bribe had any useful information, and the front desk absolutely refused.

Leaving the Bahamas without that information left me sick to my stomach.

That nausea still rolls through me often. I may never see her again.

With my hands laced behind my head, I blow out a breath. I can't think like that. I've got to have hope.

I'll examine every dollar bill I come across until I find her.

My son cries, snapping me out of my obsessive thoughts. It's the reminder I need. This is why I agreed to her plan. Ollie has to come first.

One Year Later
Sienna

"How does it feel to be the top fashion designer in the world?"

There's no fighting the urge to roll my eyes at the host of the morning show. "I'm not."

"She still hasn't accepted the truth," Cat says from beside me.

We've done one interview after another since our show on Netflix premiered last week and shot to the number one spot.

The work was grueling yet incredible. We filmed for eight months, and editing took a couple more. Now that the show has premiered, I have no intention of leaving Paris. I fell in love with the city immediately and quickly purchased my own apartment. Fortunately, Cat and her family spend almost all their time here as well, so I'm not lonely.

Though I've barely seen my brothers. The same guys who swore they'd visit all the time.

My life is busy. I spend my days in meetings preparing for my next launch and I spend my nights drawing.

I rarely have a moment to think of anything but my designs, but when I do, my mind immediately goes to Noah.

When I have a second to breathe, all I can think is: will he see this interview? Or watch my show?

It's doubtful. More than once, he mentioned that he never watches television. But a girl can hope.

Though it's been a year since we said goodbye, I swear sometimes I can still taste him on my lips.

"Now that you've got an award-winning fashion line and a hit television show," the host says, "what's next? Announcing a new relationship, maybe?" She smiles like an idiot, as if finding a man is every woman's end goal.

Then again, I've already determined that I'm the idiot, because I found the perfect one and let him go.

"A woman never kisses and tells," Cat says when I don't respond right away, her raspy voice a bit chiding.

The host looks from Cat to me, still expectant.

I affect an aloof smile that mirrors the one my mentor so often wears even as I consider launching into a detailed description of Noah in hopes that someone watching knows him and can find him for me.

It's tempting, but if I did that, I'd be cheating.

If we're meant to be, he'll find me. Or I'll find that book.

Another year later

"Where are we going to dinner?" my intern Millie asks as she turns off the studio lights.

I'm going to miss her terribly. Cat hired her last year, and the two of us clicked right away.

When she first showed up in Paris, we rented one floor of the building. Now we've taken over the entire thing. We're in the process of bringing on more designers, and soon, I'll officially launch my own fashion house. It's thrilling and beyond scary at the same time.

Especially because Cat's gone back to Boston. Now that Millie is leaving too, I'll be in Paris without any true friends.

But Millie's move is a good one. She and my brother Gavin spent months sneaking around, which had to have been tricky, since they live on different continents. Though they thought they were being discreet, I'm not an idiot.

When their relationship fell apart, she was devastated. The pain was only compounded by the fact that she had no one to talk to about the secret affair.

She's going back to Boston to—hopefully—win him back. I couldn't be more excited for her. They deserve to be happy. I just hope it's not too late for them.

I know a thing or two about regret and I don't want her to live like that.

Before allowing the thought of Noah to bring me down, I mentally shake it off and smile at my friend. It's spring in Paris; the best time of year. I'm determined to enjoy it.

"The piano bar, of course. I want to hear you play one last time," I tell her as we step out into the beautiful night.

I had no idea how talented Millie was until several months ago, when Gavin came to visit. She sat down behind the piano and sang the most gorgeous song. That was the night I knew for sure that she was sleeping with him. She forgot that I speak fluent French and understood every word she sang.

Lucky for her, her father, who also happens to be my brother's best friend, doesn't speak the language. If he did, he also would have figured out his forty-year-old best friend was sleeping with his twenty-two-year-old daughter that night.

I suppose he'll find that out soon enough. Hopefully Beckett is around to defuse that. And Brooks. If Beckett can't talk some sense into her father, then at least my goalie of a brother can protect Gavin.

Aiden might be able to tell a joke or sing a song, but fighting isn't really his strong suit.

God, I miss my brothers.

As we head toward the bar, Millie pulls her curly brown hair back into a low ponytail. The peach sweater she's paired with tight black pants that are cinched tightly at the waist looks incredible with her flawless skin. "Fine, but I'll only play if you let me stop at the bookstore first. I need something to read on the plane."

She doesn't have to twist my arm. I sneak into the shop almost daily. The habit is so obsessive that the owner knows exactly what I'm looking for. Stopping to check myself is pointless. If the book Noah sold, with his name and number scrawled on the title page, showed up, she'd have called. Still, sometimes I wonder if the book will just appear on the shelves. It's silly, really. It's been two years. The book probably ended up on a shelf in someone's home in Boston. I'm in Paris.

It's time to move on.

That's what I tell myself at least once a day.

Even so, the moment we step into the bookstore and I'm overwhelmed by the scent of the pages, old and new, overtaken by nostalgia, that familiar zing of hope settles in my bones. The romantic girl from the Bahamas returns, and the jaded Parisian disappears.

While Millie scans the new release shelf, I head straight to the romance section and run my fingers down the spines until I find the name of the author I'm looking for. In the two years since I met Noah, this author has written several more books, but I only look for that first title.

And as I find a copy, my heart flutters. I slide the book out of its spot and close my eyes. Then I turn that first page. When I open them again, all the air leaves my lungs.

It's blank.

The familiar sight leaves my throat tight. Of course it's blank. With every day that passes, the chances that I'll find it seem to dwindle.

While Millie continues perusing, I pick up another of the author's titles and read the blurb. I set it back on the shelf and go for another, then another. Eventually, I collect a few that sound good, including that first book, and head to the counter.

A few feet away, the sight of a familiar face stops me in my tracks. What is *he* doing here?

Garreth Hanson, one of Beckett's best friends, catches sight of me too and breaks into a smile. He's classically handsome, his dirty blond hair just beginning to gray at the temples. His short beard is neatly trimmed and his blue eyes are as hard as they've always been, even when he's smiling. Immediately, I compare him to Noah. Lighter hair and a smaller frame. And though his irises are a similar color, Noah's were soft, inviting, comforting.

It's unfair, really, to compare the two men. It's just that I compare every man to the one I left in the Bahamas.

While Noah is sweet, Garreth is grumpy. An asshole, even. Today, he's wearing a custom navy suit that screams *billionaire* and is leaning casually against the counter, one hand in his pocket.

And he's still smiling at me.

Why is he smiling at me?

"Sienna, this is a surprise."

Frowning, I look over one shoulder, then the other, searching for a hidden camera. The man is never friendly. What is happening?

"Is it?" I set my stack of books on the counter and greet him the way my family would expect me to, with a kiss on each cheek.

As I step back, his blue eyes are intent on me. "Okay, maybe for you, but not for me."

"I'm confused," I admit.

He slips his hands into his pockets, the picture of confidence, and proceeds to shock the shit out of me. "I saw you walk in here," he says. "So I followed you. I was hoping I could take you to dinner."

CHAPTER 14
NOAH

"I CAN'T BELIEVE you're really here."

I grin at War as I slide onto a barstool at Ground Zero. The bar is a bit of a secret, I guess. It's open to players and staff of the Boston Bolts and the Boston Revs, as well as their guests. Hannah talks about hanging out here from time to time, but this is the first time I've had the pleasure.

I can't believe I'm here either. Here, as in Boston, not Ground Zero. Here, as in playing for the Boston Bolts. Here, as in *home*.

Ted was transferred to Boston, to Jen's delight. For four years, the three of us have raised Oliver in Minnesota, though Jen's dream of moving here never faded.

I could have fought them when they wanted to take my son out of state, but that's not how Jen and I co-parent.

Instead I did everything in my power to secure a trade. For a while there, I was certain it wouldn't happen. Because I was still under the contract I signed not long before Oliver was born, the Bolts were held to its terms, meaning they'd have to pay me a lot. And to be honest, they don't really even need me.

They've got enough great wingers to fill the first and second lines already, so while I may be one of the best—according to the pundits— investing in me wasn't necessary to secure their success.

Yet here I am. If I believed in fate, I'd say there was a bigger force at work when the trade went through.

Though I suppose maybe I do.

Because when I order a drink and the bartender gives me my change, I check every single dollar. I never use credit cards. I carry large bills and request as many ones as an establishment will allow when receiving my change. Do they sometimes get annoyed? Yup. Do I give a fuck? I guess not, since I carry more ones than a stripper.

I flip over each bill, then stack them and stuff them into my wallet. "I can't believe you're married with three kids," I say as I pick up my beer.

"And one on the way." He breaks into the biggest grin I've ever seen from the guy.

I never imagined War would settle down, yet not only did he do it eagerly, but he went and adopted two kids without blinking and has legal custody of a third. Though he's always hidden behind the bad-boy image the media gave him early on, he's got the biggest of hearts.

I shake my head. "It's wild. And Brooks is engaged. Shit, I'm the last man standing."

War waggles his brows. "Don't you worry, we'll find you a good woman yet."

I take a long pull of my beer, swallowing the urge to tell him that I already found her. I don't mention that I haven't looked at another woman since.

That last part doesn't bother me anyway. When I'm not playing hockey, I focus all my attention on my son, and I wouldn't have it any other way. The only person who'd rank right up there in importance with Ollie is the woman I can't find, so it's a moot point.

"You're really moving in with Hannah? With a contract like yours? You have a gambling problem I don't know about?"

Chuckling, I spin my beer on the bar top. My stepsister Hannah has the space, and she wants Ollie and me close by.

As luck would have it, we now work for the same entity. She still handles PR for the Langfields' baseball team, while I'm the Bolts' newest player.

Her career is as hectic as ever. She travels more than she's home, so even living together, we won't see each other often. Do I need to live with her? No. But after years apart, I want as much time as I can get with her. And it'll be good for Oliver to get to know her even better too.

"No gambling problem. I swear. But for now, I'm not ready to settle on a place. Not until I know where Ollie's going to school next year or where Jen is going to live. If it's possible, I'd like to be next door to her."

He barks out a laugh. The guy thinks I'm kidding. Now that he's a dad, he should understand that nothing matters more to me than my kid. If that means living next door to my former one-night stand and her husband for the rest of my life, I'll do it.

A heavy hand lands on my shoulder, snagging my attention. I turn on my stool and find my buddy Brooks looming over me.

The guy is a giant. He's got his light brown hair pulled back in his typical man bun and a big smile on his face. "I can't believe you're really back."

I stand and offer him a hug. "Feels good. The three of us haven't played together since college."

Those days were some of the best I've ever experienced. I've never enjoyed playing with anybody more than the two of them.

The hope is that I'll end my career with them by my side, here in Boston. At thirty-four, I'm inching closer to retirement age. There's a good chance that the contract I just signed with the Bolts will be my last. Even if it's not, I don't see myself leaving Boston unless Jen relocates again.

"What are you drinking?" War asks, holding up a hand to the bartender.

As Brooks orders, I pull out my wallet. "Drinks are on me."

War drops his head back and laughs. "The guy's family owns the place. You definitely don't have to buy him a drink."

I glare at him. He knows the rule. We go to a bar, I pay with cash. "Right, and his family just made my dream come true. Let me thank him."

Brooks grins as the bartender sets his Moscow mule in front of him. "I'll drink to that."

The three of us tap our glasses and fall into silence, surveying the scene around us while I wait for my change.

It seems that's all I ever do. Wait for another chance.

Now that I'm in Boston, I can't help but think maybe she's closer than ever before.

Chapter 15
Sienna

"PROMISE YOU WON'T MENTION a word of it while we're in Boston." I clutch my wrist and bring it to my chest, my nerves getting the better of me.

Garreth grasps my hand and runs his thumb over the top of it, easing my anxiety. He has the innate ability to sense when I'm about to spiral and knows exactly how to calm me down. Especially in the months since my life went to shit.

His gentleness instantly causes guilt to flare inside me. Because even after two years with this man, a man who treats me well, who respects me and supports me, I find myself scanning the wall of books inside the shop in the airport. No matter where I go, I'm always searching for *the* book. I'm an asshole. Truly.

It's been almost five years. I should have given up by now. I'm never going to find the book. And even if I did, would I really call him?

Garreth is a good man. He doesn't ask for much. He hops a jet to visit when I have time and he never pressures me to step away from work. He's content with what I have to offer. If there's another person in this world who understands the importance of hard work and running a business, it's him. He puts just as much energy into his whiskey company as I put into my designs.

Designs. Just the thought causes a pit to open up in my stomach. The time and energy I've put into my business no longer matter. Not after the bad investment decision I made. When I asked Beckett for a recommendation, I never imagined that it would cost me everything. While the authorities are working on locating my money, I'm not holding my breath. If the scam had only impacted me, I wouldn't even care. Maybe that makes me sound spoiled, but money is replaceable. I've had several successful years. I could have several more. Unfortunately, the money I invested belonged to the co-op I created for up-and-coming artists, which means all their money got caught in this scheme too. It's bad. *Really bad.*

"I wish you'd let me handle it." With a squeeze of my hand, Garreth pulls me against his chest and kisses my forehead.

I step back, and he releases me, wearing a concerned frown.

"No." My tone is firm, and I can't help the rush of annoyance that hits me. This isn't the first time he's offered to help. He's a good man. And I appreciate it. But I won't change my mind.

"Would you at least consider allowing me to tell Beckett about us?" He maintains an even expression, though I know he's itching to do it. He's wanted to tell him since we became exclusive over a year and a half ago.

There's no reasonable excuse not to tell him, or the rest of my brothers. Garreth may be fourteen years older than me, but none of the guys would care about that—especially Gavin, whose wife is close to twenty years younger than he is. Garreth is wonderful, and my brothers would all be thrilled that I'm happy.

Yet I'm still not ready to admit to our families and friends that we're together.

I'm an asshole.

I suck in a breath and put on my proverbial big-girl panties. "After the wedding," I promise. "I don't want anything to take away from Brooks and Sara's big day."

Grinning, he leans down and presses his lips to mine. "Whatever you want."

I close my eyes and will myself to sink into the kiss. To relax and think of only Garreth.

But no matter how hard I try, every time Garreth kisses me, I think of *him*.

CHAPTER 16
NOAH

THERE'S JUST something about weddings. About how two people decide that against all odds, they're going to give it a shot.

The first time I met the woman standing at the altar with Brooks, I knew they'd make it. It's the way my friend lights up around her and how fiercely protective she is of him. Sara couldn't care less about the millions he has in the bank. She's enamored. It's evident in the way she looks at him, the way she talks about him, and in the respect she has for one of the kindest, most caring men I know. And it's more than obvious that his heart beats wildly for her.

It's the way they smile at one another like they've won the lottery as Beckett Langfield pronounces them husband and wife.

And the way she leaps into his arms with the biggest of smiles. And how his full attention remains fixed on her as he carries her up the aisle.

It's hard not to believe that soulmates exist in the presence of Brooks and Sara.

"Now, that's a wedding," I say, holding out a hand to Hannah. We stayed in our seats as we waited for the aisles to clear, but it looks like our row is next.

Hannah shocked the shit out of me when she announced that she was pregnant. My stepsister has never been one for relationships.

What was even more surprising was the identity of the father. Daniel Hall, my teammate, is often referred to as Playboy by fans and commentators. He's young, really young, and though I don't know him well yet, I admit that I judged him based on his nickname and reputation. I was sure he wouldn't take her pregnancy seriously, but I couldn't have been more wrong. Hall is all-in, and he's just as head over heels for Hannah as Brooks is for Sara.

"I don't know." Hannah sighs as she takes my hand and lets me help her up. "The way Ava and War did it was ridiculously romantic."

"Didn't their marriage start out as a contract?"

"Well, yes." She shrugs. "But it was just the two of them at city hall. I love the simplicity of it. Doing away with the whole pomp and circumstance so it's nothing more than two people pledging to do their best for one another."

"That is beautiful, Han," I tease. "Spoken like a true romantic."

She lets out a throaty laugh, the sound a bit too loud for the moment. That's Hannah to a T. She's got a big personality. "I'm an author, not a romantic. I don't actually believe in all that stuff."

With a smirk, I shake my head. "Sure you do. You write love stories about the most improbable couples. You create characters who overcome their traumas, then end up finding the love they deserve without having to change who they are."

It's what I'd wish for myself if I thought I had a chance at any of that.

Her mouth hangs open. "That's what you get from my writing?"

"Actually," I tell her, "it's how Daniel described it when he was telling the guys about you during morning skate last week."

Hannah lifts her chin and scans the room. Daniel was running late, so he didn't make it in time to sit with us. While she looks for him, I scan the crowd for a familiar face, figuring I'll bow out and give them some time alone. The bond between them is growing, whether Hannah wants to believe it or not, and since I live with her, I'm always in their space.

I'm leaning in, ready to tell her I'll catch up with her later, when my attention snags on a figure at the front of the room and my heart stops.

Because the beautiful woman standing in front of the pergola is more familiar to me than anyone in this room.

But it can't be her.

I squeeze my eyes shut, and when I open them again, she's still there. What the fuck?

Her high cheekbones and porcelain skin look exactly as I remember. Her dark hair is down and wavy and far longer than it was the last time I saw her. The petite frame and curvy hips are the same. But her big smile and stunning green eyes are what finally convince me that I haven't lost my mind. She's really here. She's gesticulating wildly as she talks to Gavin Langfield, part-owner of the Bolts and my coach. Beckett, his brother and the other co-owner, is there too, as well as his wife.

What is she doing here? And how the hell does she know the Langfields?

"You okay?" Hannah squeezes my arm, pulling me from my spiraling thoughts. "You look like you've seen a ghost."

I'm afraid to look away from the woman I've been dreaming of for years, worried that she'll vanish, but with a shake of my head, I garner the strength to turn to Hannah.

"Might have." I rub a hand over my face, already working on a way to get Sienna alone. In a room full of people, including all the bigwigs who have the power to make or break my career, I can't just rush up to her and scoop her up into a hug. But I need to know why she's here. "I'm going to splash some water on my face."

Daniel appears, cupping Hannah's arm. "I've got her."

With a wooden nod, I stalk away. Fuck, I need a moment to think. To breathe. To figure out my next fucking move. Sienna is here. My Sienna.

Finally.

All the ridiculous searching I've done for years finally feels worth it. I knew our story wasn't over. I knew it wasn't a waste of time to wait for her. To ignore every woman who crossed my path because none of them were her.

She's here.

My mind is spinning as I approach the doors, but before I can exit, I run smack dab into War's chest.

"Whoa, buddy," he says, steadying me. "Where are you rushing off to? Brooks wants to take a few pictures with us before cocktail hour."

I blow out a breath, then another, willing my heart to stop racing and my ears to stop ringing. Sienna won't evaporate into thin air, and if she does, I now have connections that'll help me find her. It's safe to take some damn pictures.

Nodding, I follow War, and when I spot Brooks waiting with his new wife and the photographer, my muscles relax a fraction.

Shit, she's really here.

Nervous energy merges with excitement, and there goes my heart again, this time taking off at a gallop. Somehow I make it through pictures, though there's a chance I'll look like a maniac in every one. But for the most part, I rein in all the emotions overtaking me while I congratulate the couple and even join in on a conversation or two.

As Brooks and Sara move on for photos with other people, my mind whirls again, working through all the reasons Sienna could be here.

And considering the best way to approach her.

War suggests getting a drink at the open bar, and I nod quickly. It'll give me a few more minutes to figure out my next move. Maybe I'll even fill War in. He'll know what to do.

As we walk away, Sara says, "There's your sister. Do you want a photo with her alone?"

That catches my attention. I haven't seen Brooks's sister since she was a kid. I think she came to a game or two when we were in college.

"Sienna," Sara says, and I whip around. "Come grab a pic with Brooks. Your brothers are taking too long."

Sienna, *my Sienna*, is no more than twenty feet from me, rolling her eyes.

My lungs seize up and my muscles lock. I'm completely enraptured, consumed by her as she banters with my friends.

Is she friends with Sara? Fuck yes. This couldn't be more perfect. Brooks's and War's wives are best friends, along with Aiden's wife.

Even Coach's. Once again, I'm hit with how right Sienna was for me all those years ago. It's fate, pure and simple.

Fucking serendipity.

"Only because he's my favorite brother. Today, at least." Her raspy laugh washes over me, making it impossible to comprehend anything she's saying.

"Aw, you hear that, Brookie?" Sara coos. "Sienna says you're her favorite."

"Who is that?" I mumble to War. Why, I don't know. All reasonable thought has escaped me.

He turns, hands in his pockets. "Oh, that's Sienna. You haven't met her?"

I shake my head, even though, yes, I'm very well acquainted. "How does she know the Langfields?"

War laughs. "Dude. You haven't looked at a woman in years. This is not the time to change that. At least not with *that* woman."

I blink out of the fog Sienna's proximity has brought with it, my head snapping his way. "Why?"

"She doesn't *know* the Langfields," he says, his brows lifted. "She *is* a Langfield. The little princess, to be exact. Brooks's baby sister, Sienna."

My mind does a million somersaults as I put together the conversation Sienna and Sara just had.

Fuck.

The bombshell War just dropped replays in my mind. Then the conversations Sienna and I had all those years ago.

When people find out my last name, it changes things.

I have four older brothers.

Holy shit. She is Sienna *Langfield*. My best friend's younger sister. My coach's younger sister. My teammate's younger sister.

Fuck.

The difference in our ages never really concerned me. Not in the beginning, because I had no intention of having anything but a fling, and not once I got to know her, because by then, she was all that mattered.

Now? Unease slithers through me. I'm a depraved asshole. All the things we did? All the ways I took her, all the filthy words, only to find out that she was once the kid sitting in the stands watching my hockey game?

I study her again. The ruching of her tight red dress accentuates all her curves, and her breasts swell from the top in a way that makes my mouth water. Sienna is all woman. The guys must know that. They don't see her as their baby sister. They see her as an adult. Right?

I'm still trying to convince myself of that when her brothers surround her, engulfing her in hugs and smiling for the camera. Fuck. Fuck. Fuck.

She waves Sara over, and a moment later, the other Langfield women join the group. Brooks's parents make their way over, too, and the whole lot of them smile for the camera. It's a family photo that'll probably be hung on the wall in more than one Langfield house, with Sienna right in the middle. By herself.

A relieved breath escapes me. There's no partner at her side. No obvious plus-one.

I just need to get her alone. Find a way to surprise her so we can have our little reunion without the attention of the dozens of people still in this room.

A memory of what her lips felt like on mine surfaces, and my mouth waters. Fuck, I can't wait to taste her again. It's followed by a flash of her smile. The smile she'll give me when she realizes I finally found her.

From there, the thoughts turn X-rated, including a fantasy of dragging her into a dark corner, hiking that dress up, and slamming into her.

"You okay?" War asks.

My heart stutters, and I reel back. Jeez, I've got to escape this room for a second. Otherwise I'll give away all my secrets. If I'm not careful, everyone here will see how utterly obsessed I am with my best friend's younger sister. They'll sense the depraved need that's stirring to live inside me as I consider all the dirty, dirty things I want to do to her when I get her alone.

So I take a step back.

Sienna's not going to disappear. This is her brother's wedding.

"Yeah, I'm just going to run to the bathroom." I thumb over my shoulder. "I'll meet up with you out there."

War mentions something about finding his wife, but I'm too focused on getting out of here to listen. As I step into the quiet restroom, I can't help but consider that this could turn into a complete disaster. When Aiden and Brooks find out about us, will it mess with our chemistry on the ice? Will they be pissed? No, I can't imagine they'll be that angry. I'm a good guy. I'll be good to Sienna.

It may take some convincing, I guess, for them to see that this is the real deal. Gavin and Beckett need to see that too. They hold all the power when it comes to my career. And I need to keep my spot on this team. I need to stay in Boston. With Ollie.

Shit, I wonder what Ollie will think of his old man finally having a woman. I bet he'll love her.

Does she like kids? Does she want her own?

My dick thickens at just the thought. I need to talk to her. It's time to get out of my head. There's no sense in worrying and planning and spiraling until I do. I've waited almost five years for this moment. I won't waste another second.

I'm coming for you, Sienna Langfield, just like I promised.

As I step out into the hall, it's as if fate has delivered her right to me.

Sienna sashays my way, looking like a fucking siren in that dress. She hasn't seen me yet. But as I inhale, ready to call out to her, a man in a tuxedo appears out of nowhere. He's older than she is, maybe in his early forties, with blond hair and a beard. With a lascivious look, he grasps her wrist and pulls her into a corner. The same kind of dark corner I was just fantasizing about. I can still see them, but they're positioned in a way that hides them from the crowd gathered for cocktail hour.

My blood pressure spikes. Concerned for her, I stalk their way, ready to intervene, ready to rail into him about the way he manhandled her like that. But when I'm still several steps away, she laughs, and my legs lock up.

"You're going to get us caught," she breathes.

"Maybe I want to get us caught," the man says with a distinct

British accent. "Maybe you look so bloody beautiful that I can't help myself. I need you."

He leans down, and to my horror, Sienna loops her arms around his neck and kisses him.

It's effortless, as if this isn't the first time they've done it. It's clear from the way they cling to each other that they're comfortable with one another's bodies.

My stomach roils when his hand settles on her ass and squeezes, like he has every right to touch her.

Fuck. I never imagined fate could be so cruel. I finally found my Sienna, only to immediately be slapped in the face with the truth that she's no longer mine.

Maybe she never was.

My vision blurs and my heart hammers in my chest.

I have to get out of this corridor. Away from her and this man. I can't stay here. I shouldn't be here anyway. I should be at home with my son.

He's all that matters.

By some miracle, I make it down to the street without being stopped. Outside, I stop and shoot a text to War, telling him my stomach is off and that I'll see him later. I ask him to please give my love to the happy couple, then I pull out my valet ticket and collect my car.

When he holds out my keys, I take out a twenty and push it toward him.

"Do you want any change?" the kid asks, pulling out a wad of ones.

A shudder works its way through me. I've spent the last few years of my life checking every single dollar bill I found searching for a girl who probably forgot me as soon as she landed in Paris. What a wicked fool I am. "No. No more change."

No more chasing fate. No more chasing Sienna.

She looked happy. Let her be happy.

It's time to move on.

Chapter 17
Sienna

AS WE PULL up to the restaurant where we're set to meet Beckett and Liv, my phone rings and my attorney's name flashes on the screen.

With a shrug, I say, "I have to take this."

As much as I'd rather put all this off until I get back to Paris, I can't ignore him.

Garreth nods. "Go ahead."

Beckett thinks I'm coming to dinner on my own. But I figured breaking the news to him that I'm dating one of his best friends would go better if we were in public and he was forced to keep his cool.

Though I really believe he'll be happy. Especially when he learns that Garreth has been my rock through all the shit life has doled out this last year.

"Hello?"

"Hi, Sienna," the older man says. "I'm sorry to bother you, but this couldn't wait."

"What's going on?" I focus on the dashboard of the expensive rental Garreth picked up. My fingers itch to touch the real Italian leather, but I fight the urge. That would be weird, right?

"They're not willing to settle for what we offered." He's direct, which I appreciate. I don't need him to soften the blow. I just need him to handle the explosion that upended my life. Or stop it altogether. Though by now it's clear that's not possible.

"What do *they* want?" They, as in the handful of designers I brought into the co-op I created. They, as in the people I'm currently locked in a legal battle with. They, as in the people who are hellbent on putting me out of business.

"They want your ability to design."

His matter-of-fact tone makes the blow easier to take. Teeth gritted, I blink once, twice. It's all the emotion I'll let show.

Beside me, Garreth watches, his eyes narrowed and his brows furrowed in concern.

"They want what?"

"They want you to agree never to design again."

"They're insane," I mutter, my eyes falling shut.

"Yes. Obviously we won't agree to that. But I think we need something more than money."

I blow out a breath, at a complete loss for how to respond.

"Sienna," he sighs. "They know what you're worth. And…"

When he doesn't immediately continue, impatience flares, like fire in my veins.

"*And what?*"

Why the hell is he suddenly tiptoeing around the facts?

"And in discovery," he hedges, "they saw the messages that involve Beckett. They know he's the one who recommended the financial manager to you."

My vision darkens as a protective rage takes over. "Beckett has nothing to do with any of this."

"We both know that's not true," he says evenly.

Desperation claws at my chest, making it hard to breathe. Fuck. Fuck, fuck, fuck. "If they promise to leave my family alone, I'll agree to whatever they want."

Garreth glares at me. "What is happening?" he mouths.

I shake my head and turn away. "Make the deal."

"Sienna," my attorney clips out. "Let's at least agree to the mediation first. From there, we can assess whether it's possible to talk them down a bit."

"Fine." My jaw cracks as I clench my teeth harder. "But if they won't agree, we protect my family at all costs. Got it?"

"Of course."

I end the call without saying goodbye. The anger is still alive inside me, but in the silence, sadness and grief join the party. I'm spiraling. The walls of the car are closing in on me, and suddenly, I can't breathe. As I gasp for air, I claw at the door, needing out.

"What's happening?" Garreth asks.

I shake my head. "I can't do this right now."

He angles over and squeezes my knee. "Okay. Let's focus on tonight. We'll figure out the rest tomorrow."

That initial irritation rears its head, getting the best of me, and I snap. "No. You don't get it. I can't do *this*."

I'm an asshole. I know I am. But I'm not in the right headspace to focus on this relationship. I need out. Of this car and of this relationship.

"Okay," he says, his tone frustratingly calm. "Do you want me to drop you at the hotel and meet Beckett without you, or do you want to go in there by yourself?"

"I'll grab an Uber." I reach for the door handle. "I'll text Beckett and tell him I'm not feeling well. Maybe you could pretend to bump into him?" I yank on the handle, but the door is locked.

His grip on my knee tightens. "Sienna, please let me at least take you back to the hotel. Your brother is fine on his own. But I want to make sure you're okay. I care about *you*."

I peer over at him. Shit. He doesn't deserve this. He deserves a woman who can give him the love he's worthy of. Not a woman who's still half in love with a fantasy. A memory.

"You shouldn't." I offer him a sad smile.

His expression falls. It's like the rug has been pulled out from under him. Like the curtain has been lifted and he's seen behind the façade. Last night was full of celebration. Throughout the reception, we snuck away to steal kisses. We teased one another via text, the messages interspersed with serious ones about how we couldn't wait to be free of all the hiding. I spent the night in his bed, and we woke up tangled in each other's arms.

But in my heart of hearts, I've always known that what we had wouldn't last. Now, with my life falling apart, I can't push forward anymore. I can't ignore the truth.

He says nothing when I step out of the car and onto the street. He doesn't chase me. He doesn't rail against me, demanding an explanation. In this moment, he knows as well as I do that it's over.

A month later, after I've signed away my right to do the only thing I've ever loved, I walk through the streets of Paris, second-guessing my decision to end things with Garreth.

Buzzed after a few drinks, I stupidly waltz into the bookstore where our affair began. At the register, where I found him standing that night, I swear his ghost hovers, smiling at me.

My already shattered heart crumbles further. Ending things was necessary, despite the despair surrounding me now. I could never have given him the one thing he wanted: my heart.

"Sienna." The owner breaks into a smile. Then in her native tongue, she chatters on about the shipment that came in this week, asking if I'd like to look through them with her to see if my book is in there.

I know it isn't. After all this time, I don't have it in me to believe in fairy tales and fate.

"I just came to say goodbye. I'm moving back to America."

Her eyes widen and her mouth forms an *O*. "You must give me your address, then. So if I find your book, I can forward it to you."

I promise to email her with an address once I'm settled, though as I hug her and step onto the sidewalk, I know I won't follow through.

She'll never find the book. And neither will I.

I've got nothing left. No career. No hope. No faith. And certainly no dreams of happy futures and fate.

I'll never be that naive girl again. And there's no one to blame for any of this but myself.

Chapter 18
Sienna

"HOW IS it possible that you still don't have answers? It's been over a year," Millie whines as the doorman at Langfield Corp ushers us inside. Millie, my former assistant and good friend, is now my sister-in-law. She and Gavin had the most gorgeous ceremony by the water three years ago.

I tug my jacket tighter around me, like it'll help me hide from the lies I've been weaving for the past year. I'm still too much of a coward to tell my family what I did. The agreement is ironclad. I've already signed away my right to design again. If my brothers knew, they'd try to find a way to undo it. They'd try to fix it for me.

I don't want their help. I've come to terms with the end of my career. It hurts to know that I'll never design clothing again, but I'm moving on.

Or I'm trying to, at least. Though it's been a challenge, coming to terms with the reality that I can never do the only thing I've ever truly been good at. I'm no longer allowed to be the only thing I've ever aspired to be. I can't have the career I've worked my ass off for. The career I sacrificed everything for, including my social life, time with my family, and *love*.

I swallow hard on that last word. The only time I ever felt anything even close to love was so long ago, and so fleeting, that it's quite possible I imagined it.

Six years. How the fuck has it been six years?

Affecting the most impassive expression, I hit the button to summon the elevator. "Things take longer in Europe."

Millie settles a hand on her stomach while we wait. She and Gavin have a daughter, Vivi, who's almost five, and they recently announced that she's pregnant with their second child. As difficult as it was to leave Paris, I'm glad I won't miss the birth of another one of my siblings' children.

There are a lot of them now.

Beckett and Liv have five children. The oldest three, Winnie, Finn, and Addie, are not his by blood, but he loves them more than just about any parent could love a child. He fell as hard for Liv's kids as he did for her. The youngest girls, June and Maggie, are only a few months younger than Vivi.

Then there's sweet baby Taylor, the little girl Sara and Brooks welcomed just last week.

Aiden married his high school sweetheart, Lennox, but they haven't decided whether they want kids. I get it. I'm undecided too. I love my nieces and nephews more than life itself, but I'm not sure I've ever wanted to be a mother. Mine has never been very maternal. Maybe not having that role model is part of it. Though it's likely because for my whole life, I've only ever wanted to be a fashion designer.

Though that's over now, so who knows how I'll feel about kids as time goes on.

I've yet to find a job in Boston. Probably because I've yet to bother looking. For the first few months, I traveled. Then, when I couldn't avoid my brothers anymore, I begrudgingly moved back into my parents' house. In the months since then, I've done a lot of yoga and spent quite a bit of time with my family. I've also been on far more dates that I wasn't aware were dates thanks to Beckett and his meddling ways.

Recently, I've become my mother's pet project. I think it's caught up with her, how little time she spent with us when we were kids, now that my father is retired and their business and social obligations have dwindled.

My brothers are all successful and happily married, while I'm single at almost thirty, and my company is in shambles.

I've gone from the most sought-after fashion designer in the world to a pariah in the industry. My name is whispered like an infectious disease. The only person still working in fashion who hasn't turned her back on me is Cat, but I've kept my distance. The last thing I want is for her to be sucked into the nasty rhetoric by association.

If I'm not careful, she'll go toe to toe with the naysayers. My brothers all would too. But I've made peace with my decision. Now it's time for everyone else to get on board with it.

As if I've summoned my mother, my phone lights up with a message from her.

> Mom: Have you heard about maple season in Vermont? There is a spa near the Berkshire family compound. I could schedule appointments for maple facials and pedicures and wraps! Then we could go on a tour and watch how they make it. What do you think? Want to get out of town for a few days?

With a groan, I jam my phone into my pocket. I need a job. Then I'd have an excuse to say no to jet-setting around with her like a stereotypical heiress to do absolutely nothing in the middle of the freaking woods. I lived in Paris for five years. I thrived there. What makes her think spending time in nature would be appealing to me? If she understood me at all, she'd know that it sounds like my worst nightmare.

Or maybe my second worst, since I'm currently living my worst nightmare.

Like I said, I need a job.

"Do you need a nanny?" I ask Millie as the elevator ascends to the floor where Liv's office is located.

She snorts, bringing her hand to her mouth a second too late to stifle it.

I glare at her.

"I'm sorry." She holds up her hands. "It's just that after a five-minute conversation with Vivi, you're usually itching for a martini."

I pull my shoulders back and lift my chin. "I love Vivi."

My best friend tilts her head, silently calling me out on my bullshit.

"Fine," I huff. "I *do* love Vivi, but I can only talk about what Barbie wants for breakfast for so long."

"I get it." She chuckles. "Which is why you'd make a terrible nanny."

She's right. I do need an excuse to avoid my mother, though. And I need a task to keep myself busy.

We step out of the elevator, and she leads me down the hall toward Liv's office, her brown curls bouncing. Liv asked me to meet her here before lunch, and Millie wanted to pop by to visit Gavin.

Halfway down the hall, my phone buzzes again. This time, though, it's not my mother. This message is from the other woman who won't leave me alone.

> Cat: You can't avoid me forever. Meet me for drinks at Allure. It's super private. No one will overhear us. Maybe then I can talk you into getting out there again too.

With a sigh, I pocket the device again. I have no intention of doing any such thing.

Garreth is her brother-in-law, and she's one of very few people who knew about my relationship with him. And she's too damn smart for her own good. She knows how I sabotaged said relationship, just like I sabotaged my career.

But getting out there again? No thanks. I'm beginning to think I'm not cut out for love. Maybe I'll stick to being the fun aunt. Or not, since according to Millie, I'm not even good at that.

I wince at the thought. She's not wrong. I definitely do better with the older kids than the younger ones.

Though relationships and kids are out, I can't help but crave something of my own. A reason to get out of bed in the morning. A distraction from the journal in my nightstand. The one that haunts me. The one I used to doodle in daily. A distraction from the concern that I'll never again feel the itch of excitement that used to take over the minute I put pencil to paper. That the magic that once flowed through me no longer exists.

I shake out my hands, sloughing off the sensation. The move exposes the turquoise butterfly inked on the inside of my wrist, catching my attention, and my heart pangs.

It's been six years, and I can still hear the murmured lies of the man I can't forget, no matter how hard I try.

You're going to do amazing things, butterfly. You're going to soar. I can't wait to see what you do with this life. And I'm going to find you again.

He never found me. I didn't soar. And this tattoo is a permanent reminder of my naïveté. More than once, I've considered covering it with another design. Thinking of that man and that weekend and my hopeless romanticism—more like sheer stupidity—hurts more that I'll ever admit.

The *what-if*s and the *maybe*s are the work of the devil.

If I'd given him my number back then, we probably would have talked once or twice, then drifted apart naturally.

Our connection would be as dead as my career is now.

Instead, I let myself believe in fate. I came up with this romanticized notion that fate kept us apart, and therefore it wasn't my fault that we never had a shot. But the chance that a man I shared one hot weekend with could be my soulmate? Yeah, that's the stuff of romance novels. Of nineties rom-coms.

Fortunately, I am no longer naïve enough to believe in love or second chances.

These days, I am chock-full of sarcasm and jaded self-deprecation. Maybe under the right circumstances, those qualities would work on a résumé.

"Sienna." Beckett steps out of an office down the hall, and Gavin appears a second after.

"Hey, Peaches." Gavin pulls his wife to him in a sweet display of their disgustingly perfect romance and plants a kiss on her lips that has her melting into him. "You girls are going to lunch, right?"

"Yeah," I say, "but Liv asked me to come see her before we go."

Beckett folds his arms across his chest and smirks. "Did she now?"

His cocky attitude makes my stomach sink. "What do you know?" I demand, eyes narrowed. "If it's another date, I swear…"

He's driving me crazy. The man thinks he's a modern-day Hello Dolly, matching couples left and right.

Except I don't want to be matched. Especially not with any of the men he's been tossing my way. I swear the guys he forces on me don't even want to date.

"Beckett," Liv calls from her office, her tone stern.

His expression sobers instantly. "Coming, Livy." He wraps an arm around my shoulder and drags me with him. "She won't yell if you're with me."

I snort, batting him away. "She totally will."

"Yes, she totally will," Liv says as she stands and rests her hands on her desk.

Their offices are side by side, with a door connecting the two. I have no idea how she gets any work done with him around. He spends his days fawning over her, while she vacillates between being charmed by him and being annoyed. She's a saint, really, for putting up with him.

He, on the other hand, is head-over-heels in love with her. Though I'd never admit it, it's sweet. And he does mean well.

I have to remind myself of that last part often.

"Thanks for coming early," Liv says as she eases into her office chair.

Her professional tone has my hackles rising. "Is this a formal thing?"

"Yes," Beckett cuts in. "But first tell me about the date last night."

Ignoring him, I drop into the soft velvet guest chair and drag my fingers over the fabric. "This is nice."

Liv smiles. "Thanks. I redecorated a few months ago. Thought it was time for some updates."

"Hello?" Beckett huffs.

Sighing, I drop my head back and pin him with a look. "He didn't show up."

He breaks into a bewildered frown. "What do you mean he didn't show up?"

I straighten and shrug easily. It wasn't a big deal. Honestly, I was relieved. "He texted an apology, at least. He said he didn't think he could go out with Beckett's younger sister. And I quote, 'No offense, but picturing Beckett Langfield while eating dinner would be a total turnoff.'"

My brother's eyes narrow to slits, and his face turns red. "Jasper Quinn did *what*?"

Liv sucks in a harsh breath. "You did not try to set her up with Jasper *Freaking* Quinn."

He stomps to the open door and bellows, "Man Bun!"

Cortney Miller, Beckett's close friend and the GM of the baseball team, materializes out of thin air in Liv's doorway. He's giant, like Brooks, with long blond hair tied back in a bun.

Now that I think about it, Cortney might be the player Beckett was wooing all those years ago that led to me traveling to the Bahamas alone.

My wrist itches at that thought. Before I can give in to the sensation and rub my fingers across the butterfly that used to bring me such hope, I ball my hands into fists.

Cortney puts his hands on his hips, his brows lifted expectantly. "What?"

"Quinn is out. Demarco is in."

Cortney lets out a heavy sigh. "You sure?"

Liv huffs a frustrated breath. "You can't trade Jasper Quinn because he didn't go on a date with your sister."

My jaw drops. "*What?*"

"I asked him if he could be a team player," Beckett says, ignoring me. "He's been on thin ice, but I gave him one more chance to prove to me he could grow up. All he had to do was take Sienna out. Make her laugh. Show her a good time. I didn't ask him to sleep with her."

"Beckett Langfield," Liv hisses.

My brother's eyes go wide, and he takes a step back, like he suddenly realized just how much shit he's gotten himself into. "Can I have a minute to talk to my sister alone?"

"Beckett," I fume. "You can't fire a player because he didn't want to hang out with me."

My brother no longer looks contrite. "I can and I will. I hate seeing you like this, and I hate knowing that I'm to blame."

I sink into the plush velvet, wishing I could become one with the fabric. That's what should happen to designers when we can no longer design. We should be given the decency of dying a gentle death, forever being comforted by the materials that bring us joy.

"You're not to blame," I say, suddenly drained of all fight.

"I'm heading back to my office," Cortney says, pointing to the hallway. "Am I really trading Quinn?"

"Yes," my brother hisses.

At the same time, Liv smacks the top of her desk and huffs out a *no*. Then she lifts her gaze and zeroes in on her husband. "You told me I was CEO of the Boston Revs. You already have a job."

My breath catches. This is news to me. My father officially retired last year, and since then, Beckett has taken on his duties as acting CFO while also running the baseball team. I've considered offering to help a time or two over the last few months to ease the amount of work on his plate, but I've been hesitant to get involved in Langfield Corp, knowing that I may never get back out.

I don't know how he manages all the work while still being as active in his kids' lives as he is. This shake-up will help there, though if Liv is the new CEO, they've mostly just transferred heaps of work from his plate to hers.

Even so… "Congrats on the promotion."

She smiles. "Thank you. That's why we asked you to come in today."

Confusion has me tilting my head. "Hmm?"

"So yes or no?" Cortney, who's still hovering at the door, pleads.

With a growl, Beckett tips forward in his seat, staring his wife down. "I'll agree not to meddle in anyone's love life for the next month if you agree to trade Quinn."

Lips twitching, Liv eyes Cortney for a heartbeat. When she zeroes in on her husband, she matches his stance, as if she's going in for the kill. "Make it three months, and you've got a deal."

"Forty-five days." Beckett leans back in his chair, folding his arms across his chest. "It's the best I can do."

Liv shakes her head. "You really want to trade Quinn?"

"Yes. From here on out, I only want team players."

The negotiation goes on for another minute or two, each volley sending me looking from my brother to Liv and back again, like I'm watching a tennis match.

Eventually, Liv holds her hand out over her desk, and my brother shakes it. "You've got a deal." With a glance at Cortney, she adds, "Make the trade."

Just like that, the Revs are down a player.

It's wild the way they argued like that and how quickly and decisively they made the deal. It almost…god, my body buzzes with an unexpected exhilaration as I replay it in my mind.

"Now," Liv says, lacing her fingers in front of her and focusing in on me. "Onto the favor we need to ask of you."

"As I was saying before, I'll never forgive myself for what you've gone through," Beckett adds.

"Beckett—" I shake my head, willing the tears pricking at my eyes to abate. If I relive it all again, if he apologizes again, there's no way I won't break down.

"It's my fault that you hired Warren Financial to handle your investments. If I hadn't referred you to Xander Warren, you wouldn't have been caught up in his Ponzi scheme, and your company—your life's work—wouldn't be caught in this whole mess."

I clench my jaw, fighting back emotion. It's true. When my company went public, I was in need of a new financial adviser, and since Beckett funded my company after I'd asked my parents and they'd turned me down, I called him. His heart was in the right place. He thought he was helping me as well as a new family friend. But that friend turned out to be a thief.

It could have happened to anyone. Unfortunately it happened to a Langfield, and when a name like ours is involved, there's always extra scrutiny. The people who had gone in on the company with me lost everything. Yet because my personal funds remained untouched—because they remained invested elsewhere—there was speculation that I colluded with the thief.

That's when I made the deal to cover what they lost myself. If only that had been enough for them.

That last part is my secret. I won't share that information with Beckett. I won't make him feel worse than he already does. My brothers and my parents think my money is tied up while the investigation is still active and that I'm hiding from the fallout. They have no idea that the fallout includes the decimation of my entire life. That there are no assets left to recoup anymore.

I'm lost, like a stray piece of yarn fluttering in the wind. A loose thread I can't even stitch back up because I've been forced to sign away my right to design ever again.

Fuck, my head hurts, and it's got nothing on my heart.

"I really don't want to do this again," I tell them. "I don't blame you. I just want to move on."

"That's why we asked you to come in." Liv's voice is gentler now, her smile warm. "We need help."

A knock at the door interrupts us, and Gavin appears. "My turn yet?"

I frown. "Huh?"

"We'd like you to come work for Langfield Corp." Beckett thumbs over his shoulder at Gavin and smirks. "You'd be his boss."

Gavin grins. "Promise you'll be nicer than my other boss?"

"I'm the best boss," Beckett grumbles.

Liv, eyes dancing, snorts.

"I'm confused." I frown at one brother, then the other, before turning to Liv. "What is it you want me to do?"

"We want you to be *me*," Liv says, "for the hockey division."

"You?" I question.

"Yes," Gavin says. "We need you to head up the Bolts. You'd step into my old position. I've been juggling the tasks of both CEO and coach since we fired Seb. We hired a GM when I took over coaching, and it's helped cut down on my workload, but it's time I pass over the reins. The hockey division of Langfield Corp needs a dedicated CEO again."

"But I know nothing about hockey." This seems like an important detail. Sure I've been to many hockey games in my life, but I've always spent those hours sketching designs. I'd yell when the crowd around me yelled, but otherwise I paid little attention to the game.

"But you know business. You've run one for the last six years. An extremely successful business, at that. And one you built from the ground up. You're the only one of us to accomplish that feat," Beckett points out.

Sure, I built a business. A business that's now bankrupt.

I cross my arms, my fingers instinctively tracing the butterfly on my wrist.

"I can help you with the hockey knowledge," Gavin explains. "But what we really need is someone with a mind for business. Who can look at numbers, advertising budgets, and the big-picture stuff. All the stuff you've been doing for half a decade. You're qualified, Sienna. We wouldn't ask you to do this if you weren't."

"And I'm a Langfield," I point out.

Beckett shrugs. "For better or worse, yeah, you're a Langfield. Gav and I are here because of our name too. But that name means I trust you more than anyone in this world, and I'll do anything to help you succeed."

I swallow down the emotions clawing up my throat. Those words are almost identical to the ones he spoke the day he agreed to fund my business. My brothers have always believed in me. Maybe I failed once, but for the first time in a long time, I feel a flutter of excitement in my belly. Maybe it's time to attempt to fly again.

CHAPTER 19
NOAH

"OLLIE," I call. "Come on. We've got to meet your mom in fifteen minutes."

I pluck his bag off the floor and hold it out. The thing has to weigh fifteen pounds. Probably because of the damn Chromebook he has to tote back and forth to school every day. Kids his age will probably end up with back problems later in life from lugging all this stuff around.

Then again, the five textbooks I once hauled around in a tattered JanSport were likely worse.

"Ollie," I holler from the doorway.

My six-year-old saunters out of his room, the picture of nonchalance, wearing a pair of aviators, new Michael Jordan sneakers, and what I swear are skinny jeans.

Daniel, my teammate-slash-brother-in-law, took him shopping this week, and Ollie has come out in a new outfit every day since. I can already picture Jen's eye roll. She complains often about how spoiled our son is, but I swear I have no hand in it, despite my hefty salary. We're aligned when it comes to the values we want to instill in him. We both strive to shape him into a humble, hardworking person.

Hannah and Daniel are the problem. They're both over-the-top in all kinds of ways, and Ollie is good at exploiting that.

My son stops halfway across the room and waves a hand,

motioning to my stance. "You're killing my vibes, Dad. You're killing my vibes."

I groan. My kid is so much cooler than me and he knows it. Fortunately he still thinks I'm cooler than his stepdad. "You have everything you need for school tomorrow?"

Ollie's mom and I have a fifty-fifty custody arrangement. My games typically fall on Tuesdays, Thursdays, and Saturdays, so those are Jen's nights, game or not, and we trade off on weekends during the offseason. It means a lot of shuffling around, but it's important to both of us that we get quality time with our son. It hasn't always been easy, but Jen and Ted and I make a good team.

Even if I do like that Ollie thinks I'm cooler than Ted.

When I'm traveling, Jen often keeps Ollie on my assigned days, though sometimes she lets him stay with Hannah or my dad. In general, though, he bounces back and forth pretty frequently between our two homes. I bought a three-bedroom condo near the arena, and Jen and Ted live in a townhome and added a little girl to their family two years ago.

Though I don't have a game today, it's Thursday, so tonight will be a quiet, lonely night for me. I hate being off when Ollie isn't here. I rarely get out of the house these days unless it's with him because I want to be around for the little time we do have together. Fortunately, Jen had a meeting after work today and asked if I'd pick him up and keep him for a few hours. But she'll be home any minute now, so we need to head her way.

Besides, Hannah talked me into meeting her and the guys at the tattoo shop. She and Daniel are getting matching ink and have turned the event into some kind of party, hence the reason my presence is required. They turn everything into a party, so I should have known the moment she mentioned it that she wouldn't let me decline.

My phone buzzes in my pocket as I finally herd Ollie out into the hall. I'm digging the device out when he makes a beeline for the door directly across from mine. I snag him by the back of his sweatshirt, giving up on checking my phone, to keep him from walking in without knocking.

"Aunt Hannah isn't even home." Keeping hold of him, I snatch his jacket off the hook in the entryway and pull the door shut.

While I lock up, Ollie peers up at me, eyes narrowed, like he doesn't believe me. "What about Daniel?"

"Nope."

He glares at the door and sighs.

I don't know whether to laugh or shake my head when he cops an attitude like this. I swear he's six going on sixteen.

War's son Brayden is practically grown now, but already, Ollie acts just like him. Despite the sarcastic attitude, Brayden is a good kid, so I'm holding out hope that my little guy will be at that age too.

For the most part, he's polite. He just doesn't hide how he feels, and I can't fault him for that. "Fine," he says, his shoulders slumping. "Let's go. But can we get icees on the way?"

"It's almost dinnertime," I remind him. Even as I say it, I know I'll stop and pick one up for him. I'll just have him put it in the freezer until after dinner.

I slip my phone out of my pocket and shoot Jen a text to let her know we're running a couple of minutes behind, then toggle over to the group chat that's had my phone buzzing in my pocket nonstop for the last several minutes.

> War: What's the plan for tonight? Are we going out after?
>
> Aiden: Lex and I are down for that.
>
> Brooks: I'm not sure why I have to come. Have you all forgotten that I have a baby at home?
>
> Aiden: Your wife told my wife to tell everyone you're coming. She's got plans for you.
>
> Brooks: I'm sitting right next to the three of you. Why are you texting me?

Chuckling, I close out the chat and pocket the phone, which continues to buzz as the Langfield brothers argue.

I couldn't be happier about how the move to Boston has turned out.

Not only has Ollie really gotten to know Hannah and my dad—once-or-twice-a-year visits and FaceTime only do so much—but I'm once again playing with War and Brooks.

The team is incredibly tight-knit and the guys instantly brought me into the fold. We've got a good shot at the playoffs this year, and since I'm at the tail end of this contract, I'll do everything I can to make it happen. With any luck, the Bolts will renew my contract, but if they don't, then before long, I may be announcing my retirement. My kid is in Boston, so this is where I'll stay, hockey or not.

"Where are you playing this weekend?" he asks as we wait at the drive-thru window for his icee.

"Chicago. I'll be back on Sunday, though, and you and I have a date at the aquarium."

He nods. "I have baseball tryouts on Saturday."

It's T-ball, and I'm aware. My son hasn't shown much interest in hockey, but after attending a few Revs games with Hannah last season —which included being brought out onto the field and sitting in the dugout—he's obsessed with the sport. "Ted is taking you, I think."

Ollie drops his head back against the seat, his expression one of exasperation. "I don't have the energy to pretend that I believe he can handle that."

I cough out a laugh, and with a grin, I peer at him where he's buckled in behind me. "He's just got to drive you there and watch."

He slips his sunglasses down the bridge of his nose, his blue eyes shrewd, and eyes me in the rearview mirror. "As I was saying."

Over my shoulder, I assure him, "I'll come to as many games as possible. Promise."

He lets out a dramatic sigh but gives me a serious nod. He knows the drill. Unfortunately.

I pay for his icee with cash, and when the woman hands me my change, Oliver perks up.

I drop the three-quarters into the cupholder, and before I pull away, I flip each dollar bill over. With each one I examine, my disappointment grows, but I keep my expression neutral.

"No name?" Ollie asks.

I shake my head and stuff the money into my pocket. It's stupid that I still check. But for almost five years, I did it religiously.

It's possible Sienna never even wrote her name and number on one like she said, and after Brooks's wedding, I know how to find her. Hell, she's the baby sister of two of my closest friends. Two guys I'm meeting up with tonight. She lives in this city now, if what I overheard them talking about is true.

But the night I saw her kissing that man, I vowed to myself to let her go.

I should have done it long ago, really. The morning after I discovered who she was, it hit me just how difficult it would have been to date Sienna Langfield when one of her brothers is my coach, two more are my teammates, and the oldest is the head of the Bolts' parent organization. All of that equates to way too much risk to my career, and since my spot on this team keeps me in Boston near my son, I won't jeopardize it.

And she's with someone else anyway. I like to think that she's happy, though I've never asked.

Since Ollie was old enough to notice the way I study every bill, he's been invested in the search too. For the last couple of years, we've had a routine. If I find a dollar with a name and number written on it belonging to someone who isn't Sienna, then I give it to him. If it's blank, I keep it.

So he pays extra attention. Now, though it hurts to look, I do it for him. It's bittersweet and probably a habit I should break soon. It can't be healthy to still be so consumed by emotions for a woman I can never have.

By the time I pull into the lot of the tattoo shop, I have more than one hundred text notifications waiting. Almost every one of them is from the group chat. When I throw my door open and step out, the whole crowd cheers from where they wait outside the front doors.

As I approach, Hannah is eyeing Daniel with a wicked grin.

"What about a clit piercing?"

Oh, for fuck's sake. Naturally that's the part of the conversation I'd have to walk up on.

Grimacing, I let out an exaggerated sigh. "Again, why am I here?"

Brooks shakes his head. "I have no idea why any of us are here. Me especially. I'd like to get home to my wife and baby, if you all don't mind, so let's get this party started."

Hannah rolls her eyes. "Your baby is fine. She's with my baby and Liv. And your wife was very clear. Tattoo her name on your balls like War did for Ava. She birthed your progeny, so you owe her that."

War chuckles and pulls Ava, whose cheeks are crimson, against his chest.

Meanwhile my own balls have shriveled up into my body. There are things friends don't need to know about one another, this being one of them. But since my friends are far too open, I'm privy to far too many of their secrets.

Ava, sweet, angelic Ava, pinches Hannah. "Shh. I told you that in confidence when I hated him."

War buries his face in his wife's neck. "You never hated me, Vicious. But keep telling yourself those lies. You know I love it."

Hannah gives a dismissive wave. "He couldn't keep it a secret from the guys anyway. They literally see each other's balls daily."

"Not quite, dream girl." Her husband squeezes her hip, trying to tame her. It's a fruitless endeavor.

Hannah grins up at him. "As I was saying, what about a clit piercing?"

"And as I was saying," I grumble, hanging my head, "why am I here?"

"Team-building opportunity," Hannah chirps. "You're all on fire this season, and now that you have a new boss, it's time to celebrate."

New boss? With a frown, I snap up straight again. "What?"

Brooks grins. "It hasn't been announced yet, but Beckett and Gavin appointed Sienna to the head of the hockey division yesterday."

A lead weight settles in my gut. "Sienna, as in your sister, Sienna?"

Brooks nods. "Have the two of you met yet?"

I work to keep my expression neutral. Sienna is my new boss? This can't be...*fuck.*

"Not formally," I force out.

Shit. I can't exactly tell him that I'm familiar with his sister biblically. That I know every inch of her body and the sounds she makes when she comes. And I definitely can't admit that I've been dreaming of the day I can do all those filthy things to her again for longer than most of these guys have been with their wives.

"I saw her at the wedding, though. And a game or two, I think."

Hannah's eyes light up, and instantly, I know I've made a terrible mistake. Same as I did the day of Brooks's wedding when I spotted Sienna and admitted that I felt like I'd seen a ghost. Fortunately my sister was too caught up in Daniel that night to notice when I disappeared.

I threw up the second I hit the parking lot. Then I got wasted, *alone*, at a bar down the street. I missed the dinner and the cake and the dancing, but if I'd stayed another minute and had to watch Sienna in the arms of another man, I'd have lost it.

I've avoided looking her up since then. Though I earnestly hope she's happy, I can't stomach the idea of witnessing how good her life is without me in it.

The wheels are still turning in Hannah's mind when the door to the tattoo shop jangles open and Lennox appears. "Are you guys ever coming in here?"

Relieved as hell and more fond of Lennox than ever now that she's saved me from my sister's scrutiny, I stride in first. I'll tattoo whatever these idiots want on my body if it means steering the topic of conversation away from Sienna.

"Are we doing this?" Hannah asks as she steps in behind me. "Or are you gonna chicken out again, Baby Hall?"

He chuckles as he brushes a kiss against her shoulder. "Not nervous, Mrs. Hall. And of course I'm coming. I always do when I'm with you."

With bile rising in my throat, I take a giant step away from them. "Why the fuck am I here?"

They're too caught up in one another to pay me any mind. Brooks passes me, slapping me on the back on his way, and Ava steps into the shop next.

War is the last to enter. He stops beside me and grasps my shoulder. "You okay?"

I blink, my mind still spiraling. "What does Sienna Langfield know about hockey?" I ask stupidly.

"She's a Langfield. I'm pretty sure she doesn't need to know anything." He frowns, his brows pinch together. "Why do you care anyway?"

I blow out a breath and shove my hands into my pockets, going for casual. "Just strange, don't you think?"

He lifts one shoulder in an easy shrug. "If one of my kids was struggling, and I ran a business like Beckett and Gavin do, I sure as shit would offer them a job. And if Bray was the one running things, I'd hope he'd do it too. It's what siblings should do."

"She's struggling?" The words slip out before I can think them through. I'm showing too many cards. Fortunately, War's attention has caught on his wife, so he doesn't notice how bothered I am by the idea.

With a heavy sigh, he drags his hand through his dark hair. "Yeah, more fucking fallout in the Xander saga."

"As in your stepbrother? What does he have to do with Sienna Langfield?"

War blows out a breath. In college, he hated the guy with every fiber of his being. And that was before the asshole dated Ava. Though, last I heard, Xander was awaiting trial, and if I remember correctly, he was remanded in custody because he was a flight risk.

My stomach sinks. Fuck. Did Sienna get caught up in the Ponzi scheme? Is that why she moved back from Paris?

"The short story is that Beckett introduced them when he still thought Xander was a family friend. You know how Beckett is. He's always trying to bring people together. He thought he was doing me a solid by helping out my brother. I guess Xander and Sienna hit it off, and her company invested a ton of money. Then Xander lost it all." He shakes his head, his fists clenching at his sides.

"Shit." It's the only word that comes to mind.

When I met her, she was so eager, so excited about what came next in her career. I didn't know the specifics, but I knew she was taking a big step.

Now that I've found her again, now that I know she's a Langfield, I've done a little research. In Paris, her design company flourished and her reality show was a huge hit. When I discovered that little tidbit, I cursed myself for not being the kind of person who watches TV.

She had a few successful years, though I haven't found time to research what happened from there. I'm sure she's devastated. I can't imagine what I'd do if I lost hockey. Before Ollie, it was all I had.

"So if you see her," War says, his head lowered, his body angled in, "just congratulate her on the job. There will be more than enough haters out there calling her a nepo-baby. Don't be one of them. She built that company of hers from the ground up. I have no doubt she can handle the business side of things. And she's got Gavin and Beckett to help her along the way."

With that, he strides away. Apparently the conversation is over. What more is there to say anyway, since he has no clue who she is to me?

Correction: who she was.

Now she's my boss. My friends' sister. *Nothing else.*

With her new role, she can't be anything more.

"Do either of you have change for a twenty?" Aiden asks. "I want to get a soda."

I reach into my pocket, but before I can pull out the ones I shoved in there earlier, the attendant behind the counter says, "I can break change."

Aiden whips around and hands her the twenty.

As if my mind and body have been taken over, I edge closer to the counter, my eyes zeroed in on the money in the attendant's hand. When she hits number eleven and the ink on the dollar bill catches my attention, I reach across the desk and pull it from her grasp.

"Hey!" she yells, stepping back on instinct.

War waves his hand. "He's got a weird thing with writing on bills. Just keep counting. He'll give it back."

His voice fades out, along with the rest of the sounds around me, as I hold the dollar bill with shaking hands. There's no way in hell she's getting this back.

Because I'm staring at a one-dollar bill with the name *Sienna* scrawled across the front of it, complete with a heart above the *i* and a ten-digit number beneath it.

At the top of the bill is another message. One that sends me reeling back and changes everything.

For Noah.

Don't forget to come back for me. Until then, I'll soar.

Chapter 20
Sienna

Aiden: Big night tonight.

Gavin: Yeah. You have a game. That I expect you to win.

Aiden: Okay, COACH. I was talking about Sienna's first official game day as CEO! Boss-bitch level.

Brooks: LOL. Congrats, Sienna.

Beckett: Sorry I can't be there. Enjoy the game.

Gavin: Stop by the ice when you get here.

Gavin: And don't be nervous. You'll do great.

Me: I wasn't nervous until you said that. I thought I was just watching a hockey game tonight.

Beckett: Sure. Right. Of course. Enjoy the game.

Me: Beckett. What did you do?

"THIS IS WILD, RIGHT?" I ask Millie as she steps out of the black town car. If she hadn't shown up with the driver, I wouldn't have gotten in the car. I still can't believe I've agreed to do this. Also, my stomach is tangled in knots. It's nerves, yes, but it's more than that. I'm excited. For the first time in almost two years, I'm truly looking forward to something.

Millie holds out a hand to Vivi, who has already maneuvered out of her car seat and is waiting patiently. She looks totally adorable with her brown curls in pigtails and her own Bolts jersey, with an eleven on her back and *Langfield* in bold letters across her shoulders. Millie's wearing a matching one.

With two brothers on the team and a third coaching, I didn't think it was right to go with a Langfield jersey. There's no way I could pick between them, so I chose a black turtleneck with black leather pants. Millie tossed me a Bolts scarf when I climbed into the car, so I've donned that as well, though the fabric is scratchy, and I had to fight the urge not to tear it off every couple of minutes on the way over. By the time we pulled into the private lot at the back of the arena, I'd decided that my first act as CEO would be to search out better fabrics for our merch.

I'm sure that's exactly what my brothers were imagining I'd do when they put me in this position, and I'm nothing if not dependable.

Millie waves off my nerves. "It's actually one of the more brilliant plans Beckett has ever concocted."

"Uncle Becks." Vivi spins in a circle, looking for my eldest brother.

"Sorry, bestie," Millie says. "Uncle Becks is at home tonight, but we'll go over and play with Deogi and Junior tomorrow, okay?"

My brothers all officially live on the same street these days. It's strange as hell. What's even stranger is that control-freak Beckett is now the proud owner of a ginormous dog that slobbers on everything and a pet raccoon. The raccoon had babies a couple of years ago, which he and Liv now share custody of with Liv's three best friends.

Who also live on the same street.

Like I said, strange.

Junior, the raccoon, is actually ridiculously cute, and I'd trust her with my niece before Deogi. That dog would run her down and not even realize he did it.

With a deep breath, I scoot across the leather seat and force myself out of the car and into my new reality. Instinctively, I rub at my butterfly tattoo. In seconds, my nerves begin to settle.

There's no reason to panic. This is just another beginning.

I've done it before. I can do it again.

"C'mon, Auntie. Let's find Daddy." Vivi clutches my hand and tugs me forward.

Inside, every attendant and employee we pass greets her by name, and she returns the greetings with high fives.

"We'll sit up in the family box, but Gavin wants you to stop in at the players' bench first so he and the team can welcome you officially."

I side-eye her. "Right. Because you don't normally pop in to see your husband when you get here."

Her responding laugh is airy. "Well, yes, but still." Curls bouncing, she leads me through the tunnels toward the ice.

With each step we take, the air grows colder, and as the smells coming from the food vendors are slowly replaced by the crisp scent of the ice, a calmness settles over me.

Growing up, I spent a lot of time at the ice rink while Brooks and Aiden played. I might not have always paid attention to what was happening on the ice, but this smell has permanently permeated my senses. It reminds me of home. Reminds me of family.

As we close in on the entrance to the player's bench, Gavin comes into view and Vivi rushes him. "Daddy!"

"She's so in love with him," Millie says with stars in her eyes.

"Yeah, and he's so in love with the two of you." I loop an arm around her waist and rest my head on her shoulder. "I'm so happy you found each other."

Her lips twitch. "I didn't have to look too hard, considering he was my dad's best friend."

The snort that escapes me echoes off the cinderblock walls. I love how she can laugh about their story. Sure, it's unconventional, but I've never seen two people more dedicated to one another. They struggled a little with infertility, but Millie always stayed positive, and my brother was right beside her every step of the way.

They're the definition of soulmates, and honestly, if a love isn't that big and all-consuming, then I don't want it.

Not that I believe in that stuff anymore.

But if I did…

"How you feeling, Peaches?" With Vivi in one arm, Gavin approaches and presses a soft kiss to his wife's lips.

When he settles his palm on her bump and strokes a thumb across it, I practically melt.

"And how about you, little guy?" he murmurs, crouching a little. "Being good for your mama?"

"I'm good and he's fine." Millie waves him off. "Just extra hungry for dessert. It's all he wants."

Gavin chuckles. "Oh, that's what *he* wants?"

She lifts her chin. "Yup." She pops the *p*. "Oreo brownie sundae, to be exact. He's very demanding."

"I'll make sure someone from concessions brings one up." He presses another kiss to her cheek, then turns to me. "You ready for your first night on the job?"

I laugh awkwardly. "I don't have the first clue what I'm supposed to be doing, but sure."

"Half the job for any of us is being seen in public and making a good impression. Gotta keep the family name spotless, you know."

I fight back a wince. The family name isn't anywhere near spotless after my giant mistake. But I have too much to worry about to allow those intrusive thoughts into my mind tonight.

"Just enjoy yourself," Gavin says, giving me a sympathetic smile. "Watch the game. Eat a sundae or two with my wife. We'll get down to the real business tomorrow."

I shrug, trying my hardest to affect an easygoing attitude I haven't felt in months. "Whatever you say."

Vivi talks Gavin into taking her over to the bench so she can say hi to the guys, and instantly, she charms them all. One by one, they skate to the boards and give her fist bumps before heading off to continue warming up. When Brooks sees me, he pulls off his helmet and blows me a kiss. Aiden practically hauls himself over the boards and then bangs on the glass to say hello.

"Always the dramatic one," I mutter to my sister-in-law. "So who else will be upstairs?"

"Lennox, maybe. She sometimes sits down here. She'll deny it, but she loves when Aiden acts a fool for her." Millie rolls her eyes, but there's no hiding her smile. "With Sara out on maternity leave, she'll probably be in the suite. Hannah is bringing Mav and her nephew tonight, I think."

I met Hannah at Brooks's wedding. And since then, she married Millie's twin brother. From the sound of things, she's close to my brothers' wives, and if I remember correctly, she used to handle PR for the Revs. Though since she had her little boy, I'm not sure she's still on staff.

If she's married to Daniel Hall, then she doesn't need to work to live a comfortable life, but if she's as close to my sisters-in-law as it seems, then she's probably just as independent and strong as they are.

Every one of these women is married to a man who makes boat-loads of money, yet every one of them has a career of her own.

A thread of sadness dampens my mood. I used to have that kind of passion. God, I miss it. With any luck, this new job will give me some semblance of that.

"Ava and the kids may be here as well. Though if Brayden has a game, she may be watching him tonight." Ava married Tyler Warren, the team's captain. Their story is one I know. Most people are familiar with it after the media circus surrounding them two years ago. They got married so Tyler could adopt the children in his care. Fortunately, the drama died down, and as far as I know, the adoptions have been finalized. And now they have another child as well.

"Okay, so Lex, Hannah, Sara, and maybe Ava. Plus their kids?"

She laughs. "I know it seems like a lot, but you'll love the girls. When Gavin and I reconnected, they welcomed me into their little circle and seriously changed my life. They're all incredible. You should come to brunch with us on Sunday. It's our thing."

"Your thing?"

She breaks into a grin. "You'll get it when you come."

Before I can respond, movement on the ice catches my attention. All the guys on the team are on their hands and knees and…

I blink. Are they—

Yes, every one of them is thrusting their hips.

"What in the hell is happening over there?"

Thank god Aiden and Brooks are chatting with Vivi. That means none of the men out there share DNA with me. Because what they're doing is not appropriate for a sister to be watching. It almost feels inappropriate to watch, no matter *who* the men are.

"They're, like, humping the ice."

Millie nods, her lip caught between her teeth. "It's hot, right? Don't tell your brother I said this, but 69 out there"—she juts her chin—"is my favorite. Look at the hip action on that one."

My mouth goes dry. Holy shit. The way he rolls his knees in circles and thrusts his hips toward the ice is *erotic*.

The move is weirdly familiar.

What the hell? I try to pull my focus away from the man, but it's as though I've been put under a spell. I can't look away. And the more I watch, the more the feeling that his moves are familiar grows.

"Just don't mention it in front of Hannah," my friend says, her voice finally snapping me out of it.

I blink at her. "Oh, is that Daniel?"

Her eyes go wide and she gags. "No, that's Harry. *Her* brother, not mine. I think the commentators call him Beauty. These men and their nicknames. I can't keep track of them all." She glances past me, breaking into a Cheshire grin. "Actually, you *should* tell Hannah how hot Harry is doing this. She tortured me for months when she and Daniel started dating. She deserves a taste of her own medicine." Belatedly, she gasps and takes a step back, whacking my arm. "And ew. How could you think I'd talk about my brother like that?"

"Shit, sorry." I grimace. I really don't even want to think about hockey fans staring at my brothers doing this. "This is really how they stretch?"

She pins me with a look, her brows raised. "I think they ham it up for the crowds nowadays. It feels like this part of the routine gets longer every season. But yes, it's how they stretch out their hamstrings. It gets tight in there."

"That's what she said," I mutter.

With a burst of laughter, she throws her head back. "Oh, I'm going to love hanging with you during the games."

I think I'll enjoy it too.

After we've collected Vivi, we make our way upstairs where, as Millie suspected, all the women are gathered.

"I wasn't sure you'd be here," I say as I rush over to my newest sister-in-law and her brand-new baby. Taylor is decked out in Bolts blue, and her shirt says *My Dad's Better Than Your Dad*.

"I had to buy it," Sara says as I giggle over it. "Because he is."

"Obviously."

Out in the real world, at least. The fathers of the children in this room could all give Brooks a run for his money. Every one of them is incredible.

"Are you really feeling up to this?" I ask. "It's only been two weeks."

"Yes, I'm going stir-crazy." She sighs. "While the guys are on home ice, you better believe I'll be here. Especially because Brooks and Gavin have banned me from travel."

"It's because you're supposed to take an actual maternity leave," Millie reminds her. "They're doing it *for* you, not *to* you."

Sara lets out an annoyed huff. "That's not what it feels like. I'm a woman. I gave birth. I can make decisions for myself."

"She has a point," I say as I scoop my niece from her arms.

Sara winks at me. "I knew you were my favorite sister-in-law."

"Hey," Lennox hollers from the corner. Lennox and Sara were best friends long before they married brothers, so her indignation is valid.

Sara waves a hand. "You're more a sister than a sister-in-law. Also, not everything is about you." She turns back to me. "I want to hear all about your new job."

Hannah and Ava are tucked into the corner on a plush couch with two one-year-olds at their feet. Not far from them, a teenage boy is pointing down at the ice and talking quietly to another boy who must be several years younger than him.

"That's Brayden, War's son," Millie says, nodding at the teenager. "And Ollie, Hannah's nephew."

"Ah," I say, lifting my chin. "Harry's son, right?"

With a wink, she gently bumps my shoulder. "See? You're already absorbing the important info. This job is going to be a piece of cake for you."

I laugh. "Right. Let me get a drink. Then I'll tell you all about Beckett's latest scheme."

Lennox prances over, her pink hair bouncing. Her lipstick is a couple of shades brighter, and her Bolts jersey—with the number 12 on the back of it, I'm sure—has been bedazzled.

I'm immediately obsessed. "Okay, I would consider wearing a jersey if I could have one like that."

"That should be your first order of business. To create a line of bedazzled jerseys," she squeals.

"All the men have bedazzled dicks," Sara quips, "so it tracks."

My jaw drops, and I'm pretty sure my brain short-circuits. *What?*

Millie snorts. "Not the coach."

Lennox and Sara, my *brothers'* wives, stand side by side now, grinning like lunatics.

I shudder. "Ew."

"Their husbands have them too." Lennox points at Hannah and Ava, who are still seated. "It's a team thing."

"Huge fan of the sparkle," Hannah calls with a waggle of her brows.

"Okay, the little ones might not get it, but I do." The teenager, Brayden, grimaces. I've never spent much time around kids, so I could be off, but he looks fifteen or sixteen. Poor kid. I can only imagine how he feels knowing about all the guys and their jeweled dicks.

Another shudder hits me, this one more violent than the last. "That has to be painful."

"How is sparkle painful?" Ollie tips his head back and gives Brayden a questioning look.

Brayden shakes his head and glares at Hannah. "I'm telling Harry it was you who told him."

She waves a dismissive hand, unfazed.

When warm-ups are over, we all settle in with drinks and snacks. I get sucked into the game quickly, the fast-paced movements keeping me on the edge of my seat.

Millie, bless her, chirps in my ear, explaining the rules and answering my questions. Eventually, Hannah joins the conversation. Apparently, like me, they were shuttled around to hockey games for years when they were kids too. They just actually paid attention.

Tonight, though, I get the excitement. The sport is violent and beautiful. Thrilling and enraging.

When Aiden gets slammed into the glass by an opponent, Lennox and I leap to our feet, screaming for the ref to do anything but just watch.

Sara is loud the whole time. So much so that Ava takes the baby for a walk so she can actually get some rest. Within minutes of the puck drop, we've all agreed that going forward, Taylor needs headphones.

The guys win 3-1 over Colorado, and after the game, as we're heading down to the friends and family room to wait for them, a woman approaches Hannah.

"Would you sign this for me?" she asks, holding out a paperback, her expression a little sheepish.

Hannah's face lights up and she holds out her hand. "Oh, of course. And it's the original cover! I don't even sell these anymore."

"She's an author?" I ask Millie as we linger nearby, waiting.

My sister-in-law hums. "She's written several books, actually."

When Hannah flips open the cover so she can sign the title page, my heart leaps into my throat.

That's the book Noah carried onto the plane all those years ago. The one he promised he'd write his number in, then sell.

My hands itch to snatch it from Hannah, to flip it open and check for his handwriting.

For years, I looked in every used bookstore I came across, though it's been a long time since I gave up the quest.

Biting my lip, I consider how weird it would be if I asked this stranger if I could look at it.

Pretty freaking weird, I decide.

And yet, "Can I see that?"

Hannah and her fan turn to me in unison, Hannah with a confused frown and the other woman wearing a giant smile.

"Of course," the woman says. "Though be careful with it. It's a first edition."

Hannah's smile softens as she holds the book out to me. "It is."

For a moment, I simply hold the book, cataloging the way it feels in my hand. Then I do the most ridiculous thing. I make a wish.

I haven't done something like that in so long. I haven't believed in something, let alone myself, in what feels like a lifetime. Yet I find myself believing that maybe this book will have the answers I've been seeking. Suddenly, I'm certain that when I ease the cover open, his name and number will be there, waiting for me.

But if I'm right, then what? It's been six years. He'd think I was crazy if I called him after all this time.

Still, I hold my breath and thumb the edge of the cover, slowly pulling it back.

The first page is blank. The sight sends a blip of disappointment through me. But it's not the title page, right? If he left his number, surely it would be there. Right where he knew I'd find it.

Yet as I turn to the next page, only to find the title and Hannah's signature, my heart sinks.

I'm a fool for romanticizing the whole thing. Truly. Even if we'd miraculously found each other, we probably wouldn't have worked out, I remind myself.

"It's a great book," I say, handing it back.

"You've read it?" Hannah's brows arch into her hairline.

"Yeah." I force a smile. "I didn't know you wrote them, but I read the whole series. It's fantastic."

Each story was genuinely wonderful, and each time I read one, I felt just a little closer to Noah. I'd envision him lying in bed at the exact moment I was, opening up to the very same page.

"My brother loves this series too. He's single, you know," she says as her fan walks away with her autographed paperback.

"I'm not dating," I tell her. "Also, I'm CEO of the team now. It wouldn't be ethical for me to date a player."

Hannah's face falls. "Ah, you're right. And Noah's such a rule follower. He'd never."

My heart stumbles over itself. *Noah?* "I thought your brother's name was Harry."

Ollie, who's entertaining Maverick, Hannah's son, at her side, shakes his head. "I told you these nicknames get confusing."

Hannah rolls her eyes. "His name is Noah. But his last name is Harrison, so the guys call him Harry."

Noah Harrison. I roll the name around my head for a few seconds, and the naïve girl I used to be tries her best to break free from the constraints I've put on her. I shut her down quickly and let the notion go. Noah is a common name. Even if this Noah's stepsister wrote the book.

It's a coincidence. That's it.

Happy coincidences. I can practically hear Noah's teasing tone all these years later.

So when the man I've been dreaming about for six years walks into the room, my heart skips about ten thousand beats in my chest, and I forget how to breathe.

As Ollie darts toward him, shouting *"Dad,"* Noah drops to the ground and holds out his arms.

In a black suit that hugs every inch of him, especially his thick thighs, he looks absolutely delicious. His hair is longer than I remembered, but it's that sandy brown color I still see in my dreams. And he's wearing glasses, the black rims making his blue irises pop as he grins at his son.

"Hey, Han," he says, lifting his head. "How did you—"

His attention lands on me, and his eyes go wide.

As we see each other for the first time in six years, the earth tilts on its axis. Or maybe it's me. Maybe it's the lack of oxygen taking me down because I've forgotten how to breathe.

His teeth tug roughly at his bottom lip, his gaze so intense I feel it like a caress beneath my clothes.

He looks older. A little more worldly. With new lines around his eyes, probably created by happy memories he's made with his son. He looks like a dad. A hot dad, but still a dad.

"The game was fine." Hannah takes a step toward him, waving a hand in front of his face. "Hello, earth to Noah."

Ollie pokes him in the chest. "Did you just power down like Robot Sam?"

The man blinks rapidly, and when he breaks his stare, I suddenly remember that I need oxygen to live.

I suck in a breath and shake my head. This is impossible. No way is the man I've so desperately missed for years really standing here in front of me. I look at the butterfly on my wrist, brushing my thumb over it, then back up, certain he'll be gone.

But he's not. In fact, the man I've been searching for is now standing up and walking toward me.

What will he say? What will I say?

With every step he takes, my heart pounds louder.

And when he opens his mouth, he says the last thing I expect.

"Hi, I'm Noah."

CHAPTER 21
NOAH

"HI, I'M NOAH."

Devastation sweeps across Sienna's face.

Fuck.

I knew this moment would come eventually. Hell, I've seen the woman from afar more than once since she returned to Boston.

Still, I'm completely unprepared to be standing so close to her. With my son and my sister at my side.

It's been six years, yet her eyes are more familiar to me than my own. They call to me, draw me in, as if looking into them is the most natural thing in the world.

She thinks I don't remember her, like I could ever fucking forget. Like I didn't spend almost five years searching for her, only to find out she's the sister of one of my closest friends.

Forget her? It would be completely impossible.

"You have a child," she mumbles as she glances down at Ollie.

"Wait," Hannah says, her tone ticking higher, like she's onto something. "You know each other?"

My chest tightens with unease. *Now's not the time to catch on, Han.*

Sienna finally blinks and then shakes her head. "No, I just meant hockey player Noah. Noah…" She snaps her fingers like she's trying to conjure my name.

"Harrison," I supply.

This interaction and her absolute shock confirm that while I know exactly who she is, she had no idea until this moment who I was.

Sienna nods and forces a smile. "Right. I've been studying the players' pictures so I could put names with faces. I just didn't know the, uh, picture of the man Noah—this Noah—had a child."

Hannah frowns. "Why would a picture tell you he has a child?"

I let out a gruff sigh. "It's been a long day, Han. Cut her some slack."

Sienna swallows heavily, avoiding eye contact.

"Dad." Ollie tugs on my suit jacket. "Can we go home now? I'm tired."

I look down at him, taking in the dark circles beneath his eyes. Shit. It's late. Before we leave, though, I have to say *something* to Sienna. But when I look up again, she's heading toward the door, her back turned.

"Where's she going?" I ask Hannah, my heart lurching. It's been six years, and those three damn words—*Hi, I'm Noah*—can't be all I say to her when we finally find each other again. She needs to know I remember. She needs to...*fuck, I don't know.*

Hannah tilts her head, her eyes narrowing. "Um, home, I'm guessing. It's late. We should go too.'"

I nod. "Right. Did she say how she's getting home?"

"What's going on with you?" my sister demands, a hand on her hip.

"Nothing. She's just a young woman, and it's late. It's called being gentlemanly. And she's my best friend's sister," I add with a bit more force, because that fact still pisses me off. "I'd hope my friends would make sure you got home if I wasn't around."

Hannah's lips twitch like she's holding back a laugh. "Right, but her brothers are here. Right there, in fact." She points to the group of them.

All three in attendance tonight are standing around, oblivious to their sister's sudden departure.

"They don't seem the least bit concerned. Probably because she's a grown woman. A grown woman who no doubt has a driver waiting right outside the doors." With every word she speaks, her tone creeps higher and her eyes shine brighter, like she sees right through me. "Because *she's a freaking Langfield*. You realize that, right? She's a Langfield. *And your boss.*"

I blow out a breath, keeping my expression flat. "I have no idea what you're talking about."

"Sure you don't," she singsongs.

"Uncle Danny," Ollie yells, startling me.

Daniel steps into the room behind me, and my little guy darts for him.

Mav bounces in Hannah's arms, reaching for his father.

Damn. I never thought I'd be so grateful for my idiot of a brother-in-law, but when Hannah's focus turns to her husband, I'm granted a momentary reprieve.

It's the break I need to remind myself to shut the fuck up and stop talking about Sienna. She's fine. Like Hannah says, there's no way she doesn't have a driver waiting for her.

And there's no way she wants me to check on her anyway.

But now that I have her number, the dollar bill it's printed on is burning a hole in my pocket.

I itch to text her. To check in. Make sure she's okay. We need to talk. But I don't have the first clue how that will go or where to start. Or even what I want to say.

All I know is that it's been too damn long since I last touched Sienna Langfield. And now that she's within reach, I've already fucked it all up.

Chapter 22
Sienna

THE SOUND of my thigh-high black Louboutins tapping against the floor as I follow Gavin to my office soothes my raw nerves. I may not be a fashion designer anymore, but I can still dress the part.

I didn't stop being me just because I'm no longer *her*.

Or so I keep telling myself.

The truth is, I'm not sure who I am anymore. But today is the start of a new era, and what better way to kick it off than in my favorite pair of boots? Paired, of course, with a black dress made of a fabric so smooth I practically cried when I slid it over my body this morning. I finished off the look with a red lipstick that will make a statement.

Don't fuck with me.

Or maybe *I'm the boss.*

Anything, really. As long as it isn't *I'm so forgettable even the man I've been dreaming about for six years doesn't remember me.*

Yeah, I'm nowhere near ready to unpack my encounter with Noah last night.

Never in my life have I wished more for female friends to help me figure out what the fuck occurred in the family and friends suite last night.

Other than Millie, I really don't have anyone to talk to. And I can't possibly talk to her, considering who she's married to and because Hannah is her sister-in-law. I swear someone needs to make me a diagram so that I can remember who everyone is either related to or fucking.

It'd be one of those giant diagrams pinned to a wall. The kind always depicted on crime shows. With red string and pushpins.

Seven Degrees of the Langfield Brothers.

I swear, no matter who I meet, they've got some sort of connection to at least one of my brothers.

Annoyance flares to life in my chest. Can't I just have one person to myself? One memory?

Nope.

Not even Noah, apparently.

"Here's your office." Gavin stops in front of a door a few down from Liv's.

I peer in, take a step back into the hall, and eye the nameplates outside the surrounding offices. "Where's yours?"

Gavin smirks. "I have one downstairs. Near the rink. This is my old office." A smile creeps onto his face as he surveys the room, like there are real memories walking around in there.

I eye the space through his eyes, quickly racked by a full-body shudder.

"How many women have you fucked in this room?"

With a scoff, he slips his hands into his pockets and looks away.

I take a step to the side so I'm in his line of vision and arch a brow.

He was always the fuckboy of the bunch. His attempt to act like he's affronted by my question isn't fooling me.

With a sigh, he adjusts the cuffs of his sleeves. "It's been empty for years, and it's cleaned weekly."

I snort as I walk in. "Noted."

"Don't say anything to Millie," he grumbles from the doorway.

Laughing, I spin to face him. "Right, because she thought you were a saint when she seduced you all those years ago."

Gavin wanders around the office, ignoring me.

That's fine. I'm happy to move on, and honestly, bantering with him like that put me in the headspace I need to move forward with this day.

"What do I do now that I'm here?" I round the desk and run my hands over the black lacquered surface.

It's nothing like Liv's desk, or Beckett's. Theirs are standard solid-wood pieces. This one is shiny and sleek. My heart aches with affection when it hits me that he had this put in here specifically for me. That he took the time to find something he knew I'd like.

The office itself is simple, with a tall bookcase on one side and framed photos of Boston on the other, but the view of the Atlantic through the floor-to-ceiling windows behind the desk makes up for it. It may not be the Eiffel Tower, but it's no less beautiful.

As that thought runs through my mind, I make a promise to myself to stop comparing this new life to my old one.

There's no going back, and it's time to start working toward making peace with that.

"HR has a few forms for you to fill out." He slips his hands into his pockets. "I've left you a list of the contracts that are up for negotiation this year, as well as a list of positions we'll be looking to fill. Take your time. Familiarize yourself with the notes. It'll probably seem like a foreign language to you—"

I snort. "I moved to France before I could speak a lick of French. I can figure out your hockey stats."

He nods, a smirk on his face. "I have no doubt. Still." He surveys me, his expression thoughtful, caring. "It's a lot. My door is always open—"

"Are you sure about that? We've already established the kinds of activities taking place in your office—"

With a roll of his eyes, he breathes out an annoyed sigh.

Laughter bubbles out of me in response to his reaction, and his eyes light up.

"What?" I ask.

"It's nice to see you smiling. It's been a while."

That sobers me. But I won't let it ruin my day. So with a shrug, I say, "Like you guys said, this is my new start." I pick up the folder on top of the pile he's left for me. "Get out of here. I need to get up to date in your world."

As he meanders to the door, his back to me, I look at the name on the folder in my hand and immediately wince. Shit. Of course it'd have to be Noah Harrison.

"Want to do dinner with Millie and me tonight?" Gavin asks, turning in the doorway.

I force a smile. "I'll keep you posted. I've got a call in to a realtor. I want to look for a place of my own."

His lips kick up on one side. "Moving out? Mom will be beside herself."

I huff a laugh. "You have no idea what it's like living with them again. I moved out when I was eighteen, and now I'm thirty and living at home again. It's pathetic."

Gavin's smile softens. "We all need help sometimes."

Eyes closed, I suck in a steadying breath. Then I lift my chin and look him in the eye. "I think I've had enough time to lick my wounds. It's time I help myself."

He nods once and taps on the doorframe. "All right. I'll be at the rink if you need me."

With that, he's gone, leaving me alone in this new space.

With a sigh, I pick up the folder with Noah's name on it. Looking inside feels like cheating. I could have googled him last night. Anyone else probably would have. There's probably a plethora of information about him on the internet. About his son. The mother.

My throat gets tight just thinking about her.

Ollie is young. Five, maybe. Which means Noah probably met his mom not all that long after our weekend. The thought sends a wave of grief through me. While I haven't been a nun these last few years, I couldn't even look at another man for months after I left the Bahamas.

It took years to even go on a date with someone else.

I was a foolish romantic who believed we'd find one another again.

I slump back in my office chair and spin to face the ocean. Its vastness has always made me uneasy. It's always made me feel small. Especially when I was on the other side of it, far from my family and friends. Far from *him*.

"Ugh." I groan, dropping my head back. Even now, I'm behaving like a hopeless romantic. How is that still possible? How, after all this time, have I not become more jaded? I should be. The man had a child in the time since I last saw him. He's probably been married and divorced since then.

Hannah mentioned that he's single. That one detail, unfortunately, makes my heart pitter-patter like a lovesick teenager. *There's a chance*, it says. *It's not impossible*, it teases. *Maybe it's fate.*

My heart is clearly delusional. It should probably be locked up. Or at least zapped a few times.

"Knock, knock."

I spin my chair at the sound of a masculine voice.

The man standing in my doorway might be one of the most attractive humans to ever walk the earth. His dirty blond hair is thick and a tad longer in the front, though he's got it haphazardly brushed to the side. The scruff on his jaw, a couple of shades darker, makes his blue eyes extra bright. The scar across his cheekbone and the light wrinkles around his eyes make me think he's probably a former hockey player. His suit is a deep shade of blue; his tie, gray. Though with the way the light reflects off the fabric, it's almost silver.

He's got one shoulder propped against the doorframe, his stance casual, the vibe radiating off him one of complete ease. Like this man is comfortable in almost every room he enters.

Money. Every inch of him screams it. A lot of it.

It's the least attractive thing about him.

"How can I help you?" I push off the desk and stand, holding his gaze.

"Wanted to introduce myself. I'm Ezra Bardot, the Bolts' GM." He straightens to full height and steps into the room.

I skirt my desk, keeping my shoulders pulled back, and hold out my hand. "Sienna Langfield."

He smiles, though it doesn't quite reach his eyes. "Yes, our new CEO, I'm told."

There's no hiding the hint of bitterness in his tone. This man does not like the changes my brothers have made. Noted.

I grip his hand firmly, meeting his pressure, then motion to the guest chairs. "Would you like to sit?"

Nodding, he eases into one. I settle in the seat beside him rather than on the other side of the desk with the hope that it'll earn a little goodwill. I don't know a thing about this man, but if we're going to work together, I'd prefer to get along.

"I wasn't aware that there was another Langfield interested in the sport." He infuses the comment with a bit of humor. Or he tries, at least. Though the words are more cutting than anything.

I shrug. "I honestly wasn't."

His eyes go wide, like he's shocked by my candor. But it's pointless to lie. He'll learn soon enough how little I know about hockey.

"This is a family business. My brothers need help, so here I am."

Tongue poking into his cheek, he nods. "Right. Well, I played hockey professionally for ten years and have been on the administrative end for the last fifteen." Yep, the man is definitely in his late forties. "So let me know if I can help at all."

I give him a professional smile. "I appreciate that."

We're silent for a moment. As if we've come to a stalemate.

And the tension in the air is not the good kind.

He studies the room, his focus pausing on the view I was admiring when he appeared. "Nice office they gave you."

My hackles rise. The words themselves are innocuous. But the tone is off, his eyes a little too cold.

"Yes. Though considering all the traveling the team does, I don't suppose I'll spend much time here."

Ezra lets out a derisive snort. "You intend to travel with the team?"

I shrug, keeping my expression serene. "How else will I figure out which of our guys we should be pushing to keep and which other players we should be looking at offering contracts to?"

He frowns, his brow creasing. "That's the GM's job."

"And the owners'," I point out. "And since, as CEO, I represent them, it's my job too."

That may not be completely accurate, but the idea that I'll have any say seems to addle him, and that only inspires me to dig my heels in. I can't imagine Beckett getting along with this guy, and now I can't wait to find out why they hired him.

Ezra stands, causing his chair to slide back a couple of inches. "Well, then I guess we'll be working together a lot. Welcome to the team." With a sharp nod, he turns and strides out.

When I'm sure I'm alone, I inhale deeply and let the air out slowly. I get the feeling he doesn't mean that at all.

CHAPTER 23
NOAH

"I KEEP FORGETTING to give this to you." Brooks pushes a crossword puzzle book toward me.

A wave of guilt washes over me. Again. Like it has at regular intervals for the last twenty-four hours. Because for the last twenty-four hours, I haven't stopped thinking about all the things I want to do to his little sister.

Yes, I've known for well over a year that Sienna is his sister. But now that I've decided to act, it feels different. There's no way I can't approach her, talk to her, worship her now that we'll see each other every day. Once I figure out how to get her to talk to me, of course.

"What's this?" I ask as I take it.

Morning skate was brutal, but the hot shower after helped. Now I'm itching to get out of here and plan how best to approach Sienna.

"Got it at the hospital. I might have gone a little overboard in the gift shop and saw it while I was loading up on gifts for Sara and Taylor."

Chuckling, I thumb the pages. That tracks. The man is obsessed with his wife and now his daughter.

The *Star Wars*–themed cover causes another round of guilt to pummel me. Dammit. He knows how obsessed I was with the movies growing up. I used to watch them with my dad, and now Oliver and I watch them together.

They're the only movies—other than *Serendipity*—that I actually watch.

Brooks knows these things because we're friends, and friends don't fuck their friend's little sisters.

Daniel Hall may have done it, but in his defense, he and I weren't really friends when he knocked Hannah up.

Even still, I cling to him as a defense because it makes me feel less shitty about myself.

"When I saw the cover, I knew I had to get it for you. You have it?"

I shake my head. Though I'm a little obsessive about crossword puzzles, especially when we travel because I have to be away from Oliver and need the distraction, I've never come across a whole book that's *Star Wars*–themed. "Thank you. Ollie will love it too."

Brooks dips his chin and walks off. "Anytime," he says over his shoulder. "Now I'm going home to nap. Hopefully. Taylor didn't sleep a wink last night."

"You want to grab lunch?" War calls from his locker.

"I actually have a meeting."

Though it's not officially on anyone's calendar, I'm going to make it happen.

I have to see the CEO of our team. It's completely unethical. Probably against bro code too. Definitely against hockey code. And it's risky, with the end of my contract coming up.

I could reason that the end of my contract is a legitimate excuse to show up at the executive offices, I guess, but the last thing I want to discuss with Sienna is what my future with the Bolts looks like.

War, probably eager to go home and get some alone time with his wife before the team comes over to watch tape tonight, waves me off without a second thought. "See you later, then." Before he's finished talking, he's tapping at his phone. Knowing him, he's texting Ava, demanding that she be naked by the time he pulls in the driveway.

I can't help but chuckle as I collect my things. The man has done a complete one-eighty since he settled down.

He's absolutely nothing like the guy who found himself in a

different bed just about every night while we were in college. All the guys here are dedicated to both the game and their families, and our captain leads by example.

Though I suppose I'm not the guy I was back when War and I played together before.

I pluck my phone off the bench beside me and smirk at the picture that appears when the screen lights up. Ollie was dead set on wearing a black fedora on the first day of school. When I questioned the choice, his answer was simple. *Why wouldn't I?*

My chest aches as I study the details of the image. It guts me that I can't see him all the time. And the guilt I carry about traveling, about missing out on so many things, eats at me a little more every day. He's getting older, and yet I feel like with each year that passes, I miss out on more important milestones.

I shake my head. I can't do anything about that right now. He's with Jen today, but a FaceTime call after he's home from school will ease a little of my discomfort. I'll get lots of time with him when we're home again next week. That's what I need to focus on.

Spring break is the following week, and I talked Jen into allowing him to travel with me for our away games. Our first stop is Orlando. While we're there, we'll hit the pool and do some fishing.

I take the underground walkway that connects the hockey arena and baseball stadium to the Langfield Corp building, mostly certain Sienna has set up shop on the same floor as Hannah's old office. It's a risk, trying to see her here, but if I used her number, then she'd know I had it, and I'd have to explain why I didn't call. And approaching her after a game is out of the question because her brothers are around.

I need to beg her to forgive me for fucking up so epically last night. I didn't expect to see her there, like that, standing beside my sister. And the sight of her knocked the wind out of me. It's embarrassing how off-kilter she made me. I wasn't expecting her.

I screwed up. It's that simple. And now I've got to fix it.

The receptionist, a pretty redhead with stars in her eyes, blinks up at me. "Mr. Harrison," she breathes. Suddenly, her expression goes pensive, and she runs her finger down a list on her desk. "Do you have an appointment?"

"Yes. I'm meeting Sienna Langfield. She's expecting me." Fuck, I hope my instinct is right. I hope she'll see me. If not, things are going to get really awkward up here.

The receptionist brightens, practically bouncing in her chair. "Oh, it's her first day. That must be why her appointments aren't on my list." She picks up the phone and presses a button. A moment later, she clears her throat. "Hi, Ms. Langfield. I have a Mr. Harrison here for your appointment."

I hold my breath, a niggle of doubt worming its way through me. What if she won't see me? What if she's pissed?

When the receptionist nods and says, "Okay, I'll send him back," I breathe out a sigh of relief.

One hurdle down, a fuck ton more to overcome.

With each step I take toward Sienna's office, the nervous energy zinging through me amplifies. We haven't been alone in the same room in six years.

The thought of stepping into her space turns the nervousness into excitement.

She's it for me. For years I've known that. I've hoped and wished for this outcome. For the chance to reconnect. To find her again and give us an actual chance.

I hope like hell this is it. That we really have a shot, and damn, I hope the British guy is out of the picture.

I'll deal with her brothers and I'll work through the guilt plaguing me. Her last name doesn't matter to me. Her family's status, their reputation? I couldn't give a flying fuck. I've never felt the way I do when I'm in her presence—like life makes sense, like my world is complete.

Admitting that, even to myself, is exhilarating. Freeing.

I'm not sure what our next step will be, but if she's even half as elated as I am, then I'm the luckiest man in the whole fucking world.

I'm still several feet away when she appears in her doorway. At the sight of her, my feet move faster, like my body has finally caught up with my brain.

Head tilted, she watches me, her expression unsure. But damn does she look gorgeous in that tight black dress with those thigh-high boots.

The closer I get, the stronger the gravitational pull. When I reach her, my instincts take over. I back her into her office and push her up against the wall. With one hand on her hip and the other cuffing the back of her neck, I press my forehead to hers. "I'm so fucking sorry about last night." Then my lips are on hers and I feel like I'm whole again.

Chapter 24
Sienna

THERE'S a breath between when Noah's apology slips from his lips and when his mouth is hot against mine. A single heartbeat in which I go from being certain he forgot about me to being reminded that what we experienced six years ago was unforgettable.

The ground tilts beneath me as his hold on my neck tightens, as he presses his body flush to mine and steals every one of my breaths like he can't get close enough.

I clutch at his shirt and tug him closer. I should push him away, but suddenly, touching him feels as necessary as oxygen. And with each mind-numbing kiss, he breathes life back into me, reminding me of who I am.

It takes seconds for him to restart my heart, to bring color back to the world around me. Blood rushes in my ears, the sound like ocean waves crashing around us.

I'm transported back to the feeling of possibility he inspired in me long ago. To a different time, when I was a different person with an entire new life ahead of me.

Noah licks my lips and skims a hand down my body with the confidence of a man who has every right to touch me.

There's no fumbling, no tremors. He knows my body better than I know it myself. Already my legs shake in expectation. It's been years since he touched me, but the effects of that touch still haven't worn off. They've reverberated inside my body, my mind, every day since I got on that plane in the Bahamas.

"Open your eyes, baby," he murmurs against my lips.

That moniker sounds more natural on his lips than it has any right to. God, how could I have lived without this for so long?

I blink my eyes open, and when he comes into focus, a whimper climbs up my throat. I'd forgotten how beautiful he was. His glasses are slightly fogged over from our steamy kiss, dulling the color of his eyes.

I pluck them off his face and fold them up carefully, then study him in earnest. His expression is one of awe, like the man is wonder struck, as he surveys me in return.

"Is this real?" I mumble. It sure doesn't feel real.

He towers over me, even in my five-inch heels, and crowds me against the wall, every inch of his body touching mine. Our hips press together, our chests heaving in sync, brushing against one another. He strokes a hand over my hip like he's trying to ground himself to this moment as well. Like he's searching for a sensation that will prove that this isn't a dream.

Noah's voice is all gravel when he responds. "Fuck, I hope so." He plucks my nipple, his aim deadly accurate through the fabric of my dress and bra.

The move tugs at an invisible tether linked directly to my core, and the sensation pulls a moan from me.

"It's hard to believe you're real. That you're here," he grits out. "You, after all this time. You're absolute perfection."

As if my lower half has a mind of its own, one foot moves, dragging along the floor, creating more space between my legs. He slots a leg between mine, bending his knee, and my hips roll forward, pressing into him.

His eyes flare, the blue of his irises burning with need. "Still so reactive. So obedient," he rasps. The praise is another reminder that he remembers every detail of our weekend together.

I can't help the needy whimper that it pulls from my throat.

He drags the back of one finger over my breast and down to my belly. His touch is barely there as he skims along my pubic bone, but when he reaches my clit, he adds the tiniest bit of pressure and rolls a knuckle over that spot.

"Fuck," I breathe, squirming against the wall.

"Are you going to come for me, butterfly? You know how much I love it." His breath ghosts over the shell of my ear, eliciting a full-body shiver. And the kiss he plants on the sensitive spot just below lights up my nerve endings.

"Touch me, please," I beg.

He licks the spot and nips at my earlobe before he drags his lips back to my mouth. As he fuses his mouth to mine, he slides his hand beneath my dress and trails the rough pads of his fingers against my thigh slowly, dragging out the moment, torturing me, making the burn that much hotter.

I shouldn't want this. We shouldn't be doing this. As of today, I'm his boss.

But he's so much more than a member of the hockey team I'm now overseeing. He's my Noah. The man I've spent years searching for.

When he reaches my panties, he growls into my mouth. "It's like coming home. Fuck, can I come home, baby, please?"

The way he begs, when I know he never does, cracks me wide open.

I nod, my nose brushing his. "Yes. Fuck. Yes, just touch me."

With his teeth sunk into his lip, he pushes my lace panties to the side. Then, without warning, he spears me with two fingers.

We groan in unison, and my pussy throbs.

"You're so fucking tight, Sienna. Fuck, I missed this perfect cunt. Your silky heat owns me."

The indecent wet sounds we make are loud in the quiet room.

God, after all this time, he still knows exactly how to touch me. Exactly how to get me where he wants me.

I tug on his hair, pulling him closer. He could be inside me, and he still wouldn't be close enough. Irrationally, I worry he'll disappear from beneath my fingertips. Like a mirage. Like he was never here to begin with.

With a groan, he grinds against me, his thick, hard cock trapped in the confines of his pants as he fucks me slowly with his fingers and kisses the goddamn life out of me.

"Fuck," he breathes. "The feel of your tight little cunt squeezing me is enough to make me come, baby—" His words are cut off by a guttural noise. When his mouth drops open and his eyes flare wide with heat, I come undone. My vision goes spotty, and I spasm, sinking beneath the surface of this sexed-out abyss. All the while, he rasps out my name and comes against my thigh.

When I can breathe again, I drop my head back against the wall and laugh. "Holy shit."

He squeezes his eyes shut and groans. "Sorry, I—"

I push at his chest. "Let me grab something to clean up."

The moment his body isn't pressed up against mine, awkwardness seeps in. I push down my skirt, and with a half smile, I hold out the glasses I'm still clutching in one hand.

He takes them without breaking eye contact. If he's uncomfortable with cum coating his pants, he doesn't show it. No, the man watches me like he's worried I'll escape if he looks away.

That's exactly what I did last night, so I guess I can't blame him. And suddenly, I'm considering the tactic again as I pluck a few tissues from the box on my desk.

As I turn back, my attention snags on the stack of folders. On the one on top, with his name emblazoned on it.

My stomach plummets. Shit. What was I thinking?

I whip around and sit on the edge of the desk, hiding the folder from his line of sight, and hold out the tissues.

He stalks across the room without an ounce of shame, and when he stops in front of me, he undoes his buckle and opens his pants, exposing his still half-hard cock, then uses the tissue to wipe himself clean.

The moment is so intimate, so personal. I should look away. But I can't. I can't focus on anything but the ease with which he moves and the length I still feel branded inside me six years later.

The hunger that I thought was sated only seconds ago dials up again.

He tosses the tissue in the trash beside my new desk and tucks himself back in, like all of this is completely normal.

Then again, maybe it is to him. Maybe he's a player like so many of the pro athletes my brothers have always warned me about.

I dismiss the idea as quickly as it appears. We may have only spent a couple of days together, but I know better than that.

Once his glasses are back in place, he meets my eye and gives me a lazy smile. "Hi."

The nerves winding tight inside me break free and rush out with a giggle. "Hello again, Noah Harrison." I like saying his name. Knowing his last name is like finding the last puzzle piece and popping it into place.

"Hello again, Sienna Langfield." As he forces out my last name, his voice goes hoarse, like it's a problem. Though I already knew it would be.

A lump forms in my throat, but I swallow past it. "I told you the name would change things."

He gives me a simple nod.

"I know it's a lot to wrap your head around and you've only had a few hours to deal with it, but—"

He steps forward and places one of his big hands on my thigh.

I can't help but study the spot, relishing the sight of his hand on me.

"I've had a bit longer than that to think about it," he says evenly.

Blinking, I zero in on his face. "What?"

He nods slowly, his eyes darting between mine like he's considering what he wants to say next.

Like whatever it is, I won't like it.

The earth shifts beneath me again. At least I'm sitting this time.

"I discovered who you were a while ago."

Confusion and concern grow in my chest. "How?"

He swipes the glasses off his face and wipes at his eyes with a groan. "I saw you at Brooks's wedding."

"Wait, that was—" I do the math and my stomach tumbles. "That was over a year ago."

He presses his teeth into his bottom lip and nods solemnly.

Moment after moment flashes through my mind. Times over the last year when I wished and hoped that I'd find Noah. Moments when I was at my weakest, when I berated myself for wanting him there to comfort me.

My return to Paris after the wedding, when it was time to face the music. The moment I gave up on my dreams and my business for good. The instant everything I'd worked for went up in flames. The day I moved home, broken, my only solace was the thought that being stateside might increase my chances of locating that stupid book with his information in it.

God, I was so naïve. All that time, he knew who I was and he chose not to reach out.

He chose to keep me in the dark.

To stay away.

I push back, scrambling off the desk.

Before I can, Noah grips my hips tightly, holding me in place. "Please give me a second to explain."

I shake my head, my hair tumbling around me, and squeeze my eyes shut. "There's nothing to explain."

He lets out a gruff sigh. "Of course there is. It's not as simple as choosing not to reach out."

My responding laugh is anything but humorous. It's angry and sarcastic. Over the years, I've become jaded. More so since I lost everything. But for one stupid moment, when his body was pressed to mine, I allowed myself to believe I'd moved past it. It's clear now that the emotion still has a firm hold on me.

"It is simple," I say, unwilling to let my voice waver. "I told you years ago that my name would be a problem for you. And that was before I became your boss." I clutch the file with his name on it and drag it around, flipping it open. I will my vision to clear so I can tick off the information listed, ensuring he feels as uncomfortable as I do.

"Sienna, stop." His harsh growl takes me by surprise, making me suck in a breath. His nostrils flare, like he's reining in his emotions, and a heartbeat later, his face softens. "Your last name doesn't matter to me. I told you years ago I don't sleep with just anyone. And I'm here, willing to risk everything because you are worth the risk."

I cough out a laugh. "Oh, thanks. I'm glad my magical pussy made you change your mind."

He grinds his molars. "You know it's not like that."

"Isn't it, though?" I narrow my eyes. "What did you say while you had your fingers inside me? That you missed my perfect cunt?" I sigh. "You got swept up in it. It's fine. I get it. I did too. It won't happen again."

I slap the folder shut, the rage draining out of me. All that's left now is exhaustion. I'm so tired of holding it together. I'm tired of being hurt over and over again. Of having my dreams, my so-called destiny, ripped away. But I'm determined. I survived after I lost the career that felt like part of my soul, so I can survive this too.

Instinctively, my thumb finds the ink on my wrist, the tattooed reminder of all I've lost.

Noah sighs. "It's not your body I crave; it's you. I'm sorry I've upset you. I'm sorry I didn't come for you sooner." He drops his head and drags a hand over the back of his neck. Then he straightens again, his expression firm. "But when I say I don't think it was our time, I mean it." He reaches into his pocket and pulls out his wallet, but when my intercom buzzes, he freezes.

A rush of relief swamps me as the receptionist's voice echoes around the room.

"Sienna, sorry to bother you," she says.

I pick up the phone, avoiding Noah's gaze. "No problem. What do you need?"

"Ezra mentioned that you were interested in learning more about the players, so he's having us pull tape from every prospect for this year's draft so you can review and discuss this weekend when you travel with the team."

I roll my eyes. God, that man works quickly. He was in this office an hour ago, and he's already presenting me with my first challenge. Seems he's determined to prove that I'm not capable of doing this job.

And I'm just determined enough to prove him wrong.

"Not a problem," I say, keeping my tone light. "Send it over to my email when it's ready."

"I'll send it via Dropbox since the files are so large." She lowers her voice to just above a whisper. "It's hours of footage. I have no idea how you'll get through it all."

I can't help but smile. What an asshole. "I'll figure it out. Thanks, Beth."

She hums. "Anytime. By the way, sorry I didn't have Mr. Harrison on the schedule this morning. If you forward your calendar to me and a list of visitors that are allowed to come and go, I'll have them added."

She drags out the last few words, like she's fishing for information. Honestly, I don't mind. She seems friendly enough. "It's not a problem," I assure her. "And no need to put Mr. Harrison on that list. I have a feeling we've already covered all the topics we need to discuss. We won't need to meet again."

Noah's eyes bore into the side of my head, but with each word I speak, my confidence grows. This was a mistake. I should never have let him back into my life, let alone allowed him to touch me. Now that the facts have been laid out, we can both move on.

Just as I suspected would have happened all those years ago if I'd been open about who I was.

We were nothing but a beautiful idea. And that's what we'll remain.

Once I've set the phone in its cradle, I push off the desk, creating space. "I need to get back to work, and really, there's nothing to apologize for. We were both taken by surprise and we let our emotions get the best of us."

"That's not what happened," he says in that deep, husky voice that's liable to get me pregnant if I stand too close.

He takes another step toward me, but I back away. If I let him touch me, I'm afraid I'll give in. So I utter the one word that I know will stop him. My safe word.

"Butterfly."

He clenches his hand into a fist, the move creating a crinkling sound, as if he's balled up a piece of paper, and his eyes fall shut.

He swallows audibly, his throat working, and sucks in a long breath. When he opens his eyes, determination shines in them rather than defeat. "Fine. But we're not done here."

"We are." I skirt around my desk, needing a physical barrier to keep me from going to him.

With a shake of his head, he storms out of my office. At the threshold, he pauses, and without turning around, he says, "No we're not, butterfly. We'll never be done."

Chapter 25
Sienna

"THIS ONE ISN'T HALF BAD."

Cat's right. And it's a hell of a lot better than everything else the realtor has shown us so far.

I'm still hesitant to consider it a possibility, though, after the last apartment she showed us. It seemed like a winner until Cat noticed how clearly she could see into the apartment across the way. Obviously, curtains could solve that issue. But the real problem was the obese man who appeared in the apartment, completely nude, and wandered around that way for some time. Cat insisted the agent get more information from the landlord, and when she did, we discovered that the man never wore clothes or used blinds.

So, unwilling to live in darkness or be mooned by a man across the way constantly, I moved on.

It was crushing, really, since the closet in that apartment was big enough to house every pair of shoes I own and had lights to illuminate each shelf.

Both Cat and I cried over that.

After she'd wiped away her tears, she texted a picture of it to her husband. Knowing Jay Hanson, Cat's closet will be upgraded within the week.

"Anything is better than living with my mom." I turn toward the agent and take the leap. "I'll take it."

She clasps her hands and breaks into a wide smile. "Okay, I'll go get the paperwork for you to sign."

Cat lets out a loud whistle. "Look at you doing big things."

I snort. "Right. Moving out of one's childhood bedroom at thirty is not a milestone to be celebrated."

She rolls her eyes. "At twenty-two, you built a fashion empire. At twenty-five, you starred on a hit show that dominated all the charts. For the last five years, you've been the number one designer on the who-to-watch list of everyone who matters."

"And now I'm starting over." I sigh, my chest aching.

"They say women can reinvent themselves as many times as they want. It's hot. A new trend." She gives me a cocky smirk.

A watery laugh bubbles out of me. "Who's *they*?"

She points at herself. "Me, Sienna. And we all know—"

"What Catherine Bouvier says goes," I chime in.

As our laughter fades, I take in the view of Boston from here. It's nothing glamorous. Just a city street, and the place doesn't even have a balcony, but Cat's right; it's a start.

Today's been full of firsts. My first day at my new job, my first non-self-induced orgasm in god knows how long, and the first time a man has ever truly hurt me.

Have I been disappointed by men in the past? Sure. But finding out that while I was searching for him, he knew where I was but chose not to reach out was devastating.

He's wrong when he says it's not over. It is. It has to be.

Cat bumps her shoulder against mine. "What are you thinking about?"

I sigh and survey my friend. She may be the most incredible person I know. With long, thick, wavy dark hair, striking whiskey-colored eyes, and curves that anyone would envy, she's gorgeous. But it's her kindness and the way she carries herself that really set her apart.

Maybe the similar dynamics of our families are what drew us to one another, or maybe it was the fashion thing, but Cat has always been the older sister I never had. Showing her the worst parts of myself, letting her in when I'm at my lowest, is hard.

"It's just a lot, you know."

She nods, surveying the street below. "Did I tell you that J.J. and your niece play hockey together?"

"Oh yeah?" I ask, shocked that she isn't hounding me for details but happy to follow along with this change of subject. Poor Beckett so badly wants his kids to play baseball, but Addie wants to be a goalie like her Uncle Brooks. "What position does he play?"

"He's a goalie as well," she says, her eyes dancing with humor. "The two of them are more competitive than any adults I know. And Addie is good. I'll give her that."

"I didn't know you liked hockey," I muse.

She laughs. "I didn't either until I watched my husband playing a pickup game with your brothers. Now that it's consumed J.J.'s life, we have no choice but to be invested. Not that Jay minds one bit. Though with as busy as we are, it can be a challenge to get him to every practice and all their games. Beckett pulled some strings and got the two of them on the same team, so that helps. He makes sure to get J.J. there when we can't."

"Sounds like my brother." I smile. The man is always meddling. "Beckett talked me into coming to work for Langfield Corp."

Her lips twitch, like this isn't new information. That shouldn't surprise me. She's connected to almost everyone I know, as well as the media. She knows things before they're ever made public. "How do you feel about that? Is it really what you want?"

With a shrug, I let out a long breath. "I don't know. But since I can't design anymore, I need *something*."

Eyes flashing with anger, she says, "You could if you'd let me fix this."

I take a step back and cross my arms. "No. I shouldn't have brought it up. We promised we wouldn't discuss this again."

She snorts. "No, you insisted that I not bring it up, but I never agreed to your demand."

My responding laugh echoes off the ceiling. "Please."

She sighs, her expression easing. "Fine. But really, CEO of the hockey team?"

That's all the confirmation I need. Of course she knew.

"Yeah. Bizarre, right? My initial instinct was to flat-out turn the offer down, but then I watched Beckett and Liv discuss trades for the baseball team and it was almost"—my heart rate ramps up a little, just like it did that day, when the memory surfaces—"exhilarating."

Her eyes widen. "That's something, huh?"

"Yup."

"You know what else is something?" she hedges.

"What?"

She grins. "Orgasms."

Heat floods my body. She can't know, right? There's no way. "Excuse me?"

She takes my hand and squeezes gently. "Come on, let's go to Allure. You'll love it."

I shake my head. Cat and her sex clubs. God, just the idea freaks me out. "No."

She lifts a shoulder and drops it easily. "Garreth is coming to town next weekend."

I wince. "I hope it's not for me."

"Still hung up on book boy?"

I bristle. She's one of very, very few people who know about that weekend and my search for Noah.

If I told her I found him, I can only imagine the meddling she'd do. She'd be worse than Beckett. For as tough as she is, her love story is epic. Years after the love of her life vanished, he resurfaced and absolutely wooed the shit out of her. Now they're living the quintessential happily ever after, with three children and a brownstone in the city. But that's not in the cards for me. Not anymore.

"Well," she says, knowing me well enough to understand that I'm not interested in delving into my past, "if you are determined to make it in the family business, then there's one more thing you need to do."

"And what is that?"

She grins. "Talk to your family."

Chapter 26
Sienna

AFTER A CELEBRATORY DRINK with Cat to celebrate my new apartment, I text my two oldest brothers, then ask my driver to drop me at Beckett's house.

Cat is right. I want to succeed in this position, and in order to do that, I need their support and I need to know what they expect from me.

Beckett's home is filled with life when I arrive. Finn, my eleven-year-old nephew and my brother's shadow, gives me a nod so reminiscent of my brother's it's uncanny. They may not share DNA, but he's a mini-Beckett to the core. Before I can wave in return, he's focused on the baseball game playing on the TV.

The twins, who are almost five, rush into the hallway, squealing, with Vivi hot on their heels. Gavin lumbers into the small space next, his arms outstretched and making monster noises.

He dips his chin, though he doesn't break character as he follows the girls into the living room.

At the kitchen doorway, I stop and peer around the frame, making sure I won't get bowled over by anyone else involved in their game.

Addie sits at the kitchen counter with a notebook open in front of her, and Liv is pulling out drawers, one after another, muttering to herself. Their kitchen never fails to lift my spirits. The room is gorgeous, with white cabinets up top with brassy handles and marble countertops marred with jagged black lines. The half dozen stools around the island are black, and the lower cabinets are as well. Beckett gained access to the Pinterest boards Liv created while still married to her ex—probably daydreaming of a life she never thought she'd have, only for my brother to eagerly give it to her years later.

God, I love them.

When I realize Liv's still in the dress and blazer she wore to the office today, guilt gnaws at my stomach. I should have been more respectful of their family time. It is a school night, after all. And this probably could have waited until business hours.

Liv spots me, and her eyes light up. "Oh my god, are you any good at math? Addie needs help. Winnie's the resident math whiz around here, but she's not home from debate team yet."

"Debate team?" I muse, a smile teasing at my lips.

She sighs, her shoulders dropping. "Right? Like anyone in this house needs to hone their arguing skills."

Beckett appears in the doorway, one brow raised. "Every one of our children should be an expert at winning a debate. It'll serve them well in the future." He gives me a peck on the cheek and squeezes my shoulders, then heads for Addie, who looks up at him and grins.

Warmth blooms in my chest as I study my niece. Addie is tiny, with long brown waves cascading around her shoulders. She's got a fantastic sense of style too. She tends to dress more on the girly side, yet she's obsessed with hockey. I love that she proudly displays both facets of her personality. The generation of girls growing up today is given so many more options and is encouraged to be everything they want rather than being pigeonholed.

It gives me hope that even though my background is in fashion, I can eventually find my place in the sports world.

Beckett rounds the counter and buries his face in Liv's neck, murmuring words I can't make out.

"I'm thinking Chinese," she says as he steps away. She drags a menu from the edge of the counter and offers it to me.

"I'm good with whatever." I take the stool next to Addie and rest my elbows on the cool marble. "Sorry if I threw off your night by showing up like this."

Laughing, Liv holds out an arm and pans the space. "Do you see my life?"

As if on cue, Gavin and the three little girls tumble into the room, the lot of them screaming.

Beckett snags June and Vivi around the waist and hauls them up, rescuing them from Gavin. That leaves poor Maggie on her own, crying about how Daddy forgot her.

Liv scoops her up and positions her on her hip, then points at Gavin. "Stop scaring them."

Addie shakes her head. "Why would you *want* to come over here?"

Giggling, I swivel to face her. "I heard you're a little hockey star."

Her eyes light up, but behind her, Beckett makes a growling sound. "She's a great softball player too."

"My Addie girl knows that hockey is the superior sport," Gavin says, sweeping an arm around her shoulder.

Genuine happiness courses through my veins as the decades-long battle continues. My oldest brothers have been arguing about this for as long as I can remember.

"Before you boys get into this," Liv says, using the mom tone that instantly causes us all to toe the line, "circle what you want so we can call in the food. I'm starving."

I snag a pen from the collection in front of Addie and quickly mark my selection, then pass the menu off to Gavin to do the same. None of us argues with Liv. She's a saint as far as I'm concerned.

Beckett disappears for a moment, and when he returns, he's cradling a bottle of red wine. I don't need to see the label to know what it is. My brother only stocks one type of wine, and that's the Jackson pinot noir his wife was drinking the night they "accidentally" got married in Vegas. He serves his wife first, then offers me a glass, which I eagerly take.

I take a sip and close my eyes, willing my muscles to relax. When I feel marginally more at ease, I turn back to Addie. "I'll help you with your homework if you agree to help me with hockey."

Her lips curl up on one side. "Deal."

Gavin grunts. "I can help you with hockey. I taught this one"—he squeezes Addie's side, making her squeal—"everything she knows."

"Actually, Uncle Brooks did," she teases.

"I'm sticking with her," I tell my brother. "Now go. We need girl time."

Shoulders slumped, he retreats, dragging his feet the whole way and grumbling about being forced to watch baseball with Finn and Beckett.

Liv calls in our order, then heads upstairs to change, leaving Addie and me on our own. After her math is done—the girl was mostly on her own; turns out math has changed—she grills me about hockey jargon to see what I know.

After she tries to explain a term involving the word hat, we determine that I know absolutely nothing.

"Am I a lost cause?" I ask as we head into the dining room for dinner.

She shakes her head. "Don't worry, Auntie. I've got you."

"What's Millie up to?" Liv asks once we're all seated, our plates full.

Gavin sets his wineglass on the table. "Napping. The pregnancy is taking a lot out of her. Especially since Vivi never stops."

"It's wild to think that next year, they'll all be in kindergarten," Liv says wistfully. "They grow up so quick."

Gavin shoots me a wink and shovels a bite of food onto his fork. "That's how we feel about Sienna."

Liv shifts in her seat, giving me an expectant smile. "So how was the first day?"

Based on the way Gavin's expression goes pensive, it's safe to say he's already heard from his GM. "It was fine. I met Ezra."

Beckett holds his fork aloft and frowns. "What happened?"

In those two words alone, I can hear the protective big brother fighting his way out. But that's not why I came over. So I school my features. "Nothing. He seems nice. Said he's happy to help me get adjusted."

My oldest brother practically sags with relief. "Good."

"He's lucky he didn't have to deal with a CEO like you," Liv tells her husband. She picks up her wineglass and swirls it gently. "Just ask Cortney how much he prefers my style of CEOing."

Beckett scoffs. "I was a great CEO. Very helpful."

"You were better at interfering than helping," she says pointedly. "If you'd asked Cortney, he probably would have told you he didn't need your help."

Beckett narrows his eyes. "Does he or does he not come into your office to ask for your opinion?"

She shrugs. "He does."

"And do you think you provide good advice?"

"I do my best," Liv admits.

My brother looks at me, the lines on his face easing a little. "Here's the thing: none of our decision-making is done in a vacuum. Conclusions made regarding money and team dynamics are all influenced by the coaches, the chemistry of the players, and the amount of money in the cap. Sometimes one person sees it differently from another. It's why it's called a team."

Beside me, Gavin smirks. "He's not wrong."

Liv sighs into her wineglass. "No, I don't suppose he is."

"But I don't know hockey," I admit.

"So learn." Beckett says it like it's so easy. "You don't think Liv grew up thinking she'd be running a baseball team, do you?"

I eye my sister-in-law. I guess I've never thought about it.

She lets out a breathy laugh. "No. When I stepped into that elevator all those years ago, it was for a position with the *corporation's* PR department. *Not* the team's."

The two of them share a look. A memory maybe. I have no idea what happened on that elevator, but whatever it was, it feels big.

Beckett takes his wife's hand, his green eyes—the same color as mine—warm as he presses his lips to her knuckles. Then he turns to me. "Now she's one of the most respected owners in the league. And not just because she's my wife."

Liv rolls her eyes, though there's nothing but adoration in her expression. "I love the game. I love our team. But yes, before I found myself handling PR for the Revs, I didn't even like baseball. But I learned all I could as quickly as I could because I wanted to succeed.

Maybe I'm the CEO today because I'm Mrs. Beckett Langfield, but either way, I want people to respect me and I want to be helpful. The only way to do that was to learn the game."

"Right. And to insert yourself in those discussions," Beckett adds.

"But you had years," I say to Liv.

Gavin hums, sitting back in his chair. "So start small. Focus on the players whose contracts are coming to an end. You've got their files. Study them. Their positions and stats. Then compare them with others in the league. Now that we're past the trade deadline, we're focusing on what changes we'll make next year. You've got time."

Beckett brings his whiskey glass to his lips. "Isn't Harrison's contract up this year?"

At the sound of his name, my muscles lock up. Shit. I can only pray my expression hasn't given away my reaction.

Gavin nods. "Yup. Brooks too—"

"Sienna can't be involved in that decision. It's a conflict of interest," Liv chimes in.

I laugh. "It's a conflict of interest for every person with the power to make big decisions, wouldn't you say? So if I can't, then who can?"

The Langfields could give two shits about being accused of nepotism, but even so, this is one more reason to steer clear of Noah. The last thing I need is to be accused of favoritism.

Beckett grunts. "That's why we brought in Ezra. He'll make the final decision when Brooks's or Aiden's contracts are up for renegotiation."

"Or mine," Gavin adds.

Beckett nods. "Or his."

"Wow, that's—" I blow out a breath. "He has the power to fire you?"

Gavin dips his chin. "If I'm not doing my job."

"And then I'd fire him," Beckett growls.

The four of us burst into laughter. Beckett is fiercely protective of his family.

"Except that would negate the whole reason we brought him on," Gavin points out. "I'm not planning to make the kind of epic mistakes that would lead to being fired from a team I actually own."

A lump forms in my throat. And now I'm CEO of that team. This conversation makes my situation feel so much more real. I've never put much thought into the business side of the teams my family owns, yet it's clear that Langfield Corp means just as much to my brothers as my company meant to me. And I want to make them proud.

"Thank you for giving me this opportunity," I tell them. "I won't let you down."

Gavin nudges me with his elbow. "We know."

Their trust in me is incredible. And it's a reminder to stand firmly on principle when it comes to Noah. Nothing can happen with us, not only because I'm angry with him but because I refuse to let anyone down again.

Before leaving the table, I text my real estate agent and ask to get into the apartment to take measurements. This is my fresh start. I'm ready to move forward.

Thirty minutes after I leave Beckett's, I collect the keys to my new place from the building manager and hit the button to call the elevator. The whole way up, I wear a stupid smile, giddy about what's to come for me.

As I pad toward the apartment, a door nearby swings open and a man steps out into the hall. I'm so lost in my thoughts that his identity doesn't register until he says my name. "Sienna?"

Heart stuttering, I blink up at the man I've just sworn to myself I'd stop thinking about.

Noah's jeans are worn in all the right places, and the sleeves of his black shirt are rolled to his elbows. Dammit. Why does he have to look so good?

"Sienna?" he says again, snapping me out of my stupor. "Are you here to see me?" His brows are furrowed, but there's a hint of hopefulness in his eyes behind those black glasses that I swear will be the death of me.

"You live here?" I mumble.

"Yeah?" He says it like it's a question. "Why are you here?"

Eyes shuttering closed, I sigh. "I just signed a lease." My arm feels weighted down as I point to my new place.

He chuckles and slips his hands into his pockets. "You know, I once knew a girl who would swear this is fate."

I huff a breath. "More like a coincidence."

"Really? That same girl swore she didn't believe in coincidences. Though this certainly feels like a happy coincidence, doesn't it?" He's full-on grinning now.

"Yup, another freaking happy coincidence," I grind out.

Lucky me.

CHAPTER 27
NOAH

ON THE WAY to morning skate, I can't help but glance at the door that will soon be Sienna's. If I thought she had slept there last night, I'd be standing outside with a coffee, waiting to offer her a ride to work.

She may not be here now, but soon enough, it's going to be damn hard for her to avoid me.

I couldn't wipe the smile from my face last night as I fell asleep. Not only did I kiss Sienna again, but I felt her come around my fingers and swallowed her moans. Then I got to watch her pretty cheeks flush pink as she came against the wall in her office.

That moment alone would have kept me soaring for days. But then the universe stepped in with another message, reminding us that we are fated to be together. Now that she's my neighbor, I'm not sure I'll ever come down from this high.

What are the fucking chances we end up not only in the same building but on the same floor?

Damn near impossible, that's what.

There's a chance Hannah mentioned the available unit, but from what I can tell, she and Sienna haven't interacted much. Plus she's too busy being a mom and an author and a husband-obsessed wife to meddle like that.

Halfway to the elevator, I turn around and stride for her door, just to confirm.

From out here, I can hear some character on their television singing a ridiculous tune and Mav babbling along with the lyrics. Then Daniel calls out—to Hannah, I presume—that he's leaving in two minutes.

The chaos inside their apartment couldn't be more different from the mostly quiet existence I lead. Even when I lived with my sister, the apartment only came to life when Daniel and Ollie were there.

My chest pinches with a longing for that kind of disorder. For a partner to do life with. For more time with my child. The custody arrangement isn't the problem; it's my job. It's not seeing Ollie for days at a time when I'm traveling and sitting in silence on Jen's days with him when I'm not. Daniel may travel too, but when he comes home, Mav and Hannah are always there waiting.

As long as I play hockey, I'll never have that kind of life. It wouldn't be fair to force a custody arrangement that revolved around my schedule. Ollie thrives on structure. Interrupting his schedule and asking Jen to jump through hoops to make it work would be a disservice to all of us. But damn does it suck not having my boy here when I'm not traveling. As it is, I already miss so much of his life.

The door swings open, but rather than greet me, Daniel practically barrels into me, his bag slung over his shoulder and his head down.

"Shit, sorry," he says, pulling up short.

I chuckle. "It's okay. Sounds like you guys had a busy morning."

In the instant before the door closes, my sister breezes into the living room and drops a kiss on Mav's head.

That pinch in my chest is back. This time, though, it's a little softer. It's accompanied by a gratefulness I wish I could feel in my own life. For so long, Hannah had no one but herself. Daniel and Mav have brought out a side of her I didn't even know existed.

"You ready?" Daniel glances back at the now-closed door, then gives me a concerned frown.

I blink myself back to reality. "Yeah, sorry. Didn't sleep much last night. I guess I'm still waking up."

He cocks his head to the side. "Was Ollie over?"

"Um, no."

"Why the hell didn't you sleep, then?" Eyes widening, he rears back. "Wait, did you get laid?"

With a shake of my head, I stride toward the elevator. "No."

"Then I'm not following," he says, trailing me.

"Sleep can be disrupted even when women and children aren't involved." I stab the call button a little too forcefully. After the reminder of how empty my life is, my mood has officially tanked.

Chuckling, Daniel sidles up beside me. "Not me. I sleep like a baby when Mav is quiet and your sister isn't—"

I jab him in the chest the same way I jabbed the elevator button. "Do not finish that sentence."

He rubs at the spot, his tongue pushing against the inside of his cheek. I know the look. He's trying like hell not to blab all the details of what my sister did to him last night.

I don't think anything could surprise me anymore. In the months I lived with them, I heard far too much. Hannah is not quiet in any facet of her life.

"So were you just craving my company, or did you stop by for a reason?"

I focus forward as we step onto the elevator, keeping my expression neutral. "I ran into Sienna Langfield in the hall last night. Was wondering if Hannah was the one who told her about the building."

Daniel shrugs. "No idea. She's moving in here?"

"Guess so."

"Hmm." He grins. "That'll be nice for Hannah."

I dip my chin, leaving it at that. He'll find out eventually why Sienna's whereabouts concern me, but I'm not ready to lay my cards out just yet.

Hours later, as I lace up my skates, I'm focused and ready to win tonight's game.

Everyone has their own pregame ritual. Aiden sings, Daniel

dances, War plays cards, Brooks puts his headphones on and zones out, and I do a crossword puzzle.

Yup. I'm aware that it's a weird fucking ritual, but pouring all my focus into the task keeps me from worrying about what's going to happen on the ice. Once I step into the arena, I divert my full attention to the game ahead. The routine allows me to channel all my energy more efficiently, I guess.

"Nervous about playing Minnesota tonight, boys?" Camden crows.

War chuckles as he deals a hand of cards. "When have you ever seen me nervous?"

Daniel surveys him. "Every time your wife yells at you."

My best friend's lips kick up on one side. "I love when my wife is vicious, so I assure you, that doesn't bother me."

Camden picks up the cards in front of him and eyes me, like he's waiting for me to respond.

I shake my head at the kid. He was traded to Las Vegas shortly after I came to Boston, but a year later, he came back. He and Daniel are really tight. He's a winger like the three of us, but War and I have ten years on Daniel and Camden. While we're coming close to the tail end of our careers, they're just getting started.

"I'm not worried," I tell him. "Vetters is weak on his left side," I say of the defenseman that Cam or I will face tonight. "And Tatty hates when people play with the puck." Minnesota's goalie is adamant that hockey is a serious sport. He despises the tricks the younger guys love.

I may not play with the puck, but the showmanship doesn't bother me. I'll do whatever it takes to get the biscuit into the back of the net. And if playing with the food is the way to make it happen, I'll manage.

When a commotion rises near the front of the locker room, I fold my crossword puzzle over and turn toward the sounds.

"Looks like Ezra's bringing the new girl around." Cam sets his cards face down on the bench in front of him.

War knees him, his blue eyes hard. "Drop the *new girl* shit and show some respect. She's the fucking owner of this team."

Aiden and Brooks pass by, headed that way, though I've yet to set eyes on my girl.

Because make no mistake about it, Sienna Langfield may be their sister, and she might be the owner and CEO of this team, but she's mine.

Just need to get her on board with that little fact.

I hang back and join in with the guys, studying my cards. I try to distract myself by chatting with them, by visualizing the way the game will go, and then flip back to the crossword puzzle I was working on. But Sienna's mere presence disrupts my peace. Then her scent hits me, beckoning me to look up.

In a locker room full of smelly fucking equipment and men—seriously, hockey is hands-down the worst-smelling sport—she's like a breath of fresh air.

The black Louboutin boots register first. Fuck. The sight takes me back to how good they looked on her when she spread her legs wide so I could fuck her with my fingers.

Not much is more uncomfortable than an erection in hockey gear, but I'm a masochist. So rather than look away, I assess her slowly, taking in all her curves.

And when a shock of blue peeks out from beneath her black blazer, I give up all hope of remaining unaffected. There's a goddamn hockey jersey beneath that jacket. Tucked into those tight black leather pants. My mouth waters.

Could the number on the back of the jersey belong to one of her brothers? Sure. But which one? How would she choose?

Knowing Sienna, she couldn't. *She wouldn't.*

That knowledge gives me a full-on chub.

I drop my puzzle book and stand to greet our new CEO. It's only polite. Good business. The cup pinches my thickened cock, but with the way my heart is racing, I barely notice the discomfort.

"No need to get up, boys. Just saying hello." She offers a smile, though she pointedly avoids looking at me.

Camden, who's dressed from the waist down only, gives her a boyish grin.

Irritation flares hot in my veins. He's not all that close to any of the Langfields. He's also enough of a player not to care about the sort of rules that would deter him from hooking up with a superior. "I don't think we've formally met. I'm Camden Snow. I handle your left side."

War stands and smacks him on the back of the head. "Shut up." With a glare at the kid, he steps in front of him. "Sienna, if any of these idiots give you trouble, let me know."

She lets out a raspy laugh and shakes her head. "I'll be fine, Warren, but thank you."

Ezra appears, decked out in a suit, with his hair slicked back, and rests his hand on Sienna's lower back. "Everyone behaving for you?" he asks. "And dressed?" Eyes narrowed, he surveys us all, stopping at Camden. "At least for the most part?"

Ezra was an okay player fifteen years ago. He retired before I was drafted, but I've heard he could be a cocky bastard. The majority of hockey players are, I guess. It comes with the territory, so I never really minded.

But the way he's touching Sienna right now has my nerves on edge. I'd be itching to push any man away from her, but as she stands stock-still, wearing an expressionless mask, like she doesn't want him to touch her, my vision goes red. I'm not a fighter. In fact, I've got a pretty chill temperament for a hockey player. But I want to rip this guy's arm out of its socket and beat him with it.

"Good luck tonight," the fucker tacks on as he guides an uncomfortable Sienna toward the center of the locker room where Gavin is now standing.

"Damn, baby Langfield is *fine,*" Cam drawls.

War smacks him so hard the sound echoes off the walls. "What did I say about respect?"

"We all called Millie *Baby Hall,*" Cam points out, rubbing the back of his blond head.

Daniel puffs up, his usually easygoing expression going sour.

"Oh, stop," Cam goes on. Clearly the kid doesn't have any sense of self-preservation. "We know your wife calls you that in bed—"

This time I'm the one who smacks the back of his head. "Please, she's my sister."

Daniel grimaces like he's in pain. "That's what I'm saying about Millie."

"The point is—" War drags out. "Sisters are off-limits."

The four of us focus on the sister in question. Sienna is smiling as

Ezra and Gavin speak, but I know her well enough to know when it's forced. And Ezra still has his hand on her back. It takes effort to fight the urge to storm over and scoop her up. How the fuck hasn't Gavin noticed that she's uncomfortable?

"Someone should let Ezra know that she's off-limits, then," Cam grumbles.

Brooks wanders over to the group, his pads all in place, chuckling.

I grind my teeth. What's with her brothers' inability to show even an ounce of protective instinct where their sister is concerned? "Why are you laughing?"

"I love my sister to death, but she's an ice queen. I've never seen her with a man." He drops onto the bench and slides his headphones over his ears.

"Maybe she's a virgin like you were until you were thirty," War teases.

Brooks blinks slowly, unimpressed. "I'll pretend that's true."

"Works for me," Aiden chirps, sliding down the bench and knocking into his brother.

A little niggle of guilt pops up, but I tamp it down quick. If they only knew how wrong they are. Though if she doesn't bring men around, then there's hope that whoever that British guy was, he didn't last long.

And maybe, if I'm lucky, I still mean as much to her as she does to me.

She and Ezra hang around while Gavin gives us our game-day talking-to. I only half listen, too caught up in studying every inch of her I can see. Even as I head out of the locker room, I don't look away from her.

Nothing but hockey. For years, that was my motto. Ollie changed my mentality quickly. Now Sienna is here, doing the same. With her near, I can't focus on anything but her. I let the guys go ahead of me, and as I step up beside her, I pause and lean in.

She turns her head away, a poor attempt at looking like she's focused on something on the other side of the room.

I move another inch closer, then another, until my lips ghost over the shell of her ear, and croak, "Whose name is on the back of your jersey?"

Her body locks up and she whips around, annoyance radiating from her. "What's it to you?" she seethes, her mouth a breath from mine.

I inhale deeply through my nose and hold my breath, savoring her scent. I've never been possessive like this. And I've never understood this need to see a woman in my damn jersey. "Is it mine?"

She coughs out a laugh. "Wouldn't you like to know."

I'm pushed forward and herded out the door before I can respond. Before I can demand she take off the damn jacket and show me.

Without confirmation, there's no way I'll focus on anything but that lingering question, even once I hit the ice.

Fuck.

CHAPTER 28
NOAH

THE CHIRPING STARTS EARLY in the game.

That's no surprise. Every team has its requisite assholes. Guys who run their mouths to make up for their lackluster performance.

That's never been my style. Even if it was, I wouldn't have the ability. Not with the way our center plays the game. Aiden uses song to communicate with us wingers. It's hard enough to remember what his damn lyrics mean to focus on offering up a *your mom* joke.

Moms are sacred, so I wouldn't do that, but I can't either way.

"Boom shakalaka," Aiden calls as he skates forward with the puck.

War goes deep to the left, but it takes me a second to remember the play. When I do, I dig my skates into the ice and power forward. As I pick up speed, a flash of blue and black at our bench catches my eye.

Sure enough, Sienna's there, settling beside Gavin.

He's looking directly at me, scowling. He shouts my name, but before I can react, I'm knocked on my ass.

"Getting slow in your old age," Vetter, Minnesota's defenseman, chirps as he skates away.

War's by my side in two strides, offering me a hand. "Where's the fucking penalty call?" he grouses.

The ref circling nearby shakes his head, then takes off.

When I'm steady on my skates, War pats my shoulder. "You okay?"

"I'm fine. I got—" I snap my mouth shut. There's no way I'll tell him I was distracted. But that's exactly the problem. I was distracted by sixty-four inches of perfection.

Distracted by the powder blue jersey pulled taut across her chest, hinting at the swell of my favorite pair of tits. The frustrating need to know whose name is plastered across her back is killing me.

I shake the thoughts from my head and line up for the face-off.

There may be twenty thousand pairs of eyes locked on the ice right now, but I only feel hers. Her confusion is palpable.

My cheek twitches, the sensation urging me to turn, to let her know I'm okay.

I give in, just for a second, and relief courses through me. Her eyes lock with mine, confusion still evident there. She still doesn't get it. This pull I feel toward her. This obsession.

I warned her long ago. Warned myself too.

I'm an obsessive guy. In many ways, I use it to my advantage. It allows me to give hockey all my focus. It helps me tune out the rest of the world during the precious little time I get with Ollie.

At the same time, the compulsion that comes with it can be a challenge.

Like now. I have no choice but to hold her gaze. To reassure her that this is real.

But as with any obsession, focusing so intently on one detail leads to missing another. So while I'm staring at Sienna, the ref blows the whistle and Minnesota wins the face-off, leaving me scrambling after the puck.

The pattern continues as the game goes on, my distraction more noticeable with every play. By the end of the second period, I'm certain Gavin will bench me.

"You seem awfully obsessed with the bench, Harry," he shouts. "Want to hang out here for the rest of the game?"

Thank fuck he hasn't caught on that my preoccupation with his sister is what's causing me to lose my edge. She, on the other hand, disappears before the third period, leading me to believe she's more aware of my dilemma than my coach or teammates.

I hate and appreciate her absence in equal measure.

As much as I want her near me, always, the space allows me to finally direct all my focus to the game. Where it should be. Where it *needs* to be.

My teammates have absolutely carried me, and we're tied when we line up again. I expect the chirping to be loud. This close to the end, the stakes are higher. But I tune it out. Focus on proving to myself that I can do this. That I can be obsessed with her yet still give my full attention to other important matters. That I can do my job while allowing myself to actually have a life.

We win the face-off this time, then Aiden slashes the puck to me in a move I know by heart. I'm the team's sniper for a reason. The chanting in the stands turns into white noise as I slash my stick against the ice and send the puck flying past Tatty's left shoulder.

As the red light flashes above the net, signaling the goal, the arena erupts, the fans on their feet, clapping and stomping, the sound deafening. War and Aiden sandwich me in a hug, and then I skate in a tight circle, searching for my girl.

Is she in the owner's box?

I take a lap around the ice, looking for her, knowing that to the rest of the world, this is nothing but the celly they're used to.

When I don't spot her, my heart sinks. Though I shake off the emotion quickly, remembering that Ollie will be waiting for my signal. So I tap my chest and point to the camera when I pass it, letting him know I might not be with him, but he's always right here with me.

It's our thing. I may get distracted from time to time, but I could never forget him.

I'm heading to the bench to switch out lines when Vetter skates up behind me.

"Looking for the Bolts' new piece of ass, Harry?" he taunts.

Teeth gritted, I stupidly turn to face him. "What did you say?"

He gets up in my face, his helmet knocking against mine. "Team passing her around yet? You get the first drag?"

By the time the last word leaves him, my stick is on the ice and my gloves are too. Without hesitation, I cock my arm back and clock him in the jaw.

It's a blur from there. The man didn't expect me to react that way. I don't react to chirping. Never have. Because I've never had a weakness like her.

Later, I'll be pissed that my obsession has already been exploited, but right now, I relish in the deep thrill that overtakes me, ecstatic that he's so shocked by the hit that he's still wide-eyed and stunned when I grab his jersey and hit him again. Before I can get a third in, War pulls me away.

He's a little too late. The rest of Minnesota's line is in the mix now, and my teammates are jumping over the boards to stop them from attacking the two of us from behind.

By the time the refs break up the skirmish and they've doled out ten-minute penalties for both Vetter and me, both benches have been cleared and everyone but the coaches is panting for breath.

I skate toward the penalty box, my heart racing and anger flowing through my veins. And the emotion only grows when I search the arena and don't see her anywhere.

Chapter 29
Sienna

FOR MORE THAN A YEAR, this man chose not to make contact. He put his career and his friendships with my brothers over his promise to come for me, and now, after seeing me in a damn Bolts jersey, he's willing to risk everything to, what? God, I don't even know what he wants.

We'll never be done.

His words from the other day bounce around in my head as I press myself against the wall in the owner's suite. I ran here to hide after Gavin chewed Noah out for not focusing on the ice.

What is he thinking?

"You know you can't see the game from back there," Lex singsongs. She's the only one of my sisters-in-law without kids, so she's the only one who makes it to just about every home game these days.

I take a small step forward, though I keep my distance from the glass separating the suite from the arena. "You don't have to stay up here with me. I'm sure Aiden loves having you down there."

She grins. "Big dopey idiot runs into the boards if I'm too close. I sit up here unless Sara forces me to freeze out there."

A rush of relief I didn't expect hits me. At least I won't be alone. "Okay, good."

It's strange how quiet the owner's box is with the rest of the girls at home with their kids. Blessedly, Ezra chose to stay rink side. Listening to him mansplain the game was getting beyond old.

I'd rather learn about hockey from Addie. My nine-year-old niece probably knows as much as he does, and she's a lot less smug about it.

"Looks like whatever was irking Harry has resolved." Lennox angles in closer to the glass, her pink hair hiding her face. "Oh shit," she squeals. "Yes. Ah, get it, Beauty!" She jumps to her feet along with the rest of the crowd and screams.

Without my permission, my body glides forward. Then I'm standing beside her, my focus intent on the action as Noah slaps his stick against the ice, sending the puck flying into the back of Minnesota's net. Excitement bubbles up, and I give in to the urge to jump up and down in celebration.

Aiden and Warren smash into Noah, hugging him and jostling him. How they do it on skates I'll never know, but with the way my body is buzzing, I can't imagine the high they're riding.

This is exciting. Far more exciting than I expected it to be. If I'm honest, I'm having fun.

Noah takes a lap around the rink. I can practically feel him searching for me as he glides easily, so I take a step back from the glass. After a moment, he pauses and looks into the screen, and a heartbeat later, his face pops up on the Jumbotron. Like this, it feels like he's looking directly at me, those familiar blue eyes so knowing. Focus intent on the camera, he taps his heart.

In response, mine goes into overdrive. "What's he doing?"

Lennox brings her hands to her chest and hums. "Isn't it sweet? It's a message to Ollie. He does it after every goal."

My heart both skips and settles as I study his flushed face. Shit. Why does that have to be so cute?

I should have known it was about Ollie. The sense that he was staring right at me was all in my head. Hell, he was probably scanning the arena for a camera so he could send his son a message, not to locate me and the stupid jersey he's obsessed with revealing.

When the enlarged image of him disappears, I step up closer to Lennox again and lean against the glass, watching him skate to the bench. "Why is he going over there?"

"Line change," Lennox explains, as if that should make sense.

She probably thinks I know the rules the way she does. I did spend hours sitting beside her while Aiden played in high school, after all. I just wasn't paying attention.

I reach for my phone so I can scan the list of questions I saved in my Notes app. I might as well go through some of them with Lennox while it's just the two of us.

"Oh *fuck*," she mutters, startling me.

Heart in my throat, I peer down at the rink.

Noah's stick is on the ground and his gloves are off. And before I can make sense of why, he pulls back and punches one of Minnesota's players.

Like he didn't see it coming, the guy's head snaps back. His response is slow, giving Noah time to clutch the front of his jersey and hit him again.

I gasp. "Holy crap. What did that guy do?"

Neither of us takes our eyes off the chaotic scene in front of us.

"I have no idea," Lennox murmurs, bringing her fingers to her mouth. "Noah's never like that."

My stomach lodges itself in my throat as players from both teams converge, every one of them throwing fists. Even Brooks, the most even-keeled of my brothers, has skated toward the melee, leaving the goalie box.

Heart racing, I scan the mass of bodies for Noah. When he's finally pulled out of it and sent to the penalty box—or the sin bin, according to Lennox—the need to go to him flares inside me, burning bright.

I need to see that he's all right.

When the game is over, the urge is just as strong. But rather than give in, I pack up and force myself to head home.

Noah is not mine to check on. He *can't* be.

CHAPTER 30
NOAH

"WHAT THE FUCK happened out there tonight?" Gavin all but shouts. "I know tensions are always high when your opponents are former teammates"—he eyes me, then War—"but save the aggression for the damn game." With his hands on his hips, he tips his head back and blows out a breath. "We're lucky those penalties didn't cost us the win." He straightens, this time zeroing in on me. "Don't put us in that position again."

I nod, my jaw locked tight. I'm barely holding it together right now. Adrenaline still courses through my veins, and the comments that asshole made about Sienna play on repeat in my mind.

My anger is only compounded by her disappearance. Where the fuck did she go after the second period?

And who the fuck's jersey is she wearing?

My preoccupation with that alone makes the blood rush in my ears.

The second Gavin stalks out of the locker room, heading to the press room, I storm for my locker.

"Harrison, you're on tonight," Andi calls after me. She's filling in for Sara while she's on maternity leave. She's nice enough, and typically, my manners win out, even when I'm pissed, but there's no goddamn way I can talk to the press right now.

"War will do it," I holler without slowing.

My best friend steps in front of me, pulling me up short, and punches my shoulder. "Dick. You'll owe me."

I pull in a deep breath and hold it, looking him in the eye. Then, exhaling, I nod. "I owe you a lot. Thanks, brother."

With a shake of his head, he squeezes my shoulder. "It's what we do. When you're ready to talk about what that was all about..." He dips his chin, leaving it at that. We both know that the time is not now.

I sidestep him and shuck my gear. Then I head toward the shower.

Half an hour later, I'm dressed in my game-day suit and exiting the locker room. I'm too keyed up to play nice, so I bypass the family suite altogether and don't bother saying goodbye to any of the guys.

My pulse is still erratic when I pound on Sienna's door. There's no way I'll get an ounce of sleep until I see her. Even then, rest will not come easy.

Almost instantly, her door flies open and she appears, her expression taut and exhausted. "Noah, I can't do this tonight."

I push past her, my head a jumbled mess. "I can't *not* do it tonight. Because what happened tonight can't happen again."

"Oh, by all means, come in," she sneers, holding an arm out in a sardonic gesture. "We'll just run on your schedule again."

I spin to face her, my breaths choppy. "What the hell is that supposed to mean?"

She hasn't changed. She's still wearing those damn leather pants and that jersey under her black jacket. She looks incredible, even standing with her arms crossed, glowering at me.

"It *means,*" she drags out the word, "that apparently you decide when we talk. You decide when you're ready to deal with this. You decided to wait months and *months* to approach me. You waited until you were ready for us. Well, guess what? I'm not."

I bark out a bitter laugh. This girl. If she only knew how the dollar bill I carry in my wallet is a living, breathing entity, taunting me, telling me that this is exactly when we were supposed to meet again. Our reconnection has nothing to do with whether *I'm* ready. Fate has decided. Fate brought us together at Brooks's wedding. And since I didn't listen, fate brought the dollar bill to me. Fate put her in this role, where she's my boss. It's fate's fault that she's become friends with my sister. And when *she* tried to ignore it, fate brought her to this apartment.

None of this is happening on my timeline. I'm at the mercy of the universe, and it's only compounded by my instinct to claim her and the physical impossibility of walking away. "Whose name is on the back of your jersey?"

"Oh my god." She drops her hands to her sides and fists them. "You've got to be kidding me."

I'm not. Not a single thing about this is funny.

I stalk toward her. When I'm a foot away, she backs up, but I don't stop until I've got her pressed up against the door.

"Take off the jacket, Sienna."

"You are absolutely insane." She glares at me, chin held high. Fucking beautiful.

"I am." My control is hanging by a thread. I've never been like this over a woman, but I am 100 percent certifiable where she's concerned.

"It means nothing." She pushes me away, then darts a few steps to the side. "I didn't have a jersey," she says as she pulls the black jacket off one shoulder and the Bolts logo on the jersey comes into view. "Hannah gave me shit about it and forced me to wear hers. So don't go acting like it means anything."

Attention averted, she shucks the garment, letting it fall to the floor, and turns. I bring my fist to my mouth and bite down. *Fuck.* There, across her shoulder blades, in block letters, is *Harrison.* The sight of the number below it, the 69, my number, is almost enough to bring me to my knees.

Darting forward, I grasp her wrists and bury my face in her neck, inhaling the scent of her. I run my nose along the side of her throat and down toward her shoulder, and when goose bumps erupt beneath my palms, a heady satisfaction fills me. "Another happy coincidence, Sienna? My jersey was your only option? Is that the line we're going with now?"

"Fuck you," she pants. Like her body has taken control, her hips roll, causing her ass to brush against my already stiff cock.

Stars dance in my vision. Holy fuck. I need to be inside this woman again.

While I keep her wrists locked in one hand, I loop one arm around her waist. Then I flatten my palm over her stomach so she's flush against me. Against her ear, I murmur, "No one has ever had me like this. I don't get distracted on the ice. I don't get into fights. But one look at you, one mention of your name, and I'm ready to rip a man to shreds."

She sucks in a breath. "That's why you got into a fight?"

It's my turn to laugh bitterly. "Why else? You're my obsession. No one else has the power to make me lose my mind."

"That—" she pants. "That sounds like a problem."

I let go of her wrists and scrape her hair away from her neck. Humming, I pepper soft kisses against her skin. "It really is. And as my boss, I'd think you'd want me completely focused."

She rolls her hips again. "Maybe."

I groan. "Baby, don't tease me. I'm teetering on the damn edge right now. Will you put me out of my misery and let me in? Forgive me for not coming for you? Be with me?"

She shakes her head, the movement jerky. "Don't do that."

"Don't do what?"

In answer, she pulls away.

My heart plummets, though the free fall stops when she holds out a hand. "I'm wet."

I swear my hearing goes in and out as the words register. Holy fuck.

"I want you to fuck me. I want you to make me come the way only you know how to. Can you do that?"

I'm nodding before she finishes her sentence.

Her lips turn up into a wicked smile. "Good. But don't get emotional on me. Don't call me baby. Fuck me with the kind of force you used when you hit that player tonight. Show me how much you want me."

"Strip," I grind out as I yank at my tie and pull it off in one quick move. "Everything off but my jersey." I loop the silk around my fist.

I want so much more than to make her come, but I'm not strong enough to say no to that request.

Without breaking eye contact, she shimmies her pants down her hips, then kicks them off.

"Bend yourself over the couch. Let me see the way my name and number look above that perfect fucking ass."

She listens without argument, stalking to the couch, her hips swaying beneath my jersey, the number 69 a sick taunt. My mouth waters at the sight.

One day Gavin'll regret having assigned me that number.

With a quick shake of my head, I push that thought away. Then I lock up any and all thoughts of her brothers. They may be my team-mates and friends, but she's the elixir to the poison coursing through my veins. Or maybe she's the accelerant.

Blood singing and body humming, I step up behind her and skim the smooth globes of her ass.

"Remember, you asked for this."

I pull back and bring my hand down on her ass cheek. She cries out, and her ivory skin turns the prettiest shade of red. Without giving her time to recover, I do it again, this time marking her other side.

"This how you want it, ba—" I snap my mouth shut to keep from calling her baby.

If I'm not careful, she'll pull away. Though with the way she moans and grinds against the couch, I don't think she noticed my slip-up.

Curling around her body, I bring my mouth to her ear. "Think I can make you come like this? By spanking you alone? Reminding you that you're mine?"

"Fuck you," she growls out.

Did that last part break her rules? Maybe. But she needs to be reminded of the truth. She's mine. I won't accept any other outcome.

"Bet you're dripping all over the couch, sweet cheeks."

When she whimpers in response, all sense of self-preservation leaves me. I drop to my knees and push apart her ass cheeks so I can lick up the mess she's making. At the first taste, I groan. Her arousal is sweet against my tongue. Just like her original nickname. So fucking delicious. I only allow myself a few licks before climbing to my feet and raining down another smack.

"Jesus," she mutters.

"Noah," I remind her.

"God, you are—"

"Yours." I land another smack.

Her body shudders, her breathing choppy. "Noah, please."

I rub my hand over her flesh, smoothing the sting. "Good girl. Tell me what you want."

"*You,*" she sobs, pushing against me.

Unable to deny her, I make quick work of unbuckling my belt and shoving my pants past my hips. My aching cock pitches forward, as desperate for her as I am. "This what you want?" I clutch her wrists again, this time wrapping my tie around them and securing it tightly.

She nods, her face buried in the cushion.

I smack her ass, and she yelps. "Tell me. Is this what you want?"

"Yes," she moans. "Shove it inside me. Fuck me. Now."

This moment couldn't be more different from our last time. Or even the first. Those moments were flooded with emotion. Tonight, my sole focus is on giving her what she asked for. After this, she'll understand that no matter how I have her, she's mine. It'll never just be fucking for us.

When I finally push into the tight cunt I've been dreaming about for years, my ears ring in blinding pleasure.

Her warm body sucks me in. I let it guide me deep, only stopping when every inch of me is sheathed inside her and my pelvis hits her ass.

Her cry brings me back to earth as she squirms beneath me. Shit. I took her too fast.

I slide my hand to the front of her neck and guide her up, pressing her ass tighter to me, then drag my lips to her shoulder, her neck, her cheek. "I'm sorry, baby."

She throws her head back, huffing. "Please don't."

She only wants a fuck, and that's what I intended to give her, but now that I'm inside her, I can't hold back. I thrust forward a little, and when I slide easily through her slickness, I do it again.

"Shh, let me take care of you," I murmur.

With her wrists bound between us, I can't take her any deeper, but she still feels like heaven. I graze her breasts and continue over her abdomen, only stopping when I reach her clit. The swollen bud pulses on contact, and when I pinch it, she cries out and spasms around me.

With every swirl of my fingers, she gets wetter, drenching me in her pleasure until I'm drowning in it.

"You feel so good, sweet cheeks. So fucking tight and wet." With each gravelly word, her breathing comes faster and her pleas become more desperate. "Are you going to come for me, butterfly? You going to give me what I need?"

As a keening sound slips from her throat, she rolls her hips back, chasing her orgasm. "Yes. Please, yes," she chants.

I push her down against the couch and fuck into her hard, drawing back until the ridge of my crown teases her opening, then slam back into her. The sight of my length glistening with her arousal causes a tingling sensation in my spine. Teeth gritted to hold back the need to come, I focus on her back, where my jersey is bunched up but my name between her shoulder blades is still visible.

Sienna Harrison.

At the thought of the future I crave, my nerve endings light up and my instincts kick in. I fuck into her harder while tearing at the knot of the tie to release her arms.

"I need your mouth." I pull out and spin her around, then bury myself inside her again.

She leans in for a kiss without hesitation, and another piece of my world clicks into place. That move alone seals the deal for me. If she thought this was just about sex before, there's no way she does now. Her hot mouth is on mine, her tongue tasting, her teeth nipping. Like she needs me as badly as I need her. With the globes of her ass clutched in my hands, I stride for what I'm certain is the master bedroom based on the layout of my apartment and Hannah's.

I don't look away from her as I step into her room, though later I will want to study every detail so I can see where she finds solace. Right now my focus is on her. I lay her back on the mattress without slipping out of her and spread her out before me, my fingers finding her clit again.

As I fuck into her hard, she wraps a leg around my hip, keeping me close.

With hooded eyes, she assesses every inch of me, like she's familiarizing herself with me.

I do the same. She's the most beautiful woman in every room, but like this, with the light of the moon casting shadows across her face, she's ethereal. Just the sight of her makes it hard to breathe.

When her back bows and her neck strains, like the need inside her is coiling tight, readying to be unleashed, I lose myself in her, fucking and teasing until she's whimpering and pulsing around me, milking me of my own orgasm. White hot light greets me as my balls tighten, and with a groan, I unload deep inside her.

When I've pumped every last drop of cum into her, I collapse on top of her, careful not to crush her. Panting and breathless, I let my hands rove her again, craving the feel of her skin while I'm still inside her, our combined release seeping out around my length.

"Shit," she hisses, pushing at my shoulder.

Dazed, I pull back a fraction, frowning. "What?"

"We didn't use a condom."

The statement should concern me. It should set my heart racing. Instead, a thrill shoots through me and a smile creeps up my face. "No, we didn't."

"Get off me." She shoves me harder this time, the move causing me to slip out of her.

I wrap my arms around her and hold tight, my cock softening between us.

"What if I wasn't on birth control?" Her tone is soft, unsure.

A strange pressure builds in my chest at the notion. Heart pounding, I push up on one forearm and slide my fingers over her soaked opening. "Are you?" I circle her clit, and when she writhes against the bed, I push the leaking cum back inside her.

With her chin tucked, she watches as I do it a second time. The third time I do it, she moans.

My dick thickens in response to the sound. In response to my own actions. The idea of her pregnant with my child suddenly consumes me. I want to fuck her over and over again until I'm sure she is. Then I can keep her. Then the world will know she's mine.

"Of course I am," she whimpers, her eyes falling shut. "Fuck, don't stop."

I gather my release and tease her clit, then push my fingers back inside her and stroke. "For what it's worth, you don't have to worry about the no condom thing."

With a sigh, she shakes her head. "Same here. I've never been with anyone but you without one."

I smirk. I can't help it. The knowledge that I'm the only one to have her bare only heightens my obsession with her. "I haven't been with anyone since you, so…"

Sienna's eyes fly wide and her mouth drops open. "As in since last week? Jeez, glad you've managed to hold out so long."

With laughter rumbling up my chest, I kiss the beauty mark on one side of her mouth. I kiss her lips, taking my time there, tangling my tongue with hers.

"Sassy fucking brat." I pull back, eyes locked on hers, and make a confession that might have her running. "No, Sienna. I haven't been with anyone since *you*."

Her lashes flutter, like she's struggling to process the simple words, and she sucks in a breath. "You're not saying—" She frowns, her eyes darting between mine, then scrutinizing me, like she'll find the truth in my expression.

"Yes, baby. I've waited for you for six years."

"But—" She shifts under me, but I don't release her. "But you knew where I was, and still—" She cuts herself off, like she can't finish that thought, her face pinched.

"And still I knew you were the only one for me. And if I couldn't have you…" I trace her lips with my fingers and press my mouth to hers once again. "Then I didn't want anyone else."

Chapter 31
Sienna

I PEEK out into the hallway, and when I find it empty, I suck in a breath and grasp the handle of my suitcase.

Yes, I'm hiding in my own building.

Yes, I'll have to face Noah eventually.

Sooner than I'd like, in fact, since we'll be on the same plane this morning and in the same hotels for the next week.

But I need just a few more minutes to put my armor in place and to remind myself of all the reasons he needs to stay firmly in my past.

And still I knew you were the only one for me. And if I couldn't have you, then I didn't want anyone else.

His words have played on repeat in my head since he uttered them two nights ago. I didn't have the capacity to wrap my head around them then, and even now, I'm still lost.

He could see it that night, I'm sure. So he pressed one more kiss to my lips and offered to give me time.

I had over a year to work through this. You've had a few days. I can wait.

The thing is, I don't know that I *can* work through this. My emotions are all over the place, and, more importantly, I'm still angry. Angry at myself for missing him for so long. Angry that I suffered on my own for so long. Angry that I wasn't worth the risk to his friendship with my brothers until I was forced back into his life.

If not for my position with the Bolts, would he have ever come for me? I'm afraid to acknowledge that the likely answer is no. Because even the thought hurts. And it makes it impossible for me to forgive, let alone move on.

But every time I get within three feet of the man, I lose all sense. And my panties.

It's embarrassing.

Hot too, but so, *so* embarrassing. I'm thirty years old. I should have the capacity to maintain at least some semblance of control.

Head down, I step into the hall with my luggage and purse and lock up quickly, then stride toward the elevator.

I'm in the elevator, almost home free, when a voice echoes down the hall.

"Can you hold that?"

My shoulders sag in response to the unfamiliar female voice. Okay, I can handle a ride in an elevator with a stranger. So with a *sure*, I press the button.

A beautiful woman I haven't seen in the building before practically glides down the hallway, smiling. "Thanks," she chirps as she steps into the stainless-steel box. "Do you mind waiting one more second? They're coming."

A heartbeat later, Noah's door opens, and my fight-or-flight instinct kicks in.

I consider how she'd react if I pretended not to hear her request and let the doors shut, but before I've made a decision, Ollie comes running down the hall, making the choice for me. I can't very well let the doors close in his face. Especially after the way his eyes light up when he sees me. "Sienna, what are you doing here?"

The woman beside me tilts her head, her dark hair falling over one shoulder, and eyes me with a look of confusion.

"I live here," I say, looking from him to the woman on the other side of the elevator. "I met Ollie last week at a Bolts game. With Hannah."

Lips tipping up, she holds out a hand. "I'm Jen. Ollie's mom."

It hits me now how obvious that should have been to me. But I've been too preoccupied with bracing myself to come face to face with the man who's now appeared outside his apartment door.

Noah is dressed in a navy suit. One of those straight ones that hits his ankle, exposing bare skin in an area that shouldn't do anything for me and yet does.

It's irritating how good-looking the man is. How his black glasses only make him more handsome. He approaches with one bag slung over his shoulder and two rolling suitcases behind him.

That's a lot of luggage.

My stomach flips over as realization dawns. He's not traveling alone. Shit. Are Jen and Ollie traveling with him? Is she *with* him?

Jealousy burns up my throat, hot and acidic, making it impossible to focus on what any of the people around me are saying. Ollie is chattering, and Noah is watching me as he steps into the confined space, his brow furrowed, like I'm a scared animal at risk of snapping at them.

"I, um—" I point into the hall. "Forgot—" I bolt out of the confined space, away from Noah's family, and rush toward my door.

"It's fine. We'll hold it," Ollie singsongs.

"No need," I squeal over my shoulder, fumbling for my keys.

The door next to mine swings open, and voices echo through the hall. When I recognize one, I squeeze my eyes shut and take a steadying breath. Before I can compose myself enough to get the key into the lock, that voice calls my name, killing any chance I had at escaping.

"You haven't left yet? Yay!" Hannah says. "We can ride together."

I fight back a wince. It's way too early for her level of energy.

"That's where you're going, right?" she asks. Like everyone else I've encountered this morning, she gives me a confused look. Clearly, I'm not hiding how out of sorts I am. "Team plane?"

I open my mouth, then snap it shut again. It's better than slamming my forehead against the door in defeat. With another steadying breath, I straighten my spine and nod. "Yup. Thought I forgot something, but I was wrong." I lift the bag clutched in one hand as proof. "So I'm good to go."

She beams at me. "Thank god. Brooks has forbidden Sara from

traveling with the baby yet, and Lex is busy organizing a charity event. And Millie texted to say she's too nauseas to fly. I was nervous I'd be alone, but I love how I can always rely on one of my girls."

Her words soothe me. *My girls.* Lennox, Sara, Millie, and Liv are my people, yes, but they're married to my brothers, so they have to be nice to me. Other than Cat, I've had very few friends in my life who weren't somehow obligated or didn't have ulterior motives.

"Baby Hall, you got the other Baby Hall and the luggage?" she calls as Daniel steps out with Mav strapped to his chest. The man rolls two suitcases out, one topped with a duffel and the other a diaper bag, bumping the doorframe as he goes.

"Does he need help?" I mumble.

She shakes her head. "He likes doing this kind of stuff for me. I used to fight it, but it's pointless, so I let him do his thing. He gets so little time with Mav as it is, right, baby?"

He grins at her with stars in his deep brown eyes. "You know it, dream girl."

"C'mon." Hannah herds me toward the elevator, where three sets of eyes are fixed on us. "Hi, Jen. Hey, Ollie," Hannah chirps, her loud voice bouncing off the metal walls. "Are you excited for our week away?"

Jen gives Hannah a polite but reserved nod. If she were with Noah, she'd be more friendly with his sister, right?

And still I knew you were the only one for me. And if I couldn't have you, then I didn't want anyone else.

It's a lie. The man is good at them. He had me fooled. Had me forgetting that his son was born *after* our weekend together.

Daniel shoves his way in, dragging his luggage, causing the rest of us to step back and to the sides. Jen grabs Ollie's shoulders and pulls him to the back left corner, and Noah goes to the right. I take a step toward the front right corner, near the panel, but I stumble back when Daniel wheels the suitcase in that direction, almost taking out my toe.

I'm still off balance when a big hand clutches my hip and pulls me back into a broad, warm chest.

In the chaos of the moment, all eyes are on Daniel, but my skin prickles at the notion that any of them could see. Okay, that's a lie. My traitorous skin tingles because *he's* touching me. His hold is gentle, the squeeze he gives me soft as he brings his mouth to my ear. "Still like to be touched in a room full of people, I see."

Knees wobbling, I suck in a surprised breath and scan the small space.

"And I still love touching you." His words are a kiss against my ear. *"Only you."*

Blessedly, the elevator dings, signaling that we've reached our destination and breaking the spell he cast on me. Noah keeps one hand pressed gently to my side, and when he confirms that I'm steady, he sidesteps me, tossing a wink over his shoulder, and outstretches his arm to hold the doors open so our group can exit. Out on the street in front of the building, I try not to stare as Ollie hugs Jen. Or as she gives the rest of the group a friendly nod and walks away.

There's no long goodbye to Noah. No kiss. No words at all.

Relief and excitement hit me, one after another. Maybe she's not someone important, after all.

The moment the thought appears, I scold myself. Because it doesn't matter. Because I shouldn't care.

If only I could stop.

CHAPTER 32
NOAH

OLLIE'S never been on a private jet before, so, as is to be expected, he's got a lot to say about the team plane. "I thought it would be bigger," he muses as we stand side by side on the tarmac.

Hannah arranged for a car service to pick us up since both kids are traveling with us, along with all the luggage they require.

I don't know how my sister did it, but she convinced Sienna to send her driver home and ride with us. It's the logical choice, of course, but my girl is stubborn, and she's clearly doing everything she can to avoid me. Even in the car, she chose the seat farthest from me and sat in silence the whole way.

Now, though, she pauses on Ollie's other side and looks up at the plane too, like she's seeing it for the first time. "I can't wait to tell my brother you said that."

Hannah giggles. "Beckett will cry."

"But then he'll want to get a new plane. And if so, maybe we can convince him to get one with a hot tub." Daniel crouches down and holds out a fist for Ollie to bump. "Make sure you tell Gavin your thoughts on the plane size. Your uncle wants a new ride."

Ollie shakes his head. "You guys are so weird. Who'd want to take a bath on a plane?"

The girls are already walking away, both laughing.

"Wait," my son continues. He hasn't stopped yammering since Jen brought him over this morning. He's excited. "We have to walk up stairs? Where's the long tunnel?"

I've always done my best to give Ollie honest answers, but damn does it get hard when he asks so many questions. "Let me grab our bags, and then I'll explain."

I'm tempted to catch up to the girls so I can maneuver my way into sitting near Sienna, but the luggage slows me down, and I'd rather not garner the attention of the guys or any of the coaching staff by running after her with Ollie in tow.

So I choose to take my time, trusting that fate will step in. Just like it did this morning when I discovered her in the elevator with Jen.

I only had a moment to celebrate before I noticed the apprehension in her eyes. By the way she was covertly studying Jen, I knew she'd run. Sienna's good at that.

I'll admit that her inclination to distrust me isn't completely unwarranted. Two nights ago, I told her I hadn't been with anyone since her. Yet my son, as well as his mother, who was standing mere feet from her, gave her reason to believe otherwise. Until she hears the full story from me, she'll wonder. I'd happily tell her the truth. It's just hard when she won't talk to me.

I answer every question my little guy throws at me as we ascend the metal stairs and step onto the plane. Everyone we pass gives him a fist bump or waves, calling his name left and right. He's beaming as we shuffle our way toward where I usually sit with the guys.

Every time he looks up at me with that grin, like this is the best day ever, my heart clenches. I miss him terribly when I'm traveling, so spending an entire week with him is an incredible gift.

As we pass the area where the coaches usually sit, Gavin lights up. "Ollie! We're so excited you're coming with us. Though my sister says you thought the plane would be bigger."

Beside him, Sienna is already settled in. Two cups of coffee sit on the table in front of them, along with a leather zip-up folder, and the seats across from them are empty.

Ollie nods, his movements exaggerated. "Yes, sir. My mom always says that with all the money Dad makes, he should have a bigger place. So maybe rich people just like small things."

Gavin throws his head back and laughs.

With a groan, I slap a hand over my face. Fucking Jen.

Still chuckling, Gavin points across the table. "Sit up here with us. The seats are a little bigger."

Sienna hisses a breath, though she tries to cover it up by turning away.

I have to bite back a smile. Yeah, I knew fate would do me a solid.

Meanwhile, Ollie looks around. "There are a lot of big guys on the plane. Maybe you should put them here and we should go back there."

Sienna snorts and elbows her brother. "I think he just called you small."

With a fake glower, Gavin puffs up. "I may not be as big as Brooks and Aiden, but I'm six-one and two hundred pounds of muscle." Then, with a glance at Ollie, he leans closer to his sister and mouths, "Oh, and I'm married to a twenty-seven-year-old."

Sienna sticks out her tongue and angles away from him. "Ugh, don't remind me."

The two continue teasing each other as Ollie sits and I dig out his iPad and a couple of books. With any luck, they'll distract him from butting into conversations for the next couple of hours.

Gavin may have found my son's observations humorous, but they can be scalding at times. Jen and I have always encouraged his curiosity and critical thinking, but there are times when I wish I knew how to explain that he doesn't need to share every thought that passes through his mind.

Sienna stares at her phone, pretending to be occupied while Ollie gets situated. Only when Ezra wanders over after the attendants have taken our drink orders does she look up from the device.

"Have you seen the winger from the University of Michigan?" he asks Gavin as he rests a hand on the back of his seat for balance.

"Huey Davis?" Coach muses.

Ezra smiles. "That's the one. He's got one hell of a dangle."

"Can't forget the flow either," I chime in.

The kid is incredible on the ice, but his hair has made him famous.

It's wild how often SportsCenter plays clips of him walking out of a game shaking his damn head.

Gavin chuckles, but Ezra's not listening. He's too focused on Sienna. "What do you think about his dangle?"

She grasps her right wrist and rubs her thumb over the inside of it, staring Ezra down. She doesn't cower. I'll give her that. "I'm unfamiliar with that term."

The GM's smarmy smile makes my hackles rise, so I jump in to play down her response. "That's understandable. I doubt any of us could tell the difference between shantung and silk. We've all got our strengths."

The moment Ezra chuckles and says, "Yeah, I definitely know nothing about fashion, so it's in my best interest to stay out of the industry altogether," my gut plummets, and I know I've fucked up.

Sienna offers a fake-ass smile. "Then I guess it's a good thing no one has *asked* you to, then. Now," she says, straightening in her seat, "if you'll excuse me, I've got to use the bathroom."

Fuck.

Ezra gives us a halfhearted wave, then shuffles back to his seat.

Across from me, Gavin puts a hand on his sister's forearm and lowers his head. "Just stick to the plan."

She stands and crosses her arms, silently waiting for him to move out of her way.

I should go after her. Apologize. Fix this. Tell her the truth about Ollie.

But a plane full of our coworkers and peers is not the place.

Then again…I take in my son, who's enraptured by the video game he's playing, headphones on, then study Gavin.

As if he can sense that I'm itching to get up, he nods. "You can walk around. I've got him."

I'm not sure he'd be so keen to offer his help if he knew that my goal was to seek out his sister.

Rather than allow the guilt to settle in my stomach, I stand and dip my chin, then stride for the back of the plane.

Halfway there, Aiden catches sight of me and lights up. "Miss us?"

I roll my eyes. "Yup. Couldn't go five minutes without you."

Brooks opens one eye. "Shh, sleepy time."

I mimic zipping my lips and walk away, happy to be given an out to go wait for Sienna. Once again, not only is the universe helping me, but her own damn brothers are too.

The guys have all settled in, most sleeping or watching a movie, noise-canceling headphones in place. With as little downtime as we get, players tend to use flights like this to recharge. Whereas the people up front, the coaches and managers and owners, use the time for business, going over lines, discussing trades, and in some cases, show-boating.

Fuck, it guts me that I helped Ezra do just that.

The door to the bathroom swings open, and I use Sienna's momentary surprise to my advantage and grasp her elbow, pulling her to the back galley and out of sight.

"What the hell are you doing?" she hisses.

I place my hand over my lips to quiet her.

Her eyes go murderous. "You going to try to kiss me again? Get my panties wet?" She scoffs. "I'm not interested. In case you couldn't tell out there"—she flings an arm out—"I'm fighting for my job, and I'm failing at it. The last thing I need is for word to get out that I've slept with a player."

"I just want to talk," I urge. "I want to explain my history with Jen."

She huffs, and I swear steam comes out of her ears. "I don't care."

She's so freaking gorgeous, even when she's pissed off and pushing me away.

But I can't get lost in our chemistry. Not now. Not when I have important things to say.

"You do care," I snap back. "And it's important to me that you know the truth." I suck in a breath, waiting for her to shut me down. I'm shocked as shit when she remains silent, scrutinizing my face, but I gather my wits quickly and get on with it. "I met her before I met you. She was pregnant before I met you. *That's* why I was on that trip. Hannah sent me because I was freaking out over the idea of becoming a father. Because she wanted me to have a few days of peace before my life got turned upside down."

Her eyes widen and dart around the galley, like she's piecing it all together.

My chest tightens. Fuck. Is it possible I'm actually getting through to her?

Maybe not, but I take a risk and step closer anyway, cupping her cheek. Then, voice low, I give her the complete truth. "Jen and I were never in a relationship. I never felt for her what I feel for you. I've never felt for *anyone* what I feel for you." I brush my thumb over her beauty mark, wishing I could press my lips to it instead. "And I *haven't* been with anyone since you. You have *nothing* to be insecure or jealous about."

Sienna blinks at me, her expression unreadable. Dammit, I wish I knew what she was thinking. But for now, I take solace in the ability to touch her. She hasn't backed up, and she hasn't swatted my hand away. That has to mean something, right?

"I'm not jealous. I'm—" She blows out a breath, her body going stiff. She takes a step back, as if she's only now noticed my hand on her face.

Her jaw hardens and her glare returns, suddenly making it clear what she's thinking. She's pissed. Definitely at me and maybe at herself for allowing me to get so close.

"My entire life fell apart last year," she says. "I'm clawing my way back from a depression that I hope you never understand. I lost every-thing." Her voice warbles on the last word, but she pulls her shoulders back and continues. "My company, my designs, my ability to do the *one* thing I'm good at. Now, I'm finally feeling a little like myself again."

I reach for her hand. "I'm sorry. I had no idea."

She pulls her hand back and holds it up, keeping me in place. "We can't keep doing this. You're going to blow up both our lives." The pain in her voice, the desperation, guts me. I had no idea how difficult her life was while we were apart, and the thought of her suffering makes my chest tighten uncomfortably. So when she storms past me, I let her go.

Chapter 33
Sienna

MY PHONE CHIMES AGAIN, and a screenshot pops up. I tap on it and scan the details, eyes narrowed and assessing. The image includes several designs by artists I know well.

In fact, an email from the group of them never would have made it anywhere near Catherine Bouvier's inbox if not for the pretty settlement fund that has bankrolled their careers.

The lines are all wrong. The fabric is cheap, and the general design is shoddy. Unoriginal too. Each piece is a rip-off of items in a collection I started three years ago and scrapped.

I roll my eyes. As if taking my money wasn't enough, they took my designs and didn't even do them justice.

> Me: Can't. I'm traveling with the team. Can you do next Wednesday?

Cat: Yes! Let's go to Allure.

> Me: Stop trying to get me to go to your family's sex club. It's weird.

Cat: 😏

Cat: We can sit at the bar. I'm not asking you to play.

I roll my eyes. Why is everything that comes out of this woman's mouth laced with innuendo?

> Me: I'll keep you posted.

Cat: Please do, because there's a position I'd love to discuss with you.

> Me: I've got a job.

Cat: That's not where I was going with this…

I snort. *See, everything sounds sexual.*

Cat: I'm talking about a career.

My heart twists. A career. I had one of those. And I loved it. What I'm doing now? It's a job.

She means well. I know she hates that I've lost everything just as much as I do, but I wish she'd leave it alone. Keeping myself convinced that the designing part of my life is over is hard enough without having to constantly reassure everyone else.

My phone buzzes in my hand, and when Hannah's name appears on the notification banner, I breathe out a sigh of relief. This is the perfect excuse to ignore Cat's last message.

"Hey, I'm almost ready. Want me to meet you at your room?" I snag my purse from the bed and give myself one last look in the hotel mirror. Though I'm wearing Bolts blue, I learned my lesson this week and left the jersey at home.

In answer, a baby cries. "About that," Hannah says. "Mav is running a fever."

I wince. "Oh my gosh. How can I help?" I have almost no experience with babies, but I'd be an asshole if I didn't offer.

"Actually," she hedges. "I need a favor."

"Anything." I tap the speaker button and navigate to my Notes app so I can jot down a list of what she needs. Surely there's a pharmacy nearby.

"Can you bring Ollie to the game?" she asks as Mav's cries get louder. "Shh," she soothes him. "I hate to burden you—"

"It's not a burden at all," I say quickly.

I really don't mind bringing the little guy, and he's certainly easier to deal with than a baby. Though I'm not sure Noah will be keen on leaving his son in my care. Not after our less-than-cordial conversation on the plane.

And what if he's the overprotective type? I could see that. He probably doesn't leave his child with anyone who doesn't have babysitting certifications and Red Cross training.

Nose scrunched, I lock my phone. "Are you sure Noah would be okay with it?"

"Already texted him. He said he's okay with it as long as you don't mind. I just sent you his contact info. Text him so he has your number." A rustling sound dampens her voice for a moment, but then she's back at full volume. "I'll have Ollie ready in five. Sound good?"

My screen lights up, and when I tap on Noah Harrison's contact card, apprehension rises inside me. Texting him means he'll have my number.

But I offered to watch Ollie, and this is part of the gig. Obviously his father will need a means of contacting me. After tonight, I'll delete his number and tell him to do the same. Then forget I ever had it in the first place.

Absolutely harmless.

Right. Like anything involving Noah Harrison is harmless.

> Me: Hi, this is Sienna Langfield.

I reread the message a dozen times, second-guessing myself. It's professional enough, right? Not flirty. Not awkward.

Instead of hitting Send, I read it again. And again until the words jumble together.

I shake my head to clear my vision. This is absurd. I hit Send and then type out another message.

> Me: Hannah asked me to take Ollie to the game. If you're okay with that, I'll head over and pick him up now. Is there anything I need to watch out for? Allergies? Foods we should avoid?

I stew over that message as well, pondering whether I should include something else. Something that proves I'm a responsible adult willing to do him a favor and not a woman trying to get into his pants.

Because I'm not. *Trying*, that is.

Been there, done that, obviously, but not going there again.

With a huff, I hit the little blue arrow, and when the whooshing sound signals that the message has been sent, I sit on the edge of the bed, staring at the screen, waiting for a response.

The message shows it's been delivered, but I get nothing in return. Not even those three dancing bubbles.

I need to confirm that he's okay with this, but I really don't want to call him. Texting is one thing, but calling is a step too far. And I've already taken too many of those. Every time I'm around the man, I do stupid things. Like strip. Or orgasm.

I can't do either of those with him. Not anymore.

Knee bouncing, I wait. I'll give him a few more minutes, at least.

Just as I'm typing up another text, my phone vibrates and lights up, an unsaved number flashing on the screen.

My heart thumps heavily. Of course he'd call rather than text. I consider not answering, but I'm determined to keep this professional, so I do what a boss who doesn't know what it feels like to be touched by him would do and answer the phone.

"Hello, this is Sienna Langfield."

The moment the words come out of my mouth, I cringe. God, I'm ridiculous.

Noah's breathy laugh in response only highlights that. "And this is Noah Harrison. You know, the guy who—"

"I know who you are," I snap.

Deep voices chatter in the background, meaning he's probably in the locker room, and the last thing I need is for my brothers to question why he's calling me.

"I was just going to say the guy whose kid you're bringing to the game tonight." He sighs, his breath making the line between us crackle. "But only if you're really okay with it."

I brush at a speck of lint on my pants, needing something to do with my hands. "Yeah, of course. Is there, uh, anything I need to know?"

"No. Though I will apologize in advance for anything he says that may hurt your feelings." Noah's voice goes up an octave like he's sincerely concerned that it'll happen.

"I've got tough skin," I say with a wave of my hand. "Besides, his comment about the plane was spot-on. Can't be mad when a person points out the obvious."

Noah chuckles. "Tell that to his first-grade teacher." His tone is low, laced with both exasperation and humor. "She was less than impressed when he told her that halitosis is nothing to be ashamed of, but that she should treat it so the people around her don't have to suffer alongside her."

A laugh bubbles out of me. I slap my hand to my mouth to stifle it, then pull it back an inch and exhale into it, testing my breath. "I'll be prepared."

"Good. And seriously," he says, "thanks for this. I know this isn't in your job description, but Ollie and I don't get to spend nearly as much time together as I'd like, and he never gets to travel with me like this, so this trip is special."

Warmth blooms in my chest. "I really don't mind at all. Besides, without Hannah, I need a buddy who can explain what's happening on the ice. I assume Ollie can handle that?"

He hums. "He knows just as much as Hannah, I promise. After the game, bring him down to the locker room. He can hang with me so you don't get stuck waiting while we shower and do post-game interviews."

"I'll, uh, I'll text you," I stammer. It's a dangerous offer, because now that we've opened this line of communication, it brings the two of us a little farther into one another's orbit. But it's preferable to walking into the locker room and potentially getting an eyeful of naked asses. Especially the asses belonging to my brothers.

I shudder. My brothers have no shame. Except Brooks, though Sara makes up for it tenfold. My other sisters-in-law aren't much better either. Hence the knowledge I didn't want to possess regarding who's pierced and who has tattoos and Lennox's passion for riding said piercings.

Noah sighs into the phone. "Thanks, Sienna."

"Have a good game."

Once I've ended the call, I sit in the silence, replaying the conversation. The sound of his voice soothes me in a way I want to despise. The easy laughter lights me up.

A smile tugs at my lips without my permission. Then my fingers join in, tracing the expanse of it. Despite all the emotions that man conjures, I can't deny that the predominant one is always joy.

There isn't another soul on this earth who's ever left me feeling this way. And regardless of how much I fight it, I don't think that will ever change.

As we head into the arena, Ollie walks by my side, head held high, smile on his face, decked out in Boston Bolts blue, with his dad's name and number on his back.

He hasn't stopped talking since I picked him up. He was ready and eagerly waiting when I showed up, clearly psyched for a break from Mav's tears.

"That kid has some lungs on him," he muttered as Hannah shut the door behind us.

"Do you want to stop and grab a snack on the way in or wait until we get into the suite?"

Ollie shakes his head. "Nah, I want to get a good seat."

My chest tightens with affection. The admiration he has for his dad is adorable. "Do you want to go down to the ice and watch them warm up?"

He comes to a screeching halt, his eyes wide. "Really?"

My brothers' kids all love it, but this level of excitement is unexpected. "Sure, come on."

It takes some time to find the visitor bench, but when I do, I wave at Gavin, and he motions the security guards to let us in.

"Holy crap," Ollie says, scanning the stands. "This is so cool."

As we step up to the boards, Aiden breaks into song. I've heard all about the lyrics he makes up to get the team pumped up, but I've never seen him in action like this. Even the video of his on-ice performance when he proposed to Lennox wasn't this exciting.

He's on the ice, stick in hand, while the rest of the team stretches around him, when he launches into his version of Sabrina Carpenter's "Espresso."

"Now they're thinkin' 'bout us every game, oh
Isn't that a goal? You know so
Say they can't win, baby, we know
You're playing the Boston Bolts, though
Beauty goes up, War goes down, oh,
Slides into the goal, whoa,
Say they can't win, baby, we know,
You're playing the Boston Bolts, though."

War spots us and hops to his feet, interrupting Aiden before he can start the next verse. Then the rest of the guys follow.

"Ollie, baby!" War roars as he glides toward us.

The little boy at my side grins. "Who you calling baby?"

As the guys approach one by one in their skates and pads, I feel tiny.

Even in uniform, Noah is easy to pick out. As he skates up, he pulls off his helmet and grins at his son the same way the little guy just grinned at me. "You being good for Sienna?"

His gaze flicks to mine, the grin turning slightly lazy, and my lungs stop working. His blue eyes are breathtaking. Soul-crushing. They're lit up with genuine excitement, and when they bounce from Ollie to me and hold, the entire arena vanishes, and it's just the two of us. The pounding of my heart in my ears is the only sound. Those damn blue irises are my sole focus.

"She just picked me up. How bad could I have been?"

Ollie's one-liner and the responding howls of laughter break the spell.

"Your kid's the coolest." Aiden whacks Gavin in the chest with a gloved hand. "Let's make sure your son ends up just like him, okay?"

My heart stutters as I look from a smiling Aiden to a grimacing Gavin. "It's a boy?"

Aiden winces. "Shit."

"That's a bad word," Ollie chides.

Gavin sighs. "Millie has a whole reveal planned, keep it between us please?" He eyes me pleadingly.

With a smile, I nod. "Consider it forgotten." Then to Ollie, I add, "This is probably a good time to find our seats." I rest a hand on his shoulder. "Tell your dad good luck."

Noah, attention still fixed on me, licks his lips. "Yeah, thanks for bringing him down." Finally, he looks away, his expression going soft. "Be good," he reminds his son.

Ollie shakes his head. "Guy worries too much."

We're just exiting the visitor's bench when Ezra appears, coming the other way. He's dressed in another bespoke suit, and with the phone he's holding to his ear, I pray he's too distracted to notice me.

But as he looks from me to Ollie and back again, a bright calculation in his eyes, my hope vanishes.

"Nannying now?" He quirks a brow.

The urge to kick him in the shin with the pointy toe of my boot is strong.

Instead, I plaster on a smile, keeping it light for Ollie's sake, if not mine. "Just hanging with my friend Ollie while we cheer on our boys."

With a shrug and a dismissive nod to the little boy, he strides away.

"*Jerk.*"

Gasping, I peer down at my pint-size buddy. He looks back at me without an ounce of remorse in his expression.

I suppose I can't chastise him. If I'd been the one calling him names, I would have chosen one much more offensive.

"Yeah, he really is." I shake my head and temper my frustration with Ezra. "Do you like Boston?" I ask, eager for a change in subject. "Where did you live before?"

"Minnesota. I don't really remember it, though. We moved to Boston when I was four. I'm six now," he says with a proud grin.

Right. Almost two years ago. And it's been well over a year since Brooks and Sara's wedding, when Noah realized who I was.

I survey the ice over my shoulder, cataloging the players. The group of them is close. As Noah skates over to Brooks and the two of them eye Aiden and laugh, then go back to chatting, I see his confession in a new light.

If he'd approached me that night, he would have risked destroying the lifelong friendship he and Brooks share. And maybe his spot on the team in Boston, where his child lives. And for what? The slight chance of rekindling a connection with a woman he hadn't seen in more than four years? A woman he'd only spent days with?

My chest tightens, making it hard to breathe, but I force the cold air into my lungs, then let it out slowly and look down at Ollie. "Do you like Boston?"

He lifts his shoulders and lets them fall. "Sure."

"And when your dad is traveling, you live with your mom?"

Maybe I'm prying, but I'm genuinely interested in getting to know this boy. He's smart and funny and so damn clever.

"And my baby sister and Ted. He's failing at life, but he's a good guy."

I shouldn't be shocked by his candor anymore, yet a surprised laugh bursts out of me. "What?"

He rolls his eyes. "The guy can't even walk in a straight line. He trips over everything. I think it's because he's so distracted by how pretty my mom is."

I smile warmly at him. "That's adorable."

He scrutinizes me with a shrewdness no six-year-old should possess. "Kind of like how my dad was with you yesterday."

Cheeks heating, I shake my head. "Oh, your dad and I—"

"I know. He told me you're just friends." He sighs. "I've got lots of friends who are girls. But only one that makes my heart go *thump-thump-thump*." He pounds his chest in time with his words. "Has that ever happened to you?"

This child is so transparent, so frank, that it feels wrong to lie. "Yes. Just once."

He sighs, his body deflating. "I don't think I like it. I get all tongue-tied, and I'm never tongue-tied."

Amusement and affection for this boy bubble up inside me. "I get that too."

"Oh man, I was hoping I would grow out of it."

Same, I want to tell him. I hoped I'd one day outgrow this infatuation with his father, yet here I am. And I have a feeling this is just the beginning.

Ollie isn't quite as versed as Addie, though he still knows far more about hockey than I do. We eat nachos, then order ice cream sundaes, all while keeping our noses glued to the glass. He tells me all his favorite parts about attending games and how, when he's at home, he begs his mom to let him stay up until they're over. Sometimes he falls asleep in the middle, but Ted is great about showing him highlights in the morning.

From what I can tell, the three adults are incredible at the co-parenting thing. Though after Ollie explains his weekly schedule, I can't help but wonder how hard it is for Noah when the two of them aren't together.

Heading into the third period, the score is still 0-0, and I'm getting antsy.

What happens if neither team scores at the end of the game?

I should ask Ollie, but he's just as keyed up as I am, and he's totally locked into the action below us.

Maybe they go into overtime. Or do they end with a tie?

When War gets a hold of the puck and rushes toward the opposite end of the ice, I start to think I won't have to ask. Aiden and Noah dart that way too, their skates digging deep as they go.

My heart pounds in my ears and my muscles all tense up as they close in on the net.

A Florida defenseman catches up to War, but before he can get too close, War passes the puck to Aiden.

My brother is like a ballerina out there. His movements are fluid and beautiful. His stick work—I think that's the right term—is incredible. He slaps the puck back and forth, making it hard to follow.

I think that's a good thing, because if I can't tell where it is, then maybe the defenseman who's on him now can't either. Before the D-man and his counterpart can flank him, he slaps the puck to Noah, who I've only now realized has fallen back.

Noah hauls his stick back and brings it forward with enough force to send the puck across the ice and past the goalie's left shoulder.

When it hits the back of the net and the light on top illuminates, the crowd goes wild. Ollie and I join in. Even the fans dressed in Orlando's colors wear looks of awe as a replay appears on the Jumbotron. I can't blame them. It'd be hard not to be impressed by that shot. He was practically at center ice.

"Yeah, Dad, yeah!" Ollie screams. "He's a sniper, did you know that?"

I didn't, and I don't know what the term means, but I'll wait and ask once his excitement has worn off.

Below, Noah circles the rink, looking up at the suite where we're sitting. Then he flattens his hand over his heart.

Ollie goes even more berserk, bouncing around and mimicking the motion. "Dad does that for me every time."

Noah's slowed now, still focused on us, with his stick tucked beneath an arm now and his thumbs linked together. He splays his fingers out and flaps his hands twice.

"What's that?" I ask.

Ollie frowns, his head tilted to one side. "It's the sign for a butterfly, but I don't know why he did it."

"You know sign language?"

Suddenly, that *thump-thump-thump* feeling Ollie mentioned earlier overtakes me. Play resumes quickly, yet I'm fixated on the butterfly sign Noah made after scoring the first goal of the game.

"Yup," Ollie chirps. "Dad uses sign language during games so we can chat when I'm in the stands."

My heart pummels my rib cage, making it hard to hear even the fans in the stands. But I ask, "How do you sign great job?"

He shows me, and after the puck has dropped, I practice it. Though my fingers itch to form the butterfly sign, my brain wars with itself, half certain Noah meant that as a message to me and half certain I've lost my mind.

The Bolts win 1-0, and as we leave the suite, I text Noah like promised. When we get down to the locker room, he's waiting for us in the hall outside it, still in his hockey gear.

He's a sweaty mess, but god, is he gorgeous. All chiseled cheekbones, blue eyes, messy hair, and muscles.

"Did you have fun?" He drops to his knees and reaches for his little boy.

Ollie grins. "So much."

Noah smiles up at me, his expression softening.

I can't help but return the gesture. "We really had a blast."

"Yup." Ollie bounces in a circle, his eyes bright and his face flushed with happiness. "We talked about how Ted fails at life, and how Sienna and I both get the *thump-thump-thumps* when we like someone."

Noah's lips lift into a smirk and his eyes dance as he stands.

My cheeks burn, and as he watches me, that damn *thump-thump-thump* returns.

"Oh." Ollie comes to an abrupt stop. "And I taught her sign language."

The smirk on Noah's face morphs into a full-on grin. "Did you now?"

"Yup. She knows butterfly and great job. Which is what you did tonight. You were the best." He throws his arms around his dad's legs in the most adorable show of affection.

"Thanks, bud." He pats his son's back. "C'mon. I need a shower, then we gotta head back to the hotel and get you into bed."

I take half a step forward. "You sure you don't want me to stick around and wait with him?" It would be silly to leave Noah to wrangle the little guy while he's trying to get cleaned up.

He smiles down at his bright-eyed boy. "Nah, we'll be good. Thank you again."

A disappointment I absolutely shouldn't feel presses down on my shoulders. "Of course."

I pull out my phone to text the car service Gavin insisted on, but before I can walk away, Ollie calls out to me. "What are you doing tomorrow?"

"Um..." I want to lie. I want to pretend I won't spend the day alone, the way I spend most of my days off. But once again, his earnestness has me admitting the truth. "Nothing, actually. I thought I'd sit by the pool. Maybe read."

"You should come fishing with us." He tips his head back. "Can she, Dad?"

A slow smile creeps over Noah's face. "Yeah. If she wants to."

Well, shit. My heart does that thumping thing again, making it impossible to deny the two of them. "Yeah, I guess I could do that."

Both of their faces light up. "Great." Noah's smile turns a tiny bit wicked. "I'll text you."

As I walk away, my mind races. Because, dammit, things are about to get sticky.

CHAPTER 34
NOAH

Aiden: Who's coming to Disney?

Brooks: I'm thinking no.

Daniel: Mav still isn't feeling great, so we're a no.

Snow: Could I convince you to go to the pool bar instead?

Brooks: You can convince me, but I'll be napping at it.

Snow: Boring.

Brooks: One-month-old at home. I'm stockpiling sleep.

Snow: Pretty sure that's not a thing.

Brooks: It's worth a shot.

Aiden: War?

War: My kids would lose their minds if I went without them.

Aiden: I'm going to lose my mind. Someone needs to come to mother-ducking Disney with me. Harry? Bet Ollie will want to go!

Me: Sorry, dude. We're going fishing.

War: Oh, snap. Can I come with you and the big man?

Brooks: I could fish.

Snow: If we bring a cooler, I'm down.

SHIT.

I pace the lobby while Ollie keeps his eye on the elevator. Sienna should be down any minute.

If I ignore the group chat, I can pretend I didn't see their messages until too late.

I'm not sure who is more excited for today, Ollie or me.

Probably me, but my kid isn't playing it cool at all. He had a great time with Sienna last night, and he's chomping at the bit to teach her how to fish.

Or maybe he understands that his old man has no game and he's doing me a solid by being my wingman.

I could use the help, so I'm not complaining. Putting Sienna at ease rather than pissing her off has been my top priority since she came back into my life. Convincing her to spend time with me is a nice little bonus. She and my son hitting it off so easily? It's more than I could have asked for.

As much as I hate that Mav is still feeling bad, I'm thrilled about the turn of events. He's wingmaning me, too, and doesn't even know it. Without him, I wouldn't have even had the opportunity to ask Sienna to come with us.

I've been racking my brain for ways to get through to her, and I think yesterday was a step in the right direction.

When the elevator opens, Ollie and I whip around.

At the sight of her, I almost stagger back a step. Her jean shorts are distressed, with several holes in strategic places, and her red halter top cups her breasts in a painstakingly perfect way.

Though I want to ravage her, I remind myself that my son is with us and force my attention to her effervescent green eyes and dazzling smile.

Ollie has far less chill. He darts for her, yelling, "You look pretty!"

I can't help but chuckle, and a few people nearby join in.

"Doesn't she, Dad?" He tips his head up and loudly whispers, "Bet his heart is doing the *thump-thump-thump*."

I press my lips together. Little traitor. But he isn't wrong.

"Thank you." She gives my son a smile so bright I swear it cracks my heart in two. "Is this outfit okay for fishing? I've never gone."

He bobs his head. "Yeah, no special outfit, right, Dad?"

I take two large steps, stopping a little closer than necessary. "You're perfect," I say, my voice thick.

She sinks her teeth into her lower lip, assessing me, clearly getting the double meaning.

Ollie prattles on for the thirty minutes it takes to get to the pier. Fortunately, Sienna is a master at steering the conversation back on track when he goes off on a tangent. Only when we've got our rented poles and are out on the pier does the kid take a breath.

Sienna has gone completely silent, grimacing at the live shrimp we brought for bait.

I show Ollie how to cast, and while he dances around, his pole bouncing so violently I can't imagine any fish will get near the shrimp, I step up behind Sienna and bring my mouth to her ear. "Can I help you?"

She stiffens. "I, um…am not sure fishing is the hobby for me."

Chuckling, I reach around her, pressing my front to her back, and pluck a shrimp from the container. "That's okay, butterfly. I've got you."

As I add it to her hook, she lets out a shuddering breath.

When the bait is in place, she steps away and brings the pole back, then casts forward.

Nothing happens. For a moment, she stares out at the water.

"Dad," Ollie chides. "You didn't tell her to lift the bail."

I take the blame with a smile. "Oh, right. Silly me."

Cheeks pink, she turns and thrusts the pole at me. "Fine. Show me."

With a shake of my head, I set my pole down and crowd her space. I put my hands over hers. Then, from over her shoulder, I guide her through the steps.

"Lean back into me," I instruct. "Flick this wrist and then release."

When the lure goes flying and it hits the water with a plop, she squeals and does a little dance, her ass brushing against my dick. "Now what?"

I groan in her ear and tighten my arms around her to keep her from moving. "Now we wait."

When I step away and pick up my pole, she peers over her shoulder, her lip stuck out. "Really? Wish I had known that earlier. I'm not very patient."

Laughing, I cast my own line. Looks like she'll get a lesson in patience today. Because for the next couple of hours, all we'll do is wait.

If that isn't irony, I don't know what is.

I've become an expert at waiting, and if I have to continue waiting for Sienna, then at least I can do it with her by my side.

Waiting is my only option, because I'll never move on. She's it for me.

Now if only she'd believe it.

"You know what happened at school this week?" Ollie asks.

I don't have a clue, which is surprising. For as much as he talks, I was certain he'd replayed every moment of the time we were apart already. "What?"

He shakes his head, like the story he's about to tell me is unbelievable. "At recess. At *recess*." He smacks his head, getting himself all worked up.

Amusement floods me. Fuck, I love this kid. "What happened at recess?"

"Jack kissed a girl." He peers up at me, practically bug-eyed, like he's waiting for me to be affronted right along with him.

Sienna takes the bait. "On the lips?"

He whips his head back, his face screwed up. "No. *Ew*."

I laugh. "So on the cheek?"

"Yeah." He shudders, clearly still grossed out by the idea.

"Did he get her consent?" I hedge.

He tilts his head. "Yeah. He asked her. Actually, I asked her because he wanted to and I wanted to see if he would."

"*Ollie*." I laugh loud enough to scare the fish away. "Seriously?"

"I didn't think he'd actually do it. So weird. We were at *recess*."

With her lip caught between her teeth like she's fighting a smile, Sienna eyes me. Then she ruffles his hair. "Have you kissed the girl you like?"

My breath falters. He likes a girl? This is news to me.

He shakes his head. "Nah. But we're going to hug when I get back."

Sienna gives up the fight and breaks into a grin. "You already planned it?"

"I can't just hug her without asking first, right? So I asked her if I could hug her at recess when we get back."

Sienna's surprised giggle is like a shot of pure joy injected straight into my veins. God, what I would do to hug this girl right now. I don't even need my lips pressed to hers. Just the ability to touch her would be enough. For now.

Her fishing pole jolts, and her giggle turns into a surprised squeal as she backs up.

Just as she lets go, clearly panicked, I snag it, keeping it from clattering to the pier or ending up in the water.

She turns to me, her eyes wide. "What do I do? What do I do?"

I set my pole to the side and step behind her again. "We reel it in."

When the tiny sunfish breaches the water, making her pole bounce lightly, she and Ollie are both ecstatic.

Though as it gets close enough to really look at, she gasps, as if only now realizing the fish was truly snagged by the hook. "Oh no, is the hook hurting it?"

I take the pole from her and kneel to unhook the fish. It flops in my hand as I hold it out to her, but rather than take it, she pulls a face, like I've lost my damn mind.

"It needs water," she urges. "Toss it back."

"Don't you want a picture with it? To prove that you caught a fish?"

With her hands held out in front of her, she steps back. "I am so not touching that thing."

"Fine, a selfie." I dig my phone out of my pocket, then loop my arm over her shoulder. "Come on, Ollie. Hop in the pic."

He bounces over, popping into the frame in front of Sienna. His face is inches from the fish I'm holding, while Sienna's eyes are wide and I'm full-on grinning.

Greatest picture ever.

As I toss the fish back and pick up my pole, Ollie says, "Hey, you got a blue butterfly on your wrist."

I whip around immediately, my gaze focused on where she stands with my son, wrist up, tracing the spot I've noticed her touch several times these last few weeks. "Turquoise, actually."

Ollie grins at her. "My dad has one just like it."

Sienna's spine goes straight and her emerald eyes lock on me, swirling with questions. "Really?"

My little boy, oblivious to the sudden tension in the air, continues, "Yup. He said that he found the most beautiful butterfly a couple of weeks before I was born. But he couldn't keep her." Head tilted, he frowns in concentration. "Wait, what else did you say, Dad?"

I step forward, my heart in my throat. "I said I wanted to remember her magic. I wanted to remember how I felt when I saw her, that I hoped the reminder of her on my skin would make me feel a little less lonely."

"Why do you have a butterfly?" he asks Sienna, the question one of pure innocence.

"The same reason." Her admission is barely a whisper.

"Seriously?" Ollie rears back. "Maybe it was the same butterfly. Maybe I'll see her one day too!"

Without missing a beat, he turns back to his pole and casts the line.

I move to her, like the two of us are tethered, like she's reeling me in. "Tell me what you're thinking."

She wrings her hands and licks her lips, her chest rising and falling with uneven breaths.

"Did you really never date his mother?"

I shake my head. "I haven't dated anyone since you. Hell, I never dated anyone before you."

Sienna nibbles on her lip, and the action goes straight to my dick. "Are you having fun today?"

I smile. That's an easy question. "This is the best date I've ever had."

She huffs lightly and rolls her eyes, but she's smiling. "This isn't a date."

I shrug and take another step closer. "Still the best one."

Her cheeks go pink and her eyes flash with mischief as she leans in close. "Better than when we fooled around while out to dinner?"

Fuck, my heart races at the memory of her in my lap. But the way she looks at me now makes it go absolutely wild.

"Yes, because that wasn't real. I didn't know your name then. And our time was limited. You weren't mine to keep." A shot of anger courses through me at that last part. Because it's still true today. "But you here, with my son? This is the dream I've had every day since you left me in the Bahamas. Having you here with us? That alone makes it the best day ever."

"*Noah.*" My name is a plea on her lips. She's begging me not to push past the boundary she's drawn.

I clear my throat and tamp down on the need to pull her into me, to bury my face in her neck and breathe her in. "I know. We're just friends."

She frowns, suddenly wary, like she's not sure we're even that.

But I refuse to give that up. "I'll take friends over not knowing you."

Her emerald irises darken, luring me in, pulling me into their depths. There, hidden behind fear and hurt, is a flicker of hope that tells me there's a chance that this can be so much more than friendship.

I ignore it. For now. "Okay?"

She nods. "Okay."

When Ollie interrupts us this time, I'm grateful for it. I need a few seconds to breathe.

As I assist him, I feel Sienna's gaze on me. As the day goes on, it continues.

I find myself watching her just as often, trying to catch glimpses of the design she permanently imprinted on her skin.

When we return to the hotel, I'm not ready to say goodbye. Though since I've avoided the group chat all day, I'm slightly concerned they'll all be waiting for me in the lobby.

Fortunately, the coast is clear.

"What are you doing tonight?" Ollie asks Sienna as we take the elevator up to our floor.

Her eyes flit to me, then back to him again. "I'll probably grab dinner at the bar and get to bed early. Spending time in the sun always wears me out."

He nods thoughtfully, though his next comment is utterly off the wall. "You should come with us to meet my grandpas."

I cough to keep from laughing. Damn, this kid is too smooth. He's doing my job for me.

"Your grandpas?" She peeks over at me again. "I thought your dad lived in Boston."

"Oh, these aren't my real grandpas," Ollie explains. "They're just old and they're friends of Dad's."

Sienna snorts. This time I don't fight the laugh. Bert is going to be so pissed when I tell him that Ollie thinks he's old.

"It's Bert and Ernie," I tell her. "They live in the area."

Sienna sucks in a breath. "You still talk to them?"

"You *know* them?" Ollie asks, wonder in his tone.

It would be best to skirt around the truth here. If our past comes out, I don't know how her brothers will take it. Still, I don't believe in lying to my kid.

Apparently, Sienna has similar beliefs. "I met them a long time ago. Briefly," she says.

"We ran into each other on a snorkeling trip," I tell him. "Wasn't planned at all."

Sienna's responding smile is so big the skin around her eyes crinkles. "Personally, I think your dad was following me, but he swears it was a coincidence."

I hum. "A happy coincidence."

"You guys are weird," Ollie mutters. "So," he hedges, peering up at Sienna, "you coming?"

She gives me an uncertain look, like she's worried I won't want her there.

Fuck. How could I not? So I dip my chin once.

Even after that silent exchange, I'm certain she'll turn us down. So I'm shocked when she says yes.

Then again, everything about Sienna tends to shock me.

Chapter 35
Sienna

Aiden: Sienna, what are you doing today? Want to go to Disney?

Aiden: Hello?

Gavin: Maybe she's sleeping.

Aiden: Do you want to go to Disney with me?

Gavin: No.

Brooks: LOL

Beckett: I'd go to Disney with you if I was there. Remember that. I'm the best of your brothers.

Gavin: Ass.

Brooks: You can have the best brother title. I'll take the extra sleep.

Beckett: Sienna, call me. I want to talk to you about designing a dress for Liv for the Josie Gala.

Brooks: War said Josie is psyched. It's a great thing you're doing, brother.

Gavin: Agreed.

Aiden: Do you custom-make suits? I'd definitely rock a pink one to match Lex.

Aiden: Sienna?

Aiden: That's it, I'm going looking for her.

I CLOSE out the text thread and quickly navigate to Aiden's name in my list of contacts. I left without my phone and missed a whole slew of messages. Hopefully Aiden hasn't sent out a search party already.

"Where the hell have you been?" he booms.

I wince. The tone is so unlike my happy-go-lucky brother.

"Sorry, I left my phone in my room."

"That doesn't answer my question."

I don't know how he'll react if I admit that I spent the day with Noah, but since Ollie was with us, I can't lie about it. With as much as he talks, I can't imagine he'll keep that factoid to himself. "Ollie invited me to go fishing, so I spent the day with him."

"And Noah?" he asks, his voice full of confusion.

"I didn't just steal his kid for the day, if that's what you're asking." I huff a breath, going for annoyed when, inside, I'm squirming.

"Are you guys like, friends?"

Friends. That's what we agreed on, but why does the word feel so wrong? "He's my neighbor, and he's a player on the team, and he's Hannah's brother—"

"I'm aware of his many roles, Sienna."

"*Okay.*" I drag out the word.

"It's just weird, I guess."

I cringe, but I tamp down the anxiety his questioning brings. "Why is it weird? His kid asked me to hang out, and I said yes. I say yes to everyone else's kids, so why not him?"

Aiden sighs. "Sure, whatever. What are you doing now?" he asks, blessedly moving on. "Want to come to dinner with Brooks and me? Gavin's going out with Ezra."

My mood sours at the mention of our GM. I really don't like him.

But I push those thoughts aside and focus on the topic at hand. "Oh, I'm, uh, grabbing dinner with Ollie," I stammer.

I don't know why I leave Noah's name out. It's idiotic.

My brother clearly thinks so too. I can envision exactly how his brows jump to his hairline. "Just Ollie?"

"Well, no. And his dad and his…grandpas?" That's what the little guy called them, so I roll with it. Plus, this way, there's no implication that I know the guys.

"You're going to a family dinner with Noah?"

"Ollie," I correct him. "Ollie invited me, and I said yes." Knee bouncing, I exhale loudly. "Sorry, I really have to get ready. Talk to you later?"

"Yeah, okay. Give me a call when you aren't so busy with *Ollie*." He's teasing me now. I'll take it over the suspicion any day.

I laugh, feeling slightly more at ease. "Will do."

Next I message Beckett.

> Me: Does Liv want me to design a dress for her, or is this one of your harebrained schemes to make me feel better?

> Beckett: Liv's been looking for a dress for a month, and she says nothing she tries on is made to fit her curves. It's driving me nuts. The woman seems to think there's something wrong with HER rather than the dresses she's looking at. So no, this isn't a scheme to make you feel better, though if this helps with that, then I really am a genius.

I snort. My oldest brother may be ridiculous most of the time, but he's got a big heart. My initial instinct was to say no, so I'm glad I asked him to clarify. What he's doing for Liv is sweet, and maybe it'll be good to design something again. It's not a violation of the agreement because I won't profit from it.

I worry my lip as I respond and hit Send before I can talk myself out of it.

Me: Okay. Make sure Liv is all right with it, though. If so, I'll have some designs for her to look over when I get back.

Beckett: You're the best.

Me: I know. You're not so bad yourself.

Beckett: We're Langfields. Of course we're the best.

Chuckling, I set my phone on the nightstand. I need to focus on getting ready, but more than that, I need to prepare myself for another few hours with Noah.

I pad into the bathroom and turn on the shower. As I step back, I catch sight of my butterfly tattoo. Standing in the middle of the tile room, I survey it.

Does Noah really have one like it? He must, since Ollie is the one who mentioned it. And I'm dying to see it.

I shouldn't be. I promised myself that I was done seeing any and all parts of that man unless they're visible when he's clothed.

Though there's a voice in the back of my head, one I try my best to ignore, calling me out on my bullshit, insisting that before long, I'll be breaking that pact.

"I never thought we'd actually find you," says the man with a shock of white hair. "But you are just as pretty as I remember. I'm Ernie, by the way. Figure it's been a few years. Though I am pretty unforgettable." With a wink, Ted Danson's lookalike leans in and kisses my cheek.

The man beside him is a little rounder, a little shorter, and bald. But he's got the biggest smile. "And I'm Bert."

I give them an awkward little wave. "I remember."

We were a few minutes early, so while we waited for Bert and Ernie to arrive, Ollie pitched his summer trip idea to Noah. From what I gather, the two of them take a trip after school gets out, and this year, he wants to try horseback riding in Montana.

Bert claps Noah on the shoulder. "Woulda been nice to know we could stop checking dollar bills." He eyes me, his lips kicked up on one side. "Six years we've been looking for you."

The confession knocks the air from my lungs

Before I can recover, Ollie's voice snaps me out of my stupor. "What are you talking about?"

Noah stands, patting his son on the shoulder. "Remember how there are grown-up things we don't always explain? This is one of them."

Ollie scowls. "You said it's rude to talk about secrets and not share them."

Noah nods, his hands on his hips. "You're right, bud. We're sorry." He ruffles the little guy's hair.

He embraces both men, exchanging words I don't catch.

Maybe if I weren't so thrown off by Bert's confession, they'd register.

And by being in the presence of these men all these years later.

Noah fits so well in the world I've just slipped back into, with my brothers and hockey and my new career, but as I watch him interact with Bert and Ernie, I'm hurtled back to another time. A time when Noah was not a threat to my happiness, but the source of it. The two days where my world began and ended with him. A world in which only the two of us existed. That's what made it feel so mystical, almost as if I'd made it up. But I'd forgotten about Bert and Ernie, and if what they are saying is true, that Noah truly looked for me for years, it makes that encounter feel less like a fantasy and more like my true past. And damn, is that doing a number on my heart.

We settle at the round table so I'm flanked by Ollie and Ernie, with Bert on the other side of his friend and Noah almost directly across from me, giving me the perfect angle to study his every reaction.

Unlike the man I met years ago, this one doesn't hide many of his thoughts. He's no longer guarded. He laughs openly and often, and he's affectionate, squeezing Ollie's shoulder, rubbing his head when he cracks a joke or makes a sarcastic comment. And he's kind when he has to correct the little guy when he tells Bert that if he wants to see seventy-five, he should probably reconsider the dessert.

I spend the meal laughing at stories the older men share of the time they've spent with Noah and Ollie over the years and sniffing back tears when I realize just how genuine the affection they all share is.

"You like this new job?" Bert asks as he digs into the berries and whipped cream the server brought out for him. He listened to Ollie and went with the healthier option.

I take a sip of my espresso while I consider how to answer. It's not nearly as good as what the cafés in Paris serve, but it'll do. "Honestly, this isn't what I thought I'd be doing with my life, so transitioning hasn't been all that natural."

Noah frowns, worry radiating from him. I don't know why he's so surprised. He can't honestly think this is what I had planned for my life. Though I suppose that since we've barely spoken since coming back into each other's lives, he knows very little about me.

"What's so unnatural about it?" Ernie asks, his tone and expression earnest, caring.

Every person at the table, including Ollie, looks at me with genuine interest and concern.

As I look from face to face, I find that being honest with them doesn't feel so scary. "I don't know hockey," I admit. I set my cup down and lay my hands flat on the table. "Like, at all."

Noah tilts his head, studying me. "But your brothers have played their entire lives."

I shrug. "And while they did that, I was doodling designs. I didn't think I needed to know any of the terms or how the business was run. I was focused on my own thing." What I don't say is how I hate not being successful at something, that the frustration has only made the transition more difficult. It's better if I stay focused on the job rather than on how I feel.

As if he can hear that thought turning over in my mind, Noah gives me a gentle nod.

"Your brothers knew that when they hired you, didn't they?" Ernie prods.

I hum. "My brothers are great. And they hired me for my business acumen, not my knowledge of the sport. But the GM, Ezra Bardot…" His name leaves a bad taste in my mouth, so I pick up my water and take a small sip. "Ezra," I continue, "doesn't believe I have what it takes to run the organization."

"Ah." Ernie lifts his chin. "So he's a real pri—" He darts a look at Ollie and winces. "He's a jerk."

Ollie nods. "I don't like him."

Noah squeezes his son's shoulder.

"So you need to brush up on your hockey knowledge so you can prove to him you belong," Bert says evenly, like it makes all the sense in the world.

I blow out a breath. "I'm trying. I go to all the games. I'm studying the players' files"—though I've avoided Noah's thus far—"and I'm trying to find ways to use what I know about business to help the organization."

"Noah can help you," Ernie offers.

Ollie nods. "Yeah, Dad can help. He knows hockey better than anyone."

Noah grins down at his son, his eyes shining with pride. "Thanks, bud. I wouldn't go that far, though."

His little guy blinks up at him. "But you'll help her, right, Dad?"

The gorgeous man across the table looks at me, his lips tipped up on one side. "Of course. I can teach Sienna *everything* I know."

CHAPTER 36
NOAH

BEDTIME IS ALWAYS AN EVENT. My kid has so much to say. Tonight, the conversation went on for a solid hour. The topic: how amazing Sienna is.

I listened patiently, but with every new detail he raved about, all I could think was, *Yeah, I feel the same.*

He wants to know if we can spend more time with her, if I think she likes Dungeons and Dragons like us, and *Star Wars*. He hopes she likes to try new recipes like we do and begs me to invite her to come with us to Montana this summer.

Once again, our thoughts are aligned. But I don't want to get my kid's hopes up, so I answer with a vague *We'll see, buddy.*

Knowing my kid loves her only solidifies my plan. I've got to find a way to convince Sienna to give us a real shot. To understand that her last name doesn't scare me. Though I hope it doesn't come to it, if I'm forced to choose between her and her brothers, Sienna wins, hands down. No hesitation. No second-guessing.

As I'm rinsing my toothbrush, my phone lights up on the counter. And when her name appears on the screen, a shot of fucking elation zips through me. For the second time this week, she's reaching out. It's another step in the right direction.

Sienna: Can you come to the door?

Grinning, I type out a quick *yes*. Then I hustle toward the door, and without pausing to check the peephole, I throw it open.

In a pair of white linen pajamas, with her hair up in a high ponytail, she stands at my door, face flushed. At the sight of her, my heart takes off at a gallop. Without fail, when I look into those green eyes of hers, my pulse races. She owns me.

"Did you mean it?" Her voice is quiet, her question direct.

But my brain glitches while I search for a response.

"Mean what?" I mean everything I say, but I want to be clear with her right now.

She takes me in from head to toe. "The butterfly. The reason you have the tattoo."

I step a little closer, keeping the door propped open with one foot. "I probably would have phrased my explanation a little differently if Ollie hadn't been there, but yes, I meant every word."

With her head tipped back, and her green eyes so focused, it feels like she's searching my soul. "How would you have phrased it?"

"I would have told you that I inked the butterfly on my skin so that every time I looked in the mirror, I'd remember the most beautiful woman I'd ever met. A striking, charming person I was lucky enough to share two perfect days with. A woman I didn't want to cage, which meant I had to let her go. I didn't tell you about Ollie then because you had so many big things coming for you. But I never, *not for one single day*, forgot you. I wanted you close. So I got this tattoo to keep you with me."

I press my hand to my chest, over the spot where she's memorialized.

"I got it so I'd remember that I'm not broken. That I know love because of you."

Her eyes sparkle like turquoise waters late in the evening, her hand drifting out in front of her. She flexes it into a fist like she's both eager to touch me and a little afraid. She stares at my chest, at the spot she's almost touching, then lifts her eyes to mine. "Can I see it?"

With my eyes on hers, I drag my shirt up over my head and then toss it inside the room. We're still in the doorway, my foot holding it open just a smidge.

Sienna steps forward, and her fingers brush my skin with the barest of touches. She pulls back a fraction, but then she's pressing her fingers to the tattoo in earnest. I hiss as a jolt of electricity shocks my heart.

Slowly, she traces the outline of the butterfly inked over my heart with her nails. It's the only tattoo on my chest. I have others on my back and arms, but this spot is reserved for her and her alone. My heart. My butterfly. And hopefully, one day, my girl.

When her eyes meet mine again, they're glassy, and as she gives me the softest of smiles, her lips tremble. "Thank you."

Between one breath and the next, she's gone, dashing down the hall, like if she stays any longer, she knows she'll latch on to me and never let go.

All week, during our downtime, Sienna joins us on our adventures.

In Chicago, we eat deep-dish pizza and visit the Willis Tower, the tallest building in the city. There are little glass enclosures at the top, and as we step out onto the glass floor more than one hundred levels up, Sienna and Ollie discover I have a fear of heights. The two of them gang up on me, bouncing and snapping photos while I press my hands to the glass and beg the universe not to send us all tumbling fourteen hundred feet to our deaths so soon after bringing Sienna back to me.

In Nashville, we listen to honky-tonk and take Ollie out for biscuits and gravy with fried chicken for breakfast. He's a huge fan. Then we hit up the zoo that afternoon.

During all our adventures, we talk about hockey. At breakfast, I use salt and pepper shakers to demonstrate plays. At lunch, I use a pizza crust hockey stick and a chunk of sausage to represent the puck.

After Ollie goes to bed, we watch film. While I prepare for upcoming games, I explain the plays, the terminology, and the general culture.

We don't touch. We definitely don't kiss. And I try to keep the flirting to a minimum. She, on the other hand, slips up pretty regularly, and fuck if I don't love every second of it.

I have to drop my little guy off with Jen before our game in Minnesota, so I leave Sienna with the rest of the team and hope that all the progress we made wasn't for nothing.

She has to return to Boston the day I'm headed to Minnesota, so we miss each other completely. When she texts to tell me, disappointment is a heavy weight in my gut. After spending so much time together, I crave her more than I ever did.

When my phone lights up with a text from her two days later, I scramble for it, acting like a damn teenager, my heart thumping in my chest.

> Sienna: I have to know, how did the hug go?

I laugh out loud and all my worries fade away.

> Me: Apparently, there's a whole story that goes along with it, so he won't share until I see him in person.

> Sienna: Oh my god, I love that kid. He's hysterical.

Pride and affection swell within me. Ollie *is* great. And knowing Sienna recognizes that only makes me more desperate to see her, to push this thing along.

> Me: What are you doing?

> Sienna: Like currently?

I laugh at her question.

> Me: Yes. Though if you want to talk about life goals and what you want your future to look like or where you see us in five years, I'm down for that too.

The dots dance on my screen, then stop. They start up again, and when they disappear a second time, my heart sinks. Shit. Maybe I pushed it too far, flirted too overtly.

Just as the thought crosses my mind, a message appears.

Sienna: I'm sketching a dress for Liv.

She may have ignored the flirting, but getting a response at all is a win.

Me: For what?

Sienna: Can I call you? It's hard to type and draw at the same time. If you're busy, though, we can talk later.

I hang my head and grin. As if I'd ever be too busy for her.

I settle back on my hotel bed and click the icon to call her.

Sienna picks up right away, but she's wearing a scowl. She's still gorgeous. Her dark hair is up in a messy bun on top of her head, with soft wisps framing her makeup-free face. I'm pretty sure there's a smudge of chocolate on her chin, and her green eyes are vibrant. The icing on the cake of this incredible view is the way her black sweater falls off one shoulder, hinting at the absence of a bra.

"You don't FaceTime someone without warning," she admonishes.

"You accepted."

Her eyes widen. "Still. I could have been naked."

I cough out a laugh. "Again. You didn't have to answer. And you won't hear me complaining."

"*Noah.*" There's that chiding tone again that makes my cock ache.

"Sienna."

She rolls her eyes and looks away, but there's no hiding the grin splitting her face.

I can't look away from her. Not after six long years of wanting. Of dreaming I'd get a simple moment like this with her one day. I won't take one second for granted.

"You got me to call you," I tease. "So go on. Tell me what you're working on."

She breathes out a surprised laugh. "*Got* you to call me?"

"You asked me to, didn't you?"

She rolls her eyes again.

Fuck, it's fun talking to her. Outside the guys, I spend very little time talking to adults. But it's easy sinking back into this banter with her.

I wish I didn't have to work so hard to get her here, but I can't deny I'm enjoying the hell out of the chase.

The screen gets blurry for a moment, and when it clears again, she sits back, her hands free, giving me an even better view. She's seated on the floor in her living room, leaning against the couch, with the phone propped up on the coffee table. Nearby, there's a set of colored pencils laid out and a pad of paper.

"So tell me about this dress," I prod.

She picks up a pencil and leans forward, focusing on her drawing rather than on the screen. "Beckett asked me to design a dress for Liv for this gala my family is throwing. It's for a little girl, Josie. I think you know her—"

I nod. "War's daughter."

"Yup." Her lips tip up lightly. "Everyone will be dressed in varying shades of pink, since that's her favorite color."

"It is." I grin at her. "Everything that girl owns is pink. Pretty sure she paints War's nails pink before every game and insists he does it when he travels."

Sienna lifts her chin, eyeing me. "Really?"

"Yeah, War's an awesome dad. Josie's foster parents abandoned her when she was diagnosed with cancer. Did you know that?"

Lips parted in shock, she shakes her head.

I settle back against the couch cushion. "The team—*your brother*—stepped up and made sure she got everything she needed."

Her eyes fill with tears. "My brother's got a big heart."

"Yup. And that's how War met Josie. He and Ava officially adopted her last year."

"That's so incredible." She ducks her head and wipes at her cheeks.

"I've met them a few times, but I never knew that story. Thanks for sharing it with me."

"Of course." I clear the emotion from my throat and squint at the pad in front of her. "So what kind of design are you thinking?"

She gives me a look that says *Like you actually care.*

The truth is I do. If Sienna is involved, then I'm interested.

Rather than tell her that—she won't believe it anyway—I arch a brow and wait her out.

Eventually, she relents and turns the sketchpad around.

The woman she's drawn is curvy, her dress cutting across one shoulder and tightening at the waist before flowing to the floor.

"This is one option." She goes on to explain how the lines of the top and the way the dress is cut should accentuate her sister-in-law's figure while drawing attention away from the parts of her body she doesn't love.

Damn. Sometimes I forget how much effort women have to put into a night at a gala like this one.

And even before the woman slips the dress on, there's another person designing it with her insecurities in mind.

She shows me a wrap dress next. This one has an oversized bow that ties at the waist. The shantung fabric, she explains, won't show every dimple but rather hang elegantly, creating cleaner lines. The shimmery shantung she has in mind would cause the dress to look deep purple from one angle, a deep magenta from another, and a deep pink from a third.

Honestly, that one sounds like a winner to me, but she's not done. The next dress is a halter. The top is black, and the bottom is made with the same shantung fabric as the previous dress.

All are considered ball gowns, she explains, and her plan is to make all three so Liv can try them on and pick the one she likes best.

"So you cut the fabric and just sew it together?" I probably sound like an idiot, but this is my introduction to fashion. I guess I have a lot to learn.

Sienna laughs. "Yes. My friend Cat owns *Jolie* magazine. She has an entire crew of tailors on staff. I'll give them the designs and the fabric, and we'll work on it together."

"That's so cool." The statement is pitiful, really. But I don't have the words to describe how impressive she is. "I want to watch that. Bet a lot of other people would want to as well."

She laughs again. "Yeah, it's like someone could create a whole show about it."

I drop my head back with a groan. Shit. I forgot. "I never watched."

She bites her lip and nods. "I figured."

But now I want to. God, I want to watch every second of it.

It should have been the first thing I did once I realized who she was.

"Bet you Ollie would love it."

Her cheeks go pink. "Don't force your son to watch my show. And don't go thinking that you have to either."

"Have to? Please. It's the next best thing to having you on FaceTime."

She ducks, hiding a smile. "Ready for the game tomorrow?"

"Yeah. I'm also ready to get home."

"Miss Ollie?"

My chest constricts. *I miss you* is what I want to say. But if I tell her that, I'll scare her off. So I nod and leave it at that.

"How's the hockey studying going?"

She shrugs. "I had a documentary on before you called. Figured I could listen while I worked."

"You'll be an expert by the end of the season."

"Better be, or Ezra will have my head." Her shoulders sink. "The dick had the audacity to ask me if I'd taken up nannying since I was hanging out with Ollie in Orlando."

"Asshole," I mutter through my teeth.

I'm a level-headed guy, and I'm always good with management, but Ezra has been an absolute prick to Sienna.

I'd be pissed that her brothers haven't spoken up for her yet, but I have a feeling she has told them to keep their mouths shut. She wants to prove she can do this, and she thinks that means she has to handle everything without backup.

"Can I ask you something?"

Sienna laughs. "As my father always says, you just did."

"What happened in Paris?"

Right before my eyes, all the joy drains from her expression and her shoulders tense. "I'd rather not talk about it."

"Please," I say, infusing as much sincerity into my voice as I can. "I want to know you. I've missed so much—"

Her eyes cut to mine aggressively, and she opens her mouth like she's going to shut me down.

Before she can, I barrel on. "And a lot of that was my fault. I should have spoken up sooner. I would have if—"

I squeeze my eyes shut and roll my neck. I can't find it in me to bring up what I saw the night I finally found her. The other guy doesn't matter. Previous relationships don't matter. It's obviously over with him or she wouldn't have let me touch her.

I clear my throat. "The point is, I should have been there for you. And I want to be now."

Head lowered, she focuses on her drawing, though the pencil in her hand doesn't move. "They took everything," she says so quietly it's hard to make out the words. "Everything I worked for, everything I am." She looks up, pain and devastation swimming in her watery eyes. "But they didn't take this." She nods at her drawing. "I'm only now realizing that. I've been so angry that I couldn't see what I still had."

My chest aches and my hands itch to hold her. "You're incredibly talented."

She gives me a tentative smile. "For most of my life, it was the only thing I was good at. But I'm finding new things, and I'm rediscovering my love for old ones."

This time the words don't feel so sad. And they don't feel like they're only about her career.

"I hope you do."

With a shake of her head, she pulls her shoulders back, clearly ready to move on, and launches into a recap of the documentary she had on when I called. That conversation evolves into one regarding the teams I've played for through the years, which morphs into a discussion about the places we've traveled and our favorite foods in each location. When she yawns for the third time, I realize we've been on the phone for three hours.

"You should get some sleep," I tell her as a yawn sneaks up on me too.

"Shit, you've got a game tomorrow." She straightens and gathers her pencils into a neater pile. "I'm the worst owner ever, keeping you up all night."

I bring the phone close to my face, ensuring she's looking at me. "I'd fight the sun with you every night, butterfly."

"*Noah*," she chides, her attention darting away, like she can hide from me.

"Good night, Sienna."

Two days later, that conversation runs on repeat in my head. And when we touch down in Boston, all I want is to see her.

I'm praying to the elevator gods as I step into the building, hoping the doors will open and she'll be there. Ollie FaceTimes me as I step out into the hall, so I deviate from the plan and unlock my door so I can talk to him about his day. The whole time, I leave my door ajar, certain I'll catch her coming home. When that doesn't pan out, and after I've said good night to my son, I stalk down the hall and knock on her door.

Screw serendipity. I'm making my own luck.

Chapter 37
Sienna

"THEY'RE GORGEOUS," Liv breathes as she flips through the designs.

"How in god's name are you going to choose between them?" Lennox leans over her shoulder, her lips parted in what might actually be wonder.

Internally, I squeal.

I nailed it.

The girls came over to see my new place since their men are still traveling, and after a tour, we relocated to Hannah's apartment. It's easier this way, since her place is babyproofed. Millie left Vivi with Beckett and Winnie so she could play with the twins, but Taylor, Maverick, and Beckham are all here.

It's wild the way my family exploded practically overnight. And I'm constantly impressed with how hands-on my brothers are with their kids. Especially since our parents were never around. They clearly didn't model the nurturing ways the guys have all adopted.

"The better question is, can you make one before the gala? It's in two weeks." Liv flips through the designs again, a longing look on her face.

Warmth blooms in my chest. It makes me happy to do this for her. Honestly, I missed working with individual clients once my brand took off. Creating designs for mass consumption meant I missed out on moments like this.

Taylor is snoozing in my arms while Sara takes a break. She's across the room on the couch, eyes closed, wineglass in hand, and a smile on her face. According to her, she's immersing herself in this moment and memorizing what it's like to have four free limbs again.

I think she might have a bit of a buzz going.

"It's not a problem. I'll have all three made by then. That way you can try them on before you decide."

"Oh my god, seriously? I'm so jealous," Lennox whines. "If she doesn't like one, can I have it? I don't care which. I'll wear any of them."

Liv giggles, picking up her glass of wine. "Pick your favorite. I'll choose between the other two." Nose scrunched, she turns to me. "If that's okay with you."

"Hey, what about me?" Sara whimpers, her eyes still closed. "I need a dress."

Hannah appears with a platter of cheese, laughing. "Look what you started."

Ava follows her in and sets a bottle of wine on the table. Then she takes the spot next to me on the floor and settles Beckham in her lap.

"Let me put Beck in the playpen with Mav," Hannah says, holding her arms out. "Then you can relax."

With a shrug, Ava hands off her son. Then she takes a long, slow sip of her wine, like maybe she's almost as overstimulated as Sara is after all the solo parenting she's done this week. "Josie is so excited for the gala. Our final dress fittings are on Saturday."

Lennox bounces, her smile bright. "What is our little princess wearing?"

Ava pulls her phone out of the side pocket of her cream-colored leggings and swipes a few times, then holds it out to us. In the image, Josie is wearing a hot pink dress with sequins on top and a puffy skirt created by layers of chiffon over tulle to keep its shape. Her strawberry blond hair is pulled back in a long braid, and the smile on her face is infectious. "Scar's is the same style in light pink. They're both thrilled."

"Oh my god, they are my favorite ever." Hannah groans. "Tell me your dress matches."

Ava laughs, her shoulders bouncing, and tucks her loose red hair behind her ears. "If it came in my size, I'm sure they would have insisted. Mine isn't quite so poofy, and it's a much deeper pink."

"I'm thinking of wearing magenta," I tell her. "I'm not really a pinky-pink girl."

"I am." With a saucy wave of her hand, Lennox flips her bright pink hair.

The room erupts in laughter, and when we settle down, I promise Lex and Sara that I'll design whatever they want.

"Me too?" Millie asks as she settles a hand on her small bump.

"Of course. A peachy pink color, right?"

She waggles her brows. "Gotta keep your brother happy."

"Ew," I groan.

Hannah cackles as she drops onto the couch.

"Speaking of brothers," Lennox interjects. "My husband told me you spent some time with Noah while you were traveling."

Every person in the room turns their attention on me, their scrutiny like a physical weight.

Keeping my expression neutral, I lift my chin. "Because Mav was sick and Hannah asked me to hang with Ollie, right?"

"Yup, she did me a solid." Hannah nods and gives me a smile, though it quickly morphs into something more devious. "That one time. You decided to spend all that *extra* time with him all on your own."

Sara sits up, finally forcing her eyes open. "Oh, do tell. What did you do, exactly?"

I slump back against the couch. "Nothing. We went fishing. Did touristy things. Ollie told him how little I know about hockey, so he offered to help me so I don't lose my job."

And then we spent hours talking over FaceTime. About everything and absolutely nothing. The ease I feel when I'm with Noah is nonsensical. And the frequency with which I think about him when we're not together? It's downright ludicrous. So is how badly I crave him even after all this time.

I'd convinced myself that he wasn't as perfect as my memories made him out to be. That the missed opportunity only added to the appeal. But I'm beginning to think he really was meant for me. That he's my person. And I'm not sure what to do about that.

"You aren't going to lose any job," Liv says pointedly.

Unease swirls in my stomach. "Yeah, well, I don't like not knowing things. Call it a personality defect."

She lifts one shoulder. "I get it. And as a female CEO, I appreciate it. But your brothers wouldn't have put you in this position if they didn't think you could do it. You and I both know that."

She's right. And I know I can be useful. Still, the idea that any of my peers could think otherwise stings.

"Harry is single, though," Lennox sings. "And oh so fine."

"It's the glasses," Ava murmurs.

Hannah jackknifes up, her spine stick-straight. "*Ava.*"

Our redheaded friend's cheeks go pink. "What?"

"He's your husband's best friend," she shouts. "And your best friend's brother."

Lennox snickers. "Sounds like a trope you'd love."

Ava eyes her best friend over her wineglass. "Sorry, but your brother is hot. I'd have to be dead not to notice. Every guy on that team is good-looking."

"And off-limits," I remind them all. "Because I'm their boss."

Liv tilts her head thoughtfully. "Not exactly."

"Right," Millie chimes in, wearing a wicked grin. "And since when do you Langfields worry about inappropriate relationships?"

"Of course the woman who seduced her dad's best friend would ask that," Lennox teases.

I groan. "Can we not use the word *seduced* when we're talking about my brothers?"

Millie and Hannah break into matching cackles. One would think the two of them would understand my plight, considering Hannah married Millie's twin and the girls are talking about how hot Hannah's stepbrother is, but apparently they're all delinquents.

When my phone lights up, I lunge for it, thankful for the distraction.

Cat: I know we planned to meet tomorrow
night, but I need you tonight.

I roll my eyes. She's so dramatic.

Me: You NEED me?

Cat: I have a surprise, and you are going to
want to be available. PLEASE be available!

"Why are you smiling?" Hannah picks up a cracker, tops it with a slice of cheese, and pops it into her mouth.

I look up, only to realize every eye is focused on me again, and grimace. "A friend asked me to meet her tonight."

"Sounds scandalous," Sara jokes, her cheeks flushed from the wine.

I roll my eyes. "It's where she wants to meet that's the issue. Her brother-in-law owns an exclusive club, and I'm not sure how I feel about going."

Lennox tilts her head, her expression suddenly shrewd. "What kind of club?"

I shrug. "It's called Allure."

"Oh my *god*," Hannah squeals. "That's a sex club. I've always wanted to go to a sex club."

"It's a *what* club?" Liv's eyes go wide. "Doesn't Hayden Hanson own that?"

Ah, fuck. Hayden Hanson. As in Garreth's twin brother. Of course he's friends with Beckett. Surely he's mentioned the nature of the place. Shit. If not, I may have just caused a fight.

But there's no way my brother has been there without his wife. Although he was single for a long, long—nope. I'm not going there.

So I nod and leave it at that.

Liv bursts into laughter. "Oh my god, your brother is dead. He tried to convince me to go last month, but he failed to mention that specific detail."

Millie hums. "I don't know. This place looks hot." She holds up her phone. There's a graphic of a golden lock in the middle, and the rest of the screen is black. "I wonder what the password is to get in. Maybe when I'm not preggo, I'll convince Gavin to take me."

I glare at her. "Rules, Mills. Follow the damn rules."

She gives me a salacious smile. "But I'm so good at breaking them."

"Well, I'm not pregnant. I want to go." Lennox launches herself off one couch and plops down beside Millie on the other. She buries her face in her device, and ten seconds later, she pops up and crows, "Got it!"

"The password? How the hell did you do that so quickly?" Ava muses.

Lennox flips her hair over her shoulder. "Perks of being the Kennedy princess."

Her family has more connections than even ours, and that's saying something.

"So the gimmick here is that when women walk in, they're given a card to use when they choose who they interact with. Like a man literally can't approach them. It's all about women being in control. This is so fucking hot." She looks up, her pupils blown wide. "If you don't go, I'll kill you."

"We're having a girls' night," I remind her lamely.

Hannah claps, startling the babies. "Fine. Girls' night is over."

"Stop," I whine. "Seriously, I don't want to go."

"Why?"

The question from Liv stops me in my tracks. Out of everyone in this room, I figured she'd be the most understanding.

"You just said you wouldn't go," I point out.

"Because I'm a mom of five. This"—she drags a hand up and down in front of her, gesturing to her body—"does not belong in a sex club."

"Bullshit," Hannah spews. "You're gorgeous. And your husband is utterly obsessed with you. If you want to keep all that sex between the two of you in your bedroom, there's no shame in that. But if you don't want to try something like this because of your body, then it's bullshit."

"I agree," Ava says. For the second time in as many minutes, I'm shocked silent. Ava is the most reserved of the group by far.

"You do?" Liv says, leaning forward.

"Yeah. I don't think you shouldn't go because you're a mom. I personally don't think I'd like something like that, but it's not because I have kids."

"Bullshit," Hannah mutters again. "You'd love it."

Ava bats at her best friend. "My husband is hot. I don't think I'd like it if other women looked at him."

"Oh, I'd have no problem with it," Hannah says. "I'd want every woman there to see my husband's massive cock and be jealous as fuck that I'm the only one who gets to suck it."

"*Hannah.*" Millie throws a pillow at our unrepentant friend.

Sara nods. "I'm with Hannah. Though Brooks would *never.*" She sighs, like being with a man as obsessed with her as he is, who wants her all to himself, is a burden.

My phone lights up again.

Cat: Pretty, pretty please.

"What does it say?" Hannah leans forward, peering over my shoulder. "Oh, she's *begging.*"

The room breaks into a cacophony of squeals and giggles.

"Come on," Lennox says. "You should go. If only so you can report back and tell us what it was like."

I bury my head in my hands. "What does one even wear to a sex club?"

CHAPTER 38
NOAH

IDEALLY, going after what I want was a genius plan. In reality, I'm only one-half of the equation, and when the other half doesn't answer the door, it puts a hitch in my plans.

So what now? Do I text her? Call?

Talk about taking the wind out of a guy's sails. I've been envisioning one of those big, dramatic moments like in Hannah's books. She'd open the door, and I'd spill my guts and confess all my feelings. I'd ask her if she's ready to stop playing games. Then we'd kiss, because of course she'd be ready. And the night would look a hell of a lot different from this.

I've been so sure that fate is on our side. Now I'm wondering if it's been working against us all this time.

How the hell has it taken us this long to reach this point? I'm ready to start my life with her, yet she's nowhere to be found.

I stalk back to my door. As I pass by Hannah and Daniel's apartment, I pull up short. Should I talk to them? Am I ready to open up about this to my sister? Maybe not. But if I don't talk to someone, I'm going to lose my mind.

I knock lightly, not wanting to wake Maverick if he's sleeping.

"Forget your key, babe?" Hannah calls. "I'm not wearing any panties, and I've got—"

"Please don't finish that sentence." I squeeze my eyes shut as the knob turns and the door opens.

"Noah," Hannah squeals. "What the hell? Why didn't you say it was you?"

"Why wouldn't you check the peephole before talking like that? I could have been *anyone*."

She huffs an impatient breath. "Come inside and open your damn eyes so you don't trip over the toys. I'm dressed."

I ease one eye open to confirm before committing to it. When I notice the candles on almost every surface, I grimace and take a step back. "Sorry, I'll get out of your hair."

"Have a drink with me before you go." She flicks on a light in the kitchen and nods toward the fridge. "I'm guessing Daniel got held up at the arena?"

I shrug. "Probably." I raced out of there, singularly focused on getting to Sienna. Though clearly that was a pointless endeavor.

Hannah holds up an open bottle of red. "You just missed the girls. Everybody rushed out of here, in a hurry to see their husbands."

I rough a hand over the back of my neck. "Oh yeah? Who was here?"

She opens a cabinet and pops up on her toes. While she struggles to reach the glasses, I bump her out of the way and pull two down. "The usual suspects. Plus Liv and Sienna."

Excitement pulses through me, but I do my best to hide it. "Oh yeah? I didn't see Sienna in the hall. When did she leave?"

My segue is ridiculous. Why would I see her in the hall? It's not like she camps out there. But it's the best I can come up with, and I fucking need to know where she is.

She breaks into a grin that makes my stomach sink. Shit. I've been caught. Though maybe this is a good thing. I came over because I needed to unload my feelings anyway.

"Oh," she says, her eyes flashing. "Sienna has a hot date at a sex club tonight."

What. The. Fuck?

I stagger back, my vision going blurry. "What do you mean she went to a sex club?"

She fills two glasses and slides one down the counter to me.

"Hannah," I grit out through clenched teeth, taking a step closer. "Explain."

She has to tip her head back to look me in the eye when we're this close. "What is there to explain? She's a hot single female and she was invited to play. Honestly you should check this place out. Maybe it'd help you relax."

Ignoring the casual way my stepsister mentions my sex life, and beyond irritated that she won't just answer my fucking question, I chug half my glass of wine. I doubt it'll do me much good, but one can hope it'll soothe my nerves a little.

Instead, it only further raises my body temperature. "Where is this place? And who was she going with? Did she specifically say it was a date?"

Hannah leans back against the counter, a smirk playing on her lips. "Oh my god, I thought I saw some interest there, but this is worse than I thought. You have it *bad*."

I shake my head, teeth gritted. The moment she used the words *sex club* in relation to Sienna, all interest in discussing my feelings vanished.

"I haven't seen you like this since you came back from the Bahamas all those years ago," she says, practically vibrating with excitement. "It's like your *have a day* girl all over again."

I down the rest of my wine and wipe my mouth with the back of my hand. Fuck it. "She *is* my have a day girl."

For the first time in the more than two decades I've known her, Hannah looks truly at a loss for words.

She blinks, her mouth dropping open. "What?"

"Sienna is the girl I met in the Bahamas," I say. Fuck. I don't have time for this. I need to know where she is. "Sienna is *the* girl."

"Why didn't you ever mention your have a day girl was Sienna Langfield?" my sister grouses. "That's a big part of the story to leave out. And how come you didn't just call her?" She straightens, her face lighting up. "Oh my god, have you been secretly seeing one another for all these years? Is that why you both moved back to Boston?"

Fuck. If only that were true.

"No." I deflate, sinking back against the counter. "We didn't share our last names. It was just the two of us. No interference from the outside world. No real lives to think about. We both had a lot going on, though we steered clear of all of that too."

Hannah nibbles on her lip. "So she didn't know about Ollie?"

I hang my head. "And I didn't know who her brothers were. If I had, I probably would have stayed away like she said I would."

She hums sympathetically. "So you walked away from each other? You gave up a connection? Because clearly that's what you had. That weekend has haunted you ever since. And she's the only woman you've ever so much as smiled about."

"Not exactly." For a moment I consider not sharing the rest. Not all of it is my story to tell. But it's been so damn long, and that weekend *has* haunted me. I rub a hand across my face, take a steadying breath, and put it all out there.

I tell her about meeting her on the plane, then bumping into her at the hotel. And the side-by-side villas. I tell her how after I tried to escape by switching rooms—a detail she finds hysterical—we ended up on the same snorkeling excursion. I explain how torn I was. How part of me wanted to go after her, because clearly we had more than a spark, while the other part knew it was unfair because of the baby carriage–size baggage waiting for me at home. Though I keep it brief, I also touch on Sienna's reasoning. About the big opportunity and how it wouldn't allow her time for more than a weekend distraction.

I admit that when I kissed her, I immediately knew I never wanted to kiss another person again. And I haven't.

That made my sister swoon. And then she punched me.

"I can't believe you've been hiding this from me for years." Her eyes go glassy, and I swear her lip quivers. "Oh my god, how did you say goodbye? That must have been awful."

A bittersweet sensation blooms in my chest when I think back on that day. Sienna was so hopeful. And she was certain that fate would bring us back together.

The dollar bill in my wallet proves just how right she was. She just doesn't know it yet.

"Sienna watched *Serendipity* on the flight there—"

Hannah whacks me again, cutting me off mid-sentence. *"That's* why you're always looking at dollar bills. Oh my god." She throws her head back. "It all makes so much sense now. I thought you had developed a compulsion or something."

Hands stuffed in my pockets, I sigh. She's so dramatic. "She put her name and number on a dollar bill, and I put mine in a copy of your first book."

Hannah's face lights up. "Oh my gosh, I'm part of your story. This is so romantic. So she found it and came back to find you?"

I cock a brow and wait for her to stop interrupting so I can finish.

She holds up a hand and takes a deep breath. "Okay, go on."

"No. I saw her at Brooks and Sara's wedding."

She blinks and breaks into a look of recognition. "You said you'd seen a ghost."

Lips pressed together, I dip my chin. "Something like that."

"Aw, I'm so sorry." She clutches my arm. "I was so focused on my own stuff that I didn't even realize you were having, like, an emotional breakthrough."

"Not exactly. At first I was ecstatic. Even after I realized she was a Langfield. Maybe I shouldn't have been, but I was just so damn happy to see her again. Until I saw her with someone else."

"Who?" She frowns. "I don't remember her bringing a date to the wedding."

I shrug. "He was older. English. It looked like they were keeping it a secret. We've never talked about it."

Hannah taps her finger against her chin. "Intriguing."

"Not exactly. But please keep that part to yourself. We haven't talked about it." I give her a pointed look. "So now that you know everything, please tell me where she went. And any details you have about her plans."

Hannah pulls out her phone, and after a few swipes, she hands it to me. "It's called Allure. It's part of the Londoner hotel—" She gasps and slaps her hand over her mouth. "Oh my god. The club's owner is an older British guy. Hayden Hanson."

She plucks the phone out of my hand and taps the screen a few more times. When she hands it back with a picture pulled up, my stomach drops.

Fuck.

This guy doesn't have a beard, and he's got a hell of a lot more hair than he did that night, but he's definitely the man Sienna was sneaking around with at the wedding.

Nausea rolls through me as I push the device back into my sister's hands.

"It doesn't make sense," she muses. "She was invited by a girlfriend, and she was pretty apprehensive about going."

"Wouldn't you be apprehensive about showing up at a sex club your ex owns?"

Hannah winces. "Uh, yeah. Talk about awkward. Shit. What are you going to do?"

"What I didn't do that night. I'm going to speak up. I'm going to make sure she knows that he's not her only option. Hell, I'll beg. I'll get down on my knees if I have to—"

With a pump of her fist, Hannah hoots. "Yeah, you will."

I pin her with a glare, but it does nothing to curb her excitement.

"What? I can't let a good sex pun go unused."

I rub at the back of my neck. "I'll do whatever's necessary. I can't lose her again."

Chapter 39
Sienna

BEFORE I'VE EVEN SEEN the place, I consider turning around and going home.

But as I step into the lobby of the Londoner, I keep my head high and my shoulders back. I'm Sienna Fucking Langfield. Not the Sienna Langfield who used to blush when men would flirt, and not the Sienna Langfield whose life was recently in shambles. Tonight, dressed in a curve-hugging black dress and a pair of red-bottomed stilettos, I'm the Sienna Langfield who lived in Paris for five years. The woman who had sex in public in the Bahamas with a man I barely knew. The woman others would kill to take the place of. The woman men would kill to have on their arm.

With that mantra playing in my mind, I stride across the marble floor like I belong.

Inside, I'm a big ball of nerves, seriously freaked out about what I might be in for.

I spot Cat immediately. Her long dark hair is pulled back and twisted up into a braided bun. Her black leather pants are tight and her bustier top is practically see-through. Her lips are painted a deep red and curled up in a wicked grin as she wiggles her fingers in greeting.

"You are the hardest woman to nail down," she teases.

"Once again, your ability to make any phrase sexual astounds me."

She leans in and kisses my left cheek, then my right. "Please, you are so not my type."

"Rude."

She loops her arm through mine and guides me toward a host stand at one end of the lobby. The blond man stationed there is dressed in an expensive black suit and wearing an earpiece. Behind him, crushed velvet curtains flank a lacquered black door.

As we approach, the man nods once. "Mrs. B."

"Evening, Lars. I've got a guest tonight. Put her under Ms. P."

I side-eye my friend. What's with all the cloak-and-dagger shit?

She only smirks at me.

The man taps at the iPad on the host stand, and the machine beside it lights up. It beeps quietly, then pushes out a black and gold card.

He hands it to her, and after she's taken it, she surveys me, tapping it against her lips. "This is your play card."

"My play card?" I parrot.

With a smirk, she leads me toward the curtains. Though before she pushes through, she tips the card in my direction. "Men aren't allowed to approach women here. We hold all the cards. Literally." She grins. "So if you see someone you're interested in, hand them the card. If they want to play, they'll accept, and off you go to the room designated for that card."

My insides war, half intrigued and half terrified. Though when I consider just how many people have probably used those rooms—

She glares at me as if she can read my thoughts. "Don't judge."

I wince. "You're right. But the card's not necessary. I'm just here to have a drink with my friend."

She hums. "So long as you keep an open mind."

I nod, and she waves her hand through the curtain, parting it easily. She waits for me to go first, and what I find inside is completely unexpected. The black walls with gold teardrops catch my attention first. The design makes it look as though the gold really is liquid. Like it's melting down the walls. As my eyes adjust to the burgundy lighting, I catalog the pair of booths in each corner. Cat grasps me by the elbow and leads me deeper into the room, but not before I catch sight of a woman with her top off in one booth. And is that a man between her legs?

"Holy shit," I mutter.

"You promised no judging."

"I didn't think I'd have a front-row seat to an orgy," I hiss.

She drags me to the black lacquered bar and gestures for me to sit on one of the golden tufted stools. The wall ahead of us is lit up and stocked with dozens of bottles of liquor. In the middle, what looks like a cauldron bubbles.

"If you put a spell on me, I'm out," I mutter.

She lets out a loud, raspy laugh.

At the sound, the female bartender looks our way, and her eyes light up with recognition. "Mrs. B, good to see you."

Cat orders two extra dirty martinis, and once our drinks have been served, she turns to me, all business. "Sophie is retiring."

I frown. "*Why?*"

Sophie and Cat started as interns at *Jolie* at the same time, and for the last several years, Cat has been editor-in-chief of the exclusive magazine and Sophie has been the creative director. It's one of the most coveted roles in the entire fashion industry. While Cat's simple nod toward a design could make a designer's career, she won't even see the design unless Sophie thinks it's worth her time. She's the visionary.

"Her husband is several years older than she is. He wants to retire, and she wants to enjoy his retirement." She shrugs. "I'll miss her tremendously, obviously, but Dex deserves his wife's attention. I've been stealing it for decades now."

I smile. Theirs is a friendship to truly admire. "Good for her, then."

Cat drags her martini stick through her drink, then lifts it to her mouth and slides one olive off with her teeth. "This is when you ask me what any of that has to do with you."

I dip my chin. "Well, yeah. What does this have to do with me?"

She sips her drink, then takes my hands in hers. "I want you to be *Jolie*'s next creative director."

My breath catches in my throat. When I can breathe again, I squeeze her hands. "Are you out of your mind?" She has to be. I've never worked for a magazine. Hell, the closest I've come is reading the damn thing on the couch each month.

She takes another sip, her expression calculating. "No, I'm brilliant. We've been over this. If I believe you're the right person for the creative director position, then it's fact."

I sigh. "I appreciate all the faith you have in me, but you're wrong about this. This is your magazine. *The* fashion magazine of our generation. Of our grandmothers' generation. It's the bright beacon to which all designers look in order to determine what comes next."

Her expression turns to one of pride. One of pure arrogance, really. "Exactly. And with you as creative director, a woman I've watched break rules and push boundaries and twist designs in a way that even has me blinking and then thinking *Oh, okay, that more than works; that's incredible*, imagine all the amazing things we could do."

I lean back in my chair. Holy shit. This isn't the kind of offer a person says no to. But how the hell can I say yes? This is so far beyond even the biggest dreams I had for myself before my life fell apart. And yet my dreams keep changing. And as I let the idea marinate, a hunger I haven't felt in two years flares to life.

"You love it," she says, her smile wide. "You love it and you want to say yes."

I lower my focus to the bar to hide my smile. "I didn't say that."

"But you didn't say no."

A scoff escapes me. "Who the hell says no to you?"

Both she and the bartender laugh.

"No one who knows what's good for them," a deep voice says.

Jay Hanson appears on Cat's other side, looming over her and laying an indecent kiss on her lips.

Jay is gorgeous, with dirty blond hair that always looks as if he or Cat has recently run a hand through it. He's tall and broad, his icy blue eyes extra bright against his crisp blue shirt. The chiseled jawline covered in a light scruff is in complete juxtaposition to the puffy lips that any woman would kill to have, yet they work together perfectly.

He bites her lip, then sucks it into his mouth without an ounce of concern about who's watching.

I flush with heat, torn between gawking and looking away. They're always like this, so I should be used to it by now. Still, when two of the most gorgeous people I know make out in front of me, it's nearly impossible not to get hot and bothered.

"Hi, Sienna." He stands at his full height, though he doesn't take his eyes off his wife. "Did my kitten fill you in on her wonderful idea?"

Oh, and he calls her kitten. It's nauseatingly adorable, considering they've been married for years.

"Yes," Cat says. "And she's taking it under consideration, right?" She eyes me, swiping at her mouth, fixing the lipstick Jay smudged.

He watches her, his teeth sunken into his own lip, like he likes that she marked him.

"Right." With a sigh, I pick up my glass and tip it back.

"Then we're all done here." Cat stands and takes Jay's outstretched hand. She leans in and kisses my cheek, this time hovering for a moment to whisper in my ear. "Stay awhile. Maybe use the card."

She pulls back, and as I turn to tell her I'm all set, my attention snags on a man standing behind Jay, a man I hadn't noticed until now, and my heart thuds heavily.

Garreth Hanson.

Chapter 40
Sienna

I GLARE AT CAT, but she merely waggles those damn fingers again and sashays away.

Alone with my ex-boyfriend, unease rolls through me. It's been a long time since I saw him, and I don't have any idea what to say.

Thankfully he takes the lead.

"You look stunning, as always," he says in that sexy British lilt. He's wearing his requisite suit. The man is never not dressed for business. This one is herringbone gray. One I helped him pick out, if I'm not mistaken.

He looks exactly like he did when we ended things almost two years ago. His well-groomed beard still hasn't started turning gray, and those silverfish blue eyes are as unreadable as ever. Though there's a hint of kindness there, it's reserved only for the people he's closest to.

They're only a few shades off from the eyes I've been dreaming about for years, but Noah's are filled with kindness for everyone he meets.

A pang of guilt hits me as I picture what they'd look like if he saw me now. I can't imagine there'd be much warmth in them. And I couldn't blame him for it.

What am I doing here?

Garreth steps forward and motions to the chair Cat just deserted. "May I?"

"Can we, uh, go to a booth?" I peer over my shoulder, feeling a little too exposed out here.

While there's nothing wrong with being seen with a man like this, considering I'm single, being in Garreth's presence stirs up the need to find a place a little more hidden. A leftover habit after hiding our relationship for so long, I suppose.

He nods, then asks the server to send over a whiskey and a fresh martini.

"Mine is fine," I argue. I reach for it to prove that fact, though I overshoot a little and send the liquid sloshing. On second thought, it probably isn't safe for me to carry it across the room. "Right." I huff. "You know me."

He smiles. "I do."

We're quiet as he leads me to one of the tables off to the side. He's familiar with the place; that's obvious. Not that it's any of my business. And it's my genuine hope that he's moved on. He deserves to have a wonderful partner. It was just never going to be me.

"I can practically hear the thoughts racing through your head, so spill them," he says as we settle at the table.

I glance over my shoulder, apprehension flaring again. "This just isn't my scene."

He nods once. "Mine either."

My eyes widen without my permission, making him chuckle.

"I haven't changed that much since we broke up. You know I like my privacy."

I nod. He's always valued it above just about everything else. "So why are you here?" I ask, getting right to the point.

"For you."

Those two simple words set my nerves on edge instantly. The ease with which he said them, as if the statement is a well-established fact, only adds to my discomfort.

"Garreth, I—" I close my eyes. The fact that he thinks there's still a chance leaves me feeling utterly bewildered. We cut ties cleanly, with no loose ends, and in truth, I haven't thought about him except in passing since I walked away.

"I did some digging into the settlement agreement you signed."

My body goes rigid. "You *what?*"

I ensured the terms of the agreement were confidential. Because if my brothers caught wind of them, especially Beckett, they would have lost their minds. I did it to protect them, and I'd do it again, but I lost everything in the process.

Back then it felt like I'd lost a piece of myself, a limb. Like *that* Sienna had died. Now? With time and distance, I realize that though the loss was real, it constituted a much smaller part of me than I believed it would. I can still create, and I am. I just can't sell my designs. No, it isn't ideal, and yes, it hurts, but I can live a full life without it.

"I didn't understand how you could have just walked away from it all. I know you, Sienna. You wouldn't give up your company unless you were forced to." He stares at me, the look far too knowing. "It didn't sit right with me, so I hired an investigator."

Stomach plummeting, I lurch forward. "You had no right."

He nods. "I'm aware. But I did it anyway. We both know I've never been great at accepting what I don't want to hear. Case in point: You told me over and over that your heart wasn't up for grabs, yet I foolishly tried to win it anyway."

I slump, the fight draining from me. "*Garreth.*"

He shakes his head and picks up his whiskey. "You were honest from the beginning. Things may not have gone the way I'd like, but I still care about you. And I can still give you *this.*" He pulls an envelope from the inner pocket of his suit jacket and pushes it across the table. "You didn't deserve what happened to you. It wasn't right and I couldn't leave it be. I'm sorry."

Frowning, I ease the envelope open and pull out the document folded neatly inside. "What is this?" I ask as I squint at the small print.

"It's a rescission of the settlement agreement. I located the funds that were stolen from you. While the authorities deal with the victims' recompense, yours included, I took what I found to the artists who sued you. Presented them with the proof that you had also been defrauded. I made them see that what they did to you was no better than what that charlatan of a financial planner did."

My heart hammers in my chest and my mind whirls, making me lightheaded. "D-does this mean what I think it means?"

"It means you're free to return to your company. Free to return to Paris. Or stay here. Or go to London." Hope flashes in his eyes, though it's gone quickly. "The point is that you're free to design, to create, to rebuild."

Choking on a sob, I launch myself over the table and into his arms and hug him fiercely. "Thank you. Thank you. *Thank you.*"

He chuckles as he squeezes me, and as I pull back, those usually shrewd eyes soften. "I'd do anything for you."

His focus drops to my mouth, and my stomach flips over on itself. Shit. He's going to kiss me.

I rear back, but before I can put a safe distance between us, the scraping of chair legs against the floor startles me.

The two of us turn at the same time, our cheeks so close that I can feel the warmth of his skin.

A large figure looms over us in the dim room, but as the man drops into the chair, straddling the seat, his arms resting on the back, his identity is revealed.

Noah.

His expression is one of indifference, his eyes unreadable. Still, I find myself cataloging every inch of him. He's wearing black pants and a black Oxford. The top two buttons are undone, exposing his thick, gorgeous neck and collarbone. His glasses are firmly in place, the black frames casting shadows on his face. Every inch of him screams sex. *And anger.*

"Can I join you?"

Scrambling, I push away from Garreth. While I may technically still be single, my body knows who I truly belong to.

"What are you doing here?" I say by way of greeting.

"Do you know him?" Garreth asks, straightening beside me.

Noah breaks into a smile. It's one I've never seen before, and it looks all wrong. This isn't the friendly one he uses at the arena when dealing with fans, and it most certainly isn't the gentle one he uses with his son. It's not unfriendly, though there's a mocking quality to it, I suppose. It's cocky. And sexy as fuck, if I'm honest.

"She does." He holds out his hand. "I'm Noah. I'm Sienna's."

Garreth glances from Noah's outstretched hand to me and then back again. "Sienna's what?"

"*Just* Sienna's." Noah sears me with a look full of dirty, filthy, painful promise.

I've never even considered categorizing this…connection between us. Or maybe I have. More than once, I told him to stay away from me. I told him we couldn't be anything more than friends.

But it's obvious now that his statement is 100 percent accurate. He's mine and I've only ever been his. Outside of that, I don't have the first clue what we are. But from the moment we met six years ago, those two things have been categorically true.

He's mine.

As if he can sense the moment I come to that realization, a proud smirk creeps onto his face and his blue eyes warm.

That warmth pulls a smile from deep within me. The news Garreth just shared is incredible. Truly. But only this man has ever left me feeling this light. This right within myself. It makes even the brightest moments in my life pale in comparison.

"Okay," Garreth says slowly, once again glancing at me.

I feel bad, truly. But I'm as lost by this turn of events as he is.

"I'm Sienna's—"

"Ex," Noah interjects.

My heart stutters in surprise. How does he—

"Garreth Hanson." Jaw locked, said ex finally shakes Noah's hand. "And yes, Sienna's ex."

"Yup. And I'm her future." Noah looks at me, a brow arched, like he's waiting for me to object.

But my mouth couldn't formulate a sentence, even if I tried. The air thickens with tension and my pulse thrums wildly. This is so unlike the calm, collected man I'm used to. Then again, maybe this is the man who fought on the ice after seeing me in a jersey that may or may not have belonged to him. Maybe his possessive side is more savage than I realized. If that's the case, I should probably rein them both in.

"Garreth was just giving me some good news," I explain.

Beside me, Garreth straightens and adjusts his jacket.

"And I appreciate it immensely." I give him a grateful look. "I don't know how I'll ever be able to thank you."

"Just be happy."

My heart cracks at the genuine affection in his voice.

"I will. I *am*." I hug him gently.

I think we both know this is our true goodbye.

When I release him, he eyes Noah, his mask of professionalism in place. "Be good to her."

Noah nods. "Always."

Without another word, Garreth pushes out of the booth and disappears.

"What was that about?" Noah asks.

My mind is still reeling. Over the course of the last hour, I've been offered an incredible career, I've been given back my ability to chase my old dreams, and I've found closure with an ex.

And now this man is here, flipping the script. Again.

"I could ask the same thing of you."

Looking unremorseful, he angles closer, his forearms on the table, and zeroes in on me, his usually warm eyes hard. "Is it over with him?"

I lick my lips and nod. "For a long time."

"And us?"

Eyes shut, I sigh. To say this evening has been eventful would be the understatement of the century. And this is not the place to have this conversation.

As if the universe wants to emphasize that point, a sexy redhead in an indecently low-cut dress appears beside our table. As she eyes me up and down, I can't help but do the same. Her tits are practically in my face as she leans forward and pulls a black card from between them. "Interested?"

My mouth drops open and a shocked sound escapes me. I don't think I've ever been propositioned by a woman before. At least not this blatantly.

"What's happening?" Noah mutters.

I shake my head and inhale deeply, finding my bearings. "Um, no thank you. Not tonight. Appreciate it, though," I add awkwardly.

When her attention drifts to Noah and she adjusts the card, like she's considering holding it out to him, I reach across the table and set my hand on his, squeezing, claiming. And with the slightest shake of my head, I let her know he's off-limits.

The woman saunters off, unbothered by our rejection, and when she's out of earshot, Noah lets out a breath. "That was hot."

"She was?" I dart a look at him, my brows pulled low.

With a breathy laugh, he shakes his head. He stands and saunters over to my side of the table to join me in the booth, then drapes one arm over my shoulders and rests the other on the table, effectively blocking my view of the bar. Demanding my full attention. "No. *You.* The way you just told her I was yours." He presses a kiss to my shoulder.

The tension is so thick, I can barely breathe.

"And you're right," he murmurs. "I am."

"Do you want to get out of here?" I need oxygen. If I don't clear my head, I'm liable to maul this man in public.

He slides his hot mouth across my bare shoulder and up my neck, then kisses the sensitive spot below my ear. "No. I want you to tell me what this place is, butterfly, because right now, my mind is racing with all sorts of wild ideas."

"They might not be so wild," I mutter, my mouth going dry. "The card she just showed me? The man at the door gives them out to the women who come in. The rule here is that women can approach the people they're interested in. Men cannot. And the card unlocks a room for—" I shrug. The last part seems pretty self-explanatory.

If Noah came here looking for me, then he has to know what this place is.

A slow, wicked smile pulls at his lips. "You have a card?"

"They give them to every woman who enters." The rasp in my voice is inadvertent and a little embarrassing. I swallow thickly to clear the sex from my tone. To get a hold of my runaway thoughts.

It's no use. Being this close to this man, here, surrounded by his warm, musky scent, makes me a bit reckless. Makes me lean in a bit closer, chasing the feeling of his lips on my body.

"Give me your card, Sienna."

Lost in thought, I blink up at him. "What?"

"You want me to touch you. I see it in the way your pupils are blown out. In the way you're licking those lips. And the way your pulse thrums against your throat." He inches closer and runs his nose up my neck. "You want me to taste you. Slide the card my way, baby. Let me make you feel good."

My pulse takes off at a sprint, my heart pounding so wildly I worry it will burst out of my chest.

But I hold back. He can't be serious. This isn't a random bar in the Bahamas, where everyone is a perfect stranger. This is a fucking *sex club* in the heart of Boston. Frequented by the city's elite. My best friend is here with her husband, probably fucking as we speak.

"Anyone could see us," I whisper.

His lips turn up in a salacious grin. "And that makes you wet."

He knows it's true. He knows I love when he takes me in public. Fuck, what is wrong with me? Am I really considering this?

"I won't let anyone see a single inch of you," he whispers against my neck, his breath sending goose bumps skittering down my arm. "But I will have you writhing. So unless you want the people nearby to know what I do to you, you'll have to keep those moans to a whimper."

He rests a hand on my thigh and squeezes gently. The feel of it, warm and heavy against my heated skin, pulls an embarrassing groan from me. "Give me the card."

I fumble for my purse and dig it out.

He plucks it from my hold, then bites down on my neck and sucks. Then he licks away the sting. "*Good girl.*"

My pussy spasms around absolutely nothing. "Oh god, please."

He inches higher, teasing the hem of my dress, teasing me, his movements painfully slow. When he finally pushes my thighs apart, I clutch at him, urging him on. As he nuzzles my neck, spots dance in my vision. I suck in a harsh breath, my brain and body starved of oxygen. I'm drunk on desire. Dizzy with want. All concerns about what's right and who could see have been erased. All I want is for Noah to touch me. To make me come.

"How 'bout we play a little game?" he suggests as he cups my pussy.

A shudder rolls through me. "A game?"

Noah flicks his thumb up and down over my pubic bone. "Yes. I want you to look around the room and tell me exactly what the people around us are doing."

Brow furrowed, I frown up at him. "That's it?"

He spears me with a finger, and I turn into him, bringing my mouth to his to stifle the sound with a kiss.

With a nip to my lip, he pulls back. "Face forward. Tell me what you see. If your descriptions are detailed enough, if you answer all my questions, then I'll let you come."

A huff of a laugh escapes me. This man is so fucking—

He adds a second finger and curls them together, making it impossible to even finish a thought. "Holy shit," I mumble.

"Tell me," he demands. "What do you see?"

With a heavy swallow, I force my attention to a table to the side of us. Only when the sight registers do I understand the game he wants to play.

There are three people in that booth. One woman—

He gives my clit a sharp tug. "Tell me what you see."

I hiss, the pain and pleasure sending a thrill through me. "That hurt."

One side of his mouth tips up. "Want me to lick it better? I'm happy to lay you out on the table."

Pussy clenching, I drop my head back and moan.

As thrilling as the idea is, in reality, I'm not ready to be spread out for everyone to see. So I force my eyes open and play along. "There are two men," I tell him. "One is leaning back against the booth. And there's a woman leaning against him, between his legs." I'm panting, my words coming out breathy and disjointed.

"Good girl, keep talking." He rubs circles over my clit while slowly fucking me with both fingers.

I swallow another moan and clench around him tightly. "The other man just pulled her top down. He's sucking on her nipple."

"What do you think of her tits? Are they nice?"

"Um—" I lick my lips. The simplest words are hard to form in this state. "Yes. Really nice. You should look."

He chuckles. "The only set of tits I want to look at are right here in front of me. Want to give me a better peek, though?"

If the question had been demanding, I would shoot him down instantly. Instead, his voice is soft and suggestive, making me actually consider his request. Do I want my breasts out like her?

The idea alone sets my skin on fire. Yes. The answer is an easy one. Especially knowing that Noah's large frame is blocking my body from view. I can see the people mingling nearby, but they can't see me. At least that's what I tell myself as I push the soft fabric of my dress down my shoulder, dragging my bra strap with it and freeing my tits.

Instantly, Noah's hot mouth surrounds my nipple, swirling over the hard peak and sending me into a tizzy.

I clutch at his hair. "Yes, please don't stop."

"Then keep talking," he says against my sensitive flesh. He flicks my nipple back and forth with his tongue. The sensation and the juxtaposition of the cool air of the club and his hot mouth send me spiraling.

"She's spreading her legs wide," I mumble. "She's wearing pink panties."

"Are they wet?"

"I can't tell." My breath is choppy, my vision going a little hazy. "The man behind her is pushing them down now."

"Is he going to lick her pussy?"

He flicks my nipple again, right as he finds the perfect spot inside me, and a wave of heat overtakes me.

"I think so." I drop my head back, delirious. "I can't think when you—"

"Don't think, butterfly. Just relax and tell me what they're doing." His hold on me loosens a fraction. "Unless you'd rather stop?"

"No." I grab his wrist to keep him from pulling out.

He brings his mouth to mine in a slow, erotic kiss, using his tongue the way I imagine he would if his head were buried between my thighs. When he pulls back, he holds my gaze. "I love how desperate you are for my touch."

"I am," I admit. "I have been."

"Good. Shall we continue?"

I nod, and when he cocks a brow, silently telling me to continue with my description of the people in the nearby booth, I look back at the table.

The air is stolen from my lungs instantly. The woman is on all fours, her head low over the man's crotch, bobbing slightly. The second man, the one behind her, grips her ass, pulling her cheeks apart, his face buried between them.

"Um, he's eating her ass." The words tumble out, my heart hammering wildly. Though I don't even have the good sense to be embarrassed.

"Fuck," he growls into my ear, adding more pressure. "I wish I was eating yours right now."

Stars dance in my vision, and another moan slips out.

"Look to your left," he tells me.

I do as I'm told, finding I have a clear view of the bar from here. It's only now that I realize that I'm not nearly as hidden as I assumed. Because if I have a clear shot of the bar, then the people there can see me just as easily.

And the man sitting on one of those plush stools is looking right at me.

Garreth.

The desire coiled tight in my belly suddenly wars with a sinking sensation. "Fuck," I mumble as our eyes connect.

"He's been watching the whole time."

"Noah," I grind out, my eyes falling shut. I don't want to be with Garreth, but letting another man touch me in front of him is cruel.

"Open your eyes, butterfly," Noah demands. "I'm not being an asshole. He chose to sit there."

I arch back, searching his face. Then I focus on my ex again. Is that true?

His stool is pushed back from the bar, his body shifted completely in our direction and a whiskey glass dangling from his fingers.

Noah's right. He wants to watch.

I turn back to the man still gently stroking me, keeping the fire in my core alive. "I-I don't know." My mind is too foggy, my emotions too unstable to allow me to think right now.

Behind his glasses, Noah's eyes are heavy-lidded. "Stop thinking. You want to come. He wants you to come. And I want him to watch me make you come." He presses a kiss to my lips. "Okay?"

My head bobs in acquiescence before I can second-guess myself.

His wicked grin returns, making my heart stammer. "Good girl." He presses his mouth to mine and kisses me slowly, his movements once again mimicking far dirtier acts. He works me higher and higher, the desire in my belly winding so tight it's ready to snap. Then he nudges my chin so I'm forced to look at Garreth again.

Even from across the darkened room, there's no denying the heat in his gaze. His jaw is tight and his expression is unreadable, but he doesn't bother trying to hide the large bulge in his pants.

Garreth is gifted in that area, just like Noah, and I enjoyed my time with him. But it was never more than good sex. With Noah, it's mind-blowing. It's on another level. And the connection goes far beyond the physical.

He's my soulmate, and he knows it.

Only a man secure in our connection would allow an ex to watch as he pleasured me. He knows there's no competition. There never has been, even in the years we were apart.

So I do as he says, and I watch the man across the room. I perform for both of them, and I love every minute of it.

As I ride Noah's hand, I lick my lips, not just parched but craving a specific taste. The whiskey in Garreth's glass calls to me, making me needier.

"What are you thinking?"

When I don't answer, too caught up in the moment, Noah nips at my ear.

"Tell me what you're thinking, butterfly, or I stop."

A shaky breath escapes me. "I'm thinking I want Garreth's whiskey on my lips."

"Dirty girl." He sucks on the sensitive spot below my ear, then laps at it, soothing the sting. "Tell him." The raspy quality of his voice, the confidence and desire there, causes goose bumps to scatter across my body.

But when his words register, my heart leaps into my throat. "What?"

"Do it." He clutches my thigh, holding me to him. "You want him to come sit by us while I get you off? I'm game. He doesn't taste you, but you can have his whiskey."

I shake my head. "No. I just." I sigh, though it sounds more like a whimper. "I don't know what I want."

"You want to lie down and let me lick you until you come for us?"

Warmth gushes from me at the thought, no doubt soaking his hand. "Fuck, I do. Shit."

"Lean back, baby."

As I ease myself onto my back on the bench, he tears my panties off.

From this angle, Garreth appears upside down. The whole world honestly feels upside down after the way Noah has edged me.

"Call him over," he rasps.

My ex is still watching, still solely fixated on me. And when I use a finger to motion him over, he stands immediately.

My lungs seize up. *Shit. Shit. Shit.* This is happening. How the fuck did I end up in a bar half naked with two men? And why am I considering the best way to get all three of us completely naked?

Noah would never.

Would he?

My heart stutters at the idea.

Would Garreth?

And is that really what I want?

The hulking presence now standing over us blocks out the majority of the dim light. "Need something?"

"She'd like a sip of your whiskey. And I thought you'd like these." Wedged between my thighs, Noah barely looks up as he tosses my panties in Garreth's direction. Then he lowers his face and licks me in one long, languid stroke.

Garreth catches my black panties and squeezes them in his fist, his eyes blazing. He's silent for what feels like an eternity before he finally says, "Is that what you want?"

The breath is stolen from my lungs as Noah sucks my clit into his mouth and then flicks it rapidly with his tongue. I can't think when he does that, let alone try to formulate a response to Garreth's question.

I squeeze my eyes shut and collect what little sense I still possess, then breathe out before meeting his gaze. "Yes."

With a muttered *fuck*, he presses my panties to his nose and inhales.

In that moment, I go up in flames. It's a wonder this entire place isn't burning down around us.

With painfully slow movements, Garreth positions a knee on the cushion near my head and leans over me. "Open."

I obey, and he tips his glass carefully, slowly pouring the whiskey into my mouth. A splash of it hits my cheek, but his aim is accurate. The majority coats my tongue, and the taste, the way it burns, over-loads my senses.

Noah, clearly a master at reading my body, fucks me violently with two fingers and sucks hard on my clit.

The telltale tingle of an impending orgasm turns into a full-body spasm, stealing my breath and my vision. I clutch at Garreth's thigh to ground myself as Noah brutally drags pleasure from my body. As a jolt of pure ecstasy overtakes me, I suck in a breath.

A scream builds in my throat, but before it escapes me, Noah hisses, "Shut her up."

Garreth drops the glass to the floor with a thunk and cuffs the front of my neck, his mouth covering mine.

Noah doesn't slow, though his grip on my hip tightens painfully, like he can't stand the sight of another man's mouth on mine, despite this moment being his doing. His movements become more feverish, giving me no time to recover before he sends me hurtling over another cliff.

Back bowing off the cushioned bench, I gasp into Garreth's mouth, shocked by the waves of rapture rolling through my body. When the last of the pleasure wanes, I sag, thoroughly spent.

Garreth pulls back and presses one gentle kiss to my lips. "Thank you." Then he releases my neck, grabs his glass from the floor, and walks away.

I blink at his retreating form, certain I've lost touch with reality. Did that really just happen?

"Are you okay?" Noah eases my skirt down and helps me into a sitting position.

When the backs of my thighs make contact with the cushion, it dawns on me that Garreth just walked off with my panties.

"Yeah, I'm okay." With a huff of a laugh, I press my hand to my racing heart.

Noah watches me from behind his glasses, studying me, taking in every detail.

I want to know what he's thinking. Did I just destroy any chance the two of us had? Or did that turn him on like it did me?

As we look at one another, silent, I'm certain that I want more than all of this. I want a life with him.

I worry my lip as the excitement of the moment fades and apprehension takes its place. "Are we done with the games?"

He tilts to one side and pulls out his wallet.

My heart lurches and my lungs spasm, making every inhale painful. "Oh my god, if you pay me right now, I will slap you."

He lowers his head and glares, as if my concern is ridiculous.

But I'm half naked in a sex club and just basically performed for two men, so excuse me if my subconscious is running wild.

Without a word, he pulls out a bill and slaps it onto the table. "I'm done with the games if you are."

I blink at him, confused, then eye the cash. When I notice the familiar writing, my mouth goes dry.

It seems impossible, but there, with a little heart over the *i*, is my name.

Sienna 508-574-6824.

My heart starts and stops again.

"You found it."

Chapter 41
Sienna

"HOW LONG?" I whisper. It's taken me close to thirty minutes to get my wits about me enough to ask. Though for most of that time, I dedicated my attention to getting out of that club. This dollar bill and this relationship have no business being in that space.

I've been silent, processing, the whole way home. But now, as the Uber driver stops in front of our building, I can't stay quiet any longer.

I hold the dollar bill out, my fingers trembling. I still can't believe he found it. And I can't get over the bright and bubbly writing. The little heart over the *i* in my name. The extra message, my plea to Noah. I was so full of hope then. I truly believed that he would find it again.

Part of me wants to scoff at the naïveté of that young woman. Yet I'm holding the proof that she wasn't so wrong. *That* Sienna wasn't a hopeless romantic. She was a believer.

The dollar is worn like it went through hell and back to get here, and god, do I feel the same. Yet it's been smoothed out, the corners flattened. As if it's been cared for. As if Noah has cherished it every moment since he found it. Treated it as his most prized possession.

Noah swallows, his throat bobbing. "Thank you." He nods to the driver, then grasps my hand. "Inside."

My instinct is to bristle at his brush-off, but I backtrack as he lowers his head and fixes those blue eyes, so full of emotion, on me.

"Please," he says. "I would rather be in private."

I'm not sure being alone with him is the wisest choice, yet I can't really throw a fit and refuse to get out of the car either. So I let him help me out.

The moment the elevator doors close and the car ascends, I turn on him. "Talk."

Rather than tense up, his body physically settles. "It was the day I found out you'd been hired as the new CEO."

I rear back. "What?"

He nods, his lips twisting.

"How the hell is that possible?"

He grins and eases his hands into his pockets. "Another happy coincidence?"

I don't smile back. I can't. This can't be real. It's too far-fetched. "No, that's…"

Noah's expression sobers. "Tell me about it."

"But how?"

"Aiden wanted a soda."

I cough out a laugh. "What?"

"Daniel and Hannah wanted matching tattoos, so they dragged the whole group of us to the shop with them. And I—" He shakes his head and rolls his shoulders. "I have no idea why they insisted I come. But all the guys were there. Brooks mentioned that you were taking over the hockey division, and I spiraled—"

"Because it meant I'd finally figure out who you were, and you didn't want that?" The words leave me of their own accord, each one laced with the pain that's plagued me since I discovered that he found me more than a year before I came to work for the Bolts, yet he never reached out. And he never came for me like he promised he would.

He pushes off the wall and brushes a nonexistent hair from my face. My instinct is to lean into his touch, but I'm confused and disoriented, so I hold strong. We've always done well when it comes to physical touch, but our communication skills are shit.

"Sienna—" The elevator dings and the door slides open, so I take the opportunity to slip past him.

Noah's quick, though. He grabs my arm and holds me in place, his eyes pleading, and the stainless-steel door closes again. "Yes, I saw you at Brooks's wedding. I was shocked and so fucking happy. I knew immediately that your last name didn't matter. That we'd make it work. That we really were meant to be. I'd been searching for you everywhere for years, and suddenly, there you were. I'd all but given up on fate, but right then, I knew you were right. I didn't care what it cost to have you in my life. All I wanted was to be near you again." Behind his glasses, I swear his eyes go misty. "*God*, just to hear your voice would have sufficed. Once I collected myself, I was on a mission to talk to you. But when I found you again, you weren't alone. Garreth was there. You were whispering to him. Touching him. *Kissing him*." He squeezes his eyes shut and rubs at them beneath his glasses, as if he's experiencing it all over again.

My stomach twists so violently I nearly double over from the pain.

I don't even remember the moment he's describing. That's how little it meant to me. And not even twenty-four hours later, I ended things with Garreth.

I tumble into a free fall as I struggle to understand the cruelty of those facts.

Twenty-four fucking hours were all that kept me from having my soulmate when my world fell apart. Twenty-four hours meant going another two years without knowing him. Having him. Touching him.

And what he saw that night? How that must have made him feel? It makes me sick to my stomach. I can't even imagine him with another woman, and he had to witness me with another man.

And I did it to him again tonight.

"I'm so sorry." My heart cracks wide open, and a sob escapes me. "A-and tonight—"

He brushes a thumb over my cheekbone, catching a tear. It does little good as another falls. But he holds my face in his hands and steps into my space. "No, baby, we're not doing that." He ducks, ensuring that I'm listening. "I wanted tonight just as much as you did. Honestly I needed to see you kiss him again to confirm that it's over."

"It is." My words are clipped, emphatic.

The hint of a smile creeps onto his face. "I know."

"You do?"

"Yes. You didn't kiss him like you need him to breathe. You didn't kiss him like this." He brings his mouth to mine, consuming me. He dominates me, and only when he's stolen my breath does he ease up and allow me to set the pace.

I wrap my arms around his neck and cling to him. "Please," I mumble against his lips.

With his hands on my ass, he hoists me up, and I wrap my legs around him. "Please what, butterfly?"

"Please don't walk away. Please, just…*please.*"

He presses the button for our floor, and the doors open again immediately. Then he adjusts his hold and strides toward his apartment.

As he fumbles with his keys with one hand and holds me up with the other, he says, "You don't have to beg, butterfly. I made you a promise and I intend to keep it. I told you I was coming for you, and now that I have you, I'm not going anywhere. But I need to hold you tonight. It's been a long six years without you, and I'm not going another night without you in my arms."

"I need you," I breathe into his neck. As he pushes the door open, I work one button through its hole with shaky fingers and relish the warm bare skin of his chest beneath it.

"We don't have to—"

"I need you," I growl. I didn't know my voice could even do that, but my hunger for him is carnal. I need him inside me. I need to be connected to him, to remind myself that this is what we waited for all these years. That the universe had its reasons for waiting so long to bring us back together.

I may not be that naïve girl anymore, but this is so much better. Because I'm a woman who's deeply in love, so completely sure that if I was made to do one thing in this world, it was to love this man. And I truly believe he was made to love me. We're soulmates. It's that simple.

I don't know what tomorrow will look like, and I don't know how we'll approach my brothers, but like Noah said, fuck my last name.

Fuck it all.

I only need him.

CHAPTER 42
NOAH

I NEED YOU.

Sienna's words echo through my apartment and latch on to my heart, unlocking what's left of my reservations.

With my lips on hers and our limbs tangled, I press her up against the back of the door. While she wiggles her ass, hiking up her dress, I undo my belt and pull out my cock. In a matter of seconds, I slide home, sheathed in her perfect heat.

She cries out, and I still inside her, holding her gaze as we finally become one again.

"I need you," I tell her. "Fuck, I've needed you for so long."

"I'm yours." She smiles against my mouth.

Standing there with my pants around my ankles, my dick inside her, and a big smile on my lips, I'm the happiest I've ever been.

"Now make me come again."

With a dark chuckle, I pull back and snap my hips, slamming into her. "Gonna fuck that sass right out of you."

"Please," she pants. "My sass is your favorite thing about me."

I lick a line up her neck. "You're not wrong."

When a breathy laugh escapes her, I seal my mouth over hers. I want to swallow all her sounds. I can't stop kissing her. I want to spend my life doing this, showing her how much she means to me.

The games are over, like she said. Her past—hell, my past—doesn't matter. We're here together. It's all I could fucking ask for.

When she goes over the edge, pulsing around me, she takes me with her. My release is so powerful I worry the two of us will go crashing to the ground. I pump faster, thrusting deeper, giving her every ounce of me.

Less than five minutes after we entered my apartment, we're breathing heavily and coated in each other's pleasure.

"Now what?" she whispers.

I bite down on her lip. "Now we live happily ever after?"

The words are a soft tease, but the way her green eyes glow in response makes my heart fucking skip.

"Maybe a shower first," she says, smile on her face.

Sienna gets carried away behind the fogged-up glass, dropping to her knees and sucking me off, her eyes never leaving mine, even as she swallows me down. The memory will live in my brain for the rest of eternity.

After, with her head on my chest, one finger tracing my tattoo, I close my eyes and soak in the moment, working to convince myself that all of this is real.

"You mentioned Garreth gave you something tonight," I eventually hedge.

Her body stiffens and her fingers stop their movement.

"It's okay, baby." I kiss her forehead. "We're good."

Muscles relaxing, she goes back to tracing my tattoo, fixing her focus on it. "Remember when I told you they took everything?"

I hum but otherwise remain quiet, giving her the time and space to explain.

"The settlement included a clause prohibiting me from ever operating another fashion house. I also had to agree to never sell my designs again."

Anger flares in my veins. "That's absurd."

Her eyes flit to mine. "Yes. They wanted to hurt me. Punish me."

I caress her bare thigh, relishing the warmth of her. "But why would you agree?"

"When they discovered that Beckett had referred me to the financial consultant who defrauded us, they saw dollar signs." She sighs. "I wanted to keep my family from being dragged into it."

I frown. "Does Beckett know that?"

"No. And you won't tell him." She lifts her head. "None of it matters anymore anyway. Garreth hired a private investigator, and not only did he find the money, but he got the designers to agree to rescind the settlement agreement." Her eyes fill with tears. "I can design again. I can do whatever I want, really."

Distrust trickles through me. The likelihood of finding that money is nearly nonexistent. He probably paid off the other side and, in return, demanded they release Sienna from the settlement.

Though I'll keep that theory to myself. There's no harm in Sienna believing his story, and I have no proof that it isn't true.

And all that matters now is that she's finally free to do what she wants. The comfort that thought brings is followed closely by a realization that makes my heart stop in my chest. "Does that mean you're going back to Paris?"

"I don't know what any of it means, really. My friend Cat offered me a position at *Jolie* Magazine tonight. A really big one. I don't know. Tonight was a lot," she says, her voice fading.

"Sounds like you have a lot of decisions to make."

She hums sleepily, her eyes fluttering closed.

I press a kiss to her temple. Regardless of what she decides, I'll support her. But the idea of her moving back to Paris is like a lead weight in my gut. I just got her back. I don't know that I can let her go again.

But between Ollie and my career, if she decides to leave, what choice will I have?

Chapter 43
Sienna

I'M EXCITED TOO. There's no denying it. About her job offer. About Noah. About the status of the settlement. After months and months of hell, things are looking up.

The thought of setting my hands on silk again, of turning a piece of cloth into a piece of art for someone I care about to wear, sets my blood on fire. My fingers can't stop twitching. All I want to do is get ahold of that fabric and start sewing and cutting and *creating*.

I just have to hold out for two more hours.

Knee bouncing with pent-up excitement, I turn back to my computer screen and click on the email from our head of marketing regarding the bedazzled jerseys I suggested. Then I respond to the one from Beckett about family dinner. There are also five emails Gavin forwarded with information about the next series of games that I have to review and one from Ezra that details the new players he's interested in drafting.

The number of players he's researched is a little alarming. It's like his goal is to build a new roster. With the already incredible team we have—a team headed for the finals, in fact—it's absurd, really.

The last email he sent focused on the high cost of keeping our first line versus drafting a new one. Is the man insane? War—the team's captain—my brother, and Noah make up the first line. Does he really think I have any interest in removing even one of them from the roster?

Noah's agent may be demanding a contract that would make him the highest-paid winger in the NHL, but based on his stats, it's worth considering.

Yes, his age is working against him, but the idea of him leaving Boston is unconscionable.

So I have to convince Ezra that keeping him is our best option. And I have to convince my brothers that he's worth the investment. And I have to do it without alerting anyone to my motives. Because they aren't the least bit professional. I can't risk losing him again. Not when I just got him back.

My cursor is hovering over Ezra's email when a knock sounds at my door and I find Garreth standing at the threshold.

Like always, he looks dashing in an expensive suit.

Nervous energy radiates through me. After last night, I don't know how to act.

Fortunately, he gives me a soft smile, putting me at ease. "Have a minute?"

I stand and motion for him to come in. "How did Beth let you by without alerting me?"

He grins. "I came to see Beckett, but I saw you sitting at your desk and thought I'd pop in."

"Oh." I suppose that makes sense. And it's a relief, really, to know he didn't come to search me out specifically.

"About last night," I say. At the same time, he murmurs, "Nice office."

Cheeks warming, I shrug. "Thanks."

We're silent then, and awkwardness grows as we stare at one another, neither knowing how to move forward.

Finally, he clears his throat. "Does your brother know?"

I frown. "Does Beckett know what?"

"About Noah. *Sienna's Noah.*" His lips quirk in amusement as he uses Noah's words from last night.

I sit back, thrown by his reaction, my protective instincts flaring to life. "There's nothing to know."

Eyes narrowed, he tilts his head. "We dated for two years, Sienna, and you didn't once look at me the way you look at him."

My cheeks heat in earnest this time. I shouldn't be surprised that he noticed. The way I feel for Noah is unlike anything I've ever felt for another person. "I'm sorry if I hurt you."

His expression grows serious. "It's okay. Honestly, you showed me what I've been missing in life. I've been so focused on repairing our family business that I didn't even notice our relationship was missing such an integral part. I enjoyed our time immensely; I hope you know that. Seeing you like this, lit up and glowing, *happy*—despite how bad things have been for you professionally—is all I could hope for. It's good to see you smile. Don't let him go."

I tip my head back, fighting back tears. He's right. Despite everything, I've never been happier than when I'm with Noah. Even if I never got to design another piece, I think I'd still be happy. Because of him.

"Thank you," I whisper.

With a nod, he heads for the door. Halfway there, he turns around, holding up a small package, and strides toward my desk. "I forgot to give you this last night."

The blue paper the package is wrapped in is familiar, as are the gold stitching and the name of the bookshop imprinted on it. "I stopped at that shop you always loved after my meeting regarding your settlement. The shop owner told me you'd want this."

My chest tightens and my breathing goes shallow. There's no way.

Though I feel as if my soul has left my body, I manage to thank him. Once he's gone, I turn away from the door, not wanting to share this moment with anyone, and tear into the paper.

As it flutters to the floor and the cover of the book in my hand is revealed, I gasp. The black background is one I recognize, and I've memorized just about every detail of the gold font and the simple design.

I run my thumb along the worn cream-colored edges of the pages and close my eyes. For a moment, I just breathe. And when I finally work up the nerve to flip open the cover and scan the title page, my legs nearly give out. Because there, right below the block letters, is Noah Harrison's name, and there's a number below it, along with a message.

One day you'll fly back to me, butterfly, and I'll never let you go again.

CHAPTER 44
NOAH

THIGHS BURNING AND PULSE POUNDING, I fold in half and set my hands on my legs. As sweat drips down my face, I heave in a deep breath. Fuck, I'm getting too old for this.

As I straighten, my best friend howls with laughter. "Trouble keeping up, Beauty?"

"Fuck, how are you barely winded?"

War and I are the same damn age. How the hell does he look like he's only taken a lap around the ice after multiple rounds of suicides and the hours we've spent running through plays with Aiden Langfield, the most competitive player I've ever met?

Our line isn't the only one still working, even though practice is long over . The entire team is out here with us.

The only person in the NHL who could get people to stay after practice is probably the damn Leprechaun. We all want to make him proud.

And he's out here singing and chirping like this shit is easy.

I won't complain. I want Aiden and all his brothers to think I'm the most agreeable, perfect human to ever exist so one day, when he finds out that I'm in love with his sister, he won't castrate me.

On our way off the ice, Camden Snow skates up beside me and nudges me. "You hear the front office is scouting Huey Davis?"

I nod. It's not a surprise after the comments Ezra made on the plane a few weeks ago.

Camden grabs the boards and steps onto the carpeting. "You nervous?"

Should I be? Probably. Am I? That's to be determined, I guess. Lately, I can't muster the hunger for the game like I used to. "Always good to have new blood."

Camden's face sours. "You don't think one of us is on the chopping block? I just came back, and you're up for renewal." He leans in close. "There's no way Gavin is getting rid of his own brother-in-law. His wife would kill him."

He's right. And on top of that, Daniel is an incredible athlete with years left to play. Besides, they just signed a deal to keep him.

"And War is like family," he adds.

I dip my chin in acknowledgment. Tyler Warren is our team's captain, and one could argue that he's the heart of this team, even if he isn't a Langfield. He isn't going anywhere. The guy spent most of his life searching for a place to belong, for a true, caring family, and here he is, with a wife and four kids and an entire team of hockey players who love him.

"But you and me." Camden sighs. "If we want to stay, we're going to have to work for it."

I squeeze his shoulder, realization dawning. He probably needs the comfort. Like War, Cam doesn't talk to his blood relatives anymore.

The only family member he was close to, his sister, disappeared after Cam's then girlfriend had an affair with his sister's boyfriend and subsequently got pregnant. Now he's got no one but hockey.

That could have been me.

Would have been if not for Ollie.

And now I have Sienna too.

So no, I'm not panicking about the possibility of being traded. This is just a job. If my options at the end of next season are accepting a trade or retiring, then yeah, I'll miss the game, but I can live without it. I can't live without Ollie and Sienna.

Fuck, just thinking of the two of them and our potential future makes me smile.

And it only grows when Sienna steps into the arena with Gavin. My girl is wearing tight black pants with a red shirt that molds to her chest and shows off her tiny curves and the swell of her breasts. With her hair pulled back in a low bun, her wicked smirk is on full display as she finds me. It's pure deviance. Like she's thinking of all the ways she can climb me. Tease me. Fuck me.

And, fuck, does the thought of any one of those light me up.

Camden nudges me. "Better be careful. Baby Langfield is giving you sex eyes."

I choke, my airway closing and panic igniting in my chest.

Behind me, Aiden groans. "That's my sister."

Sienna cocks a brow, clearly hearing our interaction, and grins.

Aiden passes us, smacking Camden on the back of the head as he goes. "And she's right there."

"Aw, Aiden," she teases. "You're such a sweet big brother." Her grin turns wicked and her eyes flash. "I hate to break it to ya, but I can hear about sex and not have my innocence rocked." Then, as if whispering, she puts a hand up and adds, "I can even have it. In fact, I did last night."

Gavin glares at her, and Brooks comes off the ice, covering his ears. "Sienna, please."

Aiden, who's stomping away now, groans. "My ears are bleeding."

Head thrown back, she laughs, the sound echoing in the giant space. "Your wives tease me incessantly. This is karma."

Brooks squirts water into his mouth and sighs. "I can't control Sara. I've tried."

Sienna gives me a salacious wink. Fuck. She's enjoying this far too much. She's also playing with fire. Her brothers aren't idiots. They'll catch on eventually. Or the other guys will, and there'll be no stopping the rumors. I'm breaking every fucking rule. A guy doesn't touch another player's sister. Especially his best friends' little sister. Especially not royalty like Sienna Fucking Langfield.

I couldn't care less.

I've touched every inch of her, and I'll do it again. Over and over.

"Last-minute request," Gavin hollers, blessedly changing the subject before we can be called out. "There's a charity event next

Saturday in Michigan, and the Bolts will be there to do a charity skate with the college to raise money. Every one of you should plan to be in attendance."

Camden nudges me. "That's where Davis goes to school. They're fucking testing him out against us. This is bad."

Frustration and disappointment bloom inside me. Shit. He's not wrong. But that's the least of my problems. Because I promised Ollie I'd be at his championship T-ball game, and now I'm going to once again let him down.

Fuck.

CHAPTER 45
NOAH

FUCK. Now I'm *hard* while her brothers mingle nearby.

I covertly eye them, making sure their attention is occupied before I reply.

A chuckle escapes me before I can stop it, snagging Snow's attention. He eyes me as he ties his shoe, then straightens and lifts his chin in question.

With a shake of my head, I slip my phone into my pocket, ensuring no one gets a peek at that message.

"Want to grab a drink?" He asks as the guys begin to file out. "I'm guessing they're all going home to their wives."

I feel for the guy. He's lonely, so when we're not playing hockey, he's looking for people to spend time with or he's out prowling for women. Though that's slowed down a bit, and even when he meets a girl, he doesn't often take her home. If I had to guess, he's looking for a real connection. One that I'm lucky enough to have found.

I shake my head. "Can't. It's my night with Ollie."

Camden nods and breaks into a small smile. "Tell him I said hi."

Lips pressed together, I assess him. "You ever think of having kids?"

That smile turns rueful. "All the damn time." He shrugs. "Just haven't found the right person to do that with yet, I guess."

I nod. "You will."

He shrugs. "Maybe. Enjoy your night, Harry."

Once the locker room has emptied out, I take out my phone again and find another message from Sienna. This one, thankfully, is much more tame.

Sienna: Dinner?

There is nothing in this world I'd rather do than spend time with Sienna. Except see my son. It's been a week, and I can't go another day without a hug from him.

It figures that the first time she initiates plans, I have to turn her down.

Me: Where are you?

Sienna: Down the hall, make a left.

Grinning, I stride out of the room. Knowing I get to see her, put my hands on her, makes me giddy. *She* makes me giddy. Happy. Fucking joy-filled.

I round the corner, and Sienna comes into view. She's pressed against the wall, phone in her hand, a smirk on her lips.

"Very covert," I tease.

Her emerald eyes glitter when they lock on me. "I would make an excellent spy," she whispers.

Fuck, she's adorable. I want to push her up against the wall and kiss the shit out of her.

Instead I slip my hands into my pockets and nod.

"So, dinner?" She gives me a hopeful smile. "I want to show you something."

My smile falls, and a heartbeat later, hers does too. "It's my night with Ollie."

I'm gearing up to explain that I want to be with her, but that my kid needs me, that the dad guilt is weighing on me more than ever now that I have to break the news that I have to miss his T-ball tournament. But before I can put my jumbled thoughts into words, she shakes her head and gives me a soft smile. "I get it. You're a dad first."

My heart sinks. Yeah, Ollie is my world. But I hate that she'd think that what we have has to take a back seat to my relationship with him. It's not one or the other. And if Sienna and I are heading in the direction I hope we are, they'll both come first. Because she isn't just a hookup or a fling. If I have it my way, she'll eventually be my family.

I take a step closer, looking down the hall to ensure we're alone. "What if," I say as I cup her cheek and revel in the feel of her smooth, warm skin, "you come over for dinner? Hang with Ollie and me?"

Her green eyes are fathomless as they widen in surprise. "Are you sure?"

Warmth blooms in my chest. "Yes, baby, I'm sure." I lean in close. "I'm a dad, but I also want to be yours."

She clutches the fabric of my shirt and tugs me closer. Lips brushing mine, she declares, "You are mine."

And fuck, now I'm hard again.

Before Sienna arrives, I sit Ollie down for a chat.

Not about Sienna. Not yet. She and I need to have a conversation before that happens.

No, it's better if I break the news about his tournament now.

He arrived this afternoon bursting with stories he's been waiting to tell me. Ted bought matching swim trunks for the two of them this week after Jen brought home a coordinating set for her and Ollie's sister.

Poor Ted. I feel bad for the guy. The gesture was a good one, and I tell my son that. But when he went on to explain that they were bright teal with pink ice cream cones, a chuckle slipped out.

"Like I'd be caught dead matching him," Ollie grouses. "Let alone in that."

I school my expression, still trying to channel benevolence. "What did you do?"

"Told him that while I think his fashion choices are daring, and he should be proud of himself for being so authentically himself, I'm a scaredy-cat who'd rather be liked by the masses." While he keeps a straight face through the whole explanation, I have to smash my lips together to keep from cackling.

"And how did your mom feel about that?" Sometimes I worry that Ted and Jen will tire of how few fucks the kid has to give, but I find it mostly hysterical.

"She pulled me aside after and thanked me and offered me twenty dollars to take the shorts with me when I came here."

"Please tell me you have them." I give up on fighting the amusement flowing through me.

"Obviously." Grinning, Ollie darts for his room and returns with his overnight bag.

He has a full wardrobe at both houses, but he still takes a bag back and forth so he has his T-ball gear and school supplies wherever he goes.

He rifles through his things and yanks out the hideous trunks with a triumphant smile.

The teal is so bright it's almost blinding, but what he failed to mention was that along with the pink ice cream cones, the fabric is printed with watermelons and strawberries. "We should send a picture to the grandpas."

Biting back a snort, I snag my phone from the table. Ollie poses with the offending suit, wearing an exaggerated look of shock, then bounces over and peers at the screen while I tap out a message.

I hit Send and set the phone down again. "They'll get a kick out of that."

He tosses the trunks onto the floor without a thought. "What are we having for dinner? I was thinking pizza. Mom's been on a health kick, and the last one she ordered had cauliflower crust." He sticks his tongue out and makes a gagging noise.

A shudder runs through me. That sounds awful. "Pizza is good. Sienna's coming over. Is that all right?"

"Really?" The way his eyes light up makes my chest warm.

"Yeah."

"What about Aunt Hannah and Uncle Danny?"

"You want me to invite them?" I'd rather not, but it's hard to say no to this kid, and he hasn't seen them in a week.

He shakes his head. "Nah, maybe just Sienna tonight. I haven't seen her in a while, and Mav hogs everyone's attention."

His words tug at my heartstrings. I can't blame him for being possessive of Sienna's attention. I feel the same way.

We still have a little time, just the two of us, so I take a deep breath and steady myself for the change in topic. "I also needed to talk to you about something."

He settles quickly, the energy radiating from him waning. The kid is so damn intuitive. He impresses me every day.

"I found out today that the team has to be in Michigan next Saturday."

A frown mars his sweet face. "But my big game is that day."

I nod, my heart clenching. "I know. And you know there's nowhere I'd rather be—"

"But you have a job," he says, his tone gentle, like he's comforting us both. Like he's the adult.

I hate it.

I love my son's sense of humor. I love how wise he is. I love his snark and his giant personality. But this part? I think I'd prefer it if he threw a fit. If he cried and begged because he's too young, too egocentric to understand. Because fuck, even I don't understand. I don't understand why I have to miss out on so much time with him. I don't understand why, no matter how hard I try, I always feel like I'm letting him down. And I don't understand how I'm *not* letting him down. It's unfair, how understanding he is.

"I'm sorry, bud. I really wish I could be there."

He nods, though he focuses somewhere over my shoulder. "Mom can send you a video so you can watch it later."

I grasp his arm and wait for him to look at me. When he does, his blue eyes are wide, depthless, and sad. In this moment, with his small body next to me, I'm reminded of how young he truly is. And how much I'm missing out on. "I'd still rather see it in person."

"Next time," he tells me.

I swallow hard and nod. "Yeah, next time."

We're still sitting quietly when the doorbell rings. And as if a switch has flipped, he perks up and darts across the apartment. "Sienna's here."

Over pizza, Ollie and Sienna carry the conversation. I'm in awe of them both, and the whole time, I'm in my head, wishing I could make this a nightly event.

"Last time I saw you, you mentioned you had plans for a hug. Did it happen?" Sienna asks as she takes her second piece of pizza.

My son sets his slice down like he's about to settle into a good story. "Oh yeah. It totally happened."

Her lips twitch and her eyes gleam. "What were you wearing?"

Without a second's hesitation, he launches into a description of the outfit. It's one that the two of them discussed as an option while we were in Florida when he was dead set on making sure his first hug went off without a hitch.

"You planning on kissing her anytime soon?" Sienna asks with a quick glance in my direction.

I fucking adore the genuine affection radiating from her. And I adore spending time with the two of them.

My little guy shakes his head. "Nah, I'm gonna make her work for that. Kissing feels like a second-grade thing."

Sienna's shocked laughter rings out, the sound lighting me up inside.

After dinner and a round of Chutes and Ladders, she offers to clean up while I get Ollie ready for bed. Before he heads to the bathroom to brush his teeth, he throws his arms around her waist, surprising us both. "I'm so glad you came to see us."

Once he's tucked in, I turn off his bedroom light, leaving only the nightlight above his bed on so he can read for another fifteen minutes, then shuffle out to find my girl.

She's settled on my couch, a full wineglass on the table in front of her, a blanket draped over her legs, and a book in her lap. She's made herself comfortable, and I like that more than I can explain.

When she spots me, she breaks into a soft smile.

Tonight was a good night. And I can't help but dream of a life where every night looks like this.

A wave of melancholy hits me next, because every night can't be like this since I don't have Ollie full time. And honestly, I'm not sure Sienna's in this wholeheartedly yet.

"What's wrong?" she asks, her brow creased.

I force a smile and ease onto the couch beside her. "Nothing. You're here. I'm happy." I pull her legs over mine, settling my hands on her bare shins. She's dressed in a pair of jean shorts and a simple black T-shirt, looking all sorts of relaxed.

"Don't lie to me. I saw the smile drop for a second. Tell me what you're thinking."

I let out a low laugh and look toward Ollie's bedroom. "I was just thinking about how nice it is having you both here and how I wish it was like this more often."

"That's not a bad thing."

Her soft tone lures me back to the moment, and I meet her inquisitive gaze. "It is for a person who travels as much as I do. I don't get enough time with him as it is, and today I found out I'll have to miss his T-ball tournament because of the charity skate Ezra coordinated in Michigan."

Lips twisting, she nods thoughtfully.

"You know what the worst part of it all is? It's how understanding my kid was when I broke the news. He didn't even get upset. More than anything, I wanted to tell Gavin that I wouldn't be there. That I had other obligations, but since I'm up for contract negotiations, I have to play ball."

Sienna's eyes widen. "We can't talk about that."

I squeeze her thigh. "You don't have to say anything. This is me talking to Sienna, the woman I can't stop thinking about. Not Sienna the CEO."

Her brows lower, her expression guarded. "You know I want you to stay."

I grin, eager to lighten the suddenly somber mood. I'm not as worried about the contract as I probably should be, and I definitely don't want her to think I expect her to do anything on my behalf. "Do you, now?"

She nods, her teeth scraping over her bottom lip. "I, uh, I wanted to show you something."

"Mmm?" I settle deeper into the cushions, relishing how right it feels to have her this close.

She tucks her chin and studies the book in her hand for several seconds. When she holds it up, there's this moment before I understand what I'm looking at. A heartbeat, really. And when it's over, I'm suddenly no longer the same man. I've changed irrevocably and completely.

The truth slams into me like a boulder, knocking the air from my lungs.

I've seen hundreds of these books. Hell, I purchased hundreds of them. But this one looks worn, and this inexplicable nudge, this voice in my head, tells me that it might actually be *the* one.

The book I brought to the Bahamas. Hannah's debut novel. The one I was reading on the plane the day I first laid eyes on Sienna.

At that time, I couldn't have fathomed what she'd come to mean to me. I never would have believed she'd be the love of my life.

Yet here we are. And I'd bet everything I have that the object in her hand is *the* book.

I grasp it, and for a moment, we hold it like that, the both of us.

"I never thought I'd find this," she whispers.

A hope stronger than any I've ever known bursts to life inside me. "But you did."

With a nod, she releases it.

I take a steadying breath, eyeing it, then her. When her lips tick up just a little, I ease the cover open.

There, in black ink, are my name and number, along with the first message I left her inside one of these paperbacks.

The first of many.

Because I cheated. I signed far more than one.

But only this one was also signed by Hannah.

This is it.

The chances that she'd find any of them are slim. But this one? It was a proverbial needle in a haystack.

Sienna's soft voice breaks through my spiraling. "I think we can both admit that we mean a lot to one another. And maybe it's time to acknowledge that the universe wants us to be together."

I smile. "Yeah, it would appear so."

She gnaws on her lip. "So please talk to me. About everything. Your concerns. Your fears. About life and Ollie and—" She shakes her head. "I know I'm not his mom, and I know he's got a great one, but I want to be there for you. I want to help in any way you'll let me. I really care about him. And you." She swipes a tear from her cheek, her lips trembling with emotion.

"Oh yeah?" Grinning, I brush away another falling tear.

Throat bobbing, she holds my gaze. "Yeah. And I want to be with you." She shrugs, suddenly radiating nervousness. "If that's what *you* want, that is."

I chuckle. "Oh, Sienna Langfield, I want to more than *be* with you."

She straightens. "Like you want to be my boyfriend?" Her eyes flash with a mix of excitement and nerves. Like she thinks a universe exists in which I don't want her with my whole damn heart. Fuck, if that's the case, then I've done a shit job of showing her how I feel.

I smooth my thumb across her damp cheek and shake my head. "No, but we could start there."

Her confidence falters, her shoulders falling. "Start?"

Angling in, ensuring her eyes are on mine, I lay it out for her. My voice doesn't shake, and my focus doesn't waver. A peace settles deep inside me, anchored with the certainty I feel when it comes to this woman. I'm confident. Settled and sure that Sienna is my future. "You're asking me if I want to be your boyfriend. I'm telling you, if it was my choice, I'd be your husband."

I wait for her to rear back. To brush off the statement. To backtrack like she has so many times since I found her again. Instead, her green eyes widen and glitter with hope. Then a wide, surprised smile splits her face.

Warmth flashes through my veins, lighting me up all over. The emotion radiating from her is one I want to hold on to forever. I want to grow old with this woman. I want her to be the last thing I see before I leave this earth.

"Okay," she rasps.

My heart stutters as the word bounces around in my brain. "Okay?"

Her smile lights up the room as it grows, and her giggle is like a perfect fucking song. She leans in, fisting my shirt, and crawls into my lap. "Okay." She drapes her arms around my neck. "We'll do it your way. But the boyfriend thing first." She shrugs like she didn't just tell me that one day she'll agree to be my wife. Like she didn't just make me the happiest fucking guy alive.

I hold her tight and close my eyes and just breathe her in. There's nothing left to be said because Sienna Fucking Langfield is officially my girlfriend.

Now, we just have to tell her brothers.

Chapter 46
Sienna

MY AFFAIR WITH THE BOLTS' winger made the following week of travel more exciting than it had any right to be. On the plane, we worked to find moments alone so we could press soft, urgent kisses against each other's mouths. We resorted to grazing pinkies during press conferences and sneaking glances during Gavin's locker room speeches. One evening, while he was out with the guys, I broke into his room and waited for him in nothing but his jersey. When he returned, we stayed up all night teasing orgasms from one another.

That night on his couch, he told me he wanted to be my husband, and with every day that passes, I want it more.

I'm in love with him. I just haven't told him yet.

Not that he's said the words either. I just know it's how we both feel. Before we can go down that path, though, we need a concrete plan for how to deal with our jobs and my family and Ollie.

Every night during the trip, he called his little guy, and more often than not, he'd ask to talk to me. Noah would pretend to send me a text, and I'd wait a minute or two before opening and closing the door and popping into the frame to say hello.

The two of them have become part of my every day, and I want a future with Ollie just as badly as I want it with Noah. They're becoming my family. My oldest brother taught me long ago that family comes first, and that's why my plan for tonight is an absolute no-brainer.

"You stole a plane?"

"I didn't steal a plane." I sigh. "It's a Langfield plane, and I'm a Langfield." With a sweep of a hand, I gesture to the private jet that I did, in fact, commandeer for the evening. "Ergo, it's my plane."

Noah chuckles. "I'm not sure that's how it works, baby."

As if the simple conversation has alerted him, Beckett's name flashes on my screen.

> Beckett: did you steal the Falcon?

Oh my god, he's so dramatic.

> Me: it's our plane. I'm merely using it.

> Beckett: Okay. For what?

> Me: Ollie has a T-ball tourney tomorrow, and if Noah had to fly commercial, he'd never make it there and back before the charity event tomorrow night.

I bite my thumb, my pulse picking up as I wait for my brother's response.

Shit. We're still on the tarmac. If he contacts the pilot and grounds us, I'll be royally pissed. It's close to midnight already, and as it is, I'm lucky the pilot agreed to fly so late. I would have loved to leave earlier, but this was as early as we could get here after tonight's game.

The tournament tomorrow should be over by noon, which means we'll have no trouble being back in Michigan before the charity skate at six.

Honestly, it's brilliant. And what's the point of having all this money if we can't help out our friends? Ollie is going to be thrilled, and that's all I truly care about.

> Beckett: why didn't you tell me? Where is it?

I frown at the phone.

Noah bumps my arm. "What?"

I shake my head and give him a small smile. The last thing I want is to stress him out. I'll make this happen one way or another. "Beckett wants to know where Ollie's tournament is."

Noah frowns. "Why?"

Good question.

> Me: why?

> Beckett: We'll all come. You know nothing is more important than family. Besides, the Revs are always looking for new players.

I laugh.

> Me: These kids are six.

> Beckett: Never too early to prepare for the draft.

Before I can respond, the pilot comes over the intercom and warns us that we'll be taking off momentarily.

I breathe out a sigh of relief. I guess he gave them the all-clear to fly. God, I love my brother.

I've always known that having our kind of money meant we could have almost anything we wanted. Deep down, though, I knew it couldn't buy true happiness. That no matter how many houses or cars or jets we had, none of it would ever compete with having love and time with family.

Beckett was the first to really show us that. All of us, really. He and Gavin were so much more than typical big brothers. They went out of their way to make sure Brooks and Aiden and I always felt special and loved.

And Beckett doubled down on the point when he married Liv and focused all that love and attention on his family.

But today, money really did buy happiness. Ollie lost his mind when Noah showed up, and he's been beaming ever since. That sight is one I'd pay millions to see again. God, what a moment.

"When are you going to tell your brothers?" Cat murmurs as the kids run the bases, warming up.

I didn't know until we got here that Cat's younger son, James, goes to school with Ollie and that the two play T-ball together.

They get along a whole lot better than Addie and J.J. Both are here today, pointedly ignoring each other. Eight-year-old drama is a riot. What I would give for life to be that simple again.

He's probably pissed because she's better than he is. She's probably pissed because he's a boy and will unquestionably get more attention on the ice because of that fact alone.

I side-eye Cat. "I don't know what you're talking about."

She snorts and shakes her head. "Jay and I always did love the sneaking around part."

Sometimes I forget that she and Jay dated behind her brothers' backs, kind of in the same way Noah and I are.

Noah rushes onto the field and lifts Ollie over his head, the two of them wearing matching bright smiles. My heart pangs at the sight. I'd love nothing more than to be out there with them. To be more than the nice boss who made this happen for a player she respects and appreciates.

The sneaking around has been fun, yes. But that excitement is tarnishing. Now I just want everyone to know he's mine. I want to be part of his little family. I want more.

Cat leans forward, getting into my line of sight, her jaw unhinged. "Shit. It's more serious than I thought."

I nudge her. "Shh, we're not talking about this."

"Not talking about what?" Beckett asks from where he's leaning against the railing overlooking the small field. He showed up with all the kids, as promised, as well as Liv and Deogi. The dog is a massive thing that slobbers everywhere, and all the kids keep trying to ride him like he's a pony.

"About Liv's dress," I say quickly. "I want you to be surprised."

Beckett hums, his focus back on the field. "Works for me. She's so excited. I really appreciate it."

A genuine smile creeps up my face. "I appreciate you asking. Seriously. I forgot how much I missed designing."

My brother nods like he's more than aware of that.

The boys are walking off the field, warm-ups apparently over, when my phone buzzes, so I check it quickly. It's an email notification, and the name of the sender instantly kills my good mood.

"What's wrong?" Beckett asks as I scan over the contents.

I scoff. "Ezra is just updating me on contract negotiations."

My brother turns to face me completely, his expression shrewd, like he knows there's more to it than that.

I sigh, annoyed. I don't know how to handle this, but I hate to ask for help. I hate to give life to the digs about nepotism that pop up here and there. Yet he's my big brother. He trusts me, but he's also more than willing to talk through any issues I have. "He says Noah's agent is asking for too much money. He wants to trade him and bring on this new kid in his place."

Beckett crosses his arms, his brow furrowed. "We worked hard to get Noah. He's the best sniper in the NHL."

I throw my hands up in the air. "Thank you. That's exactly what I said."

With his tongue pressed to the inside of his cheek, he studies me. "You and Noah have become quite close."

I shrug, playing it off. "He's Hannah's brother and my neighbor."

The ump announces the start of the game, and my brother turns his attention back to the field.

"I think it would be a mistake to let him go," I say, standing firm.

He smirks but doesn't turn to look at me. "Thought you didn't know anything about hockey."

I've already dug the hole, so I might as well keep going. "I know enough to know he's one of the best players Boston has ever had. And you brought me on because you trust my opinion, right?"

He finally turns, his lips twitching. "We did."

"So I think we should keep him."

With his mouth set in a straight line, he lowers his head. "That's Ezra's decision, really."

"Right, but maybe we could help convince him?" I suggest.

"How?"

"Maybe at the gala? Have both Ezra and Noah sit at our table. Show Ezra the chemistry he has with Aiden and War. We all know that kind of connection translates on the ice. And it can't be easily replicated."

Beckett shrugs. "Hmm, I suppose it's worth a try."

I straighten, resting my hands on my thighs. "Yes. I think so too."

Liv calls Beckett's name as Deogi drags her toward the playground, the twins running ahead, and he takes off without a word.

When it's just the two of us, Cat squeezes my arm. "Smooth."

I glare at her. "Not another word out of you."

Eyes dancing, she feigns zipping her lips shut, then turns back to the game.

Jay, who's apparently the coach, is kneeling, with the group of boys surrounding him. It's cute how they all watch him, eyes wide, eating up his every word. He holds a hand out, and the boys all pile theirs on top. Then, on the count of three, they scream, "Go Hawks." As the boys disperse, Jay stands and winks at his wife.

Beside me, Cat nibbles on her lip, her cheeks pink. Damn. After twenty years, they're still infatuated with each other.

Their love is the kind I hope Noah and I will have. Despite how successful both Cat and Jay are, both would admit without hesitation that the family they've created is by far their biggest accomplishment. And at the center of that is their marriage.

Instinctually, I scan the fence around the field for Noah. With a pair of aviator sunglasses on and wearing athletic shorts and a black T-shirt, he looks beyond hot. A total zaddy. He's on the sidelines, cheering for Ollie, who is walking up to bat.

Cat might be right. My plan for changing Ezra's mind might not be the best way to go about it, but I have to do something. I'll gladly make a fool of myself if it means my boys keep smiling like they are right now. If it means I have a shot at the happiness my best friend found with her husband.

CHAPTER 47
NOAH

AS SOON AS the last out is called and the little boys all scream because they won their first tournament, I'm rushing toward my son. Throughout the entire game, whether Ollie was chasing after a ball or swinging and missing, he'd turn and look for me on the sidelines. And every time, the way he lit up left my chest expanding.

The boys are going wild with excitement, chanting and celebrating their win. But my kid would have been just as happy if he'd lost today. My presence here was enough for him. But the smile on his face now? It makes me happier than any win I've ever had a hand in securing. I'm glad I'm here. Ecstatic, really. And I have Sienna to thank for it.

On instinct, I reach for her hand, eager for her to join me as I rush to hug my son. But realization slams into me, and I pull back just as our fingers brush.

We can't touch. I can't show her or anyone here how much she means to me. And that hits in a way I'm not comfortable with.

My disappointment over that is momentarily forgotten as Ollie launches himself at me. "Daddy, we won! I can't believe you're here. This is the bestest day ever. Can we get pizza? And ice cream?" His eyes are wide and his cheeks are flushed with exertion and joy. "Can we go to the park? And then tonight, can we watch a movie?" He doesn't even pause to catch a breath before turning to Jen. "I can sleep at Dad's tonight, right? Because he's here and he's never here for my games. Please, Mom?"

My heart cracks at the desperation in his voice. My son shouldn't have to beg to spend time with me.

Fortunately, Jen is ready with an answer, saving me from having to disappoint him before I disappear again. "Sorry, bud. We promised Nana we'd come over for dinner, remember? But Dad is picking you up tomorrow. I'm sure he'd be happy to take you for ice cream then."

Ollie's face falls. "Nana's house smells like moldy cheese."

I pull him in tight and whisper, "We can have all the ice cream and watch *Spiderman* tomorrow night."

He gasps and rips himself from my hold. "Sienna's here. Can she come over for ice cream and *Spiderman* too?"

Jen raises a brow, tamping down on a smile.

Jen may be the only person who knows exactly who Sienna is to me. As soon as I realized that she would be spending time with Ollie, I told Jen about her, as well as my hopes for the future. We agreed years ago that if I dated anyone seriously, I'd talk to Jen before introducing that person to him as my girlfriend.

"We can ask her," I tell him.

With a fist pump, he darts for her. When he flings himself at her and she wraps her arms around him, my smile grows.

"She flew you home to be here?" Jen stares at the two of them, a genuine smile on her face.

Relief washes over me. We may have had the conversation, but this is the first true interaction Jen has witnessed. "Yeah, she knew how much I wanted to be here."

"That's sweet." She takes a deep breath and lets it out slowly. "Just—"

The reticence in her tone causes dread to build in my gut, but she puts me out of my misery quickly.

"Just be careful. Ollie is really attached, and it looks like you are too."

"As far as he knows, she's just my neighbor and my friend."

Jen huffs. "Nothing gets past that boy."

With an uncomfortable laugh, I drag my hand down my face. She's not wrong. "Got it."

"I want this to work out for you," she says, her tone softer. "But until you guys go public and have really tested this relationship, I'd rather he not get any more attached. It'll hurt him if it doesn't work out."

Frustration mixes with understanding. I get it, but... "There's no testing this relationship. She's it. She's the one I'm going to marry. I didn't say a word when you told me you planned to marry Ted and raise my child with him. I jumped through the hoops you set to make it work and I moved halfway across the country so he could accept a job offer."

Her eyes go wide and she sputters.

Before she can put her thoughts into words, I hold up a hand. "I'm happy we're here. Boston is my home too. But so is Sienna. And for the last six years, I've proven to you that I'd do anything to keep Ollie well adjusted, happy, and *safe*. The last thing I'd ever want is for him to get hurt."

"I know." She gives me a conciliatory smile. "I'm sorry. You're right. And for the record, I'm happy you're happy. She seems wonderful. Truly." Her gaze turns to the field where Sienna and Ollie are chatting. "I'll take him for pizza and ice cream with the team and have Ted take Lily to dinner at his mother's."

"Thank you." I blow out a breath, relieved that he won't be completely let down. That he won't miss out on anything more. Then, while Jen wanders off to find her husband, I stride toward my two favorite people.

My heart twists as they smile and chat easily with one another. Ollie is beyond smitten with Sienna. Just like me.

Beckett beats me to them, his oversized dog dragging him around and stopping to lick Ollie's face. My kid laughs and pushes at the beast unsuccessfully, so Sienna kneels and helps him escape. As Beckett tugs on the leash, his eyes stay fixed on the two of them, his expression thoughtful.

Jen's right. We need to get ahead of this. We need to tell her brothers and hope like hell they're okay with our relationship. Because

I'm not giving up any of this. We'll be a family, Sienna and Ollie and me.

It's the only future I'll accept.

After the charity skate, we're forced to spend the next few hours rubbing elbows with donors. The whole lot of them are pompous assholes who donated so they'd feel important rather than because they actually want to do any good.

At least Sienna is here too. If I can't be with my son tonight, then I might as well show Ezra I'm a team player and want to remain one.

I've been distracted all evening, though. After the comment Jen made this afternoon, I'm fixated on coming up with a plan to move my relationship with Sienna to the next phase.

The one where people actually know we're *in* a relationship.

My phone buzzes, and when a text from the woman who's constantly on my mind pops up, I can't help the smile that hits my lips. Without reading it, I scan the room, looking for her. When I don't find her, I frown and tilt the phone close before unlocking it.

Sienna: Wanna know a secret?

The smile is back again.

Me: From you? Always, butterfly.

Sienna: I'm feeling a little needy. And cold.

A shot of lust rushes through me, heating my blood and making my cock swell.

Me: Needy for what?

Her answer comes in the form of a photo. Hissing, I study it, memorizing every detail.

Somewhere in this hotel, there's a hot tub. And Sienna is in it. The image is dark, making it impossible to see beneath the bubbles. She's wearing a teasing smile, her hair piled on top of her head, with little wisps of it clinging to her damp skin. Her cheeks are flushed and her green eyes glitter with all sorts of naughty thoughts. Fuck, I need to find her.

"Long day, huh?" Ezra's voice is like nails on a chalkboard. Not only because I don't like the guy, but because he's getting in the way of my plans to leave and finally get to my girl.

But I force a grin and play the game. "Yup."

"You seemed a little off on the ice tonight. What did you think of Davis?"

I bite back a scoff. Is this guy really asking me what I think of my potential replacement? I'm not an idiot. I know they're considering drafting him, and they haven't accepted the terms for my contract extension. After today, it's clear that if I want to remain a Bolt, I need to listen to my agent when he tells me to lower my salary expectations.

"He's a good player," I concede. "A little wet behind the ears, but as long as he doesn't let the noise surrounding him get to his head, he'll get the hang of it."

"That's what I'm thinking." Ezra slides his hands into his pockets. "I'll let you get to bed. Going back and forth to Boston must have taken a lot out of you." He lifts his chin, feigning curiosity. "How'd you manage that anyway? Seems like flying commercial would have been tricky in such a short window."

I keep my expression neutral. He clearly knows I took the Langfield jet and he's either trying to catch me in a lie or force me to explain why Sienna would arrange that for me. "You're right. I'm beat. But I'd do anything for my son and for the Bolts, so I'm happy I could make it work."

Ezra's brows arch in surprise, though there's calculation there, like he's not happy that I sidestepped his question. "Have a good night."

I book it out of there, keeping my head down so I don't catch anyone's eye. The last thing I need is to have to lie to Brooks or Aiden or Gavin about where I'm off to. Can't exactly tell them I'm on my way to do very dirty things to their sister in a hot tub.

As soon as I hit the lobby, I pull out my phone.

Me: Where is this hot tub?

Sienna: The roof.

I don't respond. She knows I'm coming for her.

"You just going to stare at me, or you going to get in here?"

Her smirk is just as sassy as her tone as she pushes up onto her knees, revealing a red bikini top reminiscent of the one she wore that first day in the Bahamas. Fucking perfection.

I pull my T-shirt over my head and slip off my shoes. I stopped by my room on the way up and changed into a pair of board shorts.

"I don't know. We're staying in a hotel with the team you oversee and I play for. You think this is a good idea?" Even as I remind her of why I shouldn't get in with her, I walk toward the bubbling water.

It's dark up here, though between the light of the half-moon that hangs sideways in the sky, the shock of glittering stars surrounding it, and the lit-up Olympic-size pool, I can see her clearly.

Other than the guard I passed on my way out here, the two of us are alone. As I approached the man just inside the door, he only let me through once I'd given my name, so I can only imagine Sienna paid him to turn other people away.

Even if he weren't there standing guard, ensuring our privacy, I would sink into this water beside my girl and risk it all. I simply don't give a fuck anymore. I want her. I want us. And I'm tired of hiding.

"I think it's an excellent idea, actually," she replies.

I don't even have time to adjust to the scorching temperature before she's straddling me. With my hands on her ass, I tug her closer and slam my lips to hers in a forceful kiss that speaks of how much we missed each other today despite spending close to twenty-four hours together before the charity event.

When my head spins from lack of oxygen, I pull back and blow out a breath, trying to get my bearings. It's so easy to get carried away when her skin touches mine.

Biting her lip, she studies me. "What's wrong?"

I rub my hands over her thighs and lean back against the wall. "Nothing. I just miss you."

She grins at me. "I'm right here."

I try to mimic the look, but it's no use. "You are, but unless we're alone, I'm not allowed to touch you, and it's fucking killing me."

Her expression sobers. "Me too."

"Really?"

She's not the most open of books, so her response surprises me. Though I know she wants to be with me, and she didn't run in the opposite direction when I told her I plan to marry her, I can't help but worry that her feelings are nowhere near as all-consuming as mine.

Nodding, she traces the shape of the butterfly inked above my heart. "I'm crazy about you, Noah. You and Ollie. I want this."

Her lips wobble as she locks eyes with me, her expression open, allowing me to see just how genuine those words are.

The look reassures me. Confirms that it's safe for me to tell her exactly how I feel.

She's ready. She won't freak out. She won't run. We're in this together.

Maybe I shouldn't be scared of the way she keeps her emotions close to the vest, because her actions over the last twenty-four hours speak far louder than any words.

Without breaking eye contact, I grasp her hand and press my lips to the butterfly on her wrist.

"I don't just want this." Another kiss against her soft, warm skin. "I ache for it. I ache for you."

A breath shudders out of her and her legs tighten around me.

"I'm in love with you, baby. I have been for years. Not just the idea of you. Not the idea of us. But *you*. I don't want to hide it anymore." I press her hand to the butterfly on my chest. "I'm yours. I love you."

Her eyes search mine like she's trying to memorize every detail of this moment, every word. She doesn't need to say it back. I can wait until she's ready to offer her own heart to me on a platter.

So when she says, "I have a plan," all I can do is smile.

"Oh yeah?"

Though there's apprehension in her eyes, her mouth tips up in a generous smile. "I'm going to use my brother's schemes against him."

"What?"

"*Beckett*. He's always trying to set people up. And this last year, he's been fixated on me."

With a growl, I wrap my arms around her. She's fucking mine, so she better not suggest he set her up with more people in some weird attempt to keep our relationship hidden.

She grinds down on me, her head tipped back and her neck exposed. "We're going to make him think he set us up."

I sit up a little straighter, blinking as I take in her suggestion.

She giggles. "See? It's a good idea." She leans in to press a kiss to my neck, her tits brushing against my chest.

My pulse picks up and my dick hardens further. Fuck, that feels good.

"You're sexy when you're plotting."

"Oh yeah?" She drags her pussy over my aching cock, whimpering.

I clamp down on her hips and hiss out a breath. "Baby, we can't."

The smile that overtakes her face is as sexy as it is innocent. "What's one more night of sneaking around? Come on, slip my bottoms to the side and have your way with me, Noah Harrison."

My blood heats, and not because of the water. Fuck. I want to. But I want to hear her plans. I want to figure this out. "*Sienna*." Her name is a desperate plea on my lips.

"You told me you love me. Prove it. Make love to me right now. Make me yours."

Possessiveness and need swamp me, and I give in to her taunting. "You are mine," I grit out as I drag my thumbs beneath the strings of her bikini bottoms, inches from my personal heaven.

She lets out a needy sigh. "Then prove it."

"Take out my cock."

With a wicked smile, she obeys, her tiny hand wrapping around my length, her tongue darting out to wet her lips as she strokes me, once, twice.

Heart pumping, I slide the scrap of fabric between her legs to the side and push a finger inside her. "Look at that. You're soaked."

She nods, eyes closed, and grinds against me like a dirty little thing, chasing an orgasm she'll never get from this alone.

"Line us up, baby," I tell her.

Her chest heaves as she pops up on her knees, and the two of us watch, rapt, as she drags my crown through her cunt, tormenting me.

Already, my need coils tight. Out of patience, I clutch her hips and pull her down hard, taking her mouth in a rough kiss before she can scream in surprise.

When we're breathless, I pull back, resting my head against the edge of the tub, and push my hips up so she's got room to work. "Ride me, baby. Fuck me until you come and tell me I get to keep you forever."

I slide the triangles of her bikini apart so I can watch her tits bounce as she moves. They're so fucking perfect. With one pinched between a thumb and finger, I roll the other one, and in response, she gushes.

"Good girl," I murmur.

In the moonlight, with her bathing suit clinging to her dewy skin, her tits out, and her cheeks flushed, she's a fucking goddess. Warmth blooms in my chest, followed by a rushing wave of pure adoration. I angle up and grip the back of her neck, pressing my forehead to hers. "I love you."

She drags her nails through the hair at my nape, licking into my mouth, rolling her hips faster.

I fuck her harder, my moves rough, her cries sharp in the quiet night.

"Fuck, I love you," I say as my balls tighten.

With my release hovering so close, I play with her clit, ensuring she gets there with me, touching her in the way I know will send her to the moon.

Ass clenched tight to stave off the need to spill into her, I channel all my focus into pleasing her. "It feels so good to fuck my girlfriend," I rasp as she whimpers into my mouth. "Now imagine how good it will feel when you're finally my *wife*." My cock stiffens as I take the dream one step further. "Or swollen with my baby."

Green eyes go wide with surprise and she cries out my name as she comes in pulsing waves around my cock. It's the hottest fucking thing, knowing that she's just as turned on by the idea of marriage. By the idea of being pregnant with *my* child.

Determined to make her come again, I focus on her clit, on keeping a steady rhythm, and soon, she's shattering above me a second time. I give her orgasm after orgasm, keeping myself on the edge, until she's babbling incoherently. Until she's begging me to fill her and give her a baby. Only then, after she's been thoroughly fucked and I've told her I love her about a hundred more times, do I fill my girl. I give her everything I have and hope one day soon she lets me give her even more.

She's boneless against my chest, my cock soft inside her, when I can finally breathe steadily again. "Okay, baby, now tell me your plan."

Chapter 48
Sienna

Aiden: Why is Noah Harrison being forced to sit at the family table?

Brooks: Huh?

Aiden: Lex just showed me the seating chart. Poor guy is stuck with us instead of the guys on the team.

Beckett: That'd be my decision.

Gavin: Why?

Beckett: Because I like the guy, but Ezra is trying to trade him.

Gavin: It's MY team.

Beckett: And I'm the brilliant one who suggested you sign him. You're welcome.

Brooks: Ezra wants to trade Harry? That's idiotic.

Aiden: Didn't think you paid that much attention to hockey, Beckett…

> Me: Hi, guys. This feels like a brothers chat. Why am I included?

> Aiden: Figured you'd want the heads-up. Looks like Beckett is trying to set you up with Harry. But I apologize for interrupting your day by having your back.

> Gavin: He wouldn't do that. He promised Liv.

> Beckett: I'm not breaking any promises.

> Me: It's okay, Beck. I trust you. Just don't make me sit next to Ezra, and we're all good.

> Gavin: He still giving you trouble?

I GRIN at my phone screen. It's like taking candy from a baby. I'm going to use my big brothers and their wild overprotectiveness against them.

Before I can reply, a set of soft, warm lips presses against my bare shoulder.

I squirm against the ticklish sensation, though I don't wiggle away.

"I wish you didn't have to leave." Noah brushes my hair away from my neck and peppers more kisses against my skin.

I drop my phone and roll so I'm facing him, draping an arm over his bare torso. "We'll get to do this again soon enough. After we've pulled off the world's greatest con tonight, we'll be free to do it all the time."

With a playful huff, he presses a kiss to my lips. "Anyone ever tell you that you are a deviant? It seems like you're truly excited to get one over on your brothers."

I beam at him. "You're not wrong."

"You know I don't care what they say, right?" He drags a finger over my ribcage and down my hip. "You're mine and I'm yours. No matter what anyone else thinks."

My heart melts inside my chest. "I know that. And I'm so grateful for it. But if this works, it'll make life easier on both of us. They can't be all dramatic about it if they think Beckett is to blame for setting us up.

He sets everyone up. And even when it isn't his idea, he takes the credit." I trace his butterfly tattoo, then kiss it for good measure. "I love my brother, but I'll gladly let him take the heat. We've had enough hard. We deserve this."

This time Noah is the one who beams at me, his smile sleepy, his hair rumpled. He's never looked better. "We do, baby. We really do."

CHAPTER 49
THE LANGFIELD BROTHERS

Aiden

THERE'S nothing like the moment I set my eyes on my wife after we've been apart. I spend far too much time away from the woman because of our schedules, so when I'm in town and she's busy like she's been today, I turn into a caged animal, pacing and waiting for her return.

As Langfield Corp's events coordinator, Lennox has been immersed in planning Josie's Gala for weeks. It's one of our family's biggest events, so naturally, my wife has been gone all day.

When I spot her, with her pink hair in a pretty updo and the deep magenta fabric of her dress cutting across her curves in a way that leaves my mouth watering, I can do nothing but stare. The woman is a fucking vision.

"Pick up your jaw, Lep." War waltzes by and snags his wife by the waist, tugging her against him.

I chuckle. As if the man isn't just as smitten with his as I am with mine.

Though when I realize his wife is free to wander around the event with him, irritation rushes through me. Because mine is still busy.

She winks at me, then turns and walks in the opposite direction, leaving me wishing I could chase after her and beg for a little attention.

It's tempting, but it would be a fruitless endeavor. So I take a look around the space instead, memorizing every detail so I can tell Lex how proud I am of the event she's thrown.

Josie's as healthy as any of the rest of our friends' kids these days, but after witnessing her battle with lymphoma, our family is dedicated to making sure no child ever suffers through an illness alone the way she did.

The room is bathed in pink light, and each table is topped with bouquets of varying sizes and bright pink candelabras that set the entire room aglow. The tablecloths are a glittering silver, and the chairs are all adorned with pink silk tied in bows.

Almost every woman is wearing some version of pink, and if I had it my way, I'd be in a magenta suit tonight. But when I asked my sister to make me a pink tux, she begged off, claiming she was too busy. So I had to settle for a pink tie to match my wife's dress.

I tap my foot, letting my knee bounce to music in my head while I continue creating the list of compliments I'll have for Lennox tonight. I wish it was time to dance. It's hard to stand in one place for this long.

As I survey the place, I catch sight of my teammates one by one. The more I find, the more obvious it is that all our ties are annoyingly similar.

I huff. I'll have to pester Sienna about the tux earlier next year. When I spot Brooks and Sara, I head for our table. If I stick close to my wife's best friend, I have a better chance of attracting my wife. Besides, Sara is entertaining as fuck.

"Thought we were supposed to be wearing pink," I say by way of greeting as I approach.

Sara grins, twirling in her Bolts blue dress. "It's got pink beading. Sienna told me that counts."

I chuckle. My sister designed dresses for all of our wives, and damn, does each one of them look good. She managed to capture each of their personalities perfectly.

Sara, my sister-in-law who dyes her hair blue at the start of every season to support the team, can wear her favorite color while sticking to tonight's theme. She's right about the color. With the pink iridescent beading covering almost every inch of fabric, the dress looks blue from one angle, but from others, it looks pink.

My sister is fucking talented.

Why she agreed to come work at the main office is beyond me. She doesn't belong there, even if I do love having her around.

When Noah joins us and eases into a chair, I shuffle closer.

"Sorry you got roped into sitting at the family table."

He shrugs, a content smile on his face. The guy is always so easygoing. And he's one hell of a winger. He never fails to set me up for a goal when the time is right, and no one can send a wicked wide shot into the back of the net as smoothly as he can. He's truly one of the best snipers the game has ever seen.

I'm bothered by the rumors that we won't extend his contract, obviously, but I think this whole setting him up with Ezra at our table thing is dumb.

"Appreciate the invite," he says.

I'm jealous of his Bolts blue tux. I didn't know that was an option. The vest underneath the jacket is a deep magenta that makes me think he had help picking it out. It'd be weird for a single guy to pick that out on his own, right?

Eh, maybe his sister is behind the outfit.

"Where's Hannah tonight?" I ask, searching the room for Daniel Hall and his wife.

"They're somewhere around here, I'm sure." Noah waves a hand.

"You didn't ride over together? Maybe get dressed over there?" I eye his vest again.

He laughs. "Nope. It's shocking, I know, but at thirty-five, I do know how to dress myself—"

He cuts himself off, his eyes going wide and his mouth falling open.

I whip around, following his line of sight. And there, at the doors, my sister stands, her dark hair down in easy waves and a deep magenta dress flowing around her.

The *exact* magenta as Noah's vest.

I peer back at my buddy to find he's frozen in place, still focused on the back of the room.

I wave, then snap my fingers, to no avail. The man is completely entranced.

After several seconds, he blinks rapidly, like he's coming back online, and breaks into a smile.

Wait. Does Harry have a thing for Sienna?

Brooks

"Are you seeing what I'm seeing?" my younger brother whisper-yells, whacking me in the chest.

Next to me, my wife leans forward, her blue hair cascading over her bare shoulders. "What are we seeing?"

Aiden eyes Noah, who's seated across from us, then turns to the back of the room.

Sara, who is about as discreet as an elephant hanging around mice, squeals. "Oh my god, I would love that."

My head has been pounding all day. After another sleepless night with Taylor and an intense morning skate, I had every intention of taking a nap. But my poor blueberry girl is having trouble with her tummy, so she screamed all afternoon. It kills me that I can't do anything to help her, but my fucking head feels like it's splitting in two right now. If my brother and my wife don't stop squealing, I'm going to leave them here and go find somewhere quiet to nap.

"Excuse me." Noah pushes back from the table. He's probably eager to get away from these two as well. Why the guy got stuck with us is beyond me. There's no fucking way management won't re-sign him. They're just playing hardball. Aiden and I leave plenty of space in the cap for the team to draft whomever we want. He and I would be set for life without pay at all, so we take the minimum. We just want to play the game.

Other than my wife, the Stanley Cup is truly the only thing I chase, and money won't help me get either.

Sara presses a kiss to my cheek and runs a hand over my hair gently. "Cocktails, dinner, and a little dancing. Then I promise we'll be out of here, and you'll be getting lucky, old man."

Chuckling, I pull her close. "I'm not that old."

The beautiful woman who has been my obsession for over half a decade bites her lip, her eyes glittering. "Whatever helps you sleep at night."

I give her a mock glare, though I wince when my head pounds again. "No sleeping lately."

"Focus, you two," my brother whines.

"On what?" I grouse. I just want to stare at my pretty wife, have a few drinks, celebrate my best friend's daughter, and get out of here. If I'm not dead on my feet by then, I might even fool around with my wife in the limo on the way home.

"Sorry." Sara leans over me, practically bouncing in her chair. "Back to Noah and Sienna. They'd be *so* hot together. Older. Forbidden. Brother's best friend and workplace romance? Get it, Sienna." She shimmies her shoulders.

Noah and Sie—*what?* "What the hell, crazy girl?"

Leg still bouncing, Aiden angles in close. "So it's not just me, right? He can't take his eyes off her. You think Noah likes Sienna?"

Gavin

"Dance with me, Peaches," I murmur in my wife's ear, needing a few seconds with her pressed up against me. All night, she's flitted around, looking like my literal wet dream, but finally, she's sitting beside me. I never could have imagined that the sight of my wife pregnant with my child would have me walking around half hard all fucking day, but here we are.

Millie's cheeks go my favorite color, a light peach. And when she licks her bottom lip, the picture of innocence, she knows precisely what it does to me. To be fair, she's gorgeous all the time. In a pair of sweats, with her journal in her hand as she hums a tune and jots down lyrics. When her dark, curly hair is a mess or when it falls past her shoulders. Millie Langfield is my obsession. Every version of her.

But tonight? *Fuck.* My sister outdid herself with Millie's dress. The peachy pink garment accentuates her tits and her curves and the swell of her stomach where my child currently grows, making her look like an ethereal goddess.

I turn to thank her again. "You outdid yourself. Every woman at this table is gorgeous."

Sienna, who's seated between Liv and Noah, wearing a big smile as Liv talks about Beckett's latest role as T-ball coach for the twins' team, dips her head in a simple nod of thanks.

"I agree," Noah says, giving her a look that lasts a second too long. "Every dress is gorgeous."

My sister's smile goes softer. "Thank you."

She holds his gaze, the two of them locked in some kind of silent interaction.

Before I can decipher what's going on between them, my wife stands and tugs on my arm. "Come on, let's dance."

I follow her, eager to get my hands on her again, and the minute her body is pressed to mine, my focus goes back to her, and all other thoughts are forgotten.

The event tonight has been nothing short of a success. Josie is in the center of the dance floor with Beckett's two older daughters, the three of them spinning in their pink dresses, having the time of their lives.

Vivi is at home with a sitter, but it's hard not to picture her out there with them in a few years. Fuck, the thought makes my throat go tight.

The crowd tonight is made up of pro hockey and baseball players, their dates, and the who's who of Boston here to help us raise money to support children fighting cancer.

We donate to research as well, but tonight's purpose is to raise funds for the extras that insurance doesn't cover. The special days that kids with cancer often miss out on. When Josie was in the hospital,

Sara and Ava brought cupcakes and movies and board games to the hospital on Sundays. Before Ava met her, she'd sometimes go days without visitors, and she's talked openly about how such simple offerings brightened her day and made it a little easier to stay optimistic, to continue to fight.

Since then, Beckett has bankrolled all kinds of upgrades to the facilities at the local hospital, including a movie theater and monthly events, like bringing in musicians to play for the kids. But this event is for a national fund that will allow us to do the same around the country.

My big brother may be a grumpy bastard sometimes, but there's a huge heart hidden behind that façade.

If I told him how proud I am of him, it'd totally go to his head, so I keep those thoughts to myself.

"Beckett did good," Millie murmurs, echoing my thoughts.

I kiss her forehead and inhale her scent. "And this is a wonderful excuse to get my beautiful wife pressed up against me."

She snorts. "My dad is *right* there."

I don't doubt that my best friend is shooting daggers at me as I pull his daughter even closer. She's my wife now. He'll have to get over it. "Like that's ever stopped you before."

Her eyes glaze over with lust and she sucks in a breath. "You are a bad influence."

"Not as bad as you, Peaches." I nuzzle her neck and nip at her ear. "Admit it, you're wet right now."

When she sucks on her bottom lip, I groan, determined to come up with an excuse to sneak out of here with her.

"Oh," she says, her pouty lips parting.

I turn, guiding her with me so I can get a look at what she sees.

All I find is the table we just left, where Sienna is chatting with Beckett and Liv and Noah.

When I don't see anything out of the ordinary, I turn back, assuming the little gasp must be in response to an idea that came to mind. "You have a dirty thought you want to share?" It's not unlike my wife to randomly come up with challenges for me that involve making her come, and I'm down for any suggestion. Pregnancy hormones have been very good to the both of us.

She giggles. "No, Coach. Head out of the gutter. Did you see the way your sister was looking at Noah? I don't think I've ever seen her smile like that." She nods to the table again.

Fuck. So much for getting laid. As all my excitement drains, I keep my focus on my wife. I'm still hard, so the last thing I want to do is look at my sister.

"Gavin," she reprimands when I don't immediately reply.

With a grunt, I adjust myself discreetly. Then I turn, following her instructions.

Noah's chair is turned so he's facing Sienna rather than the table, and he's hovering close, whispering in her ear.

Her eyes light up, and as she tosses her head back and laughs, she clutches his arm.

What the fuck?

"They look so happy," Millie muses. "Look at her. She's glowing."

My gut sinks. Sure enough, my sister's smile is brighter than any I've seen since she was a carefree little girl. *Shit.* Does Sienna like Noah?

Beckett

"So Ollie's more of a baseball fan, then?"

I rub slow circles on my wife's bare shoulder, relishing the warmth of her skin. She's a fucking dream in the deep pink dress Sienna designed for her. The silky fabric is ruched just below her breasts, putting her delicious cleavage on display. It flows out from there, camouflaging the attributes my wife seems to think are less than perfect. Every inch of her makes me weak in the knees, but I don't mind knowing I'm the only one who gets to see the soft skin beneath the dress. And I'm the only one who knows how her body feels beneath my palms as I hold her and take her from behind.

I'm just glad she didn't force herself into a stupid contraption before slipping the dress on to hide those curves. She's comfortable and gorgeous, and it's all thanks to my sister.

Noah gives Sienna a quick assessment, wearing a small smirk like he thinks he's getting one over on me. He hasn't stopped looking at her like that all night. It's the same way he watched her at the T-ball tournament last week. The man is smitten. As he should be.

"Yeah, he fell in love with baseball when Hannah worked for the Revs." He runs a hand over his mouth. "He loves watching me play, but he doesn't have any interest in doing it himself."

Sienna places her hand on his wrist and squeezes. She doesn't even realize she's doing it. Like it's a natural move. It takes a lot of fucking energy to hide how giddy that makes me. With as often as she touches him like that, discreetly but with familiarity, I don't know how my other brothers have missed it. "I think it has more to do with how much hockey steals you away from him."

Noah shrugs. "Probably."

"Get him around Addie for a few days, and he'll want to live on the ice," Livy says. "I swear that girl would wear her goalie mask to school if we'd let her."

I nod, shifting closer to her. "Yeah, our Little One is going to break some NHL records, I bet."

Noah breaks into an easy grin. "That'd be awesome. I can't wait to watch."

I like the guy. He's obviously a dedicated father. He's a great hockey player. And he's always respectful in interviews. And though I didn't know him all that well until recently, he's been around a long time. He and Brooks lived together in college, so if he had any dark secrets or problematic personality traits lingering beneath the surface, I'm certain we would have seen them long ago.

But with this guy, it's always seemed like what we see is what we get. Aside from the secret he and Sienna share, of course. But I'll let them have it. She seems genuinely happy when he's around, and considering all she's lost and how hard the last year and a half has been, I'll do anything to keep that smile on her face.

I went with her suggestion, seating Noah with us so Ezra could get a better feel for him. But our GM disappeared after entrees were served, and he's been sitting at the bar talking up the bartender for the last hour, so I think it's safe to move onto my plan for the night.

"If you'll excuse me, I'd like to take my wife out onto the dance floor. See how this gorgeous dress looks while I'm spinning her around."

Scoffing, Liv bats at my chest. "Shut up."

With a kiss to her shoulder, I push to my feet and hold out a hand to my wife. "Come on, Livy. Don't make me beg."

She looks up at me with those big, beautiful brown eyes of hers, and I swear my heart climbs into my throat. I'm so goddamn in love with this woman. "Okay, Bossman. Show me your moves."

With my wife's hand in mine, I turn back to the table. "Hey, Noah, mind taking my sister out on the dance floor? Don't want her to be stuck watching us all night."

With a whispered *Beckett*, Liv nudges me and gives me a warning look.

But my plan is already working, because Noah and Sienna are both blinking rapidly, like they've been caught stealing cookies from the cookie jar.

I chuckle to myself. This is going to be too good.

Noah recovers first, clearing his throat and adjusting his tie. "Uh, of course." He turns to my sister, his cheeks going red. "You wanna dance? I promise I only have one left foot."

Sienna peers up at me, her expression uncertain, before turning back to him, unable to meet his eye. "Only if you actually want to. Don't let my brother bully you into dancing with me. I'm fine on my own."

"I'd love to dance." He holds his hand up. "Scout's honor."

Her cheeks go rosy as she breaks into a bashful smile. "Okay."

My wife drags me to the dance floor, so I miss the rest of the beautiful interaction. She squeezes my hand hard and whisper-hisses, "You promised."

I press a kiss to my wife's cheek, and she softens immediately, just like I knew she would. "Look at them, Livy."

She doesn't take the bait. She just glares at me.

I don't lie to my wife. Ever. So I tell her the complete truth. "You are the love of my life. And you make me happier than I've ever been." I rub my hands up and down her arms. "I just want that for my sister. I want her to wake up every day feeling like she's won the lottery. Feeling like because Noah exists in this world, she knows true love. Because that's how I feel every damn day with you. Marrying you, loving you, was the best damn decision I've ever made."

"Beckett." That single word is breathless, her eyes wide.

I duck, bringing my lips to hers. "I love you."

She drapes her arms over my shoulders. "I love you too, baby."

"Forgive me?"

"Always."

Every word is true. Even six years later, I still sit in awe of this woman. Sometimes I can't believe she's my wife.

As we slowly spin, I spot my sister with her head tipped back and her arms looped around Noah's neck, with a sneaky smile on her lips.

She thinks she's gotten one over on me.

I don't even care, because Noah is staring back at her with a look of complete adoration. My sister deserves what Livy and I have. And if I was a betting man, I'd put all my money on Noah Harrison being the one to give it to her.

CHAPTER 50
NOAH

"YOUR BROTHERS ARE all staring at us."

I spin with her in my arms so she can see the four of them standing at the bar, eyes trained in our direction.

With a shrug, she focuses on me again. "Don't look at them. Look at me."

I smile. Fuck, do I love this girl. "Okay, baby. I can do that."

Tonight has been incredible. Holding her in public like this is a dream come true. It's been six years since the last time I could do it, and now that I've gotten another taste of how it feels, I'm unwilling to stop. We've danced for three songs already, and I plan to hold her for the rest of the night.

"If you couldn't play hockey, what would you do?" she asks.

Surprise flashes through me, making my heart stutter. "Still trying to make a decision about your future?"

She shakes her head. "I've made up my mind."

"Care to share?"

She tips her head back and beams up at me. "Eventually. Not tonight, though."

I nod. I'm okay with that. Honestly, she doesn't have to work, but like me, there's no way she could just sit still.

"So what would I do if I couldn't play hockey?" I repeat her question. "Maybe coach Ollie's little league?"

She giggles, the tinkling sound the prettiest music. "That doesn't pay."

"I don't need the money. And it would pay in quality time with my son, which is all I really want."

She hums. "Do you want more kids?"

The smile that splits my face is huge. I can't help it. We might have played with the kink of it all, teasing about impregnating her, but this is a real conversation, and it's the first one we've had on the subject. If it wasn't obvious to everyone in this room that I'm in love with Sienna before now, there's no way they can't see the hearts in my eyes at this moment. I tug her closer, squeezing her soft waist. "Before meeting you, no," I say honestly. "And if I never found you again, absolutely not. Ollie is my world. And if you don't want any, that's okay too."

Her lips twitch. "But?"

She knows me so well.

I lean down, my mouth at her ear. Fuck appearances. I don't care how it looks. "But if you want babies, Sienna, then I would love nothing more than to fuck you until you're carrying my child, your belly swollen with the life we created together. You're my future. With or without children." I pull back and meet her eye. "I just want you. Forever and always. My soulmate. My love. My everything."

Lips parted, speechless, she searches my face.

Fuck, what I'd do to kiss her right now.

"We need to leave," she murmurs.

"Huh?"

"Make up an excuse. Say you feel ill. Anything. But we need to go."

My heart sinks. Dammit. Did I push too hard? I thought we were past the apprehension and second-guessing. "*Sienna.*"

She shakes her head. "Now. I want all of that. Now. Take me home. Put a baby in me. Be mine forever, but it has to start *now.* Please." Her words are whispered, but they're filled with heat and desire and lust and love. She hasn't told me yet, but she's shown me.

I'm a patient man. I've been so fucking patient. But I need to hear more. I need to hear the words. So I coax her to continue. "Why, baby? Why do you want all of that?"

She gets it. She knows me. We can say all of this without words because her heart matches mine. They fit together perfectly. After years apart, she's mine. And with her in my arms and her eyes locked on mine, I can sense her every thought. Still, I need her to say it.

When she opens her mouth and the words come out, I swear my heart doubles in size.

"Because I love you, Noah Harrison," she breathes, her eyes misting over. "Because I've loved you while you were in front of me, and I loved you when we were apart. I think maybe my last name didn't matter all those years ago because I knew one day I'd have yours."

My heart pounds, my chest filling with pride, even as my cock swells, straining against my zipper. I need her so badly, but those words have healed the broken pieces inside me. They're proof that she's forgiven me. That our future is ours and ours alone.

"I love you too." I rasp the words against her ear and press the briefest of kisses to her shoulder. Then, straightening, I nod, silently communicating that I'll meet her at home. From here on out, she is my home and I am hers.

CHAPTER 51
NOAH

I'VE JUST MADE it out of the ballroom, goodbyes taking far too fucking long, when my phone pings with a notification.

The message from Sienna contains nothing but a pin notifying me of her location. With a smirk, I tap the screen. Hmm, she wants to play a little hide and seek, I see.

Me: Thought we were done with the games.

Sienna: Never. Play with me, Noah. I promise you'll like the surprise if you find me.

Chuckling, I tap the notification so it opens in my Maps app and zoom in. The gala is taking place in the ballroom on the top floor of Langfield Corp, and according to this, she hasn't gone too far. She's somewhere in this building. The question is where.

The building is made up of thirty-six floors, and I don't really feel like spending hours searching all of them, so I fire off another message.

Me: Give me a hint.

Three dots dance on my screen.

Sienna: You like me on the bottom.

Grinning, I reread the message. This fucking girl. God, I have fun with her.

Realization dawns quickly, my pulse picking up, and I race to the elevators. Once I've hit the button for the appropriate floor, I type out another message.

Me: If I find you within the next five minutes, I get to put a baby in you.

Sienna: Deal.

My heart races at her easy agreement. But it's her next words that send me running.

Sienna: You can toss the birth control yourself when we get home.

Home. That word alone makes me hard as a rock. Though the idea of fucking her tonight, knowing that every time I do from here on out, there's a chance that she'll get pregnant, that we'll make a baby, makes the need building inside me nearly unbearable.

I tug at my tie, my breaths coming out choppy. By the time I hit the bottom level, the top three buttons of my shirt are undone and my tie is wrapped around my fist. I march toward the place I'm positive I'll find Sienna without bothering to survey my surroundings.

I'm under the building, beneath the earth.

I can't deny that sneaking around is hot. It turns me the fuck on to know I'm about to fuck my girlfriend in the bar her brothers own, hell, in the building her family owns. After tonight, I won't be able to walk into Ground Zero without thinking of Sienna.

Despite how fixated I am on finding her here, I still lose my fucking breath when I open the door to the bar and find only one light on.

Because there, lying across the bar, like my wet dream, is Sienna Langfield, long hair cascading down her shoulders and over the bar, her eyes heated as she turns my way wearing nothing but a pair of high heels and a magenta G-string.

I hold up my phone, the stopwatch on the screen still running. "Still got forty-five seconds left and everything."

Her eyes flare. "Looks like you win."

I stalk toward her, tugging at the belt. "Yes, I fucking do. And what a prize this is."

She smiles at me, the expression soft, and for a moment I forget about the sex and the games. When she looks at me like that, I can't help but relax.

"I'm glad you found me," she whispers.

The words, though appropriate for this little game, hold so much weight, so much power. Because I did find her. And she found me.

It's rare for a person to find their soulmate. Rare to find this kind of love. But to find it twice? To be given this second chance? I'll never take it for granted.

I take my time appreciating the beauty that's laid out before me, studying the curve of her perfect tits as they rise and fall with her expectant breaths. The beauty mark above her lip begging to be kissed. The smooth legs that'll be wrapped around my hips in a matter of moments.

"Can I keep you?" I ask her as I drag the end of my silk tie over the curve of her hips.

She breaks into goose bumps, her body trembling. "Please."

I force my attention to her face, to her pretty green eyes. "Please what, butterfly? What do you need?"

She drags her tongue over her bottom lip. "Your mouth."

"Where?" I dip in close and brush my lips along the same path my tie just followed.

She shivers beneath me. "Between my legs."

"Lift this leg, baby." I suck on the flesh at her hip, then tap her knee and shift over the bar, giving myself better access. "You know the after-party is in here…" I glance up at the grandfather clock in the corner, noting the time. "In thirty minutes."

She digs her heel into my back and pushes me down. "Better get to work, then."

Chuckling, I nuzzle against her panties. "As you wish." I slide my tongue beneath the silky fabric and push it over, inhaling the sweet scent of her arousal. "First, I'm going to make you come with my tongue. Then I'm going to fuck you until your brothers and everyone else in the damn Bolts organization are standing right outside that door." I grin up at her. "And then we're going to play another game."

Her eyes flare. "And what is that?"

"We're going to see how prim and proper you can act with my cum leaking out of you."

She whimpers beneath me, like the thought of me filling her is enough to get her off.

"Won't be the first time," she taunts as I spear her with my tongue.

She writhes beneath me, clutching my hair and humping my chin.

I love when she's a brat. I love fucking the brat out of her even more. Spurred on by the attitude, I push two fingers inside her, then curl them in a way I know will send her hurtling straight for the edge.

She digs her heels into the bar, her hips bucking. When I suction my mouth over her clit and flick the bundle of nerves repeatedly, she gasps and squirts right into my mouth and all over my goddamn glasses.

Eyes squeezed shut, I savor the taste of her, licking and sucking until she's a whimpering, crying mess beneath me. Only when she's gone boneless do I lean up and pull off my glasses so I can see her properly.

"You did it again," I tease with a gentle kiss to her hip.

She shakes her head, her eyes closed, like she's drained of energy. "You love it."

"I really fucking do. I love when you squirt, and I love how you taste." I slide back down between her thighs and lick her again, proving my point.

"We don't have much time," she whispers.

"We can wait till we get home for the rest," I say, grasping her arm to help her up.

She shakes her head and pulls away. "No. Fuck me. Right here." With her lip caught between her teeth, she spreads her legs wider. "I don't want to wait any longer to start our life together. Put a baby in me. Or at least…try."

Fuck. A challenge like that is all it takes to get me to agree. "Ass down here." I smack the bar, then step back and shove down my pants.

But when I step up close again, it hits me that this angle is never going to work. The bar is too high. So I guide her legs around me and lift her, pulling a squeal from those pretty lips, and carry her toward the pool table.

"Beckett will kill you." There's actual panic in her tone.

"Don't care." I set her on her feet and press a kiss to her lips, then turn her so she's facing the table. With a soft smack to her ass, I silently tell her what position I want her in.

Instantly, she folds like a drunk man playing poker and peers back at me, a little smile on her lips.

The moment I slide into her, sheathing myself in her tight cunt, we both groan in relief.

"This will never get old," I mutter, kneading her ass cheeks and thrusting in and out of her slowly. Over and over, I pull back, leaving only my crown inside her, then slam back in and relish the squeals she makes. "Dirty girl. Loves when I fuck her in public."

"I do," she mumbles, easing her head to the felt of the pool table, giving me an even tighter fit between her ass cheeks.

I spank her. "I haven't fucked this in so goddamn long. That's what I'm gonna do when we get home."

She moans, like memories of the first time I fucked her ass are hitting her the way they hit me.

"But first," I grit out, squeezing my ass cheeks to keep from coming at the thought of taking her that way again, "I'm going to fill you with my cum. You're going to take every drop like the dirty girl we both know you are."

"*Yes.*" She pushes back against me, grinding against my pelvis. In seconds, her walls are pulsing around me, signaling that she's close.

Clutching her hips with enough force to leave bruises, I fuck her harder. Faster. With each thrust, I imagine her on our wedding day. Then pregnant. I imagine a full life. Spending our days teasing one another and our nights tangled up together. She topples over the edge, and when I finally come, it's to visions of our future. Dreams that I know will one day come true.

She tightens her core muscles, like she's trying to suck in every drop, making my cock twitch and my vision go dark.

"Fuck, I love you." I loop one arm around her waist and bring a hand to the place where we're connected, holding us together. After I pull out, I don't let go, ensuring that not a drop of my seed has a chance to break free. Not yet.

She spins and wraps her arms around me. "I love you too." Pushed up on her toes, she gives me a soft, easy kiss.

When we pull apart, I rest my forehead against hers and we watch as I push the cum beginning to leak out back inside her.

The sound of voices breaks the revelry between us and sends my heart racing for entirely different reasons.

"Fuck," I hiss, spinning in search of our clothes.

"Tiny problem." Sienna breaks into a mischievous smile. "My dress is in the bathroom. I don't have anything to wear." Her eyes dance like she knew this would be an issue.

With a laugh, I scoop her into my arms and rush to the bar to gather my clothes.

Then I hustle through the back and hope like hell the universe is on our side for one more night.

Chapter 52
Sienna

Beckett: Didn't Sienna and Noah look good together last night?

Brooks: Ah, man, don't start.

Aiden: Aw, I agree they were awfully cute.

Brooks: She's our sister.

Aiden: And he's Noah. Greatest guy ever.

Aiden: Don't the two of you have matching tattoos? He's practically a brother.

Beckett: We don't have matching tattoos.

Gavin: And we're not getting them. Also no. Sienna is not dating one of my players.

Beckett: Lennox did.

Beckett: Sara too.

Beckett: I think this might be the best Bolts match to date. Maybe even MY best one yet.

Brooks: Lol. There's no fighting this, is there?

> Aiden: Wait, Lex and I are definitely your best match.
>
> Aiden: Lex and I are perfect for one another.
>
> Aiden: Take it back and I'll name our first kid after you.
>
> Brooks: Lol. Lennox just smacked him.
>
> Brooks: Beckett, I'm offended.
>
> Brooks: Sorry, Sara took my phone.
>
> Aiden: So back to Sienna and Noah. Yea or nay?

OH, my god. *Wrong chat, you idiots.*

I consider allowing them to continue. The banter is comedy gold, really. But honestly, I'm not interested in how the rest of them answer that question.

> Me: Hey, big brothers, as fun as this has been—by that, I mean not at all—please, for the love of god, mind your business! You don't get a say in who I date.
>
> Aiden: I hear you, but like…what are the chances you'll go out with him again?
>
> Beckett: Duck, I texted the wrong chat. Sorry, sis. I love you and only want you to be happy. Please don't tell Liv I broke the pact!

I laugh. "Wow, they fell for it, hook, line, and sinker."

Noah snuggles into my neck, reading the text thread over my shoulder.

"I told you this would work," I say, excitement making me loopy. "Let's give it a couple of weeks, then I'll bring you to family dinner at Beckett's. We'll thank him for setting us up and give him all the credit, then *boom*, we're good." I spin around and press a kiss to his lips.

"You sure you're ready for that?" He angles back, holding his breath like he's concerned about how I'll answer.

I give him another peck, grinning. There's no thought needed. I love this man. I want a future with him. "I'm beyond ready."

After a weekend spent in bed, making love and making plans for the future, I head into work Monday morning, on cloud nine.

It's almost time to fill my brothers in on what I'm going to do about my career. With any luck, my last act as CEO of the Bolts will be signing off on the deal that will keep Noah on the team for another few years.

From there, I'll begin my next chapter.

I couldn't be more ready.

I know what I want, and as exciting as Cat's offer was, I'm not quite ready to hang up my designing hat.

Seeing my sisters-in-law in my designs this weekend cemented it for me. The way their faces lit up as they tried on pieces that made them feel both beautiful and authentic fulfilled me in ways I've never experienced.

That solidified my decision not to open another design house. I want to do what I did for them for my customers. Custom gowns and custom designs for people of all shapes and sizes. I want to work with individuals, taking into account their preferences, their comfort levels, and their figures, and find styles that will make them feel good not only in my designs but in their own skin.

Something Beckett said weeks ago resonated with me. He wants his wife to see herself the way he sees her.

And I want that for all my clients.

Beauty comes in all shapes and sizes. There is beauty in everyone, and I want to accentuate that.

Yes, my best friend will be disappointed when I break the news, but Cat will find another stellar candidate for the role. And if I know her, she'll be the biggest supporter of my new plans. I'm lucky like that. Lucky to be surrounded by a family so caring that they interfere in my life constantly. Lucky to have friends who love me and respect me enough to offer me incredible experiences and career options.

And I'm lucky I have a man who loves me and supports me and will be proud no matter what I choose to do with my life.

I'm waiting for my inbox to update when there's a quick knock on the door and Ezra appears, a smirk on his face. "You get my email?"

His expression gives me pause, and the almost giddy tone of his voice makes anxiety zip down my spine. What the hell is this man up to now?

I arch a brow and look back at my computer. "Checking my inbox now. How about we set up a meeting to discuss the topic this afternoon? That will give me time to read it first."

In other words, *go the fuck away*.

Rather than take the hint, he saunters in and sits across from me.

There is nothing I despise more than men who think they can control my time, but rather than fight with him, I give in.

"Nah, we can go over it now." He nods at my screen. "Why don't you open it up?"

I push away from my desk and cross my arms. Two can play at this stupid game. "Actually, since you're here, why don't you just tell me?"

The man smirks. "Harrison's agent is asking for ten million and a guaranteed five seasons."

I keep my expression neutral, but even I know that's a big ask. Noah is the best winger in the league. He's also thirty-five. It's hard to believe he'll play five more seasons.

"So we ask for three seasons instead."

That's probably what Noah is hoping for anyway.

Ezra scoffs. "Why would we pay him ten million a year when we could bring in Huey Davis for pennies on the dollar?"

I blink slowly. "Because Huey Davis isn't Noah Harrison."

"So we move Hall back up to the first line." He lifts a shoulder lazily. "He's got chemistry with War and Aiden. Snow's a good backup, and we can bring on a whole handful of rookies for what it would cost to keep Harrison. Hell, I could get two hall-of-famers for the same price."

It takes effort not to roll my eyes. "We should make the deal. Noah's worth it."

Ezra scrunches his nose. "I don't agree, and it's my decision."

"It's the wrong one," I grit out.

"Why do you care so much? Sparks fly during that dance on Friday night?"

I clamp down on my armrests, fighting the annoyance pushing to take over. "I care because he's the best winger we've seen in a long time. Trading him would be a mistake. Maybe we should bring Gavin in here. Get *his* opinion." I pick up my phone. "It is his team, after all."

"I saw you at Allure."

The words make my blood run cold. And I think my heart stops right there in my office at Lang Field Corp.

The phone clatters into its cradle. "What?"

Completely at ease, he kicks back in the chair. "Yup. Saw you with our star winger. The one you're so set on keeping. Willing to pay ten million just to get laid again? I woulda done it for free, ya know." He waggles his brows.

Nausea rolls in my stomach. This fucking pig. "Excuse me?"

He angles forward, his elbows hitting his knees, and stares me down. "I saw you with him." He tilts his head. "And not *just* him. If that's what you're into, I'm sure I could find a buddy to bring along."

I clasp my hands in an effort to stop them from shaking. It's no use. "What the fuck is wrong with you?"

"Nothing." He leans back and shrugs like he didn't just proposition me or call me a whore. "If that's not your thing, we can make another deal."

"Have you lost your goddamn mind?" I hiss.

He shakes his head. "Nah. I'm just the guy lucky enough to stumble upon the Langfield princess acting a certain way. Even got some grainy video." He pulls his phone out of his pocket and waves it around like it's a damn prize. "We can call your brother in now if you want. Maybe ask him for his opinion on *that*."

I tug at my shirt, in need of air. This can't be happening. Not again.

I can't put my brothers' company at risk. I can't lose everything again. Fuck.

And Noah? If that video got out? Forget his career. I have no idea how Jen would react. And one day Ollie might hear about it.

My stomach rolls at the thought. *Fuck, fuck, fuck.* What have I done?

"What do you want?" I ask, all my bravado gone. I'll give him anything if it means keeping this information private.

And he knows it. It's why he walked in here with so much swagger. He was always going to walk out of this conversation on top.

His slimy smile sends chills through me. "What I want is for you to back off. For the next year, whatever I say goes. I have plans for this team. We'll get another Stanley Cup, and you and your little boyfriend and your freaky ways won't get in the way of that." His eyes darken. His tone does too. "Harrison is gone. I have plans to restructure this team. Push out the guys already past their prime. War will be retiring soon, and Brooks won't be far behind him. If you sign off on every deal I make, then we're good."

I cycle through a thousand scenarios, but none of my options are good. If I tell my brothers, they'll have my back. But that means giving them all the nitty-gritty details. That means letting them bail me out. And if I do, there's still a chance Ezra will release the video. But staying in this position for another year? God, it's like another damn prison sentence. No matter what I do, I lose. And Noah loses too.

But what choice do I have? "I want the videos deleted and a signed agreement that you'll never so much as utter my name unless you're talking to me."

Ezra pushes up out of his chair. "You know, I thought it was a mistake when they brought you on as CEO. But in reality, this is perfect. If they'd hired someone who understands hockey, I'd have to fight them every step of the way." He nods and strolls to the door. "I'll have my attorney send over the paperwork."

My stomach rolls. Another settlement. Another damn deal. Is this ever going to end? When do I get my damn happily ever after?

CHAPTER 53
NOAH

TODAY IS SUPPOSED to be a good day. A great one, even. A day I've been anxiously anticipating for a long, long time. Today I get to tell the world that Sienna Langfield is mine.

Okay, the world might be a stretch. But I get to tell her brothers. And Ollie. So yeah, I get to tell *our* whole world.

We planned to wait a few weeks, but then, like it always does, fate intervened.

It isn't often that the Revs and Bolts have days off that coincide, but when it happens, the entire organization tends to get together to celebrate. So even though we wanted to wait a couple more weeks before we hard launched our relationship, the way things fell into place for today was too serendipitous to ignore.

Since I pitched the idea to Sienna yesterday, she's been quiet. And that's got an uneasy feeling creeping through me. To be honest, she's been quiet all week.

But she swears everything is fine and that she's happy, so I have to trust that she'll tell me if that changes. She's had a lot on her plate with contract negotiations and her other responsibilities as CEO. Plus, she's still considering what she wants to do from here. I don't think she'll stay on at Langfield Corp, but I'll support her no matter what she chooses.

Though we can't talk about contract negotiations, it's obvious they've been rough. Ezra has made it clear he's interested in drafting Huey Davis, but there's no guarantee they'll get him. And if they don't, and they haven't agreed to my extension, they'll be putting their chances of success next season at serious risk.

My agent is hounding me about alternative options. He's itching to get the deal done.

I'm just itching to get my hands on my girl again. And I'm dying to get our relationship out in the open.

The rest can wait.

"So she's, like, your girlfriend?"

My son peers down at me, wearing a thoughtful expression as I kneel in front of him and tie his shoe.

We're picking Sienna up in ten minutes, but I wanted to tell Ollie on my own. It's best if it comes from me alone, and this way, he won't be caught off guard. Although he adores Sienna, I never quite know what will come out of his mouth.

Chest tightening, I remove my glasses and use the hem of my shirt to clean them. "Yes," I say, sliding them back on and looking him in the eye. "How do you feel about that?"

He breaks into a giant grin. "I knew it."

A combination of surprise and relief rushes through me. "In a good way?"

He scoffs. "Of course. Sienna's the best."

Now I'm the one grinning. "You're not wrong."

"You're not going to kiss her, though, right?" He scrunches up his face in disgust.

He often complains about how Ted is always kissing Jen in front of him. I actually think it's a good thing that he's growing up surrounded by people in healthy, loving relationships. But I won't push it on him regularly if it makes him uncomfortable.

"If it bothers you, we'll do our best not to do it in front of you. How about that?"

He presses his lips together and squints, like he's really considering the suggestion. "I guess I can handle a little bit. But one or two kisses tops."

With a laugh, I hold out my hand. "You got a deal."

As we're gathering our things to head out, he tugs on my hand. "Hey, Dad?"

"Yeah?"

He gives me one of those wise-beyond-his-years expressions. "You seem happier."

Chest expanding, I ruffle his hair. "Ya know what? I am. I have you and Sienna, and I love our life here in Boston."

"Me too," he chirps, spinning in a circle. "Can I tell Sienna I know the secret?"

I chuckle. "It's not a secret anymore. I wanted you to know first, but after today, everyone will know."

He perks up, standing taller upon hearing that.

While I lock up, he rushes to Sienna's door and knocks. I'm still striding over when she opens the door and he lunges at her, hugging her legs. "Dad told me you're gonna be our girlfriend."

I practically swallow my tongue, but Sienna only giggles. "Did he?" She eyes me, silently asking me how the hell she's supposed to respond to that.

For as adorably bewildered as she is, she still looks damn sexy in a pair of distressed denim shorts and a black tank top. The weather has turned warm, and since we're planning to spend the day at the park across the street from Beckett's house, grilling with the team and her brothers and about a thousand kids, she's dressed perfectly.

But just looking at her has me wondering if I can cash in on one of those kisses I warned Ollie about.

"She's my girlfriend," I say, my tone a little less possessive than I feel.

Sienna ducks, hiding a smile.

"But Dad, you always said sharing is caring," he reminds me.

Damn, the kid is trolling me, but I take the bait anyway.

"Not when it comes to her," I tell him.

Sienna steps out and hugs Ollie to her side. "So I take it you're okay with me dating your dad."

He strokes his chin like he's really thinking about it. Then he smiles. "Of course. Best news ever. Welcome to the fam, Sienna." He hugs her again. "We're going to have a great time."

She turns misty eyes to me as she rubs his back.

Fuck. My kid is the best. And he's right. She's already part of the fam.

Nervous energy pours off Sienna as we park on the street.

I shut the car off and snag her hand before she can get out. "We can wait," I offer as I peek at Ollie in the rearview mirror.

He's conked out, his head tilted to one side and his mouth ajar. My heart pangs. He really is perfect.

She bites her lip. "I don't want to wait. I just—" She sighs, picking at the hem of her shorts. "I have to tell you something, but I don't want it to overshadow our day. I want my brothers to know about us. I want to have fun with you. Out in the open." She shifts in her seat, surveying my little guy. "I want Ollie to have a good day."

I don't love that she still seems uneasy, but I respect her enough to give her whatever time she needs. So without another word, I rest my elbow on the console and press a kiss to her lips. "Then we'll have a good day."

"Thank you." Her tone is so full of pain and gratefulness. Clearly, whatever has her worried is serious. Still, I don't push.

"Anything for you, baby. I love you."

She closes her eyes like she's soaking in the words. "I love you too."

We rouse Ollie, then give him a couple of minutes to really blink away the sleep before we drag him into the chaos. As expected, the moment we hit the playground, where a dozen or so kids are running around and screaming, he takes off with a burst of renewed energy.

The lawn around the pink carousel is littered with blankets. Lennox is sprawled out on one while Aiden serenades his wife obnoxiously from the stage he's created among the colorful horses.

War stands in front of a grill, shaking his head and flipping burgers.

When he sees me, he grins, and when his attention drifts to Sienna and our entwined hands, the look turns downright devilish. "I fu—" He slams his mouth shut and pounds his chest, then points an accusatory finger at us. "I ducking knew it."

Sienna lets out a light laugh. "Not you with the *ducking* too."

Aiden launches himself off the carousel. "Holy duck, they're holding hands!"

I lift our joined hands so everyone can see, and the women all whoop and holler.

Sara, of course, is the loudest. "Get it, Harry! Those glasses scream BDE."

Ava covers her mouth, her eyes dancing, while my sister lets out a loud laugh, rivaling Sara's volume.

"Happy for you," she mouths as she snatches a block from Maverick's hand a second before he sends it sailing toward Beckham. "Naughty boy," she chides lightly. "You're just like Daddy."

Daniel jogs our way. "Happy for you, man. This is what I think it is, right?"

Brooks is right behind him. Even with his tiny daughter in his arms, he's scary as fuck. His expression is wary and he looks extra huge as he scrutinizes me. He may be a gentle giant, but he's still a giant. He's been one of my best friends for years, and here I am, showing up hand in hand with his little sister. "And what exactly is it?"

My girl steps in front of me. "We're dating. You can thank Beckett for that. He's got the Midas touch or something."

Beckett himself watches from afar, pushing one of his youngest daughters on the swings, his lips tipping up in what I take as approval.

A thread of relief works its way through me. Though when Brooks clears his throat, it vanishes. "So this is serious?"

I nod, keeping my head high. "Yes."

With a subtle dip of his chin, he holds out a hand. His grip is a little too tight, but I tolerate it. All in all, I couldn't have asked for a better reaction from him. Once he releases me, he wraps his sister in a hug. "He's a good one."

She smiles over at me. "Don't I know it."

As he steps away from her, he zeroes in on me, his expression hardening. "And she's the best one of us all. Be good to her."

My heart warms at the warning. "Always."

Gavin gives me a similar lecture after we eat, but Aiden is all smiles, hugging me and welcoming me into the chaotic world of the Langfields.

A game of softball is suggested, and teams form, and when Ollie gets a hit off War's easy pitch, I throw him onto my shoulders and run the bases while all the guys "struggle" to tag us out.

It's easily one of the best days I've had in a long time.

As the sun starts to descend, Liv, Sara, Millie, and Ava take the kids over to Liv's to put on a movie, and the rest of us settle around a small fire pit in Adirondack chairs. While Gavin works on getting a fire started, Beckett hands out cigars. Lennox and Aiden share one, and Hannah snuggles on Daniel's lap while he lights his. Sienna is quiet, sticking by my side.

The longer she goes without speaking, the more the unease that's been simmering on low since her confession in the car amps up.

Finally, when I can't take it anymore, I tug her hand and nod toward the path around the small pond. "Want to walk with me for a bit?"

With a glance around the circle, she sighs. "Yeah, I could use a break."

We sneak away without being stopped, and when we're out of earshot, I tuck her into my side. "You okay?"

She's quiet at first. Like maybe she won't respond. But after a moment, she sags against me and whispers, "No."

Stomach plummeting, I stop and turn her to face me. The dim lighting of the lamps throughout the park is likely soothing to most. The lapping of the water against the small dock nearby too. But in this moment, my nerves are set on edge. "What's going on?"

Her shoulders droop. "Ezra saw us at Allure."

Fuck. My stomach lurches, but I temper my reaction. I was not expecting the conversation to go there. "What?"

She shifts on her feet, looking everywhere but at me. "He saw us.

You and me. And *Garreth*." Her eyes dart up to mine before skittering away again.

I take her hand and squeeze gently. "Okay." The situation is not fucking ideal, and it guts me that he saw Sienna like that, but the pain radiating from her now tells me there's more to the story.

"He's blackmailing me," she explains.

"What the fuck?" My muscles lock up, and it takes me a second to realize I'm crushing her hand. I ease off, but I don't drop it.

She shakes her head. "He doesn't want to renew your contract. He says if I don't go along with his plan, he'll tell my brothers."

The sound of water lapping on the dock is drowned out by a buzzing in my ears, and my vision goes hazy. "What else did he say?" I grit out.

She shrugs and licks her lips, once again avoiding eye contact. "He offered to take your place."

"That motherfucker." I finally release her hand and give in to the urge to clench mine into fists. I will kill him.

"It's fine." She gives me a pleading look. "I took care of the video, and our attorneys are working out an agreement."

"*Sienna.*"

"And I'll find a way to keep you here. A different contract—"

"Sienna," I growl. "If you think I give a fuck about my contract after what that asshole did to you, you're out of your mind."

She flings her arms out, matching my anger. "You have to care. Ollie lives in Boston. You can't leave. I won't be responsible for cutting down what little time you have with him already." She squeezes her eyes shut and heaves in breath after breath, like she's fighting the urge to cry.

Oh, my sweet girl. She's always trying so hard to keep her emotions under wraps. I love her and her big feelings so damn much.

By some miracle, I find the strength to take a calming breath. The last thing she needs is to have to manage me while I lose my mind. What she needs is my support. My encouragement.

I step closer and squeeze her hand. "Look at me."

She opens her green eyes, keeping her head lifted so the tears glistening there don't fall.

I brush my mouth over hers, and when the first tear falls, it rolls along my lip. "Baby," I coo. "I don't need the contract. I don't need the game. All I need is you and Ollie."

With jerky movements, she backs away. "What? Hockey is your life. Where will you play? What if the only offers you get come from teams on the other side of the country?"

"Then I retire." The words come out quickly, easily.

She scans my face, studying every inch, as if it'll help her make sense of my explanation. She doesn't need to decipher anything, though. I make it easy on her. "I told my agent to go in high. I—" I shake my head. "I love the game, don't get me wrong. And if I could play and still be around for all the big moments in Ollie's life, I would. But I'm missing so much. He's growing up so fast." I cup her cheek and swipe at another tear. "And if we're lucky, there will be more children who'll need me to stick close to home."

She smiles through her tears. "I'd really like that."

My vision blurs as my own eyes go misty. "I've never known a love like this. You and Ollie and our future are all I want. So even if the Bolts offered me everything my agent asked for, I think I'd still want to walk. I'm just—" I shrug. "Hockey isn't the love of my life anymore. You are."

She launches herself at me, her mouth on mine and her hands in my hair. Our tears mix, but so does our hope. It grows with every kiss, with every murmured word. So does our love. This woman is my everything, and being open with her, supporting her, being the rock she needs so she feels safe enough to open up, is only going to make us stronger.

I pull back, cupping her cheeks. "So you tell me how you want to handle the situation with Ezra. Take my career out of the equation. I want to kill him. But since going to prison would give me even less time with Ollie, I'll settle for confronting him and ensuring he knows exactly how I feel about what he's done to you. This isn't right," I urge. "I don't want to tell you what to do, but I think your brothers need to know what kind of man their GM is."

She sucks in a breath and blows it out, the sound choppy. "I always thought if I ran to them with my problems, it made me weak. That it was pathetic to ask them to fix them for me." She bites her lip. "But if the situation were reversed, I would want to know if someone was hurting one of them. I'd want to have their backs."

I press a kiss to her soft lips. "Of course you would. Because you're a natural protector." With a steadying breath, I smooth her hair away from her face. "It's one of the many reasons I love you."

"I love you too."

"I know, baby."

Movement nearby catches my eye, and when I register the source, I nod up the path. The four men who care deeply for her have wandered our way. "It looks like they have questions. Think they've figured out that we haven't just started dating?"

Another tear slips down her cheek, though as she brushes it away, she laughs. "Probably. I guess it's time to tell them everything."

Chapter 54
Sienna

WHEN WE STOP MAKING excuses for bad behavior and the truth is brought to light, darkness loses its power.

Ironically, this realization hits as I step out of the dark and onto the well-lit path, prepared to finally open up to my brothers.

Not just about Ezra, but about everything.

For so long, I thought I was protecting the people I love by keeping the pain I'd suffered locked up inside me. It's only now, after Noah's revelation about hockey, that I understand that hiding the hard truths doesn't protect people. It keeps us from truly connecting. Had I known how Noah felt about his career, we could have worked this season to help him be more present with Ollie. Hell, the team probably needs to figure out how to do that for other players too. If we want to keep good talent, that is. Of course, none of this is my problem anymore. Once I bring the truth to light, I can step aside and let someone else come up with a solution.

It's time for me to move on. I'm done living my life based on the directions of others.

Going forward, no one will have a say in my choices. Except Noah, and only because our lives will be so intertwined that all the decisions we make will affect one another. Because one day soon, I hope to be his wife.

"What's going on?" Beckett asks, his brows pulled low.

Aiden's serious expression looks so foreign on him. "Everything okay with Harry?"

I wave a dismissive hand. Noah stayed back to give me the time to talk to them.

"Yeah, we're great. We're actually—" I shake my head, garnering the courage to rip the Band-Aid off. "The truth is, we didn't just start dating."

Brooks frowns. "What do you mean?"

"We met six years ago."

"Holy fuck," Aiden crows. "You've been dating for *six* years?"

My oldest brother slaps the back of his head. "Duck."

Aiden glowers and rubs at the spot. "The kids are gone."

"When we're in public, we use the word. Besides, this is a park. It was built for children and families."

Aiden shrugs sheepishly. "Sorry."

Beckett nods at him, then turns back to me. "Go on."

"No, we haven't been together all this time. But when we met, our connection was instant and it was strong. When you brought me on as CEO, we reconnected."

"And you lied to all of us about it?" Aiden's dark eyes are almost black in the dim light along the path. "He"—he waves a hand wildly at my boyfriend—"lied to all of us?"

"Don't," I warn, my voice sharp. "We did what we thought was best for the situation. I…" I duck my head, struggling to put an explanation into words. "I didn't believe we could have this. I wasn't in the right headspace after Paris." I glance at Beckett, my heart thumping a little harder against my sternum. "I signed a deal with the artists who lost their money. I did it to protect our family. And I promised I wouldn't design anymore as long as they didn't come after Langfield Corp."

Gavin links his fingers on the top of his head and blows out a loud breath. "What?"

Brooks blinks rapidly, turning to our biggest brother. "Did you know about that?"

I step forward. "He didn't—"

"Yes," he interrupts.

The single word almost knocks me off my feet. "What?"

He nods gently. "You wanted to fix things on your own. I respect that. So I tried to stay out of it."

"Tried?" I question.

"Sienna." He drops his hands to his sides. "You were born to be a designer. I appreciate your effort to protect us, and I'm blown away by your strength. And until we found the funds that Xander had stolen, I didn't interfere. I promise."

"Wait, Garreth—"

His lips kick up on one side.

Dammit. He knew about him all along too.

With a quick shake of the head, he silently assures me that he kept the information to himself.

Tears spring to my eyes again. Dammit, do I love him even more in this moment.

"So you knew all along?" I ask softly.

He nods.

"Can we back up to the part where she and Noah lied to us?" Brooks grouses.

I wince. "I'm really sorry."

"He should have told us," he argues, his voice laced with hurt. "We were best friends."

"Enough," Beckett snaps. "She's our sister and he's your friend. You should be happy about this."

Brooks puts his hands on his hips, suddenly looking even bigger. "Happy they lied to us?"

"Happy she's happy," Beckett retorts. "If I remember correctly, you hid a relationship from us all as well."

"Right, and Gavin was pissed about it," Brooks grits out.

"Yeah. Gavin, who also hid a relationship." Beckett eyes Gav, then turns his scrutiny on Aiden. "You had your own secrets too."

"Pot meet kettle," Gavin says, though his tone is light and his eyes shine with understanding.

"Exactly," Beckett says, straightening. "We Langfields do what's necessary for the ones we love."

"Or in order to make them fall in love," Gavin teases.

Beckett shrugs. "I don't feel the slightest bit bad about how I won over my wife. I have five beautiful children and the love of the only woman I ever wanted. That kind of love is all I've ever wanted for all of you. I want you to be happy," he says, turning to me. "So yes, I interfered with the settlement you made in Paris. You built that company all on your own, and you deserve to go back to doing what you love. I'll probably interfere again if I think I can help." He eyes each one of us. "That goes for all of you. I only want you to be happy."

"You can't be a decision-maker when it comes to his contract," Gavin interjects.

Thank god for that. If he hadn't interrupted, I'd be a puddle on the path right now.

I wince. "About that…"

He gives me a sad smile. "You don't want the job anymore, do you?"

"No I don't. But that's not the issue we need to discuss. Ezra is the problem," I admit, my voice shaky. "He—"

Beckett lets out a low growl. "What the fuck did he do?"

"I thought we don't say fuck," Aiden mutters.

By the look Beckett gives him, his joke didn't land. He knows it too as he holds up his hands and backs up a step.

"He's trying to blackmail me," I blurt. "He wasn't happy when you appointed me CEO."

"What do you mean he's blackmailing you?" Brooks is the one growling now.

"We'll kill him," Aiden says, his tone pure venom.

Beckett holds a hand up to silence them. "What happened?" His voice is clipped. Deadly.

Cheeks burning, I swallow past the lump in my throat. "He saw me at Allure."

"What's Allure?" Brooks and Aiden ask in unison.

A weight the size of an anvil presses on my chest. God, I don't want to have to explain it.

"Consider it handled," Beckett says.

"Wait, what is Allure?" Aiden whines.

Gavin gives a firm shake of his head, effectively ending the conversation.

If only it would really end here. The guys will probably google it when they get home. God, this is mortifying.

"You aren't mad?" I whisper to my two oldest brothers.

"Oh, I'm livid," Beckett says, "but not at you."

He holds out his arms, and I rush into his chest, seeking comfort from the man who's always had my back.

The tension slowly eases from my body as I cry against his chest. "I'm so sorry."

He rubs comforting circles on my back. "I'm proud of you. You have nothing to be sorry for. Ezra, on the other hand, will pay."

The air shifts, and awareness settles in my bones. And then I'm guided into another set of arms. As Noah hugs me, rocking slightly, a hand lands on my shoulder. Then a figure moves in closer. Before I know it, I'm enclosed in the biggest, warmest group hug.

I allow myself a moment to soak in their love and comfort and encouragement, then I clear my throat and straighten, pulling myself together. "I'm good."

Noah's blue eyes catalog every inch of my face. "You sure?"

I nod. "Yes. Let's go relax. I'm done allowing the negativity to steal my energy."

As I pass Brooks, he gently grasps my arm. "I'm sorry."

With a smile, I pat his hand. "He's your best friend. I understand the shock."

He runs a hand over his face. "Yeah, but Beckett was right. We do what we have to for the people we love. And you love him, huh?" He surveys Noah, who's settled a hand on my hip protectively.

I peer back at the man in question. "Yeah, I love him."

"And I love her," he says without looking away from me. "More than anything."

Brooks nods. "Good."

"I say we go back to the house and make s'mores." Aiden drapes an arm over my shoulders and jostles me lightly, silently confirming that we're okay.

I chuckle. "Yeah, that sounds better than cigars anyway."

As we approach the fire pit, we discover another person has arrived. When his identity registers, my spine snaps straight.

Noah tucks me into his side protectively. "What the fuck is he doing here?"

"Shit," Gavin curses, "I invited him."

Noah's breaths come out as huffs, as if he's a bull ready to charge. But he stays put, waiting for me to lead.

I turn to him and rest my hands on his chest. "Can I handle this?"

Eyes falling shut, he dips his chin.

I scan my brothers. They all wear masks of anger, but no one moves. Beckett gives me the slightest nod, silently encouraging me to handle the situation.

My chest is tight and my heart races, but I manage to pin a smile to my face as I stride straight toward Ezra.

The move does the trick. When he notices me, he breaks into a cocky smirk, clearly believing I'm playing along with his stupid game. "Hey, Ezra."

His eyes light up. "Hi, Sienna."

"We were just talking about you."

He gives me a surprised smile, then glances at the guys. Clearly he's too vain to realize they're throwing him death glares. "Oh yeah? What about?"

I tilt my head. "I was telling them how, when they brought me on, you were worried because I didn't know much about hockey. You gave me a little shit about it, didn't you?"

His gaze snaps to mine and he gives his head a shake. "I don't know what you mean. I trust your brothers, and I trust *you* implicitly."

His tone is laced with malice. *Be careful,* it warns. *Don't fuck me over or I'll tell them everything.*

Too bad I don't give a fuck anymore.

I let out a breathy laugh. "We both know that's not true," I patronize. "But that's okay. You were right. I had a lot to learn. Fortunately, Noah was more than happy to teach me *everything* he knows."

His eyes narrow. "Yeah?"

I turn so I'm also facing my brothers. "Yup. Most important, of course, is making sure I'm familiar with the stats of everyone on the team." Smiling, I turn toward the rest of the group. "Did you know that Ezra here has quite the record in the NHL?"

Beckett presses his tongue to the inside of his cheek, his smug expression full of pride. "Oh yeah?"

"Yup. Did you know he has the third worst plus/minus record in the league?" I glance back at Ezra, whose face is red with fury. "Impressive, really. If you couldn't be the best, you probably should have tried harder to be the worst."

"What the fuck?" he mutters.

"Hey," Gavin barks, taking a step forward.

I shake my head, letting my brother know that I'm not done. "Good news is," I say to Ezra, "you are the worst GM we've ever had." I grin. "So you're fired."

"What?" His eyes go wide, but he recovers quickly, glancing at my brothers and smirking. "Nice joke. We both know you don't want them to find out about your"—lip curled, he looks at Noah—"extracurricular activities."

The smile that splits my face feels feral, powerful. I'm not even embarrassed anymore.

So I like sex. Whatever.

What I don't like is this man thinking he can use his knowledge of that against me. If I were a man and he'd seen me at Allure, he would have walked into my office the next day and given me a high five.

I did nothing wrong and I refuse to cower. "Actually, I told them all about it. And about my relationship with Noah. Turns out dating people we're not really supposed to is a Langfield tradition. It's practically a right of passage, right guys?"

When all my brothers echo my sentiments, his face falls.

"And then I told them about what you said to me. About your threats and your demands. You see, I'm tired of men screwing with my career, so although my brothers all offered to do this, as did my boyfriend, I prefer to handle it myself. So, Ezra, you've been relieved of your duties."

"You bitch," he spits, advancing on me.

Without a second thought, I knee him in the groin. While he's busy grabbing his balls, I land a punch to his nose.

The crunching sound is far more satisfying that I would have imagined.

The whimpers and screams from the weasel's mouth as he drops to the ground bring me a perverse satisfaction.

"Holy shit!" Aiden yells behind me.

Before I can kick the man while he rolls around on the ground, crying about his useless dick, Noah pulls me into his chest.

"Dammit," I growl, cradling my throbbing hand. "That hurt."

He rests his head on my shoulder and blows out a breath. "Fuck, baby. I'm so proud of you."

"He deserved it."

Hands clenched into fists, Gavin stands over the loser who's struggling to get up. "He so did."

"She hit me," he groans. "That's assault."

"Nah, I saw you fall all on your own," Gavin tells him.

"Tripped over that branch," Brooks says, pointing to a nonexistent tree limb.

Beckett holds out a hand and helps the jackass to his feet. "And this," he says before driving his fist into the man's stomach, "was obviously caused by the branch too. Now get the fuck out of here before my brothers ask for their turn, you piece of shit."

My heart stutters in response to my brother's tone. The only other time I've seen him lose it like this was when Liv's ex-husband disrespected her.

"I-I-I'll own this team when I'm done with you all," Ezra stutters, swiping at his bloody nose and stumbling backward. "You saw it," he says, pointing at War and Camden and Daniel, who are all watching with shocked expressions. "You saw the maniacs attack me for no reason."

War crosses his arms and shrugs. "I saw you trip over that branch."

Daniel nods. "Yup. And then you stepped on it, and it ricocheted up and hit you in the stomach." He winces. "That musta hurt."

Camden chuckles. "Looks like you got what you deserved."

"You're all fucking crazy," Ezra yells. "I'll own all of you."

War takes a step forward, tipping his chin the slightest bit, and Ezra yelps like a fucking chihuahua. Then, probably scared that the notorious instigator will attack, he runs off, looking back with blood dripping down his face every few steps and tripping and falling twice before he makes it out of the park.

I blow out a long breath. "Did that really just happen?"

Noah brushes my hair back from my face. "You okay?"

Every man here watches me, each wearing a concerned expression. Noah's right. We have a family here. A life. It means more than any job or any contract ever could. And thank god for that.

"Yeah," I say. "Thanks to all of you."

War pats Noah on the back. "Your girl's got quite an arm on her."

I grin at my brothers. "I learned from the best."

"You want to go home?" Noah murmurs into my neck.

It hits me in this moment, right here, surrounded by my friends and family, wrapped in Noah's arms, in this beautiful park in Boston, that I am exactly where I was always meant to be. This is my home. And that's a thing of beauty.

EPILOGUE

Noah

MY BODY BUZZES with a heavy dose of adrenaline. It's a rush I haven't felt in a long-ass time. It's the type of electric energy that could light up Bolts arena all on its own. That could cure diseases and make a man reckless enough to get down on one knee two months after hard launching a relationship.

It's the type of energy that makes a person feel immortal.

And it's exactly how every man in this locker room feels. Because today we're playing in the seventh game of the Stanley Cup Finals. It's my last game as a Bolt. My last game in the NHL. And I want this win. With this team. With the men who have become my best friends and, hopefully, future brothers-in-law.

Because yeah, I'm reckless enough to get down on my damn knee. But first things first. It's time to secure this win.

"Last game," Brooks says as he settles on the bench beside me.

His headphones are around his neck, but any minute now, he'll slip them over his ears and start his visualizing. As a goalie, Brooks has the most stressful job of us all. He'll likely be on the ice for all sixty minutes of play while the rest of us will switch out in one-minute shifts. He'll come up against two-hundred-pound opponents in head-to-toe gear and block upward of thirty shots sent toward his net.

On average, Brooks lets in one to two per game. Though he's had quite a few shutouts in his career.

I'm banking on one tonight.

Since the night Ezra was fired, we've experienced this lightness, this electricity, this deeper chemistry. Like our bond grew that night and we became more than teammates. We became brothers.

Not just me and the Langfields. Hall, Snow, and War too.

And we've brought it back to the ice. To our team. We're unstoppable.

Sure, Florida has eked out three wins in this series, but all the games have been close. Each one has come down to one flick of a damn wrist or one slip of a skate.

But it's within our grasp. I'm betting on the Bolts tonight. We're hungry, we're in love with the game, and we're itching to lift that cup over our heads to celebrate the end of a fucking era.

I meet Brooks's steady gaze. "I'm ready."

His lips twitch. "I see that." With a long breath out, he scans the locker room.

War is playing cards with Hall and Snow. They're laughing loudly, wide smiles on their faces. Aiden is talking with the other center, Keegan, their heads down. Aiden's no doubt reassuring the kid, who's playing in his first Stanley finals.

"I think I get it," Brooks murmurs. "Why you're done. It's hard, doing this when I want to be wherever Taylor and Sara are."

I nod solemnly. I'm not sad about my decision, but I am emotional. I love this game. And I'll miss it. But not nearly as much as I've missed my son during every season for the last six years.

I squeeze his shoulder. "You don't have to make any decisions tonight."

His lips lift again and his green eyes light up. "Nah, tonight we're winning the motherfucking Cup." With that, he slips on his head-phones and heads to his locker to get dressed.

I pull out my phone and dial Sienna. She and Ollie are in the owner's suite tonight, and I want to talk to them before I shut down and give 100 percent of my energy to this team for the last time.

"Look, it's Daddy," Sienna says.

Those words on her lips make my chest swell. I can't wait until she can say those words to a second child. She stopped the birth control, and we've been fucking nonstop, so with any luck, it'll happen soon.

"Hi, baby," she says to me, her smile a little wicked, like she knows what her words did to me. Like she knows she's left me tongue-tied. "Ready for your game?"

The lighthearted way she asks, as if I'm gearing up for a little league tourney, makes me chuckle. "Yeah, butterfly, I'm ready."

"Is that Sienna?" Aiden slides across the bench and leans over until his face appears in the little box in the corner of the screen.

Ollie settles on Sienna's lap, and a second later, his face fills the screen. "Hi. Aiden, did you do your song yet?"

My friend grins. "Not yet. Want to stay on the line and watch?"

The little guy's eyes go wide. "Is that allowed?"

"For you?" Aiden winks. "Of course."

"How 'bout we put it over here so all the kids can see?" Sienna reappears, and then she's moving. When she props up the device, I can pick out each of the kids in the suite. Mav sits in my sister's lap, the two of them wearing matching jerseys. The smaller Langfield cousins are running around with War's youngest kids. Brayden stopped by the locker room earlier. The kid is sixteen and obsessed with hockey. He has the potential to go pro. Who knows, maybe he'll be a Bolt one day. Addie settles in beside Sienna, probably excited about Aiden's song, since she's just as hockey-obsessed as all of her uncles.

"They're ready for you," Sienna says.

Nodding, Aiden jumps up on the bench. "All right. This is a special one," he hollers, getting the whole team's attention. "It's Harry's last game, which means it's the last time that this group of guys will ever play on the ice together." He scans the room, letting those words sink in.

Goose bumps prickle down my spine. The guys around me are all lit up, eyes bright and full of energy. Tonight is it. The last one.

"It has been a ducking honor to play with you." He winks at the screen, letting them know he's keeping it PG—the Langfield way—then lifts his chin in my direction.

"Now, for our last song, I give you the Bolts version of 'Blank Space.'"

By the time he gets to the chorus of the Taylor Swift–inspired song, every person in the room is cheering and dancing with him.

"We'll make the Bolts last forever
We won't go down in flames
This season ain't even over, mm-mm
The Stanley Cup is worth the pain

Three periods till we're legends
We're chasing eternal fame
'Cause we know we're the best players
And we love this game

Hall's young and War's reckless
Harry will take us far
Brooks will leave you breathless, mm-mm
Snow might get a nasty scar

Three periods till we're legends
We're chasing eternal fame
'Cause we know we're the best players
And we love this game!"

When it's over, the noise in the room is deafening.

On screen, Sienna is beaming. I pick my phone up and mouth an *I love you.* Then I tap my heart for Ollie. "See you after the game."

Reality doesn't set in until the last ten minutes.

Win or lose—and it's looking a lot like this will go in our favor—these are my last ten minutes on the ice as a player in the NHL.

One of the rookies chirps, "I don't want to say it, but—"

Aiden hits him in the chest, knocking him back a step. "Don't say it."

"But Brooks is—"

I glare at him. "Shut the fuck up."

Huffing, he bites down on his mouth guard, a bad habit half the league suffers from.

War looks at me, his expression saying exactly what the kid was thinking.

Is it possible that Brooks will really pull off a shutout in game seven of the Stanley Cup?

It sure fucking looks like it.

Shit. That's the stuff of legends. It'd be an incredible way to go out, too, if Brooks is serious.

I shake my head. Just like I told him, this is not the time to think about that. Right now, my focus needs to be locked on Hall and Snow, who are zig-zagging down the ice, setting up Keegan for a goal. We're up 1-0, so it's still an incredibly close game. Hall passes it to Snow, who slaps it toward the net. But it bounces off the goalpost.

That's our cue. Heart racing, I launch myself over the boards and hustle over to replace Hall.

War gets a hold of the puck with a nasty swipe at one of Florida's guys and passes it to me. I've been on the ice for less than ten seconds when I'm set up to snipe the shot. With Aiden on the ice, the defense's primary goal is to stop him. It makes sense; the kid's stick work is sick. He truly is a legend already.

His reputation works in our favor. It means Florida's not ready to defend against me all the way over here. I'm set up so far to the left that most players wouldn't even consider attempting what I'm about to do.

But War and I have played this exchange for years, and muscle memory has me pulling back my arm and slashing the puck across the ice, between Aiden's legs—with the help of a very well-timed jump—and past the goalie glove. When it hits the back of the net, the raucous cheers and chants that go up both on and off the ice are deafening.

I throw my hands up, allowing myself to celebrate what is likely my last goal. Then I brace myself to be the middle component of a War-Aiden sandwich.

After a few claps on the back, I tap my heart and point to the owner's suite, then fold my hands into the sign for a butterfly, letting the two most important people in my life know that this goal was for them.

My heart is still pounding as I take the bench again. It doesn't slow as I watch Brooks defend our goal. A minute later, I'm back on the ice, doing my job.

As the clock counts down, every single one of us skates our asses off, and when the buzzer sounds, we've left it all out on the ice. We gave it our all.

"Motherfucking champions," War howls as the two of us skate toward our goalie, who just pulled off one of the biggest games of his career.

Thanks to Brooks's shutout, the Bolts win the Stanley Cup 2-0.

Sara's screams can be heard above everyone in the crowd as she darts out onto the ice. But I'm preoccupied, waiting for the two pieces of my heart to get here.

When they finally appear, Sienna's face is tearstained, her hand locked around Ollie's. They rush toward me, and because she's the best damn woman in the world, she lets my son go in for a hug first. "You stink." He leans back, holding out a hand to stop Sienna. "Don't do it. Save yourself."

"Thanks," she laughs, even as the tears continue to fall, "but I'll risk it."

"Might want to close your eyes, bud. I'm about to take one of my two allotted kisses," I tease.

Huffing, he does as he's told. And once she's ensured she won't offend him, Sienna jumps into my arms and wraps her legs around my waist. Holding her tight, I kiss the ever-loving shit out of her. Screw the two-kiss rule.

"I'm so proud of you." She beams.

"Thank you, baby. It means the world to me that you're here. I love you."

"I wouldn't want to be anywhere else. I love *you.*"

War smacks me on the shoulder, breaking us apart. "Come on. We're gonna take the kids around the ice." He's already got Scarlett on one shoulder and Josie on the other, and Brayden has his little brother in his arms.

I eye Ollie. "You willing to risk the stench for a ride around the ice?"

He tilts his head, his lips pursed, like he actually has to think about it, then nods sharply.

One by one, the guys take off with their children, some helping those who have multiple. Brooks carries baby Taylor, who's dressed in head-to-toe blue, and Aiden has Addie on the front of his skates. Snow tosses Beckett's son Finn onto his shoulders, and the rest of the older kids rush the ice in their sneakers, making it a full-on family affair.

It's the best damn way to end my career. And as "Blank Space" plays through the speakers, we all sing the Bolts' version. We're officially legends, and we love this game.

Sienna

Aiden: So on a scale of one to ten, how late will you be?

Beckett: I'm here.

Gavin: Same.

Brooks: Walking in now.

Aiden: Obviously not talking to you.

Beckett: Which you?

Aiden: Duck.

Aiden: I mean duck.

Beckett: Hahahahaha.

Gavin: Should we say it?

Brooks: Definitely feels like he deserves it.

Me: Goose!

Beckett: There she is!

Aiden: Her! You! How late will you be?

"We're going to be late." I shift in my seat and frown at Noah.

The party is in the opposite direction, but he insisted on stopping by the arena first.

"Screw the party," he says, squeezing my hand.

"We can't ditch this. It's *your* retirement party."

With a scoff, he shifts into park.

He looks so good tonight. He's all dressed up in a black tuxedo, his brown hair swept to the side, his blue eyes dazzling behind the pair of black frames that make my knees weak. He has boxes and boxes of contacts at home, yet he chooses to wear the glasses because he knows they make me hot.

My dress is more revealing than my usual clothing choices these days, calling back to a younger, more reckless Sienna. The Sienna who reveled in taunting the man in the villa next door. It's dangerously low-cut, the V ending just above my belly button. Think JLo's green dress but red, with a gold seashell belt that I squealed when I found.

The garment is my design. The first for my new boutique based in Boston. The boutique I'll open once I've found the right space. I've done little more than tell my brothers that I'm stepping down from the organization and sketch designs.

"Can I put this on you?" He holds up a black silk blindfold.

I shimmy my shoulders. "Oh, kinky."

With a chuckle, he throws his car door open. He helps me out of the passenger side and kisses me thoroughly before placing his hands on my shoulders and spinning me to face the car.

"Just a few seconds of darkness."

He's gentle as he slips the blindfold over my eyes, careful not to mess up my hair. Then he lifts me into his arms.

Giggling, I cling to his neck. "Well, this is fun."

He hums, but as he heads toward our destination, he's silent. I listen to his footsteps the whole way, trying to discern our location.

When he finally sets my feet on the ground, he holds on tight, ensuring I'm steady. Then, with his lips against my ear, he says, "Six years ago, I met a girl on a plane, and she stole my heart."

A shiver courses up my spine.

"We had the most incredible few days," he continues, "but she had a whole new life ahead of her. So she asked me to put my name and number in a book, swearing that if she found it, we were meant to reconnect."

I grin, my eyes tearing up behind the blindfold. Our story will never not make me emotional.

"I promised I would. I'd write my name and number on the title page, then send that book out into the universe, hoping one day it would find its way to her. But I have a secret, baby." He presses a kiss below my ear. "I lied."

I suck in a shocked breath. "What—"

He eases the blindfold from my eyes, distracting me from my confusion.

I squint beneath the overhead lights, a bookshelf coming into focus as my vision clears. It's flush against the wall and it's stuffed full. There have to be a hundred paperbacks lining the shelves, each one with an identical spine.

Heart racing, I glance at Noah. "Are they—"

Nodding, he squeezes my arms. "I got back as many as I could find. Called every bookstore in Paris. Practically put out an APB."

I walk to the bookshelf, my heels clicking loudly in the quiet space, and pluck one from its shelf. It's the book he brought with him on the plane all those years ago. But not. Because the original is on a shelf in my bedroom.

"Wait, I have the original, right?"

Noah sidles up next to me and nods. "I cheated. I would have done anything to find you, sweet cheeks."

I chuckle at the old nickname.

"But yes. That's the only one signed by Hannah, so I know it's the original."

My heart takes flight. This man. He tried so hard, sending dozens upon dozens of books, maybe more, out into the world. Yet that single dollar bill and the original book are what brought us back together.

But this? His dedication? It brings tears to my eyes.

I open the book to the first page and smile at the sight of his name and number.

The message gives me pause. It's not the same as the original.

It's been two years, and still I think of you. Come back to me, butterfly.

"Noah," I breathe. "Did you write a message in them all?" I pick up the next one without waiting for a response.

"My son took his first steps today," I read, "and a butterfly landed on his shoulder. Definitely not a happy coincidence. It's fate, sweet cheeks."

My vision blurs as I turn to the love of my life. When I find him down on one knee, my heart stops and my breath catches.

"For years," he says, "I missed you. I ordered dozens of books and sent them around Boston and Paris in hopes that one day you'd find at least one of them. I added little notes about my life in some. In others, I told you how deeply I wished to find you again. How much I missed you."

The setting sun casts the room in a pink hue and turns his irises crystalline.

"You are the love of my life. I knew it then and I know it now. The universe has given me everything I could have asked for. And I'll consider myself the luckiest man alive if you'll agree to be my wife." He opens his hand, and a turquoise and diamond ring glistens in the light. "Marry me, butterfly."

With a hand to my mouth and tears in my eyes, I nod over and over. "Yes. You're all I could ask for too. You and Ollie and—" I suck in a breath. This time I'm the one with the surprise. Licking my lips, I angle closer. "Just you and Ollie and our baby."

He lets out a soft sob, his eyes welling with tears too.

"If I have nothing else, that will be enough."

He scrambles to his feet, his cheeks damp and his eyes wide. "Did you say baby?"

I grin at him through my tears. "I took the test this morning. I wanted to wait until after your party to tell you."

With a whoop, he picks me up and spins. "We're having a baby!"

I laugh. "Yes. We're having a baby."

He comes to a stop, but he doesn't put me down. "And you're going to marry me?"

I drop a kiss to his lips and angle back. "Of course I'm going to marry you."

Carefully, he eases me to the floor. He slips the ring onto my finger and kisses my knuckles. Then he flips my hand over and presses his mouth to my wrist, tracing the butterfly tattoo with his lips.

"I love you," he says, lips still on my wrist.

"I love you too." I cup his cheeks and swipe his tears away with my thumbs. "Wait." I drop my hands. "What is this place?"

He closes his eyes and shakes his head. "I had a whole thing planned, but you threw me for a loop with your news." With a hand splayed over my stomach, he rests his forehead against mine. "We're having a baby."

Fresh waves of tears crest my lashes.

"Picture this," he says, pulling me against him. "Racks filled with your designs in that corner." He points to the left, then to the window, where the sky has turned purple. "Maybe a mannequin or two in the window, showcasing your favorites." With his hands on my hips, he turns so we're facing the opposite direction. "A couch and a chair in that corner, where you can meet with clients. A dressing room back there."

I turn in his arms, my head tipped back. "This is my boutique?"

His lips quirk up on one side. "If you want it to be." He takes my hand and guides me to the window. "Look." He nods. "It's right across from Langfield Corp, and since I'll be there, I could visit you every day."

I frown and look from the Langfield structures to him and back. "Why will you be at Langfield Corp?"

"Oh, didn't I tell you? I'm the new GM of the Boston Bolts."

All the breath escapes my lungs. "Really?"

"Yup. Really." He dips in close and nuzzles my neck. "You see, my fiancée has four older brothers, and as luck would have it, they like me so much, they offered me a position in the family business."

I snort. "And to think we were afraid of how they'd react." I throw my arms around his neck and pop up on my toes. "This is the best day ever."

He laughs. "Baby, I have a feeling every day of our lives is going to be like this. So long as I have you."

The door near the front windows flies open, and Sara darts in, squealing. "Did she say yes?"

One by one, my brothers and their wives file in, then Hannah and Daniel, all wearing hopeful expressions.

Noah is right. With him, every day is better than the last. What we have is special. It's rare. Not just our love, but this family of ours.

And the family we're creating together.

Maybe it was fate. Maybe it was serendipity. Or maybe it was just a bunch of happy coincidences. Regardless, I have no doubt that we'll live happily ever after. Every single one of us.

THE END

Sixteen Years Later

"You didn't really think we were done, did you?"

Across from me, Cat shakes her head. She's wearing that signature cocky smile, like she knew all along she'd get her way. She was right. It took a little longer than she wanted, but here I am, seated in my new office as creative director of *Jolie*.

I glance around the room that I'll soon occupy two days a week. It's ostentatious because when Sophie held this position, she knocked two walls down and combined three offices. It's absolutely too big for the few hours a week I intend to spend here. "Maybe we should turn it into a closet," I muse.

Cat cackles. It's one of her throaty, sexy laughs that will have everyone on this floor humming. When she's in a good mood, everyone's happy.

And with any luck, she'll stay that way. I plan to do all I can to make Cat a very happy boss, considering she's allowing me to keep hours at my boutique.

I'll spend one day a week there as well, but the rest of my time will be spent with my family. And I need time to travel now that Ollie has been brought up from the farm team to pitch in the major leagues.

Spring training doesn't start for two months, so I'll work as much as I can now. Once he's on the mound, I'll do everything in my power to ensure I won't miss a game.

My goals may be a little lofty, considering my husband is still the GM for the Boston Bolts. There's no way he can be at every Revs game, but it's my mission.

And Beckett will be right by my side, considering his second favorite person in the world is the Revs' new catcher.

Yup, Finn and Ollie are officially Revs, and I couldn't be more excited.

Cat gets it, though. With J.J. playing for the Bolts, she works hard to make it to all the home games.

"I'll let you get settled. Remember, Savannah is doing your introduction piece."

I nod, used to giving bits and pieces of myself to the media. At least Savannah isn't a stranger. She's Addie's best friend and has been to a few family events over the last few years. She also writes *Jolie*'s Calliope Column these days. The magazine purchased it from Hannah not too long after she and Daniel got married, when she decided that she didn't want to talk about her sex life anymore.

She still overshares with my husband on the regular. He hates it. But I've learned a few things from her, so I can't complain. I just won't tell him where I learned the trick that made his toes curl last night.

At the knock on my door, we look up, and when I spot an enormous bouquet of red roses, I know my husband is the one holding them. He tilts to one side and smiles. "Hi, ladies."

"That's my cue." Cat stands, and at the door, she turns and gives me a meaningful smile. "I'm really happy you're finally here."

"Me too." It feels like I've come full circle.

She's been with me since my first few designs. Through the start of my fashion line, a television show, an incredible loss, and the aftermath. She was at my side during my highest highs and held my hand when I was at my lowest lows.

For the last sixteen years, I've ridden one high after another, though. After opening my own boutique, Noah and I were married on the beach in the Bahamas, with Bert and Ernie serving as our ring bearers.

Barefoot, hand in hand, with my rounded belly between us, we promised to love each other more every day. And he's made good on that promise. Our life isn't perfect, but we try. We show up for one another every day. We fight. With each other and for each other.

Our daughter, Sara—named after Kate Beckinsale's character in *Serendipity*—was born in February, just months after we were married.

Sara Langfield will swear to her dying day that our daughter is *her* namesake, and for the most part, we don't argue. Every time she goes on a rant, Noah grins at me like it's our little secret. We've always been fans of those.

The following year, we had another little girl. Kate. We figured we'd stick with the movie tradition.

They're thirteen and fifteen now. Each year flies by faster than the one before, so I try to soak it all in.

"I'll just shut this," Cat says as she passes Noah. "I'm sure you enjoy just how flexible our girl is."

I shake my head. How does she manage to make everything sound sexual? "You're a deviant," I yell.

She peeks in, smirking. "I meant with your schedule. But Noah, you're a lucky boy." With that, she's gone.

Chuckling, Noah sets the roses on my desk. Then he scoops me into a big hug. "So proud of you, baby."

"Thank you." I rest my chin on his chest and grin at him.

He pecks my lips, then releases me and takes in the office. "It's big."

"That's what she said."

"Fuck." He laughs. "She's going to be a bad influence, isn't she?"

Winking, I hop up onto my desk. "You love it."

Eyes heating, he stalks back toward me. In seconds, he's got me lying back, his mouth on mine and his hand up my skirt. "No panties," he rasps as he spears me with two fingers.

"They just get in the way," I say between rushed kisses. "Fuck, I have a meeting in"—I falter, eyes squeezed shut. What time did Cat say Savannah would be here?—"like five minutes."

Challenge sparks in Noah's beautiful blue eyes. "I'll get you off twice before then."

"You know what I was just thinking about?" I breathe, shuddering as he rolls his thumb over my clit.

With a hum, he bites my lip. "What?"

"Last year. Snow's party."

His chest rumbles in appreciation. "Fuck, I love his parties."

"Take your cock out," I tell him. His fingers won't be enough right now. Not when I'm like this. I need it quick and dirty.

He steps back, giving me space, and I turn around, hiking up my skirt and leaning over my desk. When his palm lands on my ass with a *crack*, the first tremors of an orgasm roll through me. "I fucked your ass that night."

I press my teeth into my lip and close my eyes, recalling those moments. Snow's house in the mountains is enormous, with far more bedrooms than the man needs, and my husband has made it his mission to fuck me in every one of them.

"I'm going to do that again this weekend." On the last word, he slams into me, the move taking my breath away.

His cock has that effect, especially with the hardware he added. Hannah wasn't wrong all those years ago when she went on about how fun it was to ride the bling.

I thank her often for the advice and tease her endlessly.

As my husband's piercing drags against my inner walls, I clench around it, savoring every delicious thrust.

"Fuck, I love you," he murmurs, his body curled around mine.

The orgasm hits me like a freight train. It isn't just the sex. It's all of it. The emotions. The love and the lust.

This man is my destiny.

I bite down on my arm to keep from crying out.

The action spurs him on, and he fucks into me harder. Thrust after thrust, he works me until I'm coming again and he's pulsing inside me.

When we're completely spent, we both collapse against the desk, panting.

I've barely caught my breath when a giggle breaks free.

Noah presses a kiss to my shoulder, then my neck, then my back, before pulling out of me. "What?" he asks as he plucks a tissue from my desk.

I straighten my dress, then dig my compact out of my desk drawer to check my makeup. "The last time I moved into a new office, we christened that one too."

"Did it at the boutique as well." With a waggle of his brows, he cleans himself up.

He's right. We snuck out of our own engagement party and fucked in one of the dressing rooms while all my brothers were toasting to us.

Aiden almost caught us when he and Lennox tried to do the same thing.

I snort at the memory. "God, I love our life."

Eyes softening, he holds out his arms to me. "Me too, baby."

I'm just resting my head against his chest when a knock sounds on the door.

I straighten, then make sure Noah looks presentable, finger-combing his hair, before leaning against my desk and saying, "Come in."

Addie's best friend, a redheaded bombshell of a woman, appears, and the second she notices Noah, her violet eyes go wide. "Shoot, I can come back."

I shake my head. "No need. My husband was just leaving."

Noah presses another kiss to my neck. "See you tonight, baby. Love you."

Sated, I sigh. "Love you too. Thank you for the…" I press my lips together, searching for a fitting term. "The *proper* congrats."

He winks. "It's tradition." With a nod to Savannah, he disappears.

"Holy shit. Your husband is hot," she says, blinking rapidly.

A laugh bubbles out of me. "Why, thank you."

She takes a step back and peers down the hall. When she returns, focusing on me, she holds her chin high. There isn't an ounce of shame in her expression.

I like that. She's not afraid to say it like it is. It's an important quality to possess when working with me. I don't want a yes-woman. I want to work with people with backbones. And it appears Savannah has a strong one.

I motion to the guest chair in front of my desk. "Do you want to chat in here, or shall we go out for coffee? Or a drink, maybe?"

Savannah's eyes dance. "That's tempting. Though I'm laid back enough as it is. Give me a drink, and I'll probably tell you that it smells like sex in here."

I cough out a laugh, my cheeks heating. That's impressive. I've spent enough time around Cat to have become mostly immune to blushing, yet here I am.

She simply shrugs.

Yup, I really like this chick.

"I guess as our resident Calliope, you'd know, huh?"

Grinning, she drops into the offered chair. "Yup."

"Any fun columns planned?"

She bites her lip, looking a little shy for the first time since she walked in. Like she's holding something close to the vest. "I'm working on something. With any luck, I'll put it into practice at the Christmas party this weekend."

I smile. "Ah, you're coming to Camden Snow's party? You're in for a treat, then. He always throws the best, most over-the-top soirées. They're often a bit taboo, so consider this your warning."

She practically bounces in her seat. "That's what I've heard. This is the first year Addie and the girls have been invited, but they've overheard all kinds of stories."

I laugh. "Yeah, you can thank Liv for invite. Now that Addie is joining the coaching staff, she realized Beckett needed to have other plans."

She shifts, straightening, like she's ready to get down to business. Instead, she holds up her finger. "Before we move on, I heard a little rumor. I was hoping you'd tell me whether it's true."

I arch a brow. Over the years, all kinds of rumors about me have flown. Most of them are probably true, but I have no intention of confirming any of them.

"Is it true that your husband wears the same suit for every special occasion?"

Ah, that rumor. Warmth fills my chest and a smile creeps up my face. Though this isn't a topic I regularly talk about, I'm feeling generous today. "He does."

"Is it true that he insisted on being your first customer when you opened Sienna's on Lexington?"

My smile gets bigger, making my cheeks ache. "Yup. And yes, that's the suit. It's also true that the lining of the jacket is made from fabric printed with the words from every note he wrote to me over the years we were apart."

With a hand to her heart, she gives me a soft smile. "That's true love."

I nod, though the emotion clogging my throat makes it impossible to respond. She's right. It is true love. And we've lived one hell of a love story. Now that we've broken the ice, I'm tempted to share a few more bits of it today. Though I think I'll keep the best parts for the two of us.

Some secrets are only meant for Noah and me.

"Will he wear it for the party?"

"It's not that kind of party," I say with a wicked grin. "Because Camden Snow is anything but a romantic."

Savannah's eyes dance. "Color me intrigued. What kind of party does the infamous Camden Snow throw?"

Want to find out what happens when Savannah meets Camden Snow? Don't forget to preorder *Snow* now!

ACKNOWLEDGMENTS

If you're done crying after Aiden's last song, I'd like to thank you for sticking with me for the last eight books so that we could get to Sienna's story. Sharing this family with you, and this team, has been the highlight of my author career. I will never forget how every one of you showed up for this team, this series, these characters and ME.

We're starting a new chapter now, entering a new era, and I can't wait to introduce you to our next FMC Savannah and for us all to finally get to know Camden Snow better. There will be some old familiar faces–literally they're older and still just as fun–and some new players to the Boston Bolts.

As always, I couldn't have done any of this without Sara. This year has been a ride. I think we said, *What do you mean?* daily. But you continue to amaze me with your friendship, your support, your marketing acumen and your ability to roll with it. Whatever IT may be.

A huge thanks to my editor Beth for always making my words beautiful and my beta readers Sarah, Glav, Madison and Michelle. My books are always better because of you! Thank you to my street teams and content creators, I truly appreciate each and every one of you. I love our conversations and all of our beautiful edits. Every release gets better because of you!

And to the lovely Elen for the gorgeous illustrated cover and all the beautiful artwork she made to go with it.

If you want to follow along on my writing journey and have sneak peeks into all the characters in my world, follow me on Instagram, join my awesome Facebook group Britt's Boozy Book Babes, sign-up for my newsletter and follow me on TikTok.

ALSO BY BRITTANÉE NICOLE

Bristol Bay Romance

She Likes Piña Coladas

Kisses Sweet Like Wine

Over the Rainbow

Love and Tequila Make Her Crazy

A Very Merry Margarita Mix-Up

Boston Billionaires

Whiskey Lies

Loving Whiskey

Wishing for Champagne Kisses

Dirty Truths

Extra Dirty

Mother Faker

(Mother Faker is Book 1 of the Mom Com Series, but is also a lead in to the Revenge Games alongside Revenge Era. This book can be read as a Standalone, or after Revenge Era and before Pucking Revenge)

Revenge Games

Revenge Era

Pucking Revenge

A Major Puck Up

Boston Bolts Hockey

Hockey Boy

Trouble

War

Playboy

Standalone Romantic Suspense

Deadly Gossip

Irish

Monhegan Summers (Co-Written with Jenni Bara)

Summer People

Dad Coms (Co-Written with Jenni Bara)

Who's Your Daddy

Better Daddy